Advance Praise for *Talk of the Town*

"*Talk of the Town* offers up a blue-plate special of romance, humor, and a rollicking good time. I absolutely loved it and highly recommend it."
 —Deeanne Gist, bestselling author of *A Bride Most Begrudging* and
  Courting Trouble

"Daily, Texas, resident Imogene Doll says, 'Small towns and Irish folks are a lot alike—full of blarney.' But Daily's characters are also full of enough heart, guts, grit, and rascallyness to outsmart those Hollywood types, and don't you forget it!"
 —Charlene Baumbich, author of the DEAREST DOROTHY series

"Lisa Wingate's *Talk of the Town* is a fun read. Daily, Texas, produces more conflict and humor than a Hollywood sound stage. These whimsical and zany characters will have you turning pages as fast as you can."
 —Rene Gutteridge, author of the OCCUPATIONAL HAZARDS series

"Wingate pens a light and entertaining story of life in a small town with Texas-sized charm."
 —*Publishers Weekly*

"Hilarious! Lisa Wingate's delightful way with words will leave you laughing and longing to visit Daily, Texas, for one of Donetta's pecan rolls! An engaging story about big dreams wrapped in small-town charm—you won't put it down, I promise!"
 —Susan May Warren, award-winning author of *Happily Ever After*

"Packed with flavorful characters, a town full of personality, and a wacky escapades of slapstick proportions, this is also a story with heart—with wounded people finding hope in the sweet and tender moments of life. A treat!"
 —Sharon Hinck, author of *Renovating Becky Miller* and *Symphony of
  Secrets*

"Lisa Wingate's entertaining story was a delight to read. . . . *Talk of the Town* is filled with integrity, love, faith and above all, hope when all seems hopeless."
 —*RomanceDesigns.com*

Other Novels
by Lisa Wingate

TENDING ROSES

Tending Roses
Good Hope Road
The Language of Sycamores
Drenched in Light
A Thousand Voices

TEXAS HILL COUNTRY

Texas Cooking
Lone Star Café
Over the Moon at the Big Lizard Diner

LISA WINGATE

Talk of the Town

BETHANYHOUSE
MINNEAPOLIS, MINNESOTA

Published by Bethany House Publishers
11400 Hampshire Avenue South
Bloomington, Minnesota 55438

Bethany House Publishers is a division of
Baker Publishing Group, Grand Rapids, Michigan.

Printed in the United States of America

Library of Congress Cataloging-in-Publication Data
Wingate, Lisa.
    Talk of the town / Lisa Wingate.
      p. cm.
    ISBN 978-0–7642–0490–6 (pbk.)
    1. Women television producers and directors—Fiction. 2. Television programs—Fiction. 3. Talent shows—Fiction. 4. Cities and towns—Fiction. 5. Texas—Fiction. I. Title.

    PS3573.I53165 T35   2008
    813'.54—dc22

                                   2007034452

To all those larger-than-life Texas girls
Who do it up big or not at all.

To Marge and Bob
In honor of a sweet, real-life love story.
And to the ladies of the
McGregor Tiara Literary Society.
Thanks for the prom dress
The tiara times
And all the great nights of book discussion.
What a hoot!

Acknowledgments

You can't create a whole town without having met some real-life characters. A few of you reading this story might think you recognize someone you know within these pages. Let me assure you that any resemblances to persons living or dead are probably exactly what they seem to be. I have, of course, changed the names to protect the innocent and altered details to salvage reputations. As always, I promise to make all participants herein even better looking, thinner, wittier, and more charming than they already are, and to give each and every one of them good hair. In return, you agree to live in the quiet town of Daily for a little while, sip coffee, eat fried food, swap stories, and tell all your friends about it, since they're probably in the book, too. We'd love to have them drop in for a big ol' Texas time.

While we're all here, I'd like to thank a few honorary citizens of Daily. My gratitude goes out to Lisa Payne, who advised me on all manner of TV terminology and equipment. Thanks to Sharon Mannion for proofreading and being my traveling buddy and to Janice Wingate for helping with address lists, stranded kids, and pretty much anything else. Thanks to our aunts, uncles, and cousins for always keeping the southern-fried stories going at family gatherings. If every family laughed so much and ate so well, we'd need a lot fewer talk shows.

My gratitude also goes out to a list of people without whom this book would not have reached publication. Thank you to my agent,

Claudia Cross, at Sterling Lord Literistic, who helped to see Daily through several stages. Thanks to author-friend Scott Walker, who introduced me to the nice folks at Bethany House. Thanks to Dave Long for believing in Daily when it was little more than an idea, for being great to work with, and for always being an encourager. Thanks also to Sarah Long for being a lovely dinner companion and for helping with editorial suggestions. My gratitude goes to Julie Klassen, editor and author in her own right. Thank you for your acute suggestions, great advice, and your depth of feeling for the characters and the story. Reading the comments in the margin has never been so much fun.

Gratitude and warm regards go out to all the folks at Bethany House, who turn ideas into books that make a difference. My special appreciation goes to those who made my visit there such a lovely, uplifting, and exciting experience. Thanks to Julie, Dave, Carol Johnson, and Dave Horton for the wonderful lunchtime conversation about books, desserts, Daily, and all things in between. Thanks also to Tim Peterson, Steve Oates, Jim Hart, Brett Benson, Debra Larsen, Linda White, and Carra Carr for taking time out to talk about the book and make plans for the future. The only thing more rewarding than spending time with imaginary believers is working alongside the real ones.

I'd be remiss if I didn't finish by sending gratitude to readers far and near. Thank you for journeying along on my imaginary adventures, for sharing them with friends, and for taking time to send notes of encouragement my way. It has been an amazing blessing to see the ways in which God connects us across the miles. I hope you'll have as much fun in Daily as I did, and of course this means that now we're neighbors. Say hi to Imagene, Donetta, and the folks for me. And watch out for Bob. He's been know to run on at the mouth and burn the lunch orders at the café. But the pie is good. Imagene made it. Don't ask her for the recipe, though. It's a secret. I hear that pie might win her a spot on *Good Morning America* one day.

But that's another story. . . .

Talk of the Town

Chapter 1

Mandalay Florentino

There is that famous moment in *Casablanca* when Bogart looks at Bergman and, in that steely way of his, delivers a penetrating question about life, about circumstance and fate.

Of all the gin joints in all the towns in all the world, why did she have to walk into his?

Bogie's question was on my mind the moment I laid eyes on the tiny town of Daily, Texas. *Of all the places in all the world, why did I have to end up here?*

I had a disquieting sense of something dark and life-altering hovering just beyond the sleepy, sun-drenched main street. The only explanation for my being sent on assignment to this middle-of-nowhere little burg was that my boss was setting me up for a full-scale F-5 disaster so she could fire me. Ursula Uberstach would do something like that. Ursula breathed in human suffering the way most people breathe oxygen. Which made her a great reality TV producer and a lousy boss. Now that she'd finished toying with

the underlings on the staff, she was sniffing around me, searching for signs of weakness, honing in on a point of attack. Ursula
delighted in messing up other people's lives just when they were
supposed to be the happiest.

If my parents had named me Ursula, Swedish or not, I would
probably have been mad at the world, too, which would have made
me perfect for reality TV. As it was, six months into my dream job
with *American Megastar*, I was struggling to acquire Ursula's taste for
blood. At the beginning of the season, she'd swept into the studio
like a svelte, perfectly dressed force of nature, while by compari-
son, I'd fumbled my way through the door wearing the sensible
shoes, brown polyblend suit, and slightly maniacal chestnut curls
of a woman accustomed to scrambling behind the scenes in the
unpredictable world of broadcast news. I'd thought the move to
a weekly show would be just the ticket for a working girl with a
slight case of daily-broadcast burnout, a yen for job advancement,
and a desire to do something glamorous for a change. *Mandalay
Florentino, Associate Producer* looks great on the desk nameplate,
but unfortunately, when you get right down to the business of
creating a show that trades on, and treads on, hopes and dreams,
the job is not so easy.

The trip to Daily, Texas, wasn't helping my morale. Twelve years
ago, when I'd started into the news business, I dreamed of being
the woman who exposed wrongdoing, defended the defenseless,
changed lives. Now here I was, helplessly watching the ruination
of my own life, and probably someone else's. The fact that our
fifth finalist, nineteen-year-old dewy-eyed gospel singer Amber
Anderson, came from a town that looked like Mayberry-well-pre-
served-on-a-studio-backlot only made my job that much more
painful. Amber's slow descent into the Hollywood muck was the
hottest thing to hit *American Megastar* in three seasons. It couldn't
have come at a better time, since the ratings for season two were
abysmal. Amber's sweet, innocent, country-girl-in-Hollywood act

was just what the doctor ordered. Everyone loves to see a would-be saint fall off the straight and narrow. That kind of drama sells magazines and brings in TV viewers by the hundreds of thousands. What an act!

Now, taking in the sun-speckled main street of Amber's birthplace, I had the startling realization that Amber might be for real. The thought was followed by a sudden and intense burst of guilt and the perverse idea that having Amber make the Final Five on the show was like throwing a lamb into a pit of hungry lions. She would be torn to pieces while all of America watched her close her big blue eyes, throw her head back, and belt out gospel music as if her heart and soul depended on it.

Ratings would skyrocket. Viewer votes might keep her in the running until the very end, assuming she didn't self-destruct before then. Over the past three months, Amber had turned my job into something between a waking nightmare and a tightrope act. Just about every week, she gave the tabloids something delicious to print and me some bizarre incident to carefully spin-doctor to the show's benefit. In her defense, Amber pleaded that every single faux pas was an innocent mistake. *American Megastar's Good Girl Detained at LAX*—Amber claimed she had completely forgotten the box knife was in her coat pocket. She'd used it to help her grandpa cut open feed sacks back home. *Gospel-Singing Goody-Two-Shoes Linked to Hollywood Brat Pack*—Amber claimed that when the gang at the studio next door invited her out clubbing, she thought it was some exotic sport, like polo or croquet. She had no idea drinking would be involved. *Gospel Girl Nabbed in Prostitution Sting*—Amber was lost and she'd only stopped to ask directions. How was she supposed to know those ladies on the corner were . . . were . . . She actually blushed and stammered and took a full minute to whisper the words *ladies of . . . ill repute.*

If it was an act, Amber was an actress worthy of an Academy Award. The show's crew even had an "Amber pool" going—a harmless little bet on when Amber's innocent façade would finally crack. Everyone except Rosita, the cleaning lady, was in. And that was only because Rosita didn't speak English. Not one crew member believed that Amber's farm girl act could last forever. Nobody short of Elly May Clampett could be that naïve.

It looked like the Amber pool might pay off pretty soon. Five days ago, Amber had been linked to Justin Shay, and reporters were hiding in bushes everywhere, trolling for pictures and details. Could the fresh-faced gospel girl really be dating a Hollywood bad boy almost twice her age?

Even I had no idea how to spin-doctor this one. When the latest Amber rumor crept into my office, I'd accepted it with a sense of resignation. She'd finally gone too far—embroiled herself in the kind of smarmy Hollywood relationship that even her honey-covered southern accent couldn't sweeten. I wasn't sad about it, really. When all was said and done Amber was an opportunist, like everyone else in LA. Why should she be any different from the rest of us? It was a cynical thought, and in the back of my mind, I was bothered by how easily it came to me, how quickly I accepted it, how I'd suspected it all along. There was a time when I was more like Amber and less like Ursula.

The lost idealism of my youth drifted back to me at the most unusual and inconvenient times, like the whiff of something sweet passing by. As I took in Amber's hometown, it left behind a vexing question—if Amber really was as innocent as her quiet little hometown appeared to be, then what did that say about those of us who were using her loss of innocence, the ultimate destruction of her dreams, to boost ratings?

If I was unsure where to stand on the issue of Amber Anderson, her hometown seemed to have no question. Hanging proudly over Main Street was a huge banner that said,

WELCOME!
DAILY REUNION DAYS FIRST WEEKEND IN APRIL

Below that, two workmen with ladders were tacking on a hand-lettered addition that read,

Birthplace of Amber Anderson,
American Megastar's Hometown Finalist

Vote for Amber!

A sick feeling gurgled in my throat and drained slowly to my stomach, producing the fleeting thought that I should have brought along the prescription ulcer medication Mother tried to give me before I left LA. She said I looked like I needed it, and now I knew I did. The Tex-Mex breakfast taco I'd eaten before taking an aerial tour of Daily in a network affiliate helicopter was rolling around in my stomach like hot lead.

My sixth sense, the one my best friend, Paula, jokingly called the Doom-o-meter, was in full emergency warning mode, which could only mean that disaster was headed my way like a freight train. I could feel it in some vague way I couldn't explain. If Paula had been standing there with me on the corner of Third and Main in Daily, Texas, she would have—after making some joke about the Doom-o-meter—filtered through her Buddhist-Kabala-New-Age spiritual philosophy and told me this place contained bad Karma. She would've dragged me off to her favorite soothsayer, Madame Murae, who told fortunes in her sandwich shop when she wasn't busy making roast beef on rye. Yesterday when Madame Murae gave me my sandwich, she turned over the love card.

"Ah, love awaits," she mused, squinting at the card as she grabbed a styro cup and put it under the Diet Coke spigot without looking.

"I'm engaged." I felt the giddy little tickle I always got when I said those words. *I'm engaged. I'm engaged. Thirty-four years old, and finally I'm engaged. I'm going to be a June bride.*

He's gorgeous, by the way.

Madame Murae turned over another card. "Ah, I see travel."

"We're going on a honeymoon right after the wedding. In a little less than three months"—*After I wrap this season of* American Megastar *and the teasers for next season, hopefully with my job and my sanity intact*—"I'll be sailing the California coast for nineteen days." *Ah, heaven. Did I mention that he owns a boat?*

Frowning at the card, Madame Murae halted the flow of Diet Coke at exactly the right moment, once again without looking.

Paula quirked a brow at me, as in, *See, I told you she has special powers*.

I rolled my eyes. Paula knew what that meant. I'm historically an Episcopalian, from a long line of Episcopalians, drawing all the way back to the pioneer days. Episcopalians, even the nonpracticing kind, do not believe in tarot cards or soda shop mysticism. Such malarkey is for people like Paula who are spiritually searching but without the benefit of any ancestral religious foundation whatsoever.

"I see travel by air." Madame Murae took a lid from under the counter, popped it on my soda, pulled my hot roast beef and Swiss from the oven, and stood speculatively studying the curlicues of slightly browned cheese. "Soon."

A sharp-edged lump formed in my throat and descended slowly to my stomach. I wasn't supposed to be traveling. I was supposed to be picking out wedding gear, reserving the Chapel-by-the-Sea's reception room, deciding how to have my hair done. "I'm not scheduled to be traveling these next three months, but with my job, it could happen." *With Ursula, anything's possible.*

"Ah." Madame Murae continued surveying my sandwich. "I see negative energy surrounding the travel card."

That would be Ursula Uberstach. Five feet eleven inches of blond, blue-eyed negative energy, with a size four waist, a perpetual tan, and men constantly groveling at her feet.

"Change, I see change."

Maybe Ursula's leaving the show. Then again, maybe I am.

"An ending, a begin—"

Setting a ten on the counter, I snatched the sandwich away in what, for me, was a surprisingly impolite maneuver. Twelve years in Episcopal school and a lifetime of competing with four disgustingly perfect older siblings had taught me manners, if nothing else. "Paula and I had better get moving. We want to do a little shopping over lunch." Madame Murae slid her hand under mine as she dropped the coins one by one and listened to the sound, her dark eyes fixating as she stroked a finger across my palm.

"Be careful," she said. "For you, the path to happiness travels uphill."

"Thanks," I muttered. *Tell me something I don't already know.*

"Isn't she great?" Paula chirped as we headed for a table on the sidewalk. "You'd be amazed how often she's right. Every time she tells me something, it happens, I swear."

Stepping into the sunshine of a beautiful LA noon, I followed my best friend and future maid of honor to a patio table. "You know I don't believe in that stuff," I said. "And you shouldn't, either. If Madame What's-her-face is so good at foretelling the future, what's she doing running a sandwich shop?" Just to prove my point, I ate a big bite of the hexed roast beef and Swiss.

Paula gave a snarky sneer and shook her head at my hopeless self, then started in on her Cobb salad. We talked about wedding plans as I consumed my Madame Murae sandwich. Pinching the last bite between my thumb and forefinger, I popped it into my mouth, smiling at Paula, who rolled her eyes and reached for her purse. "You're so . . . pragmatic."

Dabbing the corners of my mouth, I looped my bag over my shoulder and followed her out. "I have to be pragmatic. I work in reality TV."

"I liked you better back in the old days when you were writing copy in the newsroom." Paula and I had started out at a local LA affiliate twelve years ago. Two babes in the woods, fresh out of broadcasting school. Paula had always been more interested in landing a boyfriend than building a career, which was why she was still on the writing end of the business, albeit now for a prime-time soap. In soap opera land, a belief in hexes and a cursory knowledge of tarot cards was a professional advantage.

"You love me anyway," I said, then hip-butted her off the curb.

She caught a heel in a storm grate and twisted her ankle.

By the time Paula dropped me back at the studio, Ursula was waiting with airline tickets to Texas and the news that I would be the advance man for Amber's hometown segment. Given Amber's recent media glow and the fact that the Final Five had not yet been revealed, secrecy was paramount. This was too big to trust to a low-level staff member.

What Ursula wants, Ursula gets, and less than twenty-four hours later I was standing at Third and Main in Daily, Texas, watching as the *secret* Final Five news was broadcast on a banner over Main Street. How could people in Amber's hometown possibly have found out the results of the semifinals already? Even Amber hadn't been told, and wouldn't be told until Friday, the afternoon before she-was scheduled to fly to Texas. Tomorrow, at the regular Friday lunch meeting, the camera crew chiefs would receive their marching orders, but for now, the identities and hometown locations of the Final Five were known only to Ursula, two other associate producers, the director, and me. It was a closely guarded secret . . .

The Doom-o-meter screamed like a panic alarm in my head. Somewhere in there, Madame Murae whispered, *"I see negative energy surrounding the travel card."*

From the parapet of the old Daily Bank building across the street, gargoyles laughed down at me, their narrow grins saying, *Who are you to thumb your nose at fate, Mandalay Florentino?*

I should have left the roast beef and Swiss alone.

Chapter 2

Imagene Doll

Some places in this world come with grand titles, like Philadelphia and Marina Del Rey. You get the feeling that when the founding fathers named those places, they expected grand things to happen there. Hard to say what was in the minds of the folks who named our little town of Daily, Texas. Guess they expected it to be a regular kind of place. And it is. Mostly.

Every ten years or so, something really peculiar happens in Daily. There's never any telling what it's going to be, but it'd been about a decade since the Christmas lights fell off of Town Hall and landed in the shape of the Virgin Mary, and twice that long since Elvis had a flat tire on Main Street. So when Brother Ervin Hanson spotted a TV network helicopter hovering over the fairgrounds one April morning, he figured we were due for another Daily event. He pulled off the road and watched with a mix of fear and awe as that helicopter flew round and round in a blank blue sky.

When it disappeared altogether, Ervin proceeded to the café to tell everyone what he'd seen. When you're sitting on a Daily news story, that's where you go. The café can spread information faster than chaff in a brisk wind, so when Ervin showed up saying he'd seen a TV network helicopter at the fairgrounds, word was all over town lickety-split. Don't need *60 Minutes* here. We've got the café. Paul Harvey would be impressed at how quick the rest of the story gets told in Daily, Texas.

Somebody ought to have warned those TV network folks of that before they came to town.

I wasn't at the café working that morning, which is unusual during the breakfast rush, but I'd come upon a dead raccoon on my way into town, so I was next door at the Daily Hair and Body getting my car fixed and my hair redone. If you're not from Daily, you might ask what one thing has to do with the other. Long story short, the dead raccoon had attracted a big old turkey buzzard, and if there's a buzzard within fifty feet of the road, it'll fly up and hit my car. The boys at the body shop keep a road kill tally on their chalkboard next to the results of last year's Big Buck contest, and I've got the record for most buzzard collisions in a twelve-month period. My name's right there at the top, Imagene Doll, next to a stick figure (if you can imagine that) of a buzzard, and four little tally marks. That's just this year's count. And there's still eight months to go.

It's sort of embarrassing, but at nearly seventy years old, you take fame where you can get it.

This buzzard was a big one, and it hit smack in the middle of the windshield like a giant BB, then hung there in the wiper. By the time I finally got it loose, I felt like I'd been ten rounds with Muhammad Ali. Which was how I ended up needing my hair redone, even though it was only Thursday.

Sometimes it's convenient having an auto body shop and a beauty salon all in one building. You wouldn't think so, but sometimes it is.

I guess you could say that by eight-thirty that morning, it was already a pretty strange day in Daily.

I'd just come out from under the hair dryer when Brother Ervin's news made it over from the café next door, via Harlan Hanson. Harlan had started his mail route earlier than usual that morning because he was packing the biggest story to hit our town since Elvis. That was the old bloated, rhinestone-wearing Elvis, and he never got off the bus, so really, that story doesn't compare with this one, even though Elvis had supposedly been dead for eight years when he showed up in Daily.

But a posthumous Elvis can't hold a candle to a real live TV network helicopter. It's more likely that the King of Rock and Roll would rise from the grave and show up on a tour bus than a TV network would come to Daily, so I didn't believe Harlan at first.

"Oh, for heaven's sake, Harlan, you expect us to swallow that?" I said. "It's more likely Brother Ervin's been eating too many of them pickled raisins with his breakfast." Ervin soaks brown raisins in white gin and eats them for medicinal purposes. It's supposed to cure arthritis, so everyone looks the other way, even though Ervin's our Baptist preacher. I don't hold it against him, and God probably don't, either. Being the Baptist preacher in a small town would drive anyone to eat gin-soaked raisins, eventually.

"Sober as a judge," Harlan argued, and he ought to know, because he and Ervin are brothers. "Erve saw a helicopter flyin' 'round and 'round over the fairgrounds out on Cowhouse Creek. Thought he'd better check on it, it bein' almost time for the Daily Reunion Days out there and all. By the time he got down the road, the whirlybird had landed and it uz goin' up again. Erve got a clean look at it." Squinting one eye like he was sighting in a rifle, Harlan stretched out a long bony finger and reenacted the drama of Brother Ervin and the helicopter. "How 'bout them apples?"

Behind me, Lucy clucked her tongue and shook a bottle of hairspray at him. "You say to Ervin we are only fools on the *first* day of April." What she meant, of course, was that this wasn't April Fool's Day. Lucy's from Japan originally, but she's been here since the fifties, when she came over as a war bride. Her English is good, but her Texan is questionable.

"This ain't no April fools," Harlan insisted. "That helicopter had a Austin TV station sign on the side, bigger'n Dallas. Whadd'ya think that means?"

"Can't imagine," I said, and I really couldn't.

"And then"—Harlan leaned close, like this part was top secret and the Russians were on the other side of the wall with cups on their ears—"Bailey Henderson gets a call not five minutes ago, down to the Town Hall. It's some stranger with a *Los Angeles* accent, asking all about the upcomin' Daily Reunion. After that he recalled when, a few days ago, some other stranger'd called and booked the community building for a surprise fiftieth wedding anniversary party. What's that tell ya?"

"Tells me someone's having a fiftieth wedding anniversary, and someone else is wantin' information about the Daily Reunion Days, which makes sense, being as it's coming up this weekend," I said.

"Yeah, but they both had *Los Angeles* accents," Harlan repeated, like I was a little thick, not getting the point and all. "Bailey's got it figured that the fiftieth anniversary's only a cover story for Amber's hometown reunion concert."

Sometimes I'd swear Harlan would swallow a boar hog if Bailey Henderson sugarcoated it for him. "Harlan, how does a Los Angeles accent sound, exactly?"

He threw his hands in the air, knocking some letters out of his pack. Lucy picked them up. "Well I don't know, Imagene. Like TV people and stuff. Like *TV people*. What's that tell ya?"

"I don't know, Harlan. What's it tell you?" I thought we'd been at this point once already.

Leaning close again, Harlan rolled his eyes upward like a lazy old yard dog watching a squirrel run overhead. "It means Amber Anderson made it to the Final Five on *American Megastar*. They always do them hometown visit shows with the top five finalists. Heck, I bet Amber's gonna win the whole thing. That child's been singin' since she was hip high to a horned toad. You can take it to the bank, Imagene. Our little hometown girl's gonna bring the bright lights to Daily. Brother Erve and the mayor are out there right now doin' their part to make Amber's dream come true. They done got a tarp cloth and some paint from the hardware store, they painted *American Megastar Finalist* and *Vote for Amber* on it, and they're hangin' it over Main Street, right below the Daily Reunion Days banner." With a purposeful nod, he added, "How's that for a fine bushel of 'taters?"

I stood there trying to get my hat around the idea. "Don't know," I said. "Seems foolish, getting everyone's hopes up, painting signs and all. A wiggle in the water don't mean there's a fish on the hook." I wasn't sure why I felt the need to tamp down Harlan's excitement. My mama used to say the blues is an ailment that don't like no sunshine in the room.

Harlan batted a hand my direction. "Trouble with you, Imagene, is you got no imagination anymore."

That stung a bit, being as my father named me Imagene, spelled one letter from *imagine*, because he wanted me to think big thoughts and believe in wondrous possibilities. But since my husband, Jack, died, I couldn't imagine much good happening in my life, or in Daily. The town and me were both just marking time, waiting for the days to pass.

"You just wait and see, Imagene Doll. There's big things comin'." Harlan wagged a finger in the air, then headed out the door, not willing to let me dampen his excitement about Daily getting a fresh dose of fame.

I stared out the window as Harlan disappeared down the Main Street business district. That sounds grander than it is. The business district doesn't have much more than a dozen buildings that mostly sit with paint peeling off the bricks, and the grand second-story windows staring blank into space, the nameplates reminding us that there were banks, and hotels, and dry goods stores back when wool and mohair were king. Folks don't shop the hometown anymore. Mostly, they go over to Austin to the Wal-Mart Supercenter, where they can get everything fast and easy. As much as I like Wal-Mart, I miss them old times when shopping was an event you got dressed up for.

All that to say, I guess, that Daily, same as a lot of small towns, stood forgotten, a little forlorn and faded, which seemed to suit me lately. Even the Reunion Days, which once brought Dailyians home from all over the country to visit relatives, listen to music at the bandstand, ride the old Ferris wheel, and admire the yearly catch of rattlesnakes, wasn't what it used to be. But watchin' Harlan walk away, I got the sudden and strange feeling this year's festival was gonna be dig-in-your-spurs-and-hang-on, Sally. We're goin' for a ride.

I wasn't sure I was ready for it.

Donetta seemed to sense a change coming. Her hands were shaking as she teased up my hair and lowered the barber chair. "Ye-ew suppose he's ri-ight?" When Donetta talks, every word's got at least three syllables, sometimes more.

"Doubt it," I said, but I could tell that Donetta was already sniffing a rustle in the wind. Donetta often has a sense about things, so I knew what it meant when she stared hard into the old plate glass windows. She was having another one of her revelations.

"What do *you* think?" I asked carefully.

In the corner, Lucy crossed herself and kissed her locket, where she keeps a curl of hair from the baby she had to leave behind in Japan.

The room took on an eerie silence as Donetta stared at the shifting reflections in the wavy glass. "I'm not sure." She shivered, even though it was a warm day. "I see . . . people . . . a lot of people." Then she turned away, shrugged her shoulders, and sighed. "But what do I know? I could just be havin' a hot flash."

She had a heavy look that told me otherwise. And besides, Donetta's long past the age for hot flashes. She pictured more in that window than she wanted to let on.

In the corner, Lucy was quiet.

"See you two after the breakfast rush," I said and hopped up, ready to get out of there before Donetta conjured one of her wild plans about how we were gonna cash in on whatever she'd just envisioned. "When I called Bob to tell him about the buzzard, he said he'd see if Maria could come in, but I should get over there for my shift quick as I could. He's got the coffee club backed up at the counter, waiting for breakfast. I'll settle up with you later for the cut and curl."

"Sure thing," Donetta said, and headed for the back room, still looking shell-shocked from whatever she had seen in the window.

Saying good-bye to Lucy, I slipped through the hidden door between the beauty shop and the café. No one knows why that swinging bookcase is in the wall behind the cash register. It's long been the subject of Daily supposition, but the fact is that no one, not even my daddy, who was the Daily mayor for half of his life, could say for sure. He got many a laugh over the years, telling tourists and impressionable young folks all sorts of wild stories about the hidden door.

My mama never much appreciated Daddy's tendency toward wild Irish storytelling and outlandish moneymaking schemes. She said the swinging shelves were put there so after you got your hair done you could get to the café without going out in the wind. My mama was a practical woman. Some might say she lacked imagination—a little like my boss at the café, Bob Turner, who said the doorway was put there so his help could sneak over to the beauty shop, catch up on the gossip, and waste the time they should have spent getting the dishes washed.

Most days, Bob's mood was somewhere between bull and bulldog, if you know what I mean, but today he was whistling "Hollywood" behind the fry grill when I came through the bookcase. My entrance scared him, and he jerked back, flipping a sausage patty into the air. Luckily, it landed on Doyle Banes's plate at the bar, where the gents of the regular Countertop Coffee Club watch the television, eat breakfast, and solve the problems of the entire world.

"Thanks, B-B-Bob." Doyle reached for his fork. Doyle stutters, by the way. Always has.

"That ain't done," Bob warned while tending to a pile of scrambled eggs that was about to burn. "Here, hand it back."

"I ulll-like it this way." Doyle wasn't about to give up on free food. Doyle's driven a dump truck down at the lime quarry for twenty years. Eats like a horse, but he's skinny as a rail fence.

"Oh, for heaven's sake, Doyle, you'll get worms." I snatched the sausage patty off Doyle's plate and tossed it back on the fry grill. Doyle's probably already got worms—that's why he's so skinny.

Bob flipped the sausage over and glanced my way. "So, Ima, d'ya hear the big news? Hollywood's comin' to town."

"Hollywood who, Bob?" I enjoy goading Bob. Lord help me, but I can't stop myself. He's like the loud-mouthed kid on the front row in school—the one who raises his hand on all the questions and thinks he knows everything. Come to think of it, Bob *was* the annoying kid on the front row. Me and him go back a long way.

"*The* Hollywood, of course. Hollywood Cali-forn-eye-yea."

"Well, I heard that Erve saw some traffic out at the fairgrounds, and then Bailey Henderson got a call about the Daily Reunion Days. But that's all I heard. Lands, Bob, your sources must be better than mine. Did Hollywood already call and tell you they were comin'?"

Bob coughed like he'd swallowed a gnat. "Well . . . well no, of course not." It hurt Bob to admit that. Being that Bob was the president of the Daily Chamber of Commerce, and Amber Anderson had worked part-time at the café for the past year after she graduated from high school, he was mightily offended that she hadn't yet thanked him on national TV or put in a plug for the Daily Café.

"I just thought, with you bein' president of the Chamber of Commerce and Amber's former employer, and all . . ." *That wasn't nice, Imagene. Love thy neighbor. But oh, Lord, Bob's hard to love most of the time. I've got a big mouth, and there's no telling sometimes what'll tumble out. I have to repent every five minutes or so. When I get to the pearly gates, I imagine the atonement line will be long with people who don't. I'll be in the short line at the express gate, because I'm on the repent-as-you-go plan.*

"Don't need no one to call me." Bob flipped eggs and sausage onto three plates, added hash browns and the tickets, and spun them down the counter to be handed out. "Don't take no genius to add two and two and come up with four. Now that Amber's made the Final Five, it's time for them to do one of them hometown return shows—take her back to her roots, back to her Daily beginnings." Bob struck a pose with his spatula in the air, dripping bacon grease.

"Well, Bob, I didn't know she'd ever left 'em. She's still dating Buddy Ray, down at the sheriff's office. Why, I hear they call back and forth all the way to California so she can keep up on the Daily happenings. Seems like if she was coming home for a visit, she'da told Buddy Ray." I gave Bob a blank look. You can get away with a lot by acting old and addle-brained.

Huffing, like talking to me was too much effort, Bob turned back to the fry grill. "I swear, Ima, you don't know a thing about Hollywood."

"Could be," I said, delivering the plates to the countertop crowd. Doyle gave me a grateful nod for bowing out of the argument before Bob could hop onto one of his soapboxes, talk everyone's ear off, and burn the breakfast food.

Bob was, clearly enough, disappointed that I didn't have more fight in me these days. Time was, we went toe-to-toe about a lot of things. None of it seemed to matter much anymore. Mostly, I just wanted to get through my day at the café, go home and crawl into bed, and wish I could wake up the next morning in heaven with Jack.

"You can mark my words, Imagene," Bob said, slinging the spatula and scattering grease that Maria and I'd have to mop up later. "Once all them TV watchers see Amber's humble beginnings—poor orphaned girl with three little brothers, livin' in a falling-in trailer house with her old grandpappy, her mama and daddy dead in a terrible car wreck—America's gonna vote our girl straight to the top. You don't believe me, just hop on out front and take a gander at that banner they're hangin' over Main Street. We're gonna put Daily, Texas, right back on the map."

Chapter 3

Mandalay Florentino

Across the street, a woman walked out of a café next to what looked like a turn-of-the-century hotel with a hair salon downstairs. Standing under a sign that said *Daily Café*, she held down her fluffy gray 'do with one hand and shaded her eyes with the other. She studied the workmen, who had folded up their ladders and were now admiring their new banner—the one that Ursula would hang me with as soon as she heard about it. She would be certain this was somehow my fault, that I'd botched my secret mission and let the country kitten out of the bag, so to speak. She would never believe that by the time I got to town, word was already hanging over Main Street in big blocky letters.

As if on cue, my cell phone rang. Leaving the phone hooked to my purse strap, I tucked the Bluetooth into my ear to answer. Ursula was on the other end. No doubt she could smell fear and impending devastation all the way from California.

"Manda, daah-ling," Her deep voice held a false, sugary lightness that slipped through the earpiece, ping-ponged around my brain, and instantly wrenched my stomach into a twist. She only called me *daah-ling* when she was about to heap a load of Swedish-accented poop on my head. "Your trip is goingk vell?"

Oh yes, it's wonderful, I thought. *You've dropped me on a secret reconnaissance mission into* The Andy Griffith Show. *Barney and Gomer just finished hanging Amber's news on a big fat sign across Main Street, and Aunt Bee is standing on the curb. My cell phone has attracted her attention. Now she's watching me. She's wondering what I'm doing. Can I come home now?* "Fine, so far. I did an aerial tour of the staging site at the fairgrounds and rodeo arena this morning. Announcing Amber's hometown return and having her do a few songs at the afternoon performance of the rodeo should be perfect. I think we can also get some good shots on Main Street—you wouldn't believe this place. Most of the activity this weekend will be at the fair, but I'm going to poke around this afternoon and scout some downtown locales. There's no real hotel here—just an old place on Main that may or may not still be operational, so we should stage from the nearest decent-sized town. I'll book something on my way back to the airport tonight."

"No-no-no." There it was, the dreaded rapid-fire no, which meant that Ursula had already planned this caper and I was just here to be her puppet. "I vant you to book rooms in ze town. Ve must be present every minute, so as not to be scooped by ze tabloids."

As usual, my mind rushed to translate the Ursula-speak into regular English. The first few sentences were always hard. After that, things started to come in loud and clear, whether I wanted them to or not.

"We cannot have them gettingk footage we do not want them to have. Am-beer must be carefully handled on this hometown vis-eet, and *you* will be her handler." Overhead, a thundercloud clapped, punctuating Ursula's newest plan. I stumbled back under the laundromat awning, momentarily dazed.

No. No, I will be back home in sunny LA, making wedding plans and perusing coastal maps with David, selecting exotic and luxurious ports of call, and figuring out how to survive almost three weeks with a tiny closet, no Jacuzzi tub, and no dry land in sight. "What? No. Amber has a handler. Butch." *Butch, the baby-faced intern with a crush on every woman in the office—remember him?* "Butch is Amber's handler."

"Butch izz gone." The words were short and quick, as if Ursula were taking a bite out of a big, juicy steak. Butch is gone. Chomp. Who would like to be next?

Even though experience told me now was the time to shut up, I heard myself blurt, "Why? What happened? Amber likes Butch. She listens to him." Actually, I liked Butch, too. He was a nice midwestern kid from some obscure film school. He had big hopes and dreams and was patient with Amber, even when she wandered off without telling him, landed herself in the tabloids, and landed him in trouble. Now that Amber's uncanny talent for attracting controversy was translating into ratings, Butch was Ursula's favorite boy.

Accent on *was*, apparently.

"Butch izz gone." The Swedish singsong had vanished from Ursula's voice. "Apparently, Mandee-lay, you have not seen *The National Examiner* today?"

No, sorry, I've been in cabs, airplanes, helicopters, and rental cars since three a.m. "I don't think they have *The National Examiner* here." I added a nervous little laugh, trying to make it sound like a joke. Ursula was not amused.

Overhead, another clap of thunder boomed across the sky, and a gust of wind twirled the Amber banner into an unreadable tube. Maybe the storm would blow it down. . . .

"On the front cover are pictures of Am-beer with this playboy, Justin Shay," Ursula growled into the other end of the phone. "She izz with him at the beach, in the café, in the convertible on Sunset Boulevard, huggingk in front of the studio, and at a rally for his Shokahna religion. Vhere, I ask you, was Butch while this was goingk on? It izz one thing for Am-beer to step into harmless trouble, or even to date some playboy who izz old enough to be her father, but we cannot have her seen entertaining thee Shokahna idea. She izz gos-peel singer. The impression that *Ameri-keen Megastar* has turned her from her religious convictions, vhatever they are, could be bad for ratingks. When she comes to hometown, there must be careful management of theese issue. If this Justin Shay arrives there with her, you must make sure zhere are no bad reflections upon ze show. Do you understandt?"

"I . . ." *Ay-ai-ai*. How in the world could I promise that? Justin Shay's own handlers couldn't keep him under control. He'd been in and out of jail for the last twenty years, for everything from drug abuse to compulsive gambling and hiring prostitutes. "I'll do my best."

"You vill do the job." Thunder added a silent *or else*.

Aunt Bee was coming across the street, one hand still holding down her puffy hairdo, and the other waving at me. "Hey there. Do you need some help?" she called.

"No . . . uhhh . . . thank you," I hollered over the rising wind.

"Vhat!" Ursula screeched in the earpiece. "Vhat? You are tell-ingk me no?"

"Are you lost?" The woman on the street cupped her hand near her mouth as a sudden gust blew her sideways three steps.

"No," I answered, adding a friendly wave that I hoped would send her back to her own side of the road.

"Vhat!" Ursula screamed.

"I mean, I'm not. I'm not saying no," I muttered, holding my purse and the phone near my face, while trying to look inconspicuous.

"Pardon?" Aunt Bee cupped a hand to her ear, shuffling the last few steps across the street and stepping onto the curb.

"No. I'm not lost, thank you."

"Mandee-lay. Vhat is goingk on?" Ursula's voice had risen three octaves and was now vibrating with irritation. The Swedish accent was getting thick again.

"Someone's here," I whispered, turning my shoulder to the street. Aunt Bee moved closer, looking curious. "I'd better go."

"You understand this—vhat I have told you to do izz not optional. You understand this, correct?"

"Yes, I understand. I'll take care of it." *I hope.*

"Very good. Good-bye, Mandee-lay." Was it my imagination, or did that good-bye have a note of permanence in it? That didn't sound like the see-you-in-a-few days kind of good-bye. That was the good-bye of a first-class passenger waving to a peasant on the deck of the *Titanic.*

Lowering my purse, I turned around. Aunt Bee was watching me inquisitively with her hands folded over her flowered Daily Café apron.

"I'm sorry." Pulling the Bluetooth from my ear, I pointed to the phone hooked on my purse strap. "I couldn't hear over the wind."

"Ohhh," she breathed, blinking at the Bluetooth looped around my finger. "Well, lands, that thing's tiny. I thought you were over here talkin' to yourself."

I had a mental picture of how I must have looked, carrying on a conversation with my purse. "No, I was talking to my, uhhh . . . friend." No point letting the locals know I was here on business. "My boyfriend, actually my fiancé." As usual, nervousness caused me to blurt out something idiotic. I'd never been a good liar, or quick at inventing diversionary dialogue under pressure—a short-coming that had ended my college on-camera internship almost before it began. The producer of the morning show quickly moved me behind the scenes and convinced me that production was where I belonged.

"Oh, well bless your heart. Idn't that nice?" Leaning from under the canopy, she checked the sky, then fished a plastic hair bonnet from her apron pocket and unfolded it like a tiny parachute in the wind. "I just wondered if you were all right over here. It's fixin' to come a toad strangler, and the washateria's closed on Thurs-deys." She nodded over her shoulder toward the darkened building behind us. "Come about five minutes from now, you'll be stranded like a horned toad on a high rock." Tying her bonnet into place, she squinted up and down the street, her faded hazel eyes narrow and perceptive. "You got a car near here somewhere?"

"Around the corner." I thumbed vaguely toward the alley, where I'd parked so as not to be noticed while I conducted my undercover surveillance for Project Amber. Clearly, the CIA would not be call-ing me with a job offer anytime soon.

The woman craned to look past me, searching for my car over the top of her half-moon glasses. "It break down or somethin'?"

"No, I'm fine, thanks." A gust of wind blew me forward, and I had a sudden vision of the Discovery Channel's *Tornado Alley* se-ries. What time of year did those things usually happen? I couldn't remember, but that would be my luck. Less than three months from my wedding to the perfect guy, I'd be swept off the face of the earth and deposited in Oz, where the dating prospects were limited to bald wizards, scarecrows, and tin men.

"Oh goodness!" Aunt Bee grabbed my arm, waving vaguely toward the north. "Here it comes. Hurry!" Motioning frantically for me to follow, she turned and stepped off the curb, starting across the street in a flatfooted shuffle-jog.

"Wait! What . . . Is it. . . ?" A clap of thunder drowned out my tornado inquiry, and I poked my head from under the washateria awning just in time to see what looked like a wall of rain overtaking the Buy-n-Bye convenience store at the edge of town. In thirty seconds or so, it would engulf my car, and about fifteen seconds after that I was going to be stranded like a horned toad on a high rock. Faced with that prospect, I dashed across the road after Aunt Bee. Being younger and more spry, I passed her up at the center line and was waiting under the canopy of the Chamber of Commerce when she arrived. We stood watching as the leading edge of the storm swept over Main Street like the Red Sea falling back together after Moses got through with it. Overhead, the Amber banner flapped in the wind, the deluge slowly turning the letters into an unintelligible but rather interesting tie-dye.

Aunt Bee shook her head. "Guess the paint wadn't set."

"Guess not." One problem solved. That was easy.

"Figures." Shaking her head, she stepped back into the building's doorway, where the cement was dry.

Sheets of water blew horizontally under the awning, driving me into the alcove with her. "Does it always rain this hard?" I asked, and she nodded. My mind spun ahead to this weekend, the location shoot, and what I was going to do if this storm continued until then. If the Daily Reunion Days were rained out, how would we show Amber returning to her birthplace in a splash of hometown glory? Other than the high school gym, the community building, and an old movie theater that appeared to be closed down, there wasn't a building big enough to hold a decent-sized crowd. We'd already booked the community building, under the pretense of a fiftieth anniversary celebration, for Amber's surprise hometown appreciation concert. "The rain seems to be slacking off a little," I remarked hopefully, and the woman nodded, studying the clouds with a practiced eye.

"Don't reckon it'll continue long. Just a dust settler."

"Good," I breathed. "I was worried we might be in for a major storm."

She chuckled softly—a stifled sort of belly laugh that was both friendly and comforting. "You're not from around here, are ya?"

"No. I'm not."

Nodding, she indicated that my answer was pretty much a no-brainer. "You know the old sayin' about Texas weather—long foretold, long last, short foretold, quickly past. Anythin' comes in this fast, you can figure it'll blow back out quicker'n you can pull the cover off the rain barrel. Soon as it lets up a bit, we can make the dash down to the beauty shop. There's coffee there, or the café's open. There's not much left on that side of the street you were on."

Mental note—place cameras on east side of street, so as to capture vibrant, active hometown businesses rather than abandoned buildings and run-down washateria. "I hadn't noticed. Guess I pulled in on the wrong side of the road, didn't I?"

Aunt Bee nodded. I had the distinct feeling she was trying to figure me out. With a keen eye, she took in my Italian leather slingbacks, the silk slacks, the Prada handbag, the George jacket, all of which would have set me back a month's pay if they hadn't been cast-offs from Wardrobe—a perk of my glamorous new job. Was it my imagination or was she looking at my finger? The naked one that was still waiting for the engagement ring David hadn't found time to buy yet.

"So, what's the lucky fella's name? When's the big date?"

For a mortifying second, I couldn't remember. My mind had drifted to Ursula, and the idea that perhaps we should film the abandoned side of the street after all. Ursula would probably like the idea of a dying hometown. It would reinforce Amber's came-from-nothing image. "My . . . uhhh . . . pardon me?" *Focus, Mandalay, focus. Your fiancé—the man you're going to marry. Remember him? He has a name. Uhhh . . .* "David." The word popped out as fast as a rabbit from a hat, sounding false, like a magician's prop. Why did it always seem that way? *I do have a fiancé. I do. I do. I met him five months ago on* MyDestiny.com, *and we've been dating ever since. . . .*

"We're getting married on his boat in June. Then we're taking to the high seas for three weeks." A jolt of anxiety went through me, followed by a twinge of vertigo and a momentary sense of unreality during which I tried, as usual, to imagine myself drifting on a sailboat, surrounded by miles and miles and miles of water, with fish and sharks and other slimy creatures in it. *We are?* a voice whispered in my head. *Are we really going to do that?*

"Way-ul, bless yer heart," the woman was saying. "Doesn't that sound excitin'? My Jack used to dream about quittin' work at the insurance office and setting sail on a cruise ship. One day he come home and told me he was ready to retire. He said, 'Imagene'—I'm Imagene Doll, by the way. Sorry I didn't introduce myself. Anyhow, Jack said, 'Imagene, we been workin' all these years, and I've seen some of the world in the navy, but we ain't seen much of the world together. It's time.' " Letting her eyes fall closed, she laughed under her breath. "He had the tickets for a cruise and everything, but I couldn't do it." With a rueful shake of her head, she added, "I was afraid I'd get the willies, out there in the middle of that water, with sharks 'n' that sort of thing, and no dry land in sight."

Yes. Me, too. That's it exactly. I'm having a problem with the no-dry-land thing. "Mandalay Florentino," I said quickly, shaking her hand. "My fiancé is an experienced sailor. He says if you spend enough time at sea, you get used to it." Of course, even after six years of marriage, his ex-wife still hated the boat. She resented the time he spent at the marina. *I will not be that kind of wife. I will embrace the boat.*

Imagene's gaze caught mine, the creases around her eyes deepening contemplatively. "Jack told me the same thing, but I never did find out if he was ri-ight. We turned in the cruise tickets, bought us a camper, and saw places on land. Me and Jack were gen'rally pretty good at working things out so we'd both be happy."

"That's nice." What compromises would David and I face over the years? How would we have to change for each other? *Would* we change for each other?

In Hollywoodland, compromise is a dirty word. It comes wrapped in unwelcome connotations of settling for something less than perfect, of reaching for the brass ring and falling short.

Imagene stared off into the street, where the rain had tapered to a steady downpour and the Amber banner had been washed white as snow. "After Jack passed on, I always wished we'd taken the cruise. I'da liked to see those places, I think." It was hard to say whether she was talking to me or just reminiscing out loud. The melancholy tone of the words made them seem private.

"You still could," I offered.

"I might, someday." Silence fell over us, and we stood in the doorway, watching the rain, looking into the past, into the future.

Under the next canopy to the north, the door jerked open and a tall, thin woman with even taller red hair peeked through.

"Whut'na world you two doin' out'chere'n the rain?" Pushing the door open farther, the red-haired woman braced a hand on her hip. I only *thought* Imagene had an accent.

"Just passin' time, Donetta," Imagene called, moving to the edge of our dry spot. "Waitin' out the storm. I rescued this young lady from out in front of the washateria."

"Washateria's closed Thurs-deys," Donetta pointed out.

"Told her that. That's how we ended up here."

Donetta craned her neck, inspecting me as if I were an alien about to invade the Daily Chamber of Commerce. "Way-ul, y'all just git on over here. We got coffee. No sense standin' out'n the rain."

Motioning for me to do likewise, Imagene made the dash to the next awning. I followed suit, huddling my arms over my chest, protecting the Prada at all cost. Prada is not meant to be rained on.

We arrived, slightly dampened and breathless, in the beauty shop doorway. Imagene glanced at her watch. "Think I'd better git on back to work before Bob has a rigor. I'll drop over for coffee after the lunch crowd dies out." Motioning toward the café building, she turned to me. "Got a chicken-fried steak special today, comes with mashed 'taters and good cream gravy."

My stomach rolled over at the idea of deep-fried meat smothered in white flour and trans fat. No way that was on the Best Life Diet. "No thanks. I ate some kind of Mexican breakfast burrito–thing this morning." *Which isn't on the diet, either, and quite unfortunately is still with me.* "Actually, what I really need to do is get a room booked." If the weather was going to be wet and nasty, I definitely didn't want to drive the forty or so miles to the nearest real town. "Is this hotel open, or is there one close by?" Even if it was Ursula's idea, there would be advantages to stationing myself at a base of operations on Main Street.

Imagene shook her head. "Well, no, but if you go . . ."

"Actually, I do have a room available," Donetta preempted, snatching my arm and drawing me toward the beauty parlor like a fly into a web. "You just come right on in hay-er, darlin'." The next thing I knew, I was being hauled in the door so fast that I stumbled over a tiny Asian woman with permed salt-and-pepper hair. She seemed as stunned as I was.

From the sidewalk, Imagene protested, "Donetta, you don't . . ."

Kicking the door closed, my new friend slipped an arm around my shoulders. Donetta guided me through the salon toward an old hotel desk by a timeworn oak stairway in the back of the room. " 'J'like some coffee? It's hot and black. Lucy, pour this little gal a cup, would'ja? Hon, you visitin' from outta town? How long you plannin' to stay? Don't you worry 'bout a tha-ang. Here in Daily, we believe in good hospitality. Yey-us, we shore do, I'll tell ya that right now. We'll fix ye-ew up quicker'n ye-ew can say Cooter Brown."

Chapter 4

Imagene Doll

Curiosity was eating me like a winter cow on spring wheat by the time the lunch crowd tapered off, and I felt the need to slip over to the beauty shop to see what Donetta had done with that cute little girl I found outside the washateria. Grabbing the leftover pecan pie for a snack before our afternoon exercise show, I headed for the bookshelf.

When I came through the wall, Donetta was giving a haircut to some good-looking young fella in a Hawaiian shirt, starched blue jeans, and flip-flops. Definitely an out-of-towner. The bookcase creaked as I shut it, and that boy popped out of the barber chair, hit the floor flat-footed, spun around, and reached for something on his belt.

"Don't shoot!" I hollered. "I got pecan pie."

That boy got tickled at the sight of an old lady held up with a pecan pie, and he grinned as he sat down. "No thank you, ma'am," he said with a little twinkle in his eye.

Donetta finished brushing off his flowerdy shirt, then set her tools aside. "That'll do it," she said, like it was the most normal thing in the world to be cutting the hair on a fella in a Hawaiian getup and beach shoes. "Nice to meet you, Carter. Thanks for coming in." As usual, Donetta'd used the haircutting opportunity to get sociable.

"My pleasure." He smiled again as he handed her a twenty-dollar bill. On the other side of the room, Lucy fluffed her hair. Carter was a handsome fella. Too young for any of us, of course.

"Hope ya feel better." Donetta went right on chattering as she rolled the twenty around her finger. "Sorry you had such a rough flight back to Austin. Them storms just blow in like wildfire this time of year. Don't imagine it's like that where you flew in from. Where'd you say that was?"

"California," he answered pleasantly, following her to the cash register.

That cinched it. Donetta could make friends with a stump. She could get Moses to tell the secrets of the burning bush. "Oh, isn't that nice? I hear California's a real pretty place." Counting out the boy's change, she winked at Lucy.

"Yes, it is, but this trip was pretty much all airport, hotel, and high-rise—just business," he said, and started toward the door. He stopped with his hand on the knob and stood looking around the building. "Thanks for the conversation. It's good to be back in Texas."

Donetta closed the cash drawer, nodding like she understood. "Way-ul, I sure hope your brother feels better. That's awful young to have cancer. But they can do some amazin' things these days, and Austin has great hospitals. Don't lose hope. My cousin had cancer. She went with one of them stem cell transplants, too, and now she's healthy as a horse."

"Thanks," he said as he put on his sunglasses. There was a hint of moisture in his eyes before the room reflected off the mirrored lenses and he went out the door.

I wondered what else that boy had told Donetta, but I didn't question her right away. She was staring into the window glass again. She didn't flinch, even when the pie, and Lucy and I, moved to the old hotel counter by the stairs, where we keep the coffee pot and various kitchen items.

Lucy and I fixed coffee and pie, and waited. We'd learned not to disturb Donetta when she was looking into the glass. When she finally came to the counter, she had a determined expression. "Ima," she said, checking her watch, "could you sneak away for a bit tomorrow after the breakfast rush and go get some things for me at the Wal-Mart over in Austin? I'd do it myself, but I've got appointments booked solid, and tomorrow's my day to do hair at the old folks' home." Squinting hard toward the stairs, she pursed her lips and nodded. "We're gonna need paint. Lots of paint."

I hesitated for a minute, studying Donetta and wondering if sending me to Wal-Mart was another one of her little plans to get me out and about. Donetta didn't like the fact that all I did these days was go from work to home and back. "I probably could, if it's real important," I said carefully.

"It's important," Donetta answered. "I already called down to Barlinger's Hardware, but they don't have enough of any one color in stock—unless I want barn paint, and that won't do."

"I'll have to ask off from Bob," I said, still hanging back a little. Maybe the drive to Wal-Mart would do me good, though. "Bob's got Maria there with Estacio, and she could wait tables, as long as it's not too busy." I savored a bite of pie, afraid to ask, on an empty stomach, about Donetta's plans for the paint. Being an accomplice in a Donetta Bradford plan requires fortification, and lots of it.

Lucy beat me to it—the asking, that is. "What? You a-goin' to paint the old folk home?"

"Nope." Donetta scooped a bite of pie and chugged it down like a hungry field hand. "We're gonna reopen them old rooms upstairs. I rented 'em to that lady that was here this mornin'."

I choked on my coffee. "You did *what*?"

"I rented her the hotel rooms. One room for tonight and to-morrow night, then all the rooms for Saturday night, through the weekend," she stated, just as sure as if she were saying, *The sun is gonna rise in the east tomorrow*.

"Donetta!" I gasped. "Those rooms haven't been used in years. You can't rent them out to folks."

Lucy followed the conversation back and forth like a spectator at a tennis match.

"I sure enough can," Donetta declared, jerking her chin up. I almost expected her to get on her hind legs and fight. "All them rooms need is some junk cleared out from last year's parade and the church rummage sale, linens washed, and a quick coat of paint."

"By *tonight*?" What in the world was she thinking? There wasn't one of those rooms fit for habitation, much less by some lady wearing silk pants and toting a high-dollar handbag.

Donetta wagged her chin like I was half idiot. "Not by tonight. By Saturday. We can get the rooms ready by Saturday."

"What are you gonna do with that girl until Saturday?" As usual, the more Donetta talked, the less sense she made. "Keep her at your house?"

Donetta glanced away, then back at me, then cut a quick look toward the stairs. "I gave her the keys to the Beulah room."

Both Lucy and I gasped at once. Clearly, Donetta's plan had caught even Lucy unaware.

"You gave her . . . *the Beulah room*?" I repeated slowly, trying not to imagine what Beulah, Donetta's mother-in-law, would say if she knew Donetta had rented out Beulah's private shrine.

Lucy muttered something in Japanese. I think she was praying.

Chewing the side of her lip, Donetta nodded. "Mama B's in Florida for another month and a half yet. It ain't like she's usin' the room."

I wasn't sure if Donetta was trying to convince herself or me. She looked nervous, and rightly so. Beulah was about as easy to get along with as a cow with a swole-up teat, and not half as useful. When Beulah took up residence in Daily, in between her winter trips to Florida and her summer trips to New Mexico, Donetta's blood pressure went haywire.

And aside from the obvious question of Beulah's reaction to having her room rented out, there was the issue of the room itself. "Has that girl *seen* the Beulah room?"

Donetta folded her arms on the edge of the table and locked them down tight. "Well, no, but she said she wasn't particular."

"She looks particular."

"Well, she said she wasn't, and she paid in cash—for all five rooms. I gave her the key to her room, and one to the rear entry door, and she left. She said she had some tourin' to do around town and she'd be back later."

"So she ain't actually *seen* the Beulah room yet." Which made sense, considering that I hadn't heard anyone run out of the hotel screaming while I was serving lunch at the café.

"No, she ain't, actually."

The conversation dried up for a minute, and the three of us took bites of pie and swilled it around, thinking.

Even though I hated to do it, I had to bring up the subject of the rooms again. "It just don't make sense, Netta. Why do all that work, clean out and paint the rooms, just for a few days' rental? It won't pay what you put into it."

Setting down her fork, Donetta let out a long breath, the air blowing through her Rumba Red #5 lips in something between a whistle and a sigh. "That lady's from Hollywood, Ima. If she stays here and the hotel gets on *American Megastar*, it'll bring the customers back, just like the old days." Donetta'd always hated the fact that after several decades of declining business, she'd had to close down the hotel that had been in her family for over a hundred years.

"Who said she's from Hollywood?" Call me slow, but so far there hadn't been any herd of cameras showing up in Daily. So far, all we had was a lot of supposing and guessing, and a couple yay-hoos hanging a banner over Main Street.

Donetta turned slowly, her pale gray eyes reflecting the faded words *Daily Hotel* from the old plate glass window. "Nobody has to say it, GiGi." Donetta only called me GiGi during serious, emotional moments. It was a pet name from childhood, one of our sister-names for each other. DeDe and GiGi. "I just know."

The room went silent, and a draft moaned down the dumbwaiter behind the counter, as if the building itself were getting in on the conversation. The sound crept up my shirt, and I shivered head to toe. Beside me, Lucy crossed herself and kissed her locket with the baby curl in it.

"All right. I'll go to Wal-Mart for you," I said, even though I knew it was crazy. One thing we all need in this world is a friend who'll buy paint without asking questions. "Any particular color?" All right, that was one question, but I didn't ask how three old women were going to clean out four musty hotel rooms.

"What?" Donetta asked, only halfway listening. Her eyes were darting around the beauty shop, making bold plans that, if she revealed them, would probably drive me to climb to the roof and jump off.

"The paint. What color?"

"Oh . . . off white." The words were confident, like she could already see it in her mind. "That washable latex kind. Flat. Flat hides imperfections." She sighed, looking up at the ceiling, momentarily deflated by the weight of her own intentions. "I'll line up some high school kids to help us with the job. No telling what shape those rooms are in up there."

That was a point I couldn't even stand to rehash. I didn't want to think about what the rooms looked like. "All right. Flat off-white latex. How much?"

"A lot." She was too far into her own world to count up gallons.

"All right. A lot." Lucy and I traded glances like two castaways being dragged out to sea. "I'll run over and talk to Bob about getting off awhile tomorrow morning," I said, and left poor Lucy there to deal with the rest of Donetta's plan.

I caught Bob cleaning up the fry grill and asked him about taking a break tomorrow to go to Wal-Mart for Donetta. I tried to sound casual, because I didn't want any questions about Donetta and her crazy plan.

Fortunately, Bob didn't ask for details. "Sure. Not a problem," he said, as I'd expected he would. Bob's like a back-porch hound dog. Slow moving, not real smart, prone to bark whenever the wind shifts. Today he had bigger things on his mind anyway. "Hey, uhhh . . . Guess you didn't hear anything else over there at Donetta's . . . about Hollywood comin' to town, I mean."

"Well, Donetta was giving a haircut to a young fella in a flowerdy shirt when I walked in. Never seen him before. Told Donetta he just flew in from California. Seemed strange to me, because he didn't talk citified. I swear, Donetta could make friends with a stump, and . . ." *Oh shoot. Time to shut up.* Past time. If Bob's an old hound dog, I'm one of them useless little house mutts that can't stop yapping. *Yip, yip, yip, yip.*

Bob's face went gray, and I knew I'd stirred up a hornet's nest. He started pacing behind the counter, muttering to himself about how he couldn't understand why, being as he was the president of the Daily Chamber of Commerce, no one from *American Megastar* had contacted him yet, asking about permits and clearances to film on the streets of Daily. I could tell by the look in his eye that he was about to plow into the situation like a tornado down the midway of the county fair.

I did the wise thing and said, "Thanks, Bob. I'm gonna run over and finish my pie and coffee, then take an exercise class. I'll be back before the supper rush gets going." Bob didn't answer as I hurried to the shelves. He was too busy plotting his next move.

"Bob says it's fine," I told Donetta as I came back through the wall. She didn't answer me, either, but just nodded, her attention fixed on the window. She was plotting her next move, too. Which made me wonder why I was the one going to Wal-Mart tomorrow, since I wasn't plotting anything.

I knew what it must feel like to be one of the little wooden men on the chessboard when the old farts sit around in the afternoons. My job here was to do all the movin', none of the thinkin'. If someone got knocked off the table and kicked in the dirt, it'd probably be me.

I was still thinking about paint when Donetta pushed away her coffee cup, clapped her hands, and hopped out of the chair. "Guess we better get on with exercise class." She walked to the TV and turned on the VCR. "Y'all want *Sweatin' to the Oldies*, *Buns of Steel*, or *Yoga With Yahani* today?"

"Yahani have bun of steel," Lucy said without looking up. Given the choice, Lucy always picked *Yoga With Yahani*.

"Lucy!" Donetta gasped, as if she was consumed with utter mortification. Truth was, she was the one who bought *Yoga With Yahani*, and not because she thought three old ladies were gonna master yoga.

Lucy just shrugged and grinned, and they went on with a discussion about which tape to use.

I tuned it out and focused on my pecan pie. I was thinking about the mess in the rooms upstairs and getting more and more depressed, which made me want to eat. Pecan pie comforts a lot of hurts. Unfortunately, it won't paint hotel rooms or move parade decorations and yard sale leftovers to the storage shed.

"Ima!" Donetta's voice snapped me back to life, which was probably good because I could feel myself sinking deeper into a funk. "Come on. We're doin' *Yoga With Yahani.*"

Donetta had filled what used to be the back of the hotel lobby with secondhand fitness machines. At one time, she'd had visions of adding to the beauty shop income by opening a workout studio in the space that wasn't needed for the beauty shop, but so far the class had only grown to three—four, if you included Yahani.

I thought about making an excuse and going back over to the café, but I knew if I did, Donetta would be on me again about how I was letting myself go since Jack died. She'd start handing me books about depression, and calling me over for the *Dr. Phil* show, and making excuses to invite me to supper with her and her husband, Ronald, so I wouldn't be home alone all evening.

"All right, sweats on, then *Yoga With Yahani,*" Donetta said, and disappeared into the bathroom, where she kept her exercise clothes. Lucy headed for the storage closet to change, and I got my exercise suit from behind the old hotel desk, then went to the bathroom out back in the auto shop so I could change and use the restroom, which at my age is pretty much an essential precaution before vigorous movement.

"Hey there, Imagene." Donetta's brother, Frank, peeked from under the hood of a car as I came out in the ugly purple sweat suit one of the kids gave me for Christmas. "Got yer new windshield ready to put in this afternoon, then I'll pull yer car around front."

"Thanks, Frank," I said. As usual, he was looking out for me. Frank and I go back a long way.

"Put-put-put y-y-you up another buz-buzzard." Doyle was hanging around the back of the shop by the domino table. "Sure ya don-don-don't want credit for the urr-raccoon, too?" He pointed to the chalkboard, where another stick buzzard had been added beside my name.

"No, that's all right. I didn't kill the raccoon. It was dead before I got there."

"B-b-buzzard b-b-bait," Doyle joked, and Frank laughed as I headed back into the beauty shop. When I got there, Donetta was just inserting *Yoga With Yahani*. Lucy and I moved into position and we started our deep breathing.

We'd moved through a couple of stretches and were working our way into downward dog when the door opened.

"Be there in a minute," Donetta called, keeping her eyes closed so as to stay focused. Once she starts yoga class, she don't quit for anything. Folks around town know that, and usually take a seat at the front to wait.

I glanced under my armpit, and that young out-of-towner who'd had the haircut earlier was just rounding the cash register counter. He stopped midstride, looking no small bit embarrassed. I could imagine the view from where he was—one big behind and two bony ones in old sweat suits with granny panties hanging out the top.

"Uhhh . . ." He cleared his throat, trying to wipe away a grin. "I can come back later."

Donetta opened her eyes and gaped at him upside down. "No, that's all right." Walking her hands backward so that she looked like a frog on stilts, she snapped up quicker than I'd have thought was possible.

Lucy braced one hand on her knee and one on the floor, got her balance, then hauled herself to her feet with a muffled groan. I collapsed onto all fours, baby-crawled my way to the exercise bike, and used the seat to pull myself up. We stood staring at the boy, Donetta and I straightening our sweat suits and Lucy fluffing her hair.

"Well, how do, Carter," Donetta said, like she'd known him all her life. She ushered him back toward the cash register. "You're back awful soon. Did I forget to give you your change or somethin'? I been known to do that sometimes. I get to talkin' to folks and I'll tell you what, I just forget what I'm supposed to be doin'. My daddy always said I could talk the beans right off the bush and into the basket."

Carter laughed. "Well, that'd save a lot of work, wouldn't it?" He gave Donetta a wide, slow smile that was dazzling against his tanned skin.

Donetta blushed, then giggled like a teenage girl. "Well, yes. Yes, I guess that's true, isn't it? What can I do for you, Carter?" She spoke in a smooth, soft voice that wasn't hers at all. She sounded like the pastor's wife on the Sunday morning preachin' show, all sweetness and light.

Carter surveyed the room, pausing to nod at Lucy and me. "Afternoon, ladies," he said. Lucy giggled and I felt a little flutter of color rise into my cheeks. Mercy, that boy did have the prettiest blue eyes. I wondered if he was a movie star, one of those sweet-talking types who rolled into town with a big smile and mysterious ways.

He turned his attention back to Donetta. "Actually, I need to rent a hotel room." He motioned over his shoulder toward Donetta's front window. "I noticed it says *hotel*."

"Oh . . . well . . ." Donetta hesitated, no doubt hating to tell him she didn't have any rooms to rent and he'd have to stay in Austin or Waco. So far today, we'd already rented five more rooms than we actually had.

Which brought up the question of why all of a sudden everyone was interested in a hotel that had been closed for years due to lack of business.

"For how many days?" Donetta asked.

Lucy and I looked at each other with our mouths hanging open.

"Donetta," I said, "you don't have . . ."

Swatting a hand behind her back, Donetta shifted so that her shoulder was to us.

Carter chewed the side of his lip, thinking. "Through the weekend. Maybe through Monday."

"Well, let me see . . ." Donetta pulled out her date book and made a show of scanning through it, which was silly, considering there was nothing in there but beauty appointments. "I think we can handle that."

"Donetta . . ." I gasped, and Donetta shot me the *hush up or else* look, then slid around the counter, keeping her hand on the boy like she thought he might make a run for it.

Beside me, Lucy started rubbing the locket with the baby hair as Donetta reached for the ring of skeleton keys that opened the hotel doors. "Forty . . . ummm . . . five. Forty-five dollars a night, plus tax. That sound all right? There's coffee and sweet rolls here by seven in the morning, and we got an exercise room. You're welcome to use it any time."

"Sounds great."

"Wonderful!" Donetta purred like a cat being scratched behind the ears. She held up the keys. "Now, this one opens the back door in the alley, in case we're gone for the night when you come back. Then, the other one—this old timey key here, it's for your room door. Upstairs, down at the end of the hall to the left, number 2. The bathroom for that one's across the hall. I hope that's okay."

Carter held out his hand, and the keys dropped into his palm. "Sounds fine. I'll try not to be too much trouble." He winked at Donetta, and she turned pink as a baby's bottom.

"Oh, you're no trouble," she said as he turned toward the door. "Just make yourself at home. We have exercise class here at three every afternoon—no charge for hotel guests."

Carter tucked the keys into his pocket, then hooked his thumb on the rim. "I'll give that some thought." He grinned at Lucy and me as he headed toward the door. Maybe he'd just had a flash of the three of us with our rear ends in the air. "I'm not sure I can keep up."

As soon as he was gone, I lit into Donetta. "Donetta Bradford, what in the world has gotten into you? This morning you rent five hotel rooms you don't have and now you've rented six? You just gave that boy the keys to the Beulah room. You can't rent him the Beulah room." I pointed toward the back stairway that led to one end of the upstairs hall. "This morning you rented the Beulah room to that gal with the fancy suit. The one who wasn't *particular*, remember? And by the way, I think she is . . . particular, I mean, but even if she ain't, don't you think she's gonna mind having some strange man in her room?"

"It depend on the man," Lucy interjected, and both Donetta and I gave her dirty looks. Lucy shrugged and wandered off to the storage closet to change back to her regular clothes, since exercise time was over now.

Jerking her chin down, Donetta rolled her eyes up at me so they were white on the bottom and half covered with fake eyelashes on the top. When she did that, she looked like something out of a late-night horror movie. "The Beulah room's a *suite*."

"I don't think she's gonna want to share a *suite* with some man she don't know, either." The conversation was starting to spin off into an argument.

"It depend on the man," Lucy called from the closet.

Pulling the junk box from under the counter, Donetta fished out a skeleton key, shook it in my face, and grinned. "That's why I'm headed up right now to lock the door between the two rooms. The lady left without ever seeing the place, said she'd be back later. She'll never know the difference. She don't need a whole suite anyhow. Just think, GiGi, six hotel rooms rented all at once. It's just like the old days. In the morning, I'm gonna make some of my special pecan rolls and bring them in hot." She trotted off toward the back hall, just as happy as a cow in clover.

I stood there watching her go, my gut churning up what was left of my pie and coffee. Them two young folks had no idea what they were in for.

Good as Donetta's pecan rolls were, they weren't near enough to make up for an entire night in the Beulah room.

Chapter 5

Mandalay Florentino

My afternoon in Daily, Texas, was like a field trip to the set of Niceville. The storm clouds moved away and the sun came out, giving downtown a Disney World feel—a little too clean, the people militantly friendly in the grocery store, and the surreal atmosphere of the little variety shop on the corner of Second and Main, the Buy-n-Bye convenience store, the feed mill across the road with its granary silos casting long, thin shadows over Main Street. That would be a problem if we shot late in the day. In the afternoon light, the thick strips of shade looked like giant prison bars.

Then again, maybe that was an angle for the Amber segment—beautiful, talented young woman escapes the lack of opportunity in a small town, the stigmas of poverty and a difficult home life, leaves the confines of Niceville and breaks out into . . . into what, exactly? The wild rush of LA? The grit, the smog, the tabloids, the inherent dangers of the Hollywood Brat Pack, fast cars, instant fame, days and nights lived at light speed?

The truth was that LA was no place for little girls from Nice-ville. Even when you've lived there all your life, it's unpredictable at best. The city still surprises you. Hollywood had changed since my mother's days as a bit player in movies and TV shows, mostly westerns because she knew how to ride a horse. At one time, that was a marketable skill, so even though she hated horses, she took lessons and learned what to do. Ironically, she and my father were now semiretired to Sonoma Beach, where they lived across from a huge horse-showing facility, in a house that my father, as usual, had purchased during a foreclosure sale at the courthouse. Mother complained that the horsey odor of this particular locale made her allergies act up.

If she caught a whiff of the feed mill in Daily, Texas, she'd probably pass out. The breeze spun momentarily in my direction, surrounding me with what smelled like a combination of Cheerios, rotten trash, old grease, and molasses.

All scents aside, though, the place was down home and old-fashioned, a relic of bygone days when country life centered around farming—just the sort of Amber Anderson Americana that might be perfect for a passing shot, maybe a thirty-second interview spot to be cut into Amber's location piece. . . .

Picture leathery-skinned man in front of mill building, one hand hooked in overalls, other hand wrapped around hoe or plow handle, maybe a basket of fresh eggs. Shoot low angle, get the towers overhead with the faded lettering, Wool, Mohair, Cotton, Feed & Seed. *Farmer man says something like, "Yep, we always support our own here in Daily, Texas. We're behind Amber all the way. That poor little gal's had a tough life, but she's a fighter and this is the land of opportunity. God bless Amber Anderson, and God bless America!"*

I crossed the street to see what the front of the building looked like, and an old man waved at me from the porch of the feed mill. He was perfect for my imaginary shot—overalls and all. I watched with idle curiosity as he parked a dolly of heavy-looking grain bags on the loading dock, then began picking up the sacks and heaving them to a young African-American man standing in the bed of a pickup truck.

"You home helpin' your Grandpa Harve over spring break, Otis Charles?" the older man asked between throws.

Otis Charles nodded, swiping a muscular arm across his forehead. "Yes, sir, I am. Pay's not the best, but the food doesn't get any better anywhere."

The feed store man rested against his dolly, catching his breath. "Don't look like you're missin' too many meals down there at UT, son. How's off season goin'?"

"Pretty good." Otis Charles jumped onto the dock in one quick, fluid leap. "Vince Gibson's graduating, so next year I got a good shot at starting running back."

"You always been better than Vince Gibson anyway, O.C. Vince Gibson didn't spend his summertimes shovelin' rolled oats and cotton seed hulls." The feed store man gave Otis Charles an approving nod.

"True enough," O.C. agreed.

"You keepin' your grades good down there? Not falling into liquor and wild women, are ya?"

Otis Charles grinned, his dark eyes catching the uneven light. "No, sir. Gotta have the grades to get into the MBA program, so I can come home and run the feed mill. You're gettin' too old for this, right?"

The miller laughed. "You're a good kid, O.C."

Chuckling under his breath, O.C. grabbed one of the remaining sacks and tossed it into the truck like a paperweight. "I got this, Mr. O'Donnell."

Mr. O'Donnell rested a foot on the dolly wheel, holding it in place. His gaze circled vaguely in my direction, then returned to O.C. "Sure wish we still had Amber Anderson around. That girl wasn't big as a minute, but she could heft a sack of feed. She'd help get your order loaded."

Otis Charles nodded, tossing in the last sack. "Amber always did keep this old place in line. Every time I see her on TV, all I can think about is her knockin' me over and stealing my ribbon calf right out from under me in the Reunion Days calf scramble when I was seven years old. I was so mad I grabbed that ribbon outta her hand, and she wrestled me for it, too. Next thing I knew, my granny was coming over the arena fence. She pretty near jerked my ear clean off and made me give that ribbon back and tell Amber I was sorry. I didn't even get to stay for the carnival rides—Granny just marched me to the car, wearin' me out all the way, Amber followin' behind us, trying to hand that ribbon back, crying and saying, 'It's all right, Mrs. Beedie, it's all right. He got it fair and square.' I reckon she thought my granny was gonna tear me in half, the way she lit me up going across that parking lot."

Shaking his head, Otis Charles closed the tailgate. "Once we got in the car, Granny just looked at me and said, 'O.C., you oughta be ashamed. You know the Andersons need to win that calf a lot more than you do.' That was pretty much all it took. You know Grandma Beedie. You don't respect her opinion, she'll smack some respect into you."

"Yes, she will," Mr. O'Donnell agreed. "You tell Mrs. Beedie I said hi."

"I'll do that."

Stepping back with the dolly as Otis Charles drove away, Mr. O'Donnell waved at me. "Afternoon, ma'am."

"Afternoon," I said. Watching him disappear into the mill, I imagined Amber growing up in this place. Daily, Texas, a little Utopia where boys learned the lessons of humanity and charity early, black and white loaded feed in perfect harmony, and grandmothers commanded respect, one way or the other.

I had the fleeting thought that if Amber didn't make it into the Final Showdown—the point at which the two remaining performers were essentially guaranteed fame, recording contracts, and lucrative endorsement offers—she would probably come back here, hang out at the Dairy Queen, heft a few bags of corn and oats, get married, raise kids and take them to the Reunion Days calf scramble (whatever that was), and make a life. A nice, quiet little life. Maybe that wouldn't be such a bad thing.

The thought haunted me as I continued my tour of town. Over the next hour or so, my trip through the dry goods store, Barlinger's Hardware, the Dairy Queen, and the little native limestone Daily Baptist Church on the corner of Second and B streets began to develop a theme. Wherever I went, I overheard mini-trivia discussions about the life and times of Amber Anderson. She had worked at the dry goods store, the feed mill, and the Dairy Queen, where she was the best fry cook they ever had but no good at running the cash register. She'd given her first singing performance at the Daily Baptist Church during vacation Bible school, which, by the way, had gotten her involved in church and probably saved her, considering that, after the tragic deaths of her parents in an auto accident, she had no guidance at home except for her old grandfather, who drank too much and was not a churchgoer, and thus unprepared to see to the spiritual needs of a little girl.

At Barlinger's Hardware, the clerk behind the counter remembered that when Amber was little, she often came into the store with her grandfather, who painted houses and did odd jobs for people until he fell off a barn roof and crippled his leg. The clerk always bought Amber a penny candy or two, which she dutifully saved to take home and share with her three young brothers. She was such a sweet little girl, poor thing. And look at her now. She was doing the town of Daily, Texas, proud, bless her heart. If she didn't make it all the way to the top, those folks on *American Megastar* just didn't know talent when they saw it.

That last part was definitely for my benefit. The clerk glanced covertly in my direction as I pretended to be occupied with a display of dust-encrusted souvenirs. I considered buying a T-shirt to take home to Paula. *My best friend went to Daily, Texas, and all I got was this lousy T-shirt.* Paula would think it was funny. The shirt behind it said *Fun and Sun in Daily, Texas.* Fun and sun—where, exactly? Behind that, there was a purple tank top with a blingy flying saucer on the front and the words *The Dailyians Have Landed!* And under that in fine print, *Daily, Texas.* I chose that one for Paula. Before she got into New-Age mysticism, she'd been highly involved in chasing UFO sightings. She'd even begged her way into a couple of research assignments for documentary pieces on supposed UFO landings and abductions. She would probably wear *The Dailyians Have Landed!* At least she'd get a laugh out of it, and she would know that, so far this trip, I had retained my underdeveloped sense of humor.

After purchasing my shirt and evading a plethora of probing questions from the woman behind the counter, I made an exit from the hardware store. Luckily, it was closing time, six o'clock, or I probably wouldn't have gotten out at all. Clearly, word was out that there was a strange woman in town. Suspicions were that I was connected with *American Megastar* and the unexplained helicopter flyover at the fairgrounds this morning. The woman at the hardware store wanted to know if I'd heard the *big news* about *TV network helicopters* hovering over the county fairgrounds. She gave me the evil eye when I answered no.

As I walked out the door, she whispered to the clerk dusting a display of plungers nearby, "She bought the purple Dailyians shirt. Nobody from around here would do that."

I decided to get out of town for a while, drive to the fairgrounds, check the lay of the land, and see if I could figure out how to quietly stage a location shoot at the county fair without alerting everyone. The glow and excitement of the hometown return segments depended, at least in part, on the big hometown reveal being a surprise to the local population. In Amber's case, there was the additional problem of the recent media frenzy surrounding her personal activities. If the paparazzi found out she was coming here, the place would be swamped and any chance of capturing our country girl in the serene and peaceful bosom of her hometown would be gone.

When I drove up to the fairgrounds gate, a man in a John Deere ball cap was padlocking it shut. I rolled down my window and leaned out. "Hi there. Any chance I can get in for a few minutes?"

The caretaker gave me a perplexed look, his thin, weathered face all mustache and baseball cap. "Afraid not this ev'nin', ma'am. All I do's mow the grass. Fairgrounds opens at nine tomorrow for vendors. Livestock barns open at seven for sheep and goats, but you've got to have an exhibitor's pass." He looked my rental car up and down, stroking the side of his mustache. "Don't guess you're here to show sheep and goats?"

"No, but thanks for the information."

"My pleasure, ma'am." He tipped the bill of his cap. "Have a good ev'nin'." Waving over his shoulder, he crossed the driveway, climbed into a battered pickup truck, and puttered away, towing a trailer full of lawnmowers and weed trimmers.

I sat surveying the fairgrounds, looking up and down the tall chain-link fence, thinking about my aerial overview that morning. The place was huge—a maze of barns, decaying livestock corrals, a rodeo arena lined with rows of rusted metal bleachers, various carnival rides, and a group of old cinderblock structures that looked like leftovers from a bygone military installation.

Near an old rock building marked *Kiddie Korral*, a giant metal cowboy stood smiling at me, his faded gray eyes watching blankly as I rolled up my window, backed off the side of the gravel drive, and headed for the county road.

A Jeep pulled in as I stopped to check for traffic. The driver leaned out his window, the arm of his Hawaiian shirt catching the sunlight, his face shaded by the brim of a well-worn straw cowboy hat. I rolled down my window, something I never would have done back home in LA.

"Looks like the place is closed," he said, pushing back his hat so that his face was visible. He had blue eyes. *Really* blue eyes, framed by thick brown lashes and strong, straight brows darker than his hair, sandy brown and slicked back in loose curls from driving with the window open. He needed a shave, but he looked good that way, sort of rugged . . .

He blinked expectantly, waiting for me to say something. I realized I was staring. "Locked up until nine a.m.," I finally said, "unless you've brought sheep or goats along, that is. Then you can get in at seven." Something about him seemed vaguely familiar, but I couldn't decide what.

With a quick shake of his head, he snapped his fingers. "Left my sheep at home."

The comment made me chuckle. The first time I'd felt like laughing all day. "Then you're out of luck, cowboy." I caught myself doing what Paula called *the eye thing*—the up and down flutter of lashes that said, *Where ya headed, big fella?*

"Guess I'll have to give up and go get some supper." The sentence faded into a slow, one-sided grin that made his words seem like a proposal of some kind. The idea caused a little pulse to flutter in my neck. His eyes drifted downward, as if he saw it.

"It *is* supper time already, isn't it?"

"Past time." He raised a brow, waiting, his gaze meeting mine again. I tunneled in, momentarily losing track of the conversation.

A quick mental image flicked through my mind. Me, the cowboy in the Hawaiian shirt, dinner . . . *Whoa there, where did that come from? You are an engaged woman, Mandalay. Happily engaged. Engaged. Happily.*

Reality hit me like a blast of cold water. Come to think of it, what was this guy doing hanging around the fairgrounds after hours? If he was a local, would he be asking *me* if the fairgrounds were closed? Wouldn't he know the place was locked up overnight?

I quickly ricocheted from intrigued and titillated to suspicious, which was probably a safer reaction for my engaged self to be having. He registered the change in body language, apparently, and retreated into his truck, his face disappearing among the shadows as he rested his hand loosely on the gearshift. "Guess I'll come back in the morning."

"Don't forget your sheep," I said. *Or, perhaps, your camera equipment. Any chance you have scopes and a collection of long range lenses hidden in that Jeep?*

"Yes, ma'am." In the shadows, he grinned again, his teeth an even white line—not the orthodontically perfect kind—just crooked enough to be natural. "Thanks for the advice." He didn't have the same accent as the rest of the locals. His was a cross between *Big Easy* and *southern comfort.* Casual, yet proper, soft on the ear. Nice to listen to. The next thing I knew, I was leaning closer, hesitating again.

"I hear the café in town is pretty good." *Stop that, Mandalay. This is the enemy. Maybe.* "I don't know if they're open in the evenings, though. Anyway, good luck."

"You too." Sticking his hand out the window, he waved as he drifted onward toward the fairgrounds gate. He took his time there, slowly turning around. I wondered if he was scoping out the place or watching me, trying to figure out who I was and what I was up to. Just in case he was, I turned away from town and followed the fairgrounds road into the hills, glancing at my map and plotting a loop through the countryside. The drive would do me good. It would give me time to think, to clear my head of random thoughts of cowboys and cafés and concentrate instead on getting an entire production crew into the fairgrounds without causing a commotion that would spoil the big reveal at the rodeo.

Unfortunately, while plotting my next move, I lost track of the road, and before I knew it, I was driving some asphalt-and-gravel path that wasn't on the map. *It'll go back to town eventually*, I told myself. *It's headed in the right direction.*

The cell phone rang, and when I picked it up, Ursula was on the other end, sounding far away in the static.

"Mandee-lay. How izz your trip?" As usual, the first few words of Ursula-speak were like a foreign language. My mind rushed to translate.

"Good. Fine. I booked hotel rooms in town and scouted a couple of locales." The phone fuzzed out momentarily and came back. "I'll go to the fairgrounds tomorrow."

"Very goot, Mandee-lay. The crew will fly in on Saturday morn-ingk. They will film Am-beer landingk at the airport and then bring her to you in time to shoot background before her big reveal duringk ro-day-o. In the interim, we would not want anyone to discern that she is comingk, or that she is finalist, this izz clear?"

Crystal. Thank goodness Ursula hadn't seen the banner that had been hanging over Main Street until the rain washed it away. "Yes. I think the phone's going out of range. I'm out near the fairgrounds right now."

"There is one more thing I must tell you." Ursula went right on talking, certain, no doubt, that the phone wouldn't dare cut out until she was finished giving orders. "When Am-beer arrives, you must watch closely her efforts to contact people there. In her hotel today, there was left at the desk a communiqué from a recording company in Austin. If she were to exit *American Megastar* to engage with a tiny unknown company, this would reflect badly on us. If you find such to be true, you will let me know immediately."

A little ache started right between my eyes, like Chinese water torture. I didn't even want to know how Ursula had managed to see Amber's hotel messages. Surely Amber wouldn't be stupid enough to openly negotiate with a recording company just days before the announcement of the Final Five. This had to be yet more of Ursula's paranoia. "Is it possible that this company just contacted her out of the blue? Do we have proof of any ongoing dialogue?"

"Not at this time. This could be nothingk, of course."

I rubbed the thrumming in my forehead. What now? What other possible nugget of insanity could be heaped into the already-teetering Amber basket?

"Be watchful when Am-beer arrives. Marta will email the final travel schedules to you tomorrow." As usual, Ursula was through dumping and ready to have the conversation over with. She was probably headed out to some lavish dinner with one of the many vendors who serviced the production company and periodically stroked Ursula's ego with expensive perks. "Have a good eveningk, Mandee . . ." The words faded into static, and I drove with the phone pressed to my ear for a mile or so, wondering if she would come back. Finally, I set the phone down and concluded two things—Ursula had hung up, and judging by the setting sun, I wasn't headed in the right direction anymore. I'd passed through more than one fork in the road, so there was no possibility of back-tracking. Essentially, I was lost in the middle of nowhere.

An appropriate metaphor for my life lately.

The road turned into a couple of dirt ruts with a grass hump in the middle, and my hopes plummeted. I envisioned myself stuck in the car overnight with no food, no water, no help, and unfortunately, less than a quarter tank of gas. Not a pretty picture.

There were probably wild animals out here. Coyotes and mountain lions. Prowlers that came out after dark, searching the hills for stranded tourists and careless city girls with inadequate navigational skills. Taking out the map, I drove on, carefully checking occasional signs at dusty dirt-road intersections, where both paths seemed to wander off into the hills and disappear.

By the time I finally found my way back to Daily, the sun had gone down. The café, where I was going to treat myself to a nice relaxing supper, was closed. I settled for to-go food from the Dairy Queen and then drove through the darkened streets to the hotel, ravenously consuming soggy French fries. I was glad, at least, that I'd managed to secure lodging in Daily, rather than having to drive all the way to the nearest real town.

Turning the car into the alley behind Main Street, I reconsidered my lodging plans and the forty-mile drive to a Holiday Inn. The back alley was shadowy and silent, lit by the glow of a single flickering streetlamp and a faded neon sign over the hotel's rear entrance. It simply said *Hotel Welcome*—like something from a Stephen King novel. Overhead, the windows were dark, the high arches reflecting the glow of the streetlight in shifting, uneven shapes. From the end of the alleyway, the gargoyles on the bank building watched me, their fang-filled mouths hanging open, as in, *Come into my parlor, my pretty . . .*

A shudder ran over my shoulders as I worked up my courage, took a fortifying breath, and got out of the car. Grabbing my overnight bag, my purse, and my briefcase, I hurried to the door as fast as my Italian leather slingbacks would carry me. As I fiddled with the keys, someone or something knocked over a tin can near a stack of pallets not far away. I jumped, did a back flip with a triple twist, and landed in fighting position with my karate fists en garde—in my mind, anyway. In reality, I dropped the keys, said a bad word, broke a nail snatching up the key ring, and whimpered when I couldn't get the key into the lock because my hand was shaking.

Calm down, Mandalay. This is ridiculous. You live in LA, for heaven's sake.

That was exactly the problem. In LA, no matter where you went, you were always surrounded by people. Safety was mostly about learning which places to go at what times of day. Between the streetlights and the ambient glow of zillions of kilowatts of electricity flowing into homes, apartments, signs, and office buildings, LA was always well illuminated. Who knew what could happen to a lone woman here, where it was impossibly dark and there was no one to hear you scream? Ursula probably wouldn't even report me missing. I'd be like one of those people who fall off cruise ships and three days later someone says, *Hey, Joe hasn't been sleeping in his bed. Has anyone seen Joe?*

Finally, the key slipped into the lock. I turned the knob and pushed the door open in one quick motion. After wrestling my way through with my luggage, I closed the door, untangled my belongings, and caught my breath. The hallway was quiet, shadowy in the light of a dresser lamp on an old-fashioned buffet cabinet near the staircase. The click of the door latch behind me echoed against the silence. Checking to be sure it was locked, I tiptoed forward.

"Hello?" I whispered, my voice disappearing into the darkness. "Is anybody here?" It was probably a silly question. My new friend Donetta had told me no one else was staying in the hotel right now, and there was no night clerk on duty, hence the need for me to have my own key to the back entrance. According to her directions, my room was upstairs, to the left, at the end of the hall.

Up those long, dark stairs . . .

Straightening my shoulders, I tiptoed past a couple of closed doors and a storage room filled with Styrofoam heads wearing wigs of all shapes and colors. The heads watched me through formless white eyes as I continued toward the stairs. On the buffet cabinet, someone had left a plate of homemade cookies and a sign that said *Welcome. For emergencies, call Donetta.* A phone number was hastily scrawled beneath. I considered programming it into my cell, but on the vague theory that preparing for an emergency might actually cause one, I grabbed a couple of cookies and went upstairs. My room door was exactly where it was supposed to be, at the end of the second-story hall, behind a pink door with a brass 1 in the center and an engraved golden plate that read *Suite Beulahland*.

Balancing my overnight bag, my briefcase, purse, the Dairy Queen sack, and my supersize Diet Coke, I stuck the cookies in my only remaining containment device, my teeth, and wiggled the skeleton key into the door with one hand while turning the knob and pushing the door open with the other.

The room was dark, the outline of a dresser and an ornate brass bed silhouetted by the tall arched windows facing Main Street. Setting down my things as the door creaked shut behind me, I walked through the strip of light to the window and surveyed Main Street while eating one of the cookies. It tasted incredibly good. Below, the town seemed peaceful and quiet, its old street lamps casting a Norman Rockwell sheen over the empty sidewalks and silent store fronts, making the scene seem welcoming, safe, unlike the alley out back. I took a moment to admire the view while eating the other cookie. After I'd had supper and found some light switches, not necessarily in that order, I would gather my courage and venture downstairs for more cookies.

Crossing the room, I searched for a light switch by the door. Nothing visible in the slice of window light, so I widened my reconnaissance area, using my hands. Still nothing, although I did find the door to what turned out to be the bathroom. I checked the ceiling over my shoulder. There was definitely a light fixture there—something with intricate scrollwork and several glass globes. Where in the world was the switch?

Moving around the room, I searched the walls, tipping picture frames off balance, touching heavy cloth wall hangings. Something that felt like a feather boa momentarily snagged my arm, and I jumped back, getting a quick heebie-jeebie. Finally, near the bed, I found a wall lamp, investigated it with my fingers, and pulled the chain.

The bulb came to life, made an explosive pop, and went dead. In the moment of brilliant light, I took in yards and yards of pink satin, a thick plush white furry something on the bed, and a huge black velvet Elvis crooning over the headboard.

I stood frozen in place, imagining that this was some sort of weird dream and I would wake up any moment. I would find myself home in LA, safe in my bed, with the street noises, and the hum of the air system, and the occasional roar of jets headed for LAX. There would be no velvet Elvis pictures, no hairy bedspreads, no pink satin pillows and drapes.

Or maybe I was on the boat, sailing the California coast with David. The wedding was over and the season of *American Megastar* in the bag—an unqualified success, of course. We were drifting along on the breeze, carefree, happy, in love. Hundreds of miles from Ursula Uberstach. Thousands of miles from Daily, Texas. David was standing on the bow, the wind combing his dark, perfectly trimmed hair, a shirt hanging unbuttoned over his shoulders—a very G.Q. shirt. David was so G.Q.

David hadn't called all day. Why hadn't David called, especially when he knew I needed . . .

A noise in the hallway sliced the thought in half. I froze, listening. The sound came again—a stair squeaking, then another.

Someone was in the building.

Breath caught in my throat. There wasn't supposed to be anyone else in the hotel. Donetta had told me that specifically. She'd said no one would be here. But someone, or something, was coming up the stairs.

I slipped off a shoe, then bent and took off the other shoe, then tiptoed toward the door. Outside, the footsteps reached the landing.

A loose floorboard squealed under my weight, and I stopped. The noises in the hall moved closer. Holding my breath, I grabbed my purse from the chair and clutched it to my chest. Thank goodness for Prada with mace and a cell phone inside.

Inching to the wall, I squatted down, moved my face close to the doorknob, and squinted through the keyhole just in time to see a shadow pass by.

A key turned in the lock next door. Right next door. Hinges squealed as the door opened. My fingers trembled on my purse, slipped inside it, slid over my cell phone as the intruder knocked something over, crossing the room. Something rattled in the wall between my room and the next one. An adjoining door. There was an adjoining door, and someone was trying to open it.

The cell phone beeped once as I switched it to silent. Holding my breath, I crawled to the other side of the room, crouched behind the furry bed, and dialed 9-1-1.

Chapter 6

Imagene Doll

I'd just settled in to watch that good-looking football player on *Dancing With the Stars* when Jack's scanner from the volunteer fire department went to squawking in the kitchen. I got up from my chair, aggravated with myself for having turned it on to keep me company during supper. Tonight was mambo night, and unless my own house was burning down, I didn't want any interruptions. The dance-off was down to only five contestants, and it was gonna be a mambo to end all mambos. Goodness, but that football player sure could wiggle. Reckon he learned that on the football field.

The phone rang just as I got to the kitchen doorway. Couldn't be one of the kids checking on me. All four of the boys knew better than to call during *Dancing With the Stars*.

For a minute, I had the odd thought that my house really was on fire and I just hadn't noticed it yet, and Patti down at the county dispatch was calling to tell me to get out. I pictured all my things, all the memories of Jack and me and our life together, gone up in smoke, and tears rushed over me.

Oh, for heaven's sake, Imagene, some sensible part of me said, *call the psychiatric ward and see if they've noticed your mind run by, because you've sure enough lost it.*

Grabbing a towel, I wiped my eyes as I answered the phone. No doubt, Patti had slipped up and called my number again out of habit from all the years Jack was on the VFD. Patti always got embarrassed when she did that.

I picked up the phone and answered, figuring she'd launch into a wave of apologies the minute she heard my voice.

It was Forrest, the county sheriff, on the other end, which surprised me and got me worried all over again. Something had to be wrong for Forrest to call on Thursday, which was normally his poker night with the boys down at The Junction.

"Imagene?" He sounded irritated, being as whatever call was out on the scanner had probably interrupted his game. "You know anything about someone staying over to the Daily Hotel? Dispatch just got a prowler report from a lady, said she was a guest there. In the Beulah room, no less. Patti figured it was kids playing a joke, but she can't get ahold of Donetta."

"Donetta's probably on the internet." Ever since DeDe got that yard-sale computer, she's been addicted to the internet, eBay mostly, but she also liked to print out political gossip and warnings about underarm deodorant causing breast cancer—information she felt had been hidden until now by a government conspiracy to sell more deodorant.

"Figures," Forrest said. "Well, I imagine it's just a prank, or maybe kids down there lookin' for the ghost again. Usually that ain't a problem until Halloween or Elvis's birthday, but you never can tell. Heaven help us if they touch anything in the Beulah room. I had Patti dispatch Buddy Ray over there with a pass key, just in case."

"Oh, Lord have mercy! You sent Buddy Ray to the hotel?" The words exploded from my mouth just as the mambo music was starting on TV. "I've got to go, Forrest. I better get down there before Buddy Ray makes a mess of things. Donetta's got guests in those rooms." Without waiting for an answer, I grabbed my purse and hit Record on the VCR, even though that meant *Dancing With the Stars* would record over today's episode of *One Life to Live*. Sometimes you have to prioritize.

All the way to town, four miles to the crossroad and two past that, I tried not to imagine what might be going on at the hotel. *Lord have mercy,* I kept thinking, *what a mess.*

It didn't occur to me until I pulled up behind the hotel that I was in my housecoat and slippers. By then, there wasn't much I could do about it.

Buddy Ray's cruiser was parked behind the building with the driver's side door askew and the light flashing. The hotel entrance was hanging open, as if he'd burst in there like a scene from *Dragnet*, which he probably had. Buddy Ray took six months toward a criminal justice degree before he flunked out of community college. He liked to put all that higher education to use.

"Buddy Ray?" I called his name as I stepped in because I didn't want to get shot. A part of me had been wishing to go to the pearly gates ever since Jack died, but not at the hands of Buddy Ray and his peacemaker. "Buddy Ray? It's Imagene. You up there?"

The stairway was quiet, the hall empty except for a little plate of cookies Donetta'd left on the bureau. I pictured her home shopping on eBay while I was down at the hotel in my bathrobe, risking life and limb. "Buddy Ray? You upstairs? It's Imagene." Maybe he was in the beauty shop. Maybe he'd checked there first and he hadn't bothered the guests yet. Maybe he was scared speechless because he'd seen the ghost of the Daily Hotel, which some said was Elvis and some said was a Confederate soldier.

"I'm up here," Buddy Ray's voice boomed down the stairs. He didn't *sound* like he'd seen a ghost. "That you, Donetta?"

"No, it's Imagene." I moved up the stairs as quick as I could. Maybe Buddy Ray hadn't gotten into the guest rooms yet.

"Call for backup, Imagene. I got perpetrators up here." Buddy Ray was breathless with excitement. "Tell Patti to radio Forrest."

So much for hoping he hadn't disturbed the guests yet. "Buddy Ray," I hollered as I crossed the landing and hurried up the last few stairs. "You leave them people alo—" When I rounded the corner, there was Buddy Ray, with his hand on his gun. He had that sweet girl who wasn't particular and Carter, the darling boy with beach shoes and pretty blue eyes, handcuffed and spread-eagle against the wall. That poor boy wasn't wearing his Hawaiian shirt anymore. In fact, he wasn't wearing anything but some silky boxer shorts. Apparently, Buddy Ray had caught him in the middle of changing clothes.

"Buddy Ray, you turn those people loose!" I said, and all three of them looked in my direction. Staggering backward a step, Buddy Ray swung the pistol around. "Don't you point that gun at me, young man. You put that thing down and unlock them handcuffs. For heaven's sake, Buddy Ray, you might ask a few questions before you go dragging some fella into the hall in his boxers."

"Exercise shorts," Carter corrected, and grinned like he was getting a kick out of the whole thing. I had to give him credit for steady nerves, being as there was a certified idiot behind him with a loaded gun. The girl, whose name I couldn't remember right then, looked terrified and no small bit embarrassed, standing there in her nice suit with her hands braceleted behind her back. She was a good three or four inches shorter without the high heels. Kind of a petite little thing with curly reddish-brown hair and the prettiest brown eyes. Cute as a bug, but red as a beet.

"These folks are paying guests," I said, but Buddy Ray didn't look like he was ready to give up his prisoners just on my say-so. "Donetta's gonna have your hide, Buddy Ray."

"Donetta d-don't rent r-rooms anymore," Buddy Ray stammered, feeling the need, I'm sure, to defend his powers of crime scene investigation.

"Well, she does now, as of this afternoon." I pointed toward the Beulah room. Buddy Ray's eyes got wide and he froze up for a minute. "Unlock them cuffs," I said, to get him back on track.

"Oh . . . okay, Mrs. Doll, but-but-but . . ." He gaped toward the Beulah room like he was afraid Beulah herself was gonna step out and turn him into a pillar of salt. I reckon he was thinking he'd rather haul two innocent folks off to jail than risk the wrath of Beulah. "Does *she* . . . does she know about this?" His eyes cut toward Beulah's name on the door again.

"Donetta said it was okay."

Buddy put a hand to his mouth and whispered out the side, like he was worried all the little statues in the Beulah room might hear, "But does *she* know?"

"Donetta said it was all right, Buddy Ray. Turn these folks loose."

Buddy Ray shrugged and shook his head. "Okay, but I didn't have nothin' to do with it. . . . If Beulah asks, I mean."

"True enough," I agreed, to ease Buddy Ray's nerves. He'd had a run-in or two with Beulah before. Every time she came to town, she was sure thieves had snuck into and heisted some of the priceless collectibles in her suite. About the time poor Buddy Ray came around to investigate, she always found her lost treasures hidden under the chair cushions or behind the curtains or tucked under the bed covers. She usually blamed it on the ghost, but the truth was that before she left, Beulah always hid her favorite things, then forgot about it by the time she came back. The ghost got credit for a lot of activity that was really just Beulah being Beulah. Even if there was such thing as ghosts, I doubt if they'd have the guts to mess with Beulah's stuff.

The keys rattled in Buddy Ray's hands as he took the cuffs off that cute little girl, then turned to set Carter loose. Standing there in his exercise shorts, Carter looked like the cover of *Yoga With Yahani,* only with shorter hair. Anyhow, he cut a fine figure. The girl noticed that, even though she was busy rubbing her wrists and trying to shake the blood back into her hands. She looked away when Carter turned around, so he wouldn't see her watching. I reckon she forgot for a minute that I was standing behind them both, because when she saw me there, she blushed. I pretended I hadn't seen her looking at Carter. Her being an engaged girl and all, that would be a little embarrassing.

Her name came back to me out of the blue. Amanda-Lee, I think she'd said earlier on that day, but it'd been hard to hear with all the racket of the rainstorm.

Buddy Ray's radio crackled, and he had to head outside to answer it. Radio reception was never good in the Daily Hotel building.

I figured now was my chance to rattle off a heartfelt apology to the guests without having to insult Buddy Ray right to his face. I waited while Carter ducked off into his room and then come back out wearing an orange T-shirt that said SPCA on the front. "I'm real sorry for the inconvenience to you folks. I hope y'all don't take this as a sign of Daily hospitality. Donetta would be mortified, just mortified, I'll tell you—if she wasn't at the eBay, that is. She wanted y'all to enjoy your stay at the Daily Hotel."

Amanda-Lee crossed her arms over her chest and took a step toward her room, like she was about to grab her stuff and hit the road. If she did that, it'd break Donetta's heart, so I laid on some more sweet talk. "Having y'all here really did make Donetta's day— well, her week, month, and year, actually. Her family's operated this place for generations, and a lot of her childhood memories are tied up with the comings and goings of guests, sometimes even famous ones. Back in the forties, a scene of the movie *Bonnie and Clyde* was shot right down there in the hotel lobby—of course, that's the beauty shop and exercise area now. She's been awful sad about having to close down the hotel these last years."

Oh shoot, Imagene, you shouldn't have told them that. Big mouth. "I mean, not that the hotel's not open for business now, because it is. Sure enough. You're both here." I flashed a big toothy grin, but only Carter smiled back. The girl wasn't sold. Which was a problem, considering that she was the one renting all the rooms for the weekend. "By the way, Amanda-Lee—I hope I said that right—this is Carter, and Carter, this is Amanda-Lee." Couldn't hurt to perform introductions. If I was a young lady and someone introduced me to a fella that looked like Carter, I'd stay. "You two are the very first guests in the newly reopened Daily Hotel. Except for the ghost, that is." *Shoot, Imagene. Blabbermouth. You're gonna talk the guests right out the door.* "But he don't need a room, since he don't really exist." I flashed another big smile.

Carter smiled back, then turned to Amanda-Lee. "Nice to meet you . . ." He paused on the name but extended a hand. "I'm sorry, I didn't quite catch your name. I guess we're neighbors."

She didn't look one bit thrilled about the idea. She stuck out one hand halfheartedly, keeping the other crossed over her stomach. Her feet were still pointed toward the door, ready to turn tail. "Mandalay Florentino."

She had the strangest way of saying Amanda-Lee, and that last name was a mouthful.

"Carter Woods." Carter glanced down at his SPCA shirt. "Sorry about the clothes. I was just on my way down to exercise."

Amanda-Lee didn't answer, so I piped in, "*Yoga With Yahani* is still in the VCR down there. If you want, I can show you how to turn it on."

Carter grinned kind of sheepish-like. "Thanks, Imagene, but I think the exercise bike and the weight machine are about all I can handle for tonight. Have to do something to wind down before bed. Insomniac."

Lands, that boy had a smile that could melt butter. *He remembered my name*, I thought, then I pictured what he was seeing—a fat old lady in a bathrobe—and I felt a little silly. Still, it was nice that he remembered my name. It made me feel like a real person. When you're a woman past your beauty years, sometimes people look right past you. I doubted if little Amanda-Lee could have understood that.

Carter turned that charming smile on her. "Well, it's a pleasure having you next door. Sorry I scared you, coming in. I didn't realize there was anyone here."

Amanda-Lee relaxed the frosty posture, uncrossing her arms. I had a feeling she'd decided to stay. "I'm sorry I called the police." The last word came out with a chuckle. Slapping a hand over her mouth, she shook her head and giggled again, like she was picturing the two of them spread-eagle against the wall. "That was really stupid."

"I've been handcuffed in worse company," Carter said, and Amanda-Lee glanced at him in a way that brought to mind an old saying, *Engaged with words don't mean a thing. Engaged ain't engaged until sweethearts buy a ring.* Amanda-Lee wasn't wearing a ring. I saw Carter check.

Hmmm . . . Some meddlesome part of me that enjoyed sorting out other people's lives raised its head and found a voice. "Well, you two young folks just make yourselves to home here. Enjoy the exercise area. There's a TV down there, too. Y'all just use the building like it was yours."

"You're sure the ghost won't mind?" Carter checked the dark corners of the hallway and made a spooky motion with his hands.

"Oh no, he won't mind a bit."

Amanda-Lee shuddered and threaded her arms again.

"I mean, there ain't *really* a ghost," I rushed out. "That's just a legend, on account of this old building makes noise sometimes. My daddy, rest his soul, probably started some of those stories himself. Many was the evening my daddy sat in the café with Donetta and me and told us whoppers about our town." As a girl, I never gave a conscious thought to how lucky I was to have a daddy who took me to dinner. All Donetta's father ever did was work all day and fall asleep at night with a glass of whiskey in his hand.

"My daddy could weave a ghost story that'd make you feel a cold breath on the back of your neck. He used to tell us that some folks thought the swinging bookshelf downstairs was put there so settlers could escape Indian raids, or so moonshiners could hide liquor when the regulators came to town, but Daddy knew it was from the Civil War. Confederate leaders in the hotel built it so they could take secret documents and slip away if there was an attack. Daddy claimed that underneath the café was a tunnel leading to a cave on Caney Creek. He'd seen it once, back in the forties, when the café building got termites and Daddy oversaw the floor repair. Late one evening, he followed that tunnel all the way to Cancy Creek, and even saw the bones of the ghost-man down there, counting a secret stash of Confederate gold in the moonlight."

A little shiver went through me, just thinking about my daddy telling that tale, and then I wondered how I got off on that tack in the first place. I laughed, to show the guests it was just nonsense. "My mama never much appreciated him spouting that kind of stuff, but he was Irish, so he couldn't help it, I reckon." Amanda-Lee looked more nervous than ever, so I added, "I'm sure it was him that made up the ghost—all in fun, you know."

Forgive me, Lord, that was a little white lie, but I did it for Donetta. The legend of the Daily Hotel ghost had been around for at least a hundred years. "There's no tunnel, either. My daddy always claimed the hatch was hid under at least three layers of linoleum—that's why we couldn't see it—but we kids searched for the cave entrance on the creek and we never found it, just like we never saw any ghost." *Heard strange things a time or two though.* "It's all just blarney. Small towns and Irish folks are a lot alike—full of blarney."

Carter nodded, like he knew about small towns, but Amanda-Lee checked the shadows at the end of the hall, where the other rooms sat dark and empty, except for stacks of junk.

"I shouldn'ta told that story." I reached out and touched her arm, and she jumped. Her skin was cold as ice and covered with a goose rash. "You two will be just as snug as bugs in a rug here. Don't you worry about a thing."

"I'm not worried." Running her hands up and down her arms, she straightened her shoulders and smiled halfheartedly. She had the sweetest face—thick eyelashes like a little china doll's and the kind of fully, pouty lips I always wished I had. "I'm just tired. It's been a long day."

"Sure it has," I agreed.

Carter gave her a sympathetic look. "Sorry for getting you arrested."

She chuckled and shook her head.

Buddy Ray was clomping back up the stairs with his radio crackling, so I figured it was a good time to get out of there, while the guests were getting along so well and nobody had handcuffs on. "I've bent your ears enough. Y'all two have a good night. Just help yourselves to anything you need." I started backing away, and to my relief, neither one of them followed. "We'll see you in the morning. 'Night, now." Capturing Buddy Ray, I tugged him down the stairs while he babbled about having to fill out a report.

"Buddy Ray, you hush up and come on. You caused enough trouble here tonight. It ever cross your mind to ask some questions before you go pulling out your gun and slapping handcuffs on folks?"

Outside the door, Buddy Ray stood with his clipboard, his face blank as the summer sky. "Nope," he said, and I had to feel sorry for him. He looked a little crestfallen now that there was no one to take to jail.

"Well, no harm done." There really wasn't, except that I'd missed *Dancing With the Stars*.

"Mrs. Doll?" Buddy Ray's thick eyebrows knotted as I fished my keys from my purse.

"Yes, Buddy Ray?"

"Did you know you come downtown in your housecoat and slippers?" It figured that, with his keen investigation skills, he'd just now be noticing.

"I was in a hurry, Buddy Ray."

"Oh." He jotted something down as if that was valuable information.

"Probably no need to mention it in your report." Heaven forbid if this was to get around town. Folks would figure I was one biscuit short of a basket, for sure. "Matter of fact, we could just not tell Donetta about any of this. It'd only get her upset. You know what a nervous Nellie she is."

"Oh." Buddy Ray scribbled out his notation. "I reckon." Folding up his pad, he headed toward his cruiser. "'Night, Mrs. Doll."

"'Night."

He grabbed the car door handle and it was locked. Kicking the cement, he peered through the window, probably looking for his keys.

"You need a ride to the sheriff's office for the spare set?" I asked.

"Reckon," he said and headed my way, his shoulders slumped over. Sometimes it was hard to believe Buddy Ray had six whole months of criminal justice education.

"Don't guess we need to put this in the report, either," I said as we climbed into my van.

Buddy Ray nodded, looking relieved. "Reckon not, Mrs. Doll. Reckon we'd best just forget the whole thing."

Chapter 7

Mandalay Florentino

My new neighbor and I stood in the hallway, watching Imagene and the sheriff's deputy disappear down the stairs. I had the strongest urge to run after them and tell them I wanted my money back—I couldn't possibly stay here.

You're such a wimp. The voice in my head sounded like my brother and big sisters chanting *baby, baby, baby* back when they were way-cool teenagers and I was the dorky caboose kid, ten years younger, with stork legs, bad hair, and Coke-bottle glasses. Aside from that, there was Ursula, all five feet eleven inches of her, saying, *"I vant you to book rooms in the town. You vill do the job . . . understandt?"*

Carter was watching me speculatively. Come to think of it, his being here did present another reason to stay. I could keep an eye on him and try to figure out what he was up to. He was a little too smooth, a little too confident and polite to be just your average paparazzo. I couldn't picture him jumping out from behind bushes and trash barrels with a camera on rapid-repeat. Freelance celeb watchers were fast-moving and brash, rude and completely mercenary in issues of personal space and social courtesy.

Carter was none of those things. He was cordial, friendly, and charming, with a slow-talking ease that reminded me of the South Carolina bartender who'd been a contestant early in the season. Lenny worked in a cabana by the shore and was half beach bum, half southern good ol' boy. *American Megastar* had chewed him up and spit him out, just as it eventually would poor little Amber. The paparazzi had had a field day with Lenny—always convincing him to do things that looked deliciously stupid on camera.

If Carter wasn't one of those entrepreneurial photographers, who was he and why did he look vaguely familiar to me—as if I should know him? Could I have met him somewhere before, crossed paths at a convention or a studio party? Ursula had warned me about the recording company in Austin, but Carter didn't seem the type, and if he was here to secretly meet with Amber, why show up two days early? Why waste time driving out to the fairgrounds and whatnot?

Photographer or reporter was a more likely scenario. That would explain his casing the joint, doing some research before Amber showed up.

Carter clapped his hands in front of himself, sending a sharp sound echoing down the hall, and I jumped. He raised a brow, smiling slightly. "Guess the rest of the evening's going to look pretty dull after this."

I found myself smiling back, thinking maybe I was just being paranoid about Carter. Maybe he was in town visiting long-lost relatives or doing business—what kind, I couldn't imagine. "Yes, I guess it will." Part of me said, *If you'd ever seen him before, Mandalay, you'd remember. Whew.* I wished Paula were with me. I could have introduced them and won her undying gratitude. Paula would have been show-me-to-the-altar crazy over Carter. Not many guys looked like that in gym shorts and a T-shirt. And his were the bluest eyes I'd ever seen, outside of color-enhanced Hollywood headshots. I caught myself checking for tinted contacts, but Carter's eyes were natural.

The cell phone rang in my room, which was probably a good thing, because I'd just belatedly reminded myself that I was a happily engaged woman. This trip had me completely out of sorts. Not once since David and I started dating had I been tempted to check out another guy—except for the benefit of Paula, who regularly sought my opinion in restaurants, on the street, at the health club, wherever. It irritated her that these days I was detached from her informal version of *The Dating Game*.

"Guess I'd better go. That's probably my fiancé," I said, and thumbed over my shoulder toward my room. "Nice being arrested with you."

"Anytime." He waved, with a lazy wink that made me feel unexpectedly glittery. A real friend probably would have tried to get his address for Paula. Guys with that kind of charm were hard to find.

Of course, con men had charm. Con men made a living with charm. . . .

Slinging open my room door, I made a dash for the cell phone in the stream of the incoming hallway light. The door slammed shut as I grabbed the phone off the chair, where I'd dropped it when the deputy leveled his gun at me and said, "All right, lady, hands in the air. I don't know who you are, but there ain't supposed to be anyone in Suite Beulahland." Shortly thereafter, I was handcuffed next to Carter in the hall, trying to decide who I'd contact from jail.

Thank goodness for Imagene Doll. She was a little quirky, but anyone living in this town would have to be.

Putting the phone to my ear, I pictured David curled up on the warm brown leather sofa that would soon be the focal point of our living room. "Hey, baby, you won't believe—"

A pre-recorded advertisement from my cell phone company cut me off. The offer to upgrade my service for a mere $9.95 a month left me wounded in a vague way. My cell phone provider could track me down but my fiancé, the man I was pledged to marry in three months, couldn't? What was wrong with this picture?

He's probably out on the boat, Mandalay. He probably went out overnight because he was lonesome. Stop being such an infant. . . .

Something clicked in the corner of the room, and from the darkness near the bed, Elvis started singing "Love Me Tender." I could barely make out the silhouette of a moving head. Imagene's ghost story wound around me like a cold mist, and even though I don't believe in the paranormal, a creepy crawly ran from my hair to my toes. Backing away, I yanked open the door and stumbled into the corridor. Carter was just coming out of a bathroom across the hall with a towel around his neck.

He blinked at me, surprised.

"Elvis is singing in there, and I can't find the lights."

Carter observed the door with a completely unsurprised look. "You've got Elvis?" He chuckled, as if all of this were a very elaborate joke. "I've got Care Bears, Precious Moments figurines, and *Dukes of Hazzard* memorabilia, and then in the bathroom, celebrity china dolls." He pointed toward the door he'd just exited. "Marilyn Monroe loaned me a towel."

I gaped back and forth across the hall.

"No lie," he promised. "Have a look."

I shook my head. "I'm scared to."

Carter unfolded his James Dean towel and held it up, shaking it like a toreador's cape. Dean's velvet curves seemed to catch the light and come to life. "Classy stuff."

"That's just creepy," I muttered.

Carter raised a brow. "You ought to see the rest of the bathroom. Ripley's wax museum has nothing on this place. I don't have Elvis, though. Elvis must have his own room."

And I'm not staying in it. I flashed back to the huge wall hanging that had been briefly illuminated before the lamp blew up. "I don't know what I have. I can't find any light switch in there. There's a light fixture but no switch." *And it really doesn't matter, because I'm thinking I'll just sleep in my car tonight, with the gargoyles.*

"Huh . . ." Carter mused, scratching his chin and surveying my door. "Hang on a minute." Unlocking his room, he disappeared inside. I waited in the hallway and light shone under his doorway. A moment later, a pinkish glow flickered and then glowed under mine.

"That's it!" I cheered, disproportionately excited. With proper lighting, I could handle almost anything.

Exiting his room, Carter checked out the soft crimson light slipping from beneath my door and creating a tiny laser stream through the keyhole. "Your switch is on my side. Looks like you're in the red light district." He leaned close to the keyhole. "Mind if I take a peek?"

"As long as you don't do that when I'm *in* the room," I joked.

Drawing back, he gave me a flirty look over his shoulder, then said, "My mama raised me better than that, darlin'." He could turn on the southern accent when he wanted to. He sounded like a character from *Gone With the Wind*. It was nice.

I turned the knob and opened the door a crack so he could see inside. He gave a long whistle. "Woo-wee, you're in for a night."

I can imagine. "Any ghosts in there?"

He pretended to check, swiveling his head back and forth. "Not that I can see. Looks like Elvis has the place all to himself. That's an anatomical King of Rock and Roll alarm clock in the corner making the noise. Just think, in the morning, you can wake up to a rubber bust of Elvis singing 'Love Me Tender.' You might want to add one of those to your wedding gift list."

I blushed and a giggle pressed my throat. "Not likely."

"It might grow on you."

Closing my fingers over the doorknob, I opened the door a bit farther as Carter stepped out of the way. Peeking through, I took in the giant black velvet Elvis wall hanging above the bed, the heavy pink satin curtains trimmed with feather boa, the red chandelier with *Graceland* printed in gold on the globes, the bed topped with pink satin pillows and a three-inch white fur plush . . . something I hoped was synthetic.

"I'm afraid a lot of things in there might grow on me," I muttered. Fortunately, I was too exhausted to care. "I'm goin' in." Giving the door a yank, I took a step across the threshold. The door came back with surprising speed and knocked me in the rear when I turned to thank Carter.

"I'll come back and check on you in a little while," he said, wrapping James Dean around his shoulders. Together, they sauntered off down the hall. "If you don't find another switch in there, just tap on the door when you want the lights turned out."

"I'm leaving the lights on," I called after him. "All night."

Sending back a salute, he disappeared onto the stairway, whistling an old seventies song, "Knock three times on the ceiling if you want me . . ."

I listened as the sound faded away, then I wished Carter would come back. The Elvis room was even creepier now that I was alone. After bolting the door behind me, I turned off the singing alarm clock. The swish of the suitcase zipper seemed deafening as I opened my bag and took out my sweats.

While investigating the fifties diner–themed mini-shrine of my bathroom, I changed into my comfy sweats, a navy and white set I'd bought on an unexpectedly cold day at the marina, pulled on my fuzzy slipper socks, then hung my used clothes on a towel hook in the shape of an electric guitar with *Blue Hawaii* emblazoned in rhinestones. The light flickered overhead as I reentered the Beulah room and sank into a chair, taking in Elvis memorabilia of every possible description and trying to work up the energy to move the "yeti hide" away from the bed. Far, far away . . .

A noise by the window caused me to jerk upright just as I was dozing off. My arm flew out, knocking over something on the end table. Blinking the fog from my eyes, I checked the room, taking in the velvet wall hangings, the feather boa draped around a repro-duction gold album on the wall by the bathroom, the collection of miniature Elvi in a glass-fronted case by the door.

The heavy pink satin curtains stirred and puffed outward as if someone were pushing them from behind, and I sat up, shiver-ing, a rash of goose bumps traveling over my skin. I glanced at the door to Carter's room, hoping for light underneath, but there was nothing. I'd probably only been asleep for a minute or two. No doubt he was still downstairs.

My stomach rumbled, bringing to mind the Dairy Queen take-out I'd been forced to abandon during my arrest. Soggy fries and a cold burger by now. I reached for the bag on the end table, but it was wet. Everything was wet, because I'd knocked over my drink while waking up, and diet soda was slowly oozing out, drenching the food and dripping onto the white shag carpet. Fortunately, the pile of Dairy Queen napkins had caught most of it.

Turning the soda upright, I rescued the last dry napkin, sopped up the drips from the floor, then scooped the remainder of the mess into the bag and tossed it in the trash.

Lying back in my chair, I contemplated the cookies downstairs and let my eyes fall closed again. Once I was groggy enough, I could probably convince myself to move to the bed. The pillow in the shape of a rhinestone shirt with a hairy chest inside would have to go. . . .

For the first time, I found myself regretting the laser eye surgery I'd had last year. In the past, I could have taken off my contacts and turned everything into a nondescript pink and white blur. I wouldn't have been able to see the curtain swirling outward, the feather trim ruffling as if someone had just walked by, but I still would have felt the whisper of cold air moving across my head and down my neck. . . .

Stop that, Mandalay. This is juvenile. I forced myself to take a deep breath and sink toward sleep again.

Something moaned low and deep, and my eyes flew open.

I sat listening, taking in sounds, searching for confirmation that the noise was only my stomach growling, not a dead Confederate soldier roaming the halls, collecting lost gold, Care Bears, and Elvis memorabilia.

The sound came again—a long, low groan. I was out of the chair, into the hallway, and headed down the stairs before a conscious thought could register. *That was not me. I did not make that sound.*

In the hallway below, I stood for a minute and listened. Nothing. On the lamp table, the cookie plate was empty, unfortunately. A little food might have helped me relax and get to sleep. Ever since I'd joined *American Megastar*, and especially the last few months with the pressure of wedding plans, I'd had trouble falling asleep. Even though my body grew exhausted by ten o'clock, my mind raced until two or three in the morning. My mother had wanted to send prescription sleeping pills along with the ulcer medication, but I'd told her no. Maybe I shouldn't have.

The sharp clash of metal on metal echoed against the silence, and I listened, recognizing the rhythmic sound of reps on a weight machine. Carter was still in the exercise area. I moved toward the noise, traveling down a short hallway and through a swinging door into another storeroom of wigs and heads. The next swinging door deposited me into the back of the old hotel lobby, and I stood by a heavy oak stairway that probably led to the west end of the second-story hall.

Near the front windows, the beauty shop was dim except for the glow of a chrome floor lamp on the counter by the cash register. The pink gooseneck hairdryers with their cone-shaped heads took on an alien countenance in the low light, their dual adjustment knobs watching me like glassy eyes as I came closer, moving toward the exercise area. From my vantage point, I could see the weights moving up and down on the machine, but the person moving them was hidden behind an old hotel counter converted to serve as a coffee bar. I hoped that, when I rounded the partition, it was Carter and not some ghostly Confederate soldier trying to stay in shape.

The weights paused, and I stopped where I was. Maybe he was coming back upstairs now. If I knew there was someone—a living, breathing someone—in the next room, I could probably relax and turn in.

I heard metal slide against metal as he loaded up a barbell—my best guess—and then after another minute heard him exhaling at regular intervals. I swallowed my pride in one big lump, then walked around the corner. Carter lay face-up on a bench, doing chest presses with his eyes squinted shut. An impressive amount of weight moved smoothly up and down as his chest tightened and strained beneath the SPCA shirt.

"Hi," I said, so as not to startle him.

Letting the bar drop into its rack, he bolted upright and screamed, "Ahhh!"

I stumbled backward, my heart bouncing into my throat.

"Just kidding," he said wryly. "I heard someone coming in the door."

Slapping a hand over my chest, I caught my breath. "I think you just gave me a ministroke."

"Sorry." Grabbing his towel off the partition, he wiped the perspiration from his forehead, then dried the fringes of his hair, creating something between a mess and a Shirley Temple. His hair turned from wavy to curly when it was wet. "Change your mind about using the exercise equipment tonight?" He took in my sweats and fuzzy blue socks.

I considered lying and saying that I'd come down to exercise. But if there's one thing they hammer home in Episcopal school it's that lying, especially the kind of lies that you think about ahead of time and still decide to tell, is wrong. "I couldn't sleep," I told him, feeling pathetic and inept. "I'm not stalking you, I promise. It's just kind of weird up there."

"It's a little weird down here, too," he admitted, probably just to make me feel better, because he didn't look scared. "You'll be happy to know, though, that Buddy Ray has the front of the building staked out." He pointed toward a police car moving slowly down Main Street. "You might not want to dress near the window up there."

"I'll be careful," I answered, and for a minute we just stood there watching the car pass out of sight. When it was gone, I shifted uncomfortably, feeling like the dorky girl at a middle school dance. "I didn't mean to bother you."

"You're not." He motioned toward the TV in the corner, where a salesman was advertising aluminum siding on some late-night cable channel. "Turn up the sound and stay a while if you want."

"Okay." The word rushed out far too quickly, sounding terribly uncool. "I mean, if you're sure I won't be in the way."

"Not a bit."

I felt him watching me as I crossed the exercise area, but by the time I sat down in one of the sixties-style vinyl chairs at the edge of the carpet, he'd gone back to work with the weights. I concentrated on the TV so he wouldn't think I was watching him. It was surprisingly hard not to look.

An episode of *Bonanza* came on, and I focused in, a sudden sense of home and family enveloping me like a favorite blanket. "My dad and I used to watch reruns of this show. My mom had bit parts in some of the episodes."

His rhythmic breathing stopped. "Really?"

Curling my legs into the chair, I waited for the opening scene, hoping this would be one of her episodes. "Oh sure. She had little parts in a lot of old shows. She's half Italian, so she's been everything from a gypsy to an Indian princess. She even got to play Little Joe's romantic lead once. I was always jealous of that one. I had a major crush on Little Joe."

The bench squealed as Carter sat up. "Oh, you're a cowgirl, huh?"

"Hardly," I laughed. "There wasn't much chance of my having a horse in LA, but I fantasized about it a lot. I had a cousin who lived on a ranch up by Truckee, and we went there once or twice."

"Pretty country up by Truckee." He didn't return to exercising but just sat there astraddle the bench, as if he'd rather talk than work out. "I wanted to take a drive up that way when I was out in LA but couldn't spare the time last trip."

"Oh really? What brought you to LA?" Mandalay Florentino, hard-edged associate producer, reared her suspicious head. Carter had recently been to LA. Hmmm . . .

"Business. Nothing very interesting." He closed up like a clam in a riptide. The weight bench squealed as he lay down again.

"Did it work out all right?"

"We'll see." The weights started moving up and down again.

I shifted toward the TV, contemplating what *We'll see* might mean. My stomach gurgled unexpectedly, sending out a long, loud moan. I hugged my knees against my chest, but the moaning got louder.

"Is that you or the ghost?" There was a heavy clunk as he set the barbell in the rack.

"It's me," I admitted with a growing sense of humiliation. This was so undignified. I should have stayed upstairs in my room. "I dumped soda all over my takeout food, and the cookie plate downstairs is empty."

"I think Buddy Ray ate the cookies." The weight bench squealed and rattled as Carter stood up. I glanced over my shoulder, and he was watching the sheriff's car pass by outside the windows again.

"Come on," he said, giving a clandestine shrug toward the far side of the room as the car slipped out of sight.

"What?"

"Midnight snack." Shrugging again, he checked the front window, then said, "Watch this," and started across the room.

I'm not normally the adventurous type, but something about Carter's invitation was impossible to resist. Uncurling my legs, I followed him through the room, past the hair dryers that looked like alien mind-sucking devices, to a four-foot-wide bookshelf, which he proceeded to swing open, creating a doorway in the wall.

"Whoa," I gasped, standing back. "Is that the secret door Imagene was talking about?"

"Must be." He winked in a way that told me he'd seen the doorway in operation before. "Let's go see what we can rustle up in the café."

"No way!" I laughed, poking my head through the hole. The café was on the other side, the interior dimly lit by neon signs in the window and a flickering fluorescent bulb on the huge Vent-A-Hood.

"Ladies first," Carter urged.

"Huh-uh." Stepping back, I adopted what I hoped was a steadfast posture. Something in there smelled really good. . . . "That's breaking and entering."

"Not necessarily."

"It is, too."

"She said to make ourselves at home." Carter lifted his hands, indicating *It's elementary*.

"We've been arrested once tonight already," I protested, but Carter was slipping sideways through the opening, heading toward the good-smelling stuff.

"That was mostly your fault," he pointed out just before he disappeared. "Hey, there's pecan pie in the case. It looks fresh."

My stomach went wild and a slew of primal urges pulled me through the wall against all good sense. I stopped on the café side, thinking that if Buddy Ray passed by, I'd hurry back through and leave Carter to explain why he was rummaging around the café. This time, he could get arrested without me.

He didn't seem worried. In fact, he was taking his time, looking in cabinets and opening metal bins on the prep table. Momentarily, he appeared to consider turning on the cooktop.

"I'm thinking . . . nachos," he decided finally, grabbing an open bag of tortilla chips and dumping some into a paper hotdog boat. "Nachos and pecan pie." He spun a partially filled pie plate down the counter and motioned to me. "Cut a couple pieces of that."

Hesitating a few steps into the room, I tried to reconcile myself to pie larceny. My mother would be horrified. Then again, my mother wasn't the one starving in the middle of the night and standing mere feet away from a luscious dessert. "All right." In the morning, I'd confess to the café owner and pay for the pie. And the nachos.

At the prep table, Carter whistled as he sprinkled shredded cheese on the chips, popped the whole shebang into the microwave, then dropped the metal cheese lid noisily back into place.

I jumped. Again. Guilty conscience. "Sshhh. You know, there's a ghost under here counting Confederate coins."

Carter leaned over to observe the nachos, his finger poised to press the microwave button at exactly the right moment. "Let's hope the pecan pie isn't his."

Shaking my head, I finished cutting our slices and handed the pie back like a hot tamale. "Here. Put this away."

Carter set the pie in the rack, then pointed calmly toward the front window. "Down in front." Giving my shirt a quick tug, he ducked behind the counter, and I turned around just in time to see the sheriff's car passing slowly along Main Street.

I froze, silently praying that the headlights were reflecting on the window and Buddy Ray couldn't see inside. *Please, God, don't let me get arrested again tonight. Please?*

The car passed and I breathed a sigh of relief. Finally, something was going right.

Carter popped up behind the counter. His cell phone rang and I gasped, slapping a hand against my chest.

"You're not very good at this," he commented. Checking the number on his phone, he seemed to consider answering it, then he turned off the ringer and slipped the phone back into his pocket.

"I'm probably not the person you want along on your next bank robbery," I joked, catching my breath.

"I don't know. You've got possibilities." He grinned at me as he moved to the refrigerator case. "Root beer, Coke, or Dr. Pepper?"

A little tingly feeling traveled over my skin. "Root beer. Let's get out of here, all right?"

"As you wish." Balancing the nachos on his palm, he ushered me out with the two bottles of root beer laced between his fingers. As we made our getaway, he reached into the pocket of his workout shorts and left a twenty on the counter. "My treat," he said as we slipped through the bookcase and pushed it into place again.

Back in the beauty shop, Carter set the nachos on an overturned box that doubled as a magazine table. Then he opened the lids on both sodas and handed mine to me with a ceremonious flourish that made him look like a waiter serving up fine wine. He hesitated there for a moment after I took my drink, and I was afraid he was considering excusing himself and going upstairs. I wanted him to stay, but of course I couldn't tell him that. Any way I said it, *please stay* would sound like an invitation to something more than a late-night snack and an episode of *Bonanza*.

I gave myself a mental kick. That was hardly a proper line of thought for a happily engaged Episcopal-schooled girl to be descending into. What was wrong with me tonight?

Scooping up a nacho, Carter plopped down in the chair next to mine, seeming perfectly happy to spend the wee hours of the night watching *Bonanza* with me.

David wouldn't watch Bonanza. *David hates cowboy shows.* . . .

Focusing on the television, I stuffed a nacho into my mouth, hoping the food would clear my head.

Chapter 8

Imagene Doll

For a few minutes every morning I wake up and think Jack's there. In my mind, he's in the kitchen making the coffee like he always did before he headed off to the insurance office. He'd bring me a cup and we'd sit in the bed, me underneath the covers and him on top, because he was already dressed. Some mornings even yet, I hear him downstairs, whistling "Danny Boy" or "The Old Rugged Cross." I smell soap and Old Spice and I reach over and feel the sunken spot beside me in bed.

I lay there smiling, pretending I'm still asleep, waiting for him to come and kiss me and say, "Rise and shine, Majee. Coffee's on." I always loved when he used that little pet name. Nobody else ever called me that, and even though Jack wasn't a romantic man in big showy ways, those little things let me know his feelings more than any high-dollar roses on Valentine's Day ever could have. In Corinthians, Paul says love's not boastful, so I reckon Jack got it right. His love was patient and quiet, and it endured.

I never would have told anybody, but even all these months after Jack's passing, I still felt like he was with me in the house. The kids bought me a coffee pot with a timer to turn on in the mornings, but my heart said that Jack made the trip down from heaven every day to turn on the coffee, fill up the house, wake me with a kiss, and whisper, "Rise and shine, Majee. Coffee's on."

I was glad the whisper of my Jack was there to ease me into morning, but I hoped my wishing for him wasn't a burden. I wanted him to have time to enjoy his mansion up there in heaven. I hoped there was lots of open country around it, because Jack sure loved wide spaces.

Usually, about the time I was turning over to ask him what heaven was like, one of the kids would call. With all four of them living out of town, they felt the need to take turns getting me up and making sure I wasn't lying around feeling sad and lonesome.

As much as I love my boys, I always dreaded the morning phone call, because it meant my time with Jack was over. I'd get out of bed and answer, feeling like I'd woke up in the wrong place. I didn't tell the boys that, of course, but every once in a while, when it was Donetta calling first thing, I could get a little closer to the core. Donetta never hears much that I say on the phone, anyhow. Whenever she calls, it's because she's packing some news, and if she doesn't get it out, she'll explode.

When the phone rang first thing, I had an inkling it was her. Outside, it was just getting light. Too early for the kids to call, and nobody with a lick of sense would phone someone's house at the crack of daylight without an emergency.

"Well, mornin', mornin', mornin'!" As usual, Donetta sounded like she'd been pacing the stall for an hour waiting to be milked. "I wake you up?" She always pretended she didn't realize how early it was.

"I was just having coffee," I mumbled, grabbing the glass of water by my bed to wet down my throat and loosen my lips. Terrible thing, snoring in your sleep.

"Well, good. I didn't want to disturb your sleep." Considering how long we've been friends, Donetta knew she'd be waking me, calling this early. "I heard there was a little excitement down to the hotel last night."

"A little." Swinging my legs around, I sat up and put my feet on the floor without making a sound. I always kept quiet around the house in the mornings and left the curtains closed a little while. If there was even a hint of Jack still there, I didn't want to spoil it.

Donetta Bradford's voice booming through the phone spoiled the quiet anyway. "Well, you should've called me." No telling how she heard about the mess at the hotel already this morning. Maybe Buddy Ray came by her house while he was finishing his shift.

"I *tried* to call you," I told Donetta. "Your phone was busy all evening long. I figured y'all had it on the eBay again. Anyway, things down at the hotel were all taken care of. When I left, both of your guests looked pretty well settled. Carter was headed off to exercise and Amanda-Lee said she was turning in. They were probably tired, what with Buddy Ray putting them in cuffs and frisking them and all."

"Lands," Donetta sighed. "If that Buddy Ray Baldrige ain't about as thick as a pine knot on a post. Just when you think them Baldriges can't get any dumber, they go and produce Buddy Ray."

"He meant well." If I hadn't promised Buddy Ray I'd keep quiet, I would have told Donetta about him locking the keys in his cruiser. "Anyhow, both of your customers were good sports about it. I don't think that Carter fella minded much. He seemed to get a kick out of it, actually. The girl was a little put off, but not too bad. Of course, Buddy Ray caught Carter in nothing but his exercise shorts, and not too many women would mind being handcuffed next to that." Donetta gasped into the phone, and

I added, "Young women, I mean," just in case Jack actually was listening. "She looked like she had a little shine for him, actually, but that's neither here nor there."

"I thought she was engaged."

"She did say that. She's not wearing a ring, though, I noticed."

"Ooohhhh." Donetta stretched the word out until it had some drama to it. I could hear her clucking her tongue against her teeth. "Maybe that's part of her cover—you know, so folks won't know she's from *American Megastar*. She say anything about that last night—maybe about when Amber's coming for her big hometown appearance? You find out anything more about what Carter's doin' here and whether them two know each other?"

"Nope. Not a thing. Hang on a minute, I've got to visit the facilities." I set the phone down on the nightstand with Donetta complaining and reminding me that the phone was cordless, which I knew. The boys had bought me the cordless phone for Christmas so I could keep it with me around the yard and such. Still, it didn't seem proper to take someone into the bathroom with you. Donetta wouldn't have minded. She carried me into the bathtub, the kitchen, the garden shed—pretty much anywhere she went.

Donetta huffed a little when I came back on the phone. "Imagene, I swear. You got to get with the modern times."

"I'm too old and slow to get modern," I said. The sun was rising over the hills in the distance, and that heavy feeling had started to settle in. I needed to get up and get moving or it would take hold of me and I'd want to curl up in bed and lay there and pass the day and the night and wait to feel Jack close by again.

Tears stung my eyes. Sometimes it was more than I could bear, being just sixty-nine and a widow, alone for the rest of my life.

"You're not old, Imagene."

I sighed into the phone. If it was the kids, I'd have kept up a front, but Donetta knew how things were. "I feel old, Netta. I'm afraid there's nothing good left ahead of me. Some days I just wish . . ." *Some days I wish I wouldn't wake up.* "Well, it don't matter."

"GiGi, don't talk that way." Donetta knew what was in my mind. With friends like us, there's a lot that doesn't get said, just understood. "*American Megastar's* on its way to town. We got TV people staying right on the second floor of the Daily Hotel. Our own little Amber Anderson's gonna be a singin' sensation, and when they finally do break the news, our hotel will be right in the middle of it. Land sakes, what could be more excitin' than that?"

"Who knows if we're even right about everything." It wasn't nice of me to rain on Donetta's parade. Opening the curtains, I headed downstairs, hoping the sun in the kitchen would perk me up.

Donetta puffed a breath into the phone. "Pppfff. We're right about it." She said it in that mysterious tone that made me think about her staring into the window the day before. "It's quiet around here this morning, but you just wait until I get a little more time with my two new guests. I'll find out exactly what the scuttle is."

"You're down to the hotel already?" I blinked at the clock on the coffeemaker. It wasn't even seven yet.

"Buddy Ray came by the house on his way home this morning and he told me what'd happened. I figured I'd better get down here just to make sure everything was all right. Looks like maybe they were up for a while after you and Buddy Ray left. Someone had nachos and pecan pie down in the exercise room. I saw the leftovers in the trash. There was *two* root beers and *two* plastic forks."

"Oh my," I said, thinking that Bob would probably have a fit about Donetta's guests going in his café in the middle of the night.

Donetta must have heard my mind working. "They left a twenty-dollar bill on the counter, so I don't reckon Bob'll mind much. Guess they must've come in hungry last night."

"Guess so."

"Uh-oh . . ." Donetta whispered. "There's water on upstairs. I better go. I got pecan rolls, toast, and breakfast casserole all fixed to put out on the bureau before they come down. If there's any trouble with Bob about the nachos and the pie, you smooth it over when you get in to work, would'ja? I don't want him fussin' at my guests. Tonight, I'll be sure to leave a little snack down here in the exercise room in case they get hungry. Just tell Bob to behave hisself if they come over there, okay?"

"I will," I said, and I hung up.

Thinking about what might have gone on at the hotel last night, I got a little more interested in the day. By the time I'd dressed and fixed my hair, I headed to town with a fresh enthusiasm and a pretty good wind in my sails. I was looking forward to seeing what would develop.

When I got to the café, Bob had already opened and was greasing up the fry grill. He was whistling "Hollywood" again, so I could tell he was in a pretty good mood. He didn't even mind that Donetta's hotel guests had been in his café last night. First of all, they left a good tip, and second, he figured that would increase the chances of the Daily Café making it onto *American Megastar*.

"You tell 'em to come on in anytime. Anytime at all," Bob said as the crew got ready for the breakfast rush. "Anything they need—breakfast, lunch, tour of the town, Daily history, or filming permits—they can just come see me. I'll be happy to do my part to make Amber's hometown show worthy of the next *American Megastar* champion." He struck a pose as the door opened, then let his belly drop back down and returned to the grill when it was only Harlan Hanson, coming to pick up his egg on toast before heading off on his mail route west of town.

All morning long, Bob posed for the door, and he was a little disappointed when neither of those Hollywood folks came into the café. By the time breakfast was over, he looked down-in-the-mouth, muttering to himself as he scraped off the fry grill. Word was that Amanda-Lee had been all over town yesterday. Couple that with Carter showing up, not saying too much about who he was or why he was there, and Daily gossip had been at a fever pitch in the café all morning long. Belva, from down at the Daily Hardware, said that Carter sure looked familiar to her when he came in the store yesterday, but she couldn't place where from. She thought maybe she'd seen him on TV before. Bob said if he got a good look he could say for sure, since he watched a lot of TV and never forgot a face.

When someone mentioned that Donetta was handing out pecan rolls and casserole for breakfast, Bob figured out that was probably why the hotel guests hadn't showed up to take a morning meal at the café. While Bob was busy working up a head of steam about Donetta stealing his breakfast customers, I decided to scoot off to Wal-Mart. Hanging my apron on the wall, I grabbed my purse and headed for the door. "I'll be back before lunch." I didn't wait for an answer—just hurried out before Bob could blow a gasket.

On the drive to Wal-Mart down in Austin, I thought about Amanda-Lee and Carter and wondered where they were right now. The drive passed quicker than usual, and it seemed like I was pulling into Wal-Mart in just three shakes of a lamb's tail. I tried to imagine what might be going on back in Daily as I went inside to pick out Donetta's paint. My mind conjured up a picture of Bob posing with his spatula, and that made me laugh as I stood absently pulling cans of winter-white latex off the shelf, still thinking about Daily, not able to focus on calculating gallons. I was zoned out to the max, as my teenaged granddaughter would have said.

I didn't even notice at first when a stock boy came up and offered to help load paint.

"Pardon?" I said.

"I thought you might need some help."

"Oh . . ." It's hard to know how to respond to an offer like that at my age. Part of me says, *Isn't he a sweet young man, being so conscientious about his job?* But another part of me says (and I hate this part), *You look so old the boy thinks you can't heft a gallon of paint.* The two are like angel and devil on my shoulders, and it's always a toss-up as to which one gets hold of my mouth.

"How many of these do you need?" the boy asked.

"Maybe around ten." I realized I probably could use help with lugging that much paint.

Raising an eyebrow, the boy motioned down the aisle. "It'd be a lot cheaper to get two of those five-gallon buckets, ma'am."

Bless him for trying, but I'd already looked at the five-gallon buckets and decided it was a physical impossibility. "Too heavy," I confessed. There was a time when I could sling fifty-pound sacks of feed into a pickup without even a wink.

The bright-eyed boy gave an understanding nod. "I can load the buckets for you." He started to put the one-gallon cans back on the shelf, but I stopped him.

"Trouble is, son, even if you load the buckets for me, I can't get them unloaded at the other end."

The boy turned red, said, "Yes, ma'am," and finished putting in ten one-gallon cans. All that paint in one cart was quite a load, so I grabbed the front of the basket and tugged it along, while he pushed from behind, and we headed for the checkout lines. The cart was squealing like a pup with its foot in the gate by the time we made it to the cash registers.

Standing at the checkout line, I looked again at that stock boy with my load of paint. *You've done gone round the bend, Imagene,* I told myself. *The barn door's open and the cows are gone. Of all the things you've ever let Donetta Bradford talk you into, this is the craziest. How in the world are we gonna clean and paint four hotel rooms before Saturday evening?*

A weak, weighted-down feeling settled over me, as if all my muscles had suddenly gone limp. I wanted to sit down on the bench by the door and cry, which was a silly response to a load of paint.

Donetta could always return it whenever she came to her senses, but it hit me at the strangest times that I wanted Jack. He would know exactly how to handle Donetta's crazy plan, and he'd be able to lift the paint. I never pictured myself living without someone who could lift the things that were too heavy for me.

I stood there, froze up in the checkout line, trying to decide whether I should really go through with the purchase. It'd just make more complications, having to return all that paint. . . .

Still, I'd promised Donetta. . . .

Maybe all this was too heavy for the back of the van. What if I blew out a tire on the way home? I'd be stuck on the highway alone with a load of paint stacked on top of the spare.

I probably should have turned to prayer at that point, but instead I turned to the tabloid newspapers. The latest editions of *The National Examiner*, *Inside Track*, *Worldwide Scoop*, and *Celebs Magazine* were sitting there in the racks, and there's something healing about finding out that other folks have got it worse than you. It wasn't the most Christian attitude, but I was glad not to be the eighty-two-year-old Chinese grandma giving birth to a baby sumo wrestler, or the real-life mermaid living in a fountain on Long Island, or the woman who'd had her storage shed squashed by an alien landing. (Those aliens even had the nerve to take a dip in her goldfish pond, and now it was a crime scene. There was no telling what might happen to the fish, having been exposed to radioactivity and all.)

I finished the front page of *Worldwide Scoop* and moved on to *The National Examiner*. Holy mackerel, there was Amber Anderson, hugging some boy, and it wasn't Buddy Ray! Heavens to Betsy, she was on the cover of *Celebs Magazine*, too, splashing around at the beach with that same fella, next to a headline that was big enough for me to read even without my glasses. "Gospel Girl Goes Gaga," and in smaller letters I had to squint at a bit, "Amber Anderson's Romantic Romp With Justin Shay." On the cover of *The National*

Examiner, the headline read "Good Girl Gone Bad?" Below that, there was a picture of some old coot in overalls and a long beard, sighting in a rifle. He was half-covered with the headline "Amber's Family Threatens Shay—Hands Off Amber or Else!"

What a horrible lie. That wasn't Amber's grandpa any more than I was. Verl Anderson was about the mildest mannered man I'd ever met. He probably didn't even own so much as a little old twenty-two rifle for picking off snakes and armadillos—not much need for a rifle with five hundred stray cats prowling the barnyard. The only time I'd ever seen Verl Anderson get red in the face was when Ty Bennett's goats got out and ate the Andersons' garden plants. Even then, Verl was pretty forgiving, especially considering that Amber and the boys needed to sell the vegetables on the roadside to get money for school clothes and things they couldn't buy on food stamps. Which is not to say that Verl was a sterling person, being a heathen and a drunk and all. He'd never done right by those poor kids, but he sure wasn't a gun-toting hillbilly with a foot-long beard and a mean glint in his eye.

Looking around to make sure there wasn't anyone I knew in Wal-Mart, I picked up both newspapers and slid them onto the checkout stand, upside down, as the girl started with my order. She stopped for a minute to read the back cover of *The Examiner*, where a woman had lost two hundred pounds and got a bikini body just by taking pills. I couldn't help looking on with the cashier.

I checked the other cashier stands again, just to make sure no one was watching. It'd be my luck the pastor's wife or one of those uppity ladies from Betty Prine's Daily Literary Society would happen to be in the store today. All I needed was for it to get around that I was seen at Wal-Mart buying paint and smutty magazines. No telling what kind of rumors could come out of something like that.

The tension eased up a bit when the checkout girl finally tucked my magazines into a bag and gave it to me to hold. I could imagine what Donetta was going to say when she saw the headlines. If any of these reports about Amber was true, there could be trouble ahead—for Amber, and for Daily. No doubt those folks at *American Megastar* wouldn't like it that a girl who was supposed to be a fine Christian young lady was out and about with some Hollywood playboy. What in the world was going on in Amber's head? Here she was, with one chance to pull herself and her brothers out of that hardscrabble farm, and she was flushing her good fortunes, and Daily's, right down the drain.

This spate of bad news about our little hometown singing sensation might affect the need for paint. It surely might.

Chapter 9

Mandalay Florentino

After spending all morning attending the Friday logistics and production meeting via phone, I'd anticipated that a drive through the countryside to scope out Amber Anderson's childhood home would feel like a minibreak. A little fresh air and sunshine were just what I needed. I left well supplied with leftover pecan rolls, and even the lack of adequate directions and a maze of twisting, curving, poorly marked country roads did little to dampen my spirits. I wandered through the hills, taking in the landscape of clear-running streams and craggy limestone bluffs towering high over the road. At a river crossing, I slowed on an old bridge, listened to the music of the tires clicking over the weathered wooden deck, sending a soft *ping, ping, ping* along the rusted metal girders.

Near a farmhouse in the distance, a trio of young boys were wading and skipping stones. The dappled shade of overhanging live oaks and sycamores slid over their tanned skin as they ran through the water, sending up showers of sunlit drops. For a moment, I had the strongest urge to pull the car off the road, abandon my work, and join them.

Laughing at myself, I shook off the notion. I'd finally found Caney Creek Road, which meant I couldn't be far from the Anderson place. Letting my foot off the brake, I allowed the car to drift onward, up the hill and past a field where longhorn cattle grazed in a sea of blue wild flowers that seemed to stretch on forever. What a beautiful day. What a quietly breathtaking place. On camera, it would be incredible. . . .

Fifteen minutes later, stopped on a rocky slope in front of what I'd guessed was my intended destination, I experienced a wave of conflicting emotions that thickened the air in the car until it was oppressive. Opening the window might have helped, but the odor of a poultry farm down the road blanketed everything with a noxious smell. I rubbed my eyes, looking for a name on the off-kilter mailbox, an obvious victim of a drive-by box bashing that had left the door hanging permanently open, like a lolling metal tongue. There was mail inside, but without breaking a half-dozen federal laws, I couldn't check the recipient's address.

Even if this was the Anderson house, where Amber's grandfather and her brothers still lived, did we really want to bring a film crew here? It was worse than I'd ever imagined. What Amber had described as a little farm by Caney Creek was actually an ancient mobile home with faded aqua paint and a sag in the middle. The windows were covered with aluminum foil and dirt, blocking out the sun. A combination of plastic sheeting and tarps, held in place by silver tape and weighted down with twenty or so old tires, covered the roof, presumably to keep out the rain.

Behind the trailer, an old barn listed to one side like a slowly sinking ship, its damaged hull patched with road signs, scraps of plywood, metal sheeting, cardboard. A goat alternately chewed on remains of a grocery store banana box and paused to chase away a curious chicken. The entire spread, perhaps four acres or so, bounded by a chain-link fence that had seen better days, was a cacophony of dogs, cats, and farm animals. Goats, sheep, and chickens roamed freely around the place, and a black and white calf played on the front steps, climbing up, then jumping off and cavorting through the yard. The only place the animals didn't seem to be welcome was a small orchard and garden separated by a fence covered with honeysuckle and blackberry brambles.

My mind drifted to one of Amber's previous background interviews. I could picture her sitting in the confessional set we affectionately called *The Box*, smiling for the camera and, for America's viewing pleasure, painting a rosy picture of her childhood.

"In the summertime we had blackberries, and fresh lettuce, and homegrown tomatoes." The melodiousness of her voice made the words sound lyrical. "My grandaddy'd help us pick tons and tons of berries and divide them all up, and we kids would head off to town with a wagonload of the freshest blackberries, and sometimes tomatoes, and we'd sit on the street corner down by the old bank building with a sign. Folks were always so nice when they'd stop to buy some. You just haven't really lived until you've had homegrown fruits and vegetables. Those old store tomatoes are all pink and hard, and store-bought blackberries, even if you can find 'em, don't taste like anything. The wild kind taste lots better, and you know, most folks don't even know that anymore. They've never had anything but the store-bought stuff that's all sprayed with chemicals to make it grow faster. I always did feel sorry for folks like that—ones who don't know how things taste when they just have air and sunlight. And kids—I feel sorry for kids who have to live in places where they stay inside and everyone's scared of their neighbors and stuff."

Sighing, Amber looked at her shoes, kicked a stray sound cord back and forth underneath a silver cowboy boot someone in Wardrobe had given her to wear. "If I had a million dollars, I think that's one thing I'd do. I'd make a place for kids to go out in the country—all kinds of kids—little black kids, and little Chinese kids, and little kids from Iraq and other places. Kids ought to know what it's like to pack a lunch and hike off down the creek looking for good swimmin' holes, and pick wild blackberries and hog plums, and take the honeysuckle flowers and pull out the stems to taste the honey inside. When the honeysuckle blooms around our house, you can close your eyes and think you're in heaven. Every little child ought to know how that feels."

Amber's big blue eyes fell closed, and she took in a long breath of climate-controlled studio air. She looked like a little girl, her full lips pursed in a slight smile, dark lashes fluttering against her cheeks. Finally, she shook her head and opened her eyes, tucking her hands between her knees and shrugging. "I guess that sounds kind of silly." She paused, as if she were waiting for the cameraman to answer, which of course, he wouldn't. "I can't help it, I'm a dreamer." She let her hands slide further between her thighs, as if she might fold herself up and disappear. "I spent a lot of hours up and down Caney Creek, imagining things and making up games of let's pretend so we all wouldn't be bored."

Amber's giggle jingled through the studio. "Three boys can get in a lot of mischief if they're bored. Our house doesn't have ninety-seven TV channels to watch. Just four—five if the wind's from the east and you hold your tongue just right." She giggled again, and the camera operator glanced sideways covertly, as in, *Is this girl for real?* Amber didn't seem to notice. Most of the time, Amber didn't get the drift of what was going on around her. She didn't see the hidden eye rolls of the other contestants when she said hi to the folks back home in Daily every week or blew kisses to her younger brothers. She remained blissfully unaware, as far as I could tell, of the ongoing Amber pool, predicting her downfall.

The camera operator to whom she was pouring out her heart in The Box had the official Amber pool spreadsheet on his BlackBerry.

He looked as if he felt mildly guilty about it as Amber waxed nostalgic about life back home.

"I miss home sometimes at night—I don't want to go off the show or anything, because I want to go all the way—but it's really bright here at night. Back home, sometimes we'd sit out in the yard and it'd be so dark you could see a million and one stars. On Wednesdays and Sundays we could hear the singin' from the little country church just down from my house—we weren't members there or anything, because it's a black church and all—but sometimes I'd sit in when they had choir practice. Goodness, their choir can sing. They got a gospel band and everything. Sometimes during Sunday night service, I'd lay on the grass at home and look up at that big old blanket of stars and listen to the music, and it was like my heavenly Father was rockin' me off to sleep."

At that point, one of the grips handling a boom buried his face in his shoulder to stifle a guffaw. He turned away, his eyes bulging and his cheeks growing red. Amber was completely oblivious. She took a deep breath, smiling as if she were listening to the music and drinking in the scent of honeysuckle.

When Ursula saw the tape, she growled under her breath, then slammed a freshly manicured hand against her desktop, crimson fingernails extended, slowly scratching backward across the wood in a way that made my spine crawl. "We must eliminate this hayseedt. She izz makingk a mockery of my show. This izz *American Megastar*, not the Hee-Haw Hillbilly Hour. She izz gone this week, either way...." The frustration-induced accent was so thick, I missed a few closing words, but the gist was unmistakable.

At the time, I'd sat there with my clipboard, vaguely wondering what *gone this week, either way* meant. I knew better than to ask. Much of my job performance depended on my ability to quietly wait for Ursula's moods to pass. The elimination of contestants from the show was determined by an equal combination of the judge's scores and votes from the viewing public, which meant there was no way Ursula could ensure that Amber would be leaving next week, or any particular week, for that matter.

Fortunately for Amber, her viewer votes soared the week after her interview stint in The Box. Even the judges couldn't deny the quality of her rendition of "A Letter From Heaven," a song she dedicated to her parents, who'd died in a car accident when Amber was just eleven. Numbers for the show that week were up a whopping thirty percent, and two focus groups logged Amber's performance as a significant reason for continuing viewership of *American Megastar*.

Ursula was suddenly in love. If Hee-Haw Hillbilly worked for the viewers, it worked for her. "At least this izz good for now," she said. The last part, *for now*, stuck in my head.

It came back to me again as I looked at Amber's house. The place smelled like anything but honeysuckle, and there was no way Amber or anyone else could have lain in the grass and looked at the stars. There *wasn't* any grass. With so many animals running loose, anyone lying in the yard would have been reclining in a variety of poop.

Ursula would not like this. Assuming I was in the right place, this didn't fit cleanly into the Amber story we'd sold to the public. The sparkling creek she'd talked about was little more than a muddy ditch. No chance of filming there. Ursula wouldn't like the rotting trailer home, either. Amber had described her home as tiny, but kept up real nice, and it was anything but. When Ursula had said she wanted to show Amber's humble beginnings, I doubt a junk-yard filled with old boxes, farm animals, used tires, and a decaying pink porcelain toilet on the porch were what she had in mind. The place belonged in some third-world country. Ursula would never want to air this in conjunction with an *American Megastar* Final Five show. We'd be laughed out of LA.

We'd have to make the most of filming Amber in town and at the fairgrounds . . . and maybe at the little church across the creek.

From my vantage point, I could barely see it through a border of overgrown cedars I assumed marked the Andersons' property line, but the church looked picturesque enough—a sturdy antique white wooden building with a simple four-sided steeple rising upward into the overhanging branches of enormous trees. A lovely place, actually. As I let the car roll forward to get a better view of the church, it occurred to me that the church would make a nice post-card, with its expansive lawn and heavy, ancient pecans and live oaks. A foundation for some new construction had been plowed out back, but we could film at an angle so as to avoid that. In the front flower beds, a bright array of spring irises flew multicolored flags, and tulips were blooming around a wooden sign by the road. *HARVES CHAPEL*, the crudely cut metal letters read. Sort of an un-glamorous name for a church, but other than that, the place was perfect for a location piece.

A young man in orange sweat pants was mowing the grass out front, the mocha-brown skin of his arms glistening with a sheen of perspiration as he pivoted the mower. He was wearing an orange tank top, which made me think of Carter in his SPCA shirt last night. I wondered where he was today. He'd been gone by the time I'd awakened this morning. I was amazed that I'd slept so late, with the room lights blazing. It was wimpy of me to leave them on, but even after two episodes of Bonanza, I still had the creeps, and I'd hollered through the door when Carter flipped the light switch.

He'd laughed and turned it back on. "You'll be tired in the morning, Hollywood." Sometime during our conversation about my mother's career as a movie extra and my short stint as a child actor, he'd taken to calling me *Hollywood*. It occurred to me after the fact that I probably shouldn't have divulged so much infor-mation about where I was from, especially since Carter wasn't as equally forthcoming.

I pictured myself in the exercise area with him last night, chat-tering on and on about *Bonanza*, and my childhood crush on Little

Joe, and my latent desire to take a dude ranch vacation one of these days when my schedule wasn't so packed. I hadn't thought about it at the time, but reviewing the evening in my mind, I could see that it had been a one-sided yack fest—Carter making what seemed like harmless inquiries and me babbling on and on because I didn't want to go upstairs to Graceland. All I'd learned about Carter was that he'd recently moved back to Austin after living out of state for fifteen years, and he had some kind of a business appointment in Daily.

What kind of business could someone like Carter possibly have here?

Pulling up near the church sign, I stopped and rolled down my window. The man mowing released the lawnmower handle and let the engine die, then headed my way. I recognized him as he came closer—Otis Charles, the feed store customer who'd told the story about battling for Amber's calf at the Reunion Days calf scramble. His shirt said *UT Athletics* on the front.

He smiled as I leaned out the window. "Can I help you?"

I tried to look casual, pleasant. Just a run-of-the-mill tourist, out in the middle of nowhere, stopping to ask for directions. "I think I'm a little lost. I was wondering if you could tell me, is this the Caney Creek Church?" I pretended not to see the rather large sign beside us that said *HARVES CHAPEL*.

O.C. glanced at the wood and stone billboard. "Yes, ma'am, it is. Don't mind the sign. Last year, the church council voted to give the place an official name, Harvest Chapel, but the *T* fell off. Since my Grandpa Harve's the pastor, we left it for a joke. Most folks still call it Caney Creek Church, anyhow." Bracing his hands on his hips, he gave me a bemused look. "You're the third person who's asked me that today."

"I am? Is that normal?"

O.C. rolled his eyes then blinked at me as if I were daft. "Not hardly. Nobody ever comes down this road. Did you need to talk to Grandpa Harve? He's inside." He glanced toward the building, seeming ready to turn me over to someone else and finish the mowing.

"Oh, no thanks." At least for now, the less attention I called to myself, the better. "I was just trying to figure out where I was. Could you tell me how to get to the fairgrounds from here? I wanted to see the sheep . . . contest. My friend has sheep. In the contest." *That was lame.*

O.C. blinked, his lips parting into a wide, white grin that said, *Okay, lady, whatever you say.* "You're a little ways off from the fairgrounds." Scratching his forehead, he paused to think. "Let's see . . . to get there from here, you'd go down this road till you get to the T. Take a left on 2102, then right by the big old white barn and you're almost there. Can't remember the number of that road, but you'll see the barn. There's an old Mobil Oil sign painted on the side of it."

"I'm sure I can find it. Thanks," I said. "I'm sorry to have bothered you. Sounds like you've had a lot of interruptions around here today." I left the statement open-ended, waiting to see if he would volunteer more information about recent visitors.

"A bit—you, and some people in a slick-lookin' motor bus, and the dude who's in the church talking to Grandpa Harve." He motioned over his shoulder and I glanced toward the church. Two men were coming out the front door, engrossed in conversation. The older man, I guessed by his imposing stature, was O.C.'s grandfather—Harve of Harve's Chapel. The younger man, I recognized instantly. Carter Woods. In the flesh. Looking chipper today in jeans, cowboy boots, and a Hard Rock Cafe T-shirt. He'd slicked back his hair in waves that curled over his ears and caught the sunlight on the back of his neck. At the moment, he was focused on a notebook the old man was holding. The pastor turned the page and pointed at something, and both of them laughed.

"What's he doing here . . ." I muttered.

Otis Charles assumed the question was for him. "Came by to talk to Grandpa Harve. Didn't say what about."

"Huh . . ." I mused, watching Carter in the side mirror, my suspicions blooming like flowers in time-lapse photography. If I'd wanted to believe last night that Carter was just a nice guy, traveling through Daily on some unnamed business errand, the notion seemed utterly ludicrous now. What were the odds that the stranger who'd happened to show up in town when I did would also happen to turn up at some middle-of-nowhere church a few hundred yards from Amber Anderson's childhood home? A supposition of coincidence can only go so far before venturing into the realm of blind stupidity. Carter Woods was not my friend, or my protector, or my happenstance hotel mate—he was up to something.

"You can go ask him if you want," O.C. offered. "Looks like they're about done."

"Oh . . . ummm . . . no thanks. I'd better take off. Thanks for the directions, though." Best to move on while Carter was still occupied. No sense letting him know I'd seen him hanging out in Amber's neighborhood.

"You're welcome, ma'am." Backing politely away from the window, Otis Charles shielded his eyes and peered down the road toward the Anderson place. "I'll be dogged. There's that motor bus again. What'n the heck . . ."

I didn't turn around to look at the RV, just waved a thank-you to O.C., circled the sign, and pulled out, watching Carter and Pastor Harve in the mirror until a hedge blocked my view. Neither Carter nor Pastor Harve ever looked up. Whatever was in that book was not only amusing but very interesting. They kept turning the pages, pointing, nodding, and occasionally laughing.

Curiosity needled me like one of the fluffy angora sweaters my mother used to make me wear to church. LA was usually too hot for angora, but my mother thought I looked cute in fluffy pastel things. By the time I came along, she was forty-three and realizing that her days of Mary Janes and lacy skirts with petticoats were numbered. At the age of twelve, I revolted. I vowed that I'd never wear tights or angora again, and I never had, but I still remembered the feeling—hot, itchy, vaguely crawly and prickly, a sensation that stuck with you even after the garment was safely back in the closet.

Pulling over, I sat on the side of the road, watched the glistening blue motor home stop in front of the Anderson place. A woman in a brown suit got out, walked to the fence and checked out the house, then opened the gate. An assortment of dogs and farm animals bounded toward her, and she jumped back through the opening, slamming the gate shut just in time to prevent the pet calf from escaping. Checking over her shoulder, she hurried to the motor home in a high-heeled trot, then stood for a moment stroking her short, spiked blond hair, watching the trailer home as if hoping someone would come out. Finally, she disappeared into the RV.

She had *reporter* written all over her. *Great.* I waited for the RV to come closer so I could see if there was a logo, but there was nothing. The RV was probably a loaner from some local dealer, given in exchange for promotional consideration. Glare on the window blocked my view of the driver, but the woman in the brown suit was sitting in the passenger seat, alternately checking her mirror and trying to unfold a map. Spotting Otis Charles in front of the church, she pointed, and the motor home made a wide-swinging turn into the church parking lot, swaying back and forth as it bumped over the culvert.

I sat on the side of the road a moment longer observing, then finally let off the brake and drove on through the patchy sunlight, trying do some creative problem solving. There had to be a way of keeping everything under control until after we'd brought Amber home and completed her location shoot.

Unfortunately, nothing was occurring to me. I felt like a ninety-pound weakling confronted with a brawny beach bully. Any way

I played this, I was going to end up smashed to a pulp with sand in my face. I wanted to go home. I wanted to plop down on my parents' couch and have my mother offer me hot chocolate and prescription medications.

It occurred to me, as I headed toward the fairgrounds, that in my moment of desperation, I should have been yearning for David. His voice should have seemed like a comfort, his arms a refuge. Instead, the thought of him brought more stress. Where was David, anyway? I'd tried calling him six times—four yesterday and two this morning after the production meeting. All I'd gotten was David's voice mail. No answer, no call back. He had to be out on the boat. He'd probably gone on a pre-honeymoon shakedown just to make sure everything was in shape for our trip.

Even so, knowing I was traveling, couldn't he have called?

Sometimes, even though I was now one half of a couple, I felt more alone than ever. There were good things about operating with a fair amount of independence—David liked that about me, especially considering that his ex-wife had been clingy and controlling. Having spent the last twelve years of my life making my own decisions, I appreciated the fact that David saw me as an equal, capable of taking care of myself. I didn't want someone checking up on me all the time, asking where I was, demanding reports on what I was doing, delving into my checkbook and my dinner dates with Paula.

Paula predicted that when David and I actually did move into the apartment together we would have some space issues. That was perfectly natural, she said, considering my past history of trying to wrestle my independence from a pair of overprotective parents and David's past history of a nasty divorce. It would take some time to work out the details of which level of relationship was enough and which level was too much.

It bothered me a little when she said that. Could you be *too* married? Wasn't marriage supposed to be all the way?

Right now, alone in Daily, Texas, with David out of touch on the high seas, our present situation felt like too little commitment. It would probably be different when I got back home.

Sighing, I turned on the radio. Music always helped when I was descending into the blues.

"And that's your 'Mandy in the Middle,' " the DJ said. "Hey, all you listeners out there. Hope your Friday's rolling along just as fine as frog hair. The big news around Central Texas and the Hill Country today—still no official confirmation, but word is that local favorite Amber Anderson is a shoo-in for the Final Five on *American Megastar. . . .*"

Chapter 10

Imagene Doll

The lunch rush was already underway and looking busier than usual when I got back to Daily. Quite a number of cars were parked out front, and through the window I could see that the booths were already full. Some of the countertoppers had come in for lunch, which was surprising, considering that it was the opening of Reunion Days. Granted, it wasn't the big event it once was, when former Dailyians used to return from all over the country, but the fair and rattlesnake weigh-in were still pretty popular. I'd have thought Doyle, Harlan, Ervin, and the rest of them would be at the fairgrounds, buying sausage on a stick and wandering through the cow barns, trying to pick this year's sure-fire grand champion steer, or at least sizing up the yearly catch of rattlesnakes.

With the rush on in the café, I knew I shouldn't stop by the beauty shop, but I had to tell Donetta what I'd learned at the checkout stand in Wal-Mart. Before I could get a word in edgewise, she started rattling on about her plans to get the rooms painted. She'd talked to her nephew, Coach Rollins, over at the school, and she had the entire baseball team and a half-dozen cheerleaders coming to help with cleaning and painting the rooms as soon as school was out. In the meantime, she'd happened across Amber Anderson's grandpa when she was down at the hardware store, and she'd hired him to start filling the cracks in the walls, then give directions to the high school kids when they showed up.

"You hired Verl Anderson to paint your hotel rooms?" I said, even though I knew I didn't have time to get into a discussion. "Donetta, what were you thinking? That poor old man probably can't even make it up the stairs, with his leg the way it is." Years ago, Verl had slid off a barn roof and wrecked up his leg pretty bad.

Donetta put her hands on her hips. "Well, I figured he could use the work. What with Amber off in Hollywood and not bringing in a salary here at home, things must be pretty tough around the Anderson place. Besides, at least one of them Anderson boys is on the baseball team, so he'll be over here working this afternoon. Verl can keep those baseball boys in line and take on whatever work he's able enough to do."

Donetta leaned close, shutting out even Lucy, who was busy packing their supply cart to head over to wash and style hair at the old folks' home. "Besides, what with them TV folks staying upstairs, it just wouldn't hurt for them to look at the shape Amber's family is in. They might see she needs that million-dollar recording contract more than anybody else."

A sheen of moisture came into Donetta's eyes, and I got a warm, prickly feeling all over me. Donetta was always looking to do good for somebody. "DeDe. You're a wonder." I reached out and hugged her, and we just stayed that way for a minute.

A loud crash in the café pulled us apart. "I need to get over there," I said, and even though I hated to do it, I handed Donetta the sack with *The National Examiner* and *Worldwide Scoop*. "Better take a look at these."

Before she could open the sack, I hurried off through the wall, feeling like a big fat thundercloud about to douse Donetta's ray of sunshine.

Nobody even noticed when I came into the café and closed the bookshelf behind me. I could smell right away that Bob was letting something burn on the fry grill. Maria was busy trying to wait all the tables, and in the booths by the window, a couple of cowboys from the Double T Ranch were looking toward the kitchen with some concern, wondering, no doubt, if they'd ever get food.

"Hey, Ms. Doll, how about some coffee?" one of them called.

"Sure thing," I said, stopping to flip the burgers on the grill and stir the hash browns. "Comin' right up. Looks like these burgers are just about ready."

Bob didn't budge. He was caught up in a conversation with Harlan, who'd just come in from his rural mail route with the news that some out-of-towners were staying at Miss Lulu's RV camp near Boggy Bend. They'd parked three brand new RVs, still with dealer tags on, in spaces 1A through 4A, plus a truck with some kind of space-aged electronic antenna on top. Miss Lulu had kept quiet about it since yesterday, which, for Miss Lulu, was a record. Normally, she shows up in town every morning like clockwork, dressed in one of her favorite muumuus without benefit of a brassiere, and Miss Lulu's not a small woman. She's Otis Charles's aunt, and she could probably play football for UT right along with him. She always wears her hair braided in neat little rows with a big flower in the back. Most days, while picking up her mail at the post office, she makes the rounds of town, telling, in that big deep voice of hers, all sorts of wild stories about the folks staying in the campground, or teenagers skinny-dipping in the swimming hole at Boggy Bend Park, or the latest stray pooch to be abandoned on her porch. Whatever the subject, Miss Lulu loves to tell a tale.

When Harlan got to her house that Friday morning, he'd found Miss Lulu in a powerful fret, sitting on her front porch in a sweat-drenched muumuu with her hair frizzed out six inches in all directions. She hadn't even bothered to braid it or put in a flower. "Looked like a chain smoker on her third day cold turkey," Harlan said as he splayed his fingers around his head, giving an impression of Miss Lulu's hair. "She come runnin' out and give me a big sweaty hug right there in the driveway."

The other countertoppers winced, and Doyle Banes's hat-rack body convulsed in a powerful shudder. He'd been caught under the mistletoe by Miss Lulu at the Daily Downtown Christmas celebration last year after she had too much eggnog, so he knew what those hugs felt like.

Harlan went on with his story. "She calls me inside, all the while lookin' over her shoulder, and soon as she closes the door, she cracks like a rotten egg in August, spewing out words ninety-to-nothin'. She said that yesterday a lady with short white-blond hair and nice clothes showed up in a taxicab, of all things, and wanted to rent three campsites with full water and sewer hookup. Miss Lulu didn't know what to think, so she asked about the lady's business in Daily. Lady said she's on vacation, and then she offered Miss Lulu a big check to keep quiet." Harlan paused for effect, narrowing an eye and sweeping back and forth between Bob and the other fellas.

I smelled food burning again, so I started plates and took the burgers off the grill. The odor of the onions stirred an anxiousness in my stomach. I wasn't sure I wanted to know who those folks were out at Miss Lulu's. *First, all the hotel rooms booked up at Donetta's, and now there's a rush on at the RV park.* Donetta was right. Something big was in motion.

I couldn't help tuning in as I finished the plates, and Harlan went on with his story.

"So Miss Lulu takes the money, and it ain't until later that she realizes what a problem it's gonna be to keep up her end of the bargain. She figures the only way she'll be able to keep quiet is to stay out of town. Period. By the time I show up, she's breakin' out in a rash and she's got a tic in her right eye. She's worried maybe she's rented out her campsites to bank robbers or international spies, or a gang of domestic terrorists, even." Harlan pointed a finger and drummed it on the bar top. "So then this morning, in rolls three motor homes and a truck van with some kind of radar machine on top. There's at least seven fellas and the spike-haired lady, and they don't want to have nothin' to do with nobody. They don't buy no wood for a campfire or take a walk down to the park on Boggy Bend. After a while, they all get in the one motor home and drive out, lickety-split. Being as they'd left in such a hurry, Lulu checks around their campsites, just to make sure the electric and sewer are hooked up right. Every window shade on every motor home is closed. Tight."

"Uulll-land-land sakes," Doyle breathed, reaching blindly for his coffee. His fingers landed in it, then he pulled them out and wiped them on his shirt. "Won-wonder what them f-f-folks u-rrr doin' there, ya reckon?"

"TV people," Bob cut in. "Just mark my words. That's people from Hollywood." He stopped me as I stuck the tickets in the hamburger plates and started toward the cowboys. "Imagene, those folks staying at the hotel say anything about bringing in a filming crew, maybe puttin' them up out at the RV park?"

"Not that I know of, Bob." I wasn't about to tell him Donetta had the rest of the rooms rented to Amanda-Lee for the weekend. That'd send Bob into such a spin we'd never get through the lunch crowd.

Bob gave me a back-handed wave, since I didn't have any interesting stories about TV folks taking over Daily. I took the plates out to the cowboys and stopped to take an order at the next table, keeping one ear tuned toward the countertop conversation.

"So then, Miss Lulu notices that a window on one of the trailers is cracked open just a little bit, and the miniblind is broke. Being as the weather forecast was for twenty percent chance of rain, that worries her some, and she goes to the window to investigate. When she peeks through, there's computer equipment, TV screens, big wads of cable layin' everywhere, and a machine that looks like the heart monitor at the emergency clinic. There's a fella standing near the machine. He must've heard Miss Lulu, because right then he turns toward the window. She ducks off and runs for the golf cart and hurries back home, quick as she can. By the time I showed up, she had it in her mind they were terrorists for sure and she was about to be one of those people who disappear in broad daylight and never get seen again." Chuckling under his breath, Harlan took a sip of his root beer. "I explained to her about Amber's TV show and told her not to worry, and she got so relieved I was afraid she was gonna hug me again, so I got myself on outta there."

Bob scratched his chin, watching a fly crawl across the ceiling. "Can't understand why they'd be out there dealing with Miss Lulu when they didn't even come by the Daily Chamber of Commerce yet. Don't make sense." He frowned deeper, until he'd moved into a full-blown pout. "Don't make any sense at all. . . ."

"Well, you know, Miss Lulu's is only about three miles down the county road from the Anderson place," Harlan pointed out. "Less than two miles through the field, if you go as the crow flies." Being the postman, Harlan knows his geography. "It'd make sense—them wanting to be out by the Anderson place, I mean."

"P-p-p-probably doin' re-recon work. An-an advance t-t-team, advance team," Doyle chimed in.

"What in the world would they be looking for out at the Anderson place?" I asked. "Stray cats and coyotes?"

All three of them turned to me like I had corn growing out my ears.

"If they're gonna do Amber's hometown show, they gotta set up interviews, find good background scenery, get the scoop," Bob said slowly, like he was talking to the class dunce. Holding up his fingers, he made a little box and looked through it, pretending to be a movie man on the job.

"At the Anderson place?" I couldn't help coughing out loud. "Any of you seen that place lately? Four acres of bare dirt, black-berries growin' up in the fence, and animals loose all over the porch. With Amber gone and just Verl and the boys there, it's worse than ever. Who in the world would put something like that on TV?"

About that time, Brother Erve walked in, dressed in his three-piece suit, which usually meant he was headed out to preach a wedding or a funeral. "Just saw a nice-lookin' motor home out on Caney Creek Road. They were pulled up in the parking lot at Harve's Chapel, talking to O.C., and they kept pointing back toward the Anderson place."

"Guess that proves my point," Bob said triumphantly.

"Guess so" was all I could think of to say. All of a sudden, I had a sense of our quiet life being upended like a bucket under an unruly milk cow.

When the lunch rush was over and I'd helped Estacio and Maria get the dishes to the kitchen, I headed through the wall to see if Donetta was back from the old folks' home.

"We got time to sneak in a class," she said when I came in. "We'll wait while you get changed. We'll have to cut it short a bit. Got Betty Prine coming in for a cut and color in thirty minutes, and you know she'll get on her high horse if I'm not ready when she waltzes through the door. Had two other call-ins, too, so that makes a full schedule the rest of the day. All of a sudden, everybody's in a rush to get their hair done before the weekend. Getting ready for Reunion Days, I guess."

I sank down in one of the dryer chairs by the café wall. It oc-curred to me that Betty Prine probably wanted to make sure she had all her gray hairs covered just in case Hollywood really did come to town. I didn't bring it up to Donetta. That'd only get her started on a tirade about that snooty bunch in the Daily Literary

Society. I didn't have the energy for that conversation today. "Let's skip exercise and just have coffee."

Donetta pulled up her pink leg warmers. Standing there in her leotard and tights, she looked like a cocktail olive on two fluffy pink skewers. "We can't skip exercise. Besides, we're all dressed, right, Lucy?"

Lucy was already headed toward the coffee pot. She stopped midway, waiting to see how the discussion would play out.

"I'm pooped." I let my head fall back and closed my eyes. It seemed like a million years since I'd dreamed of Jack downstairs making the coffee that morning. I'd been on the run all day, and now that things had settled down, I was bushed. "Busy lunch shift at the café. Lots of out-of-towners. Bob's sure they're all from Hollywood."

"More traffic up and down the highway than normal, too. Wonder if there's something goin' on down in Austin this weekend," Donetta said as she watched a pretty silver sports car roll through town.

"Don't know," I said. "You read those newspapers I brought from Wal-Mart?"

"I did." Donetta's lips pursed into a disgusted frown. "The things they'll say! I can't feature any of that'd be true. Amber and Buddy Ray been sweet on each other since the tenth grade. I always thought they'd get married, but it's hard to say, I guess. There's been many a young girl get her head turned by that Justin Shay. Movie star, got money, smooth talker, and he ain't hard to look at, that's for sure. Little country girl like Amber might find herself caught up by someone like that."

"Lands, I hope not." I pictured Amber, with her sweet blue eyes and that smattering of freckles over her nose, falling into the trap of a fast-living dandy who'd been through at least a dozen Hollywood women already. Even I knew that Justin Shay had ex-wives and kids all over the place.

"His one wife try suicide with pill and drink," Lucy interjected with a note of concern.

Donetta took in a breath. "You don't think Amber would get took into that kind of mess? Drinkin' does run in her family. You know Amber's daddy was drunk the day he ran the car off Cowhouse Creek Bridge and killed her mama? There wasn't a skid mark on the road. He probably just passed out at the wheel, ran off the bridge, and poor Tara Lynn got pinned under the water. She wasn't even hurt much—she just drowned. If Patrick hadn't been so drunk, he mighta saved her."

"Hard to say." Years ago, I'd heard about the car crash that killed Amber's mama. Jack being with the volunteer fire department, he was there on the scene. He said there were beer cans everywhere and at least two empty bottles of whiskey. He figured both of Amber's parents had been on a drinking spree that night. He didn't want me to say anything, because word getting around wouldn't do those kids any good. "Hard to say about Amber, too. Those tabloid papers make things up. I doubt if that woman in China who birthed the baby sumo wrestler is really eighty-two."

"The picture's convincin', though," Donetta pointed out. "The baby's got her eyes."

"They make it on computer," Lucy chimed in. "I see on *Sic-ty Minute* one time."

"Let's hope," I agreed. Maybe those pictures were all made up on computers and Amber didn't even know Justin Shay.

Donetta clapped her hands together. "Well, time for exercise class. We still got twenty-one minutes."

"Not today." Every once in a while I had to stand my ground with Donetta.

"Come on, upsy-daisy."

"I'm too tired."

"Imagene . . ."

I pulled the dryer hood over my head. "I can't hear you."

Donetta leaned over and knocked on the dryer. "A little exercise will perk you right up."

I shook my head. "Sometimes I don't want to be perky, DeDe. Sometimes I just want to be me."

"Oh, for heaven's sake." I heard Donetta's footsteps cross the room. "There's not enough time now, anyway. We might as well just change back into our clothes and have coffee. I sure don't want to be in this getup when them high school boys come over."

I got a little tickled, thinking about the high school kids showing up while Donetta was in her yoga suit. "Them boys might think you look pretty good in your exercise outfit, Netta."

Donetta spat a puff of air as I pushed the dryer hood up. "Doubt that. I walked by the mirror a while ago and plumb scared myself. Looked like I'd swallowed a melon. Anymore, it seems like the less I wear, the worse I look." Snorting at the mirror, she headed off to the storeroom to change back into her pants and smock.

Lucy watched her go, frowning.

"I didn't mean to get her all upset about the exercise," I said, walking over to the coffee area. "It's all right if we skip a day once in a while, that's all."

Shrugging, Lucy picked up the coffee pot and started pouring. I always liked to watch Lucy pour coffee. She had a certain way of doing it that made me think of that old Marlon Brando movie *Sayonara*. Whenever I thought of *Sayonara,* my mind always went back to sitting in the Paramount Theatre in Abilene, Texas, with Jack. He was just out of the navy, and we'd driven over there for an interview with Farmer's Insurance Company. He didn't take the job, but we stayed long enough to go to the picture show. On the way home, he told me all about Japan and the South Pacific, and it was just like I'd been there myself. When darkness settled in, we put down the top on his old Chevy ragtop and smelled the sagebrush and looked at the stars. It's funny, the little moments you remember from a lifetime.

Lucy finished pouring the coffee, and I doctored mine up, waiting for Donetta to come back. When she did, we sat down, the three of us seeming to have run out of things to say.

Something crashed upstairs, and I jerked out of my fog, looking up at the tin ceiling. "Your hotel guests come back already?"

Donetta shook her head. "Verl's up there working. I'm hoping my guests won't come back till evening. It'd be better if they didn't see us hauling junk out of the other rooms."

"You got Verl up there alone?" I asked. "What if he falls out a window and breaks his neck or something?"

Donetta's look was reproachful. "He seemed sober enough. Matter of fact, when he showed up to work, he looked like he had a little wind in his sails. It was nice."

I scoffed at that, which wasn't a very kind thing to do, but it was hard to have much sympathy for Verl Anderson. Over the years, he'd lost job after job for drinking, and when the Johnsons took pity on him and hired him to reroof their barn, he got drunk and fell off. With no way to pay a doctor's bill, he'd been bounced between four different hospitals for six days before proper surgery was done. By then, the leg was in terrible shape and the doctors wanted to take it off.

A young lady doctor from India took hold of his case and saved the leg out of pure bulldog determination. I met her once when the Daily Auxiliary took some flowers to the hospital. That lady doctor had a dot between her eyebrows and a tiny jewel in the side of her nose, just like one of them belly dancers in the movies. I couldn't understand much she said, but she was kind to Verl, and she patted Amber's little head as she passed by.

"Is my granddad gonna lose his leg?" Amber asked.

The lady doctor looked at her chart and checked under Verl's sheet. "God willing, we will safe thees leg," she said, then smiled at Amber and left the room.

The next day in Bible study, Brother Ervin talked on the story of the Good Samaritan, and I thought of that lady doctor. Sometimes it's folks who been passed over themselves that most know how it feels to be left on the side of the road.

Donetta had a sense about things like that. She smiled in a knowing way as Verl came down the top few stairs, taking them one at a time, the game leg first and then the good one. The leg didn't seem to be slowing him down much.

"Sorry about the noise," he said, poking his head between the stairway rail and the ceiling. "Hope I'm not making too much racket."

"It's all right, Verl," Donetta said, waving off his concern. "You just do whatever you need to do up there to get those rooms right."

"You betcha," Verl answered and tipped his hat at Lucy and me. "I'll have them old window frames right as rain. You can count on that. I already filled the holes and touched up the trim here and there. You won't even know those rooms when I get through."

That was more words than I'd heard Verl string together in a sentence in twenty years.

The front door opened, and Donetta stood up as Betty Prine came in. "Thank you much, Verl. I know you will. You want a cup of coffee? It's fresh."

Verl shook his head. "Oh no, no thank you, Mrs. Bradford. No time for that. Too much work to do before my help shows up." Smiling, he tipped his ratty old cowboy hat again, then turned and headed back up the stairs, just as quick and as light as any man with two good legs.

Donetta was right. Verl Anderson did have a little wind in his sails.

By the doorway, Betty Prine stopped and craned her neck like a hawk eyeing a snake in the grass. "Was that *Verl Anderson*? What in the world is that man doing here?"

I hoped Verl was too far up the stairs to hear.

Chapter 11

Mandalay Florentino

The fairgrounds were decidedly different from the day before. When I arrived, the place was abuzz with activity. Fortunately there was no sign of reporters flocking to Daily, chasing the unconfirmed radio report of Amber's Final Five status. Everything appeared to be business as usual as I waited in a line of entry traffic comprised mostly of pickup trucks and livestock trailers filled with farm animals.

The line divided, and I pulled up behind a horse trailer. One of the horses gave the trailer a resounding kick, then raised its tail and did what horses are known for doing. The mess oozed over the door and into the street, which I thought should be illegal. Where I came from, there was a hefty fine for failing to promptly pick up your doggie droppings in the park, which was one of the reasons David and I had decided to be strictly no pets. Dogs required regular effort and attention, and a cat wouldn't like the boat. The idea of something soft and fuzzy to come home to was nice, but in reality, between David's asset management company and my job with *American Megastar*, there was no time for a furry dependent.

I occasionally wondered how we'd ever work in kids. David just laughed and said I was projecting too far into the future, but at thirty-four, there was a little tick-tock inside me. I felt it during family gatherings, when my nieces and nephews brought their schoolwork to show me or curled up on the sofa with me to watch TV. Occasionally, my mother wistfully pointed out that all the grandkids were growing up, and with my sisters and my brother now well over forty, there probably wouldn't be any more babies in the family unless I got busy. Not that she was pushing. Having been a career woman herself before falling for my father, my mother fully understood the concept of wanting to achieve success in the working world. That didn't stop her from pointing out that given David's income level, I would have options. . . .

The horse trailer moved forward, and I rolled over the road apple trail, my nose curling involuntarily. Maybe I wasn't cut out for motherhood, anyway. I wasn't very good at dealing with poop and stuff. Every once in a while on show night, one of the contestants experienced nerve-induced nausea and had to run to the bathroom to throw up. I never went in to help with cleanup or re-wardrobing.

Ursula thought I was ridiculous. "You Ameri-keen women are weak," she'd say and then intimate that, if she'd been in place when I came on staff at *American Megastar*, I wouldn't have my job. Fortunately, before Ursula came on board, the executive producer had been an old friend of mine from LA affiliate news. Unfortunately, two weeks after I was hired, he left for another job, and in came Ursula Uberstach.

My cell phone rang as I pulled up to the gate, and I thought of Ursula. I answered while paying a man in striped overalls three dollars for parking.

David was on the other end of the line. I instantly felt giddy. "Hey, baby," I said. The horse in front of me whinnied, the sound echoing through the open window and bouncing around the car.

David was laughing when the sound died. "Where in the world are you?"

"Texas. Remember?" The words came out with a mildly biting undertone. *Stop that,* I thought, quickly slipping into premarital counseling mode. *He finally calls and you're displaying resentment? That was what he didn't like about his ex-wife, remember?* "So how's your day been? Did you take the boat out?" *Was the satellite phone on the blink, was there no place to come ashore, no way to check and see how I was doing down here?*

"Nah, I had to go up the coast overnight to meet with a client."

Up the coast? Up the coast? There's phone reception all over the coast. "I called you last night."

"Yeah, I know." He yawned and sighed, and a car horn blared in the background. I pictured him driving down 101, stretching and rubbing his eyes. Those big gorgeous brown eyes. "We worked pretty late and then did a breakfast meeting again this morning. I didn't want to wake you up."

"I didn't sleep much." David would probably laugh if I admitted that an old lady told me a ghost story and I was too scared to go to bed. David had never seen the wimpy insecure twelve-year-old nerd hiding deep inside me. In our six months together, he'd only met Mandalay Florentino, assistant producer. He loved that Mandalay, and I loved the fact that being with him made me feel like I *was* that Mandalay, a hundred percent. It was hard to feel anything but successful when I was walking down the street on David's arm. "There's a two-hour time difference. I would have been up this morning."

He paused to do something, then came back as I was pulling into a parking space. "Yeah, I didn't think about that. This morning was kind of a rush, getting through a workout and then to the early meeting. How's your trip going so far?"

"Fine." *After a half-dozen missed calls and two voice mails, you couldn't have skipped the workout to call me?* "A little strange, so far."

He laughed, and a warm flutter tickled my stomach. "I can imagine."

"You wouldn't believe this little town. I'm out in the middle of nowhere."

"Hang on a minute." David moved the phone away from his mouth and ordered food from a drive-through. Thai, it sounded like. Thai food, somewhere back in the land of super-highways and multi-cultural cuisine.

Cradling the phone on my shoulder, I turned off the ignition and took in the sounds and sights of the fairgrounds. Nearby, a carnival was getting underway, complete with a huge antique-style Ferris wheel, roller coaster, bumper cars, vendors hocking chances to win giant stuffed dogs and black-velvet paintings that looked like the ones in my hotel room. Beyond that stretched acres and acres of livestock barns, numerous corrals, and the rodeo arena. Near the Kiddie Korral, the giant metal cowboy smiled, his hand raised in a perpetual greeting.

A Jeep cruised by on its way to a parking spot, and I watched it pass, my mouth dropping open as I peered at the driver. Carter. Again. Everywhere I went, there he was. Of course, with the growing speculation about Amber's Final Five status, the place would be lousy with reporters soon enough. Was that why Carter had been at the Caney Creek Church this morning? Was he trying to gain information about when Amber would come home, or perhaps looking for a spot from which to stake out the Anderson place, hoping to catch that million-dollar shot of her bringing Justin Shay to the house trailer?

Just the concept made me ill, but not in the way I would have imagined. It wasn't the idea of the photo that bothered me; it was the thought of Carter taking it. My mind flashed back to the two of us sitting in the beauty shop, watching *Bonanza* reruns and sharing a contraband midnight snack. I'd been drifting off to sleep when the show ended. He leaned over and touched my arm, whispering, "Hey," in a voice that was deep and resonant. "You missed the big finale. Little Joe's girl had to leave town with her family, so he's still on the market." He fanned an eyebrow, and I laughed, then stood up and turned off the TV as he cleaned up the paper plates and root beer bottles before we headed upstairs.

Something moaned long and low in the upper hall. Carter's eyes caught the dim light as he glanced toward the noise, then back at me. "Air coming down the dumbwaiter. I tracked that one down earlier. The tapping in the attic I'm not sure about yet. That may be the ghost counting coins." He winked when I rubbed the goose bumps on my arms, but then he offered to loan me a Care Bear from his room if I needed it to go to sleep.

In spite of the moaning building, I laughed, feeling better—at least until I was back in my room alone.

I'd tried to call David for company, but of course, he wasn't answering. I was grateful that Carter and the Care Bear collection were right next door.

Even now, in the bright light of day, I didn't want to, almost couldn't, imagine that Carter was here in Daily to prey off the mishaps of a nineteen-year-old girl whose only crime was to believe that someone from a run-down trailer house in Podunk, Texas, could become the next *American Megastar*.

If a person who seemed as genuine as Carter could do something like that, what did it say about the world? What did it say about my sense of judgment? Maybe I was as easily taken in as Ursula accused me of being. I always felt bad when contestants left the show with their dreams in tatters. Ursula said that was just part of the entertainment, and the contestants knew it. Those tearful good-byes were only the work of skilled performers hoping to leave *American Megastar* with enough public interest to generate gigs or a recording contract with a little music company somewhere. According to Ursula, every contestant was aware that a little public heartache and humiliation was good for ratings—both theirs and ours.

She was working hard to cure me of my gullibility.

"Hey, babe, you there?" David's voice shook me from my reverie. I'd forgotten he was still on the other end of the phone.

"Sorry, I got distracted for a minute." Outside, Carter was crossing the parking lot, getting in line to buy a ticket and go in the gate. I wanted to follow him and see where he was headed.

"I guess." David's words were garbled. He was eating something. I realized I was hungry. I'd missed lunch while scouting locations and looking for Amber's house.

"So," David went on, "I thought you were in Austin. It's not LA, but it's not exactly in the middle of nowhere."

"I'm in Amber Anderson's hometown—someplace called Daily, Texas. Remember? I told you about that." Actually, we'd had an entire conversation as I was packing to leave LA. Had he forgotten completely?

"I remember," he said, but his tone said that this was all new information. "So, what time are you getting into LAX tonight?"

My spirits sank with the renewed realization that I wouldn't be winging my way back to LA for a few days. "I'm here in Daily through the weekend. Thanks to Ursula. She has crowned me advance man and Amber's handler until we have this hometown segment bagged. Didn't you get my voice mail messages last night?"

"I haven't listened to the voice mails yet."

Thanks a lot. "Just delete it all. I was emotional."

He bit into something crunchy. "So you'll be gone through the weekend?"

"It looks that way."

He muttered a regretful, "Huh," and I felt fluttery again. He missed me. "There's a party Saturday night up the coast."

"What?" I felt the sting of salt in my traveling wounds. While I was stuck here, David was having fun. "A party where?"

"The client I was with last night—she's having some kind of an art charity thing. Lots of money there, if you know what I mean. Good place to network."

I barely heard the part about *art* and *charity*. I was still stuck on *she* and *the client I was with last night*. *She?* Something animalistic and fiercely territorial growled inside me. *She?* "I can't get back by tomorrow night. Amber's coming to Austin Saturday morning, and we film her big reveal at the rodeo Saturday afternoon, then her hometown concert Saturday evening. There's no way I can make it." *Please, please, please say you won't go to the party without me.*

"That's all right. I can do it solo. You probably wouldn't enjoy it much, anyway. I'll be working the crowd."

An uneasiness started in my throat and prickled all the way to my stomach. *What else will you be working besides the crowd?* The question surprised me. It sounded like something Ursula would come up with. Ursula thought the worst of everybody.

I trusted David. Didn't I?

Outside, Carter had made it through the entry line and was waiting for the gatekeeper to tear his ticket.

"I'd better go." Both David and I said it at the same time.

He chuckled. "Have a good time in Austin, babe."

I'm not in Austin. "Yeah, thanks." We exchanged the customary round of *I love you*, and *miss you, miss you, too*, then hung up. I didn't tell him to have a good time at the party. Tucking the cell phone in my purse, I rolled up the window and got out of the car.

By the time I'd purchased a ticket and made it to the gate, Carter was disappearing into the crowd somewhere near the Kiddie Korral. The old man taking tickets was painfully slow. I jittered impatiently as he chatted with the fairgoers in line ahead of me. Hands trembling, he carefully took each ticket and ripped it in half, then held both sides close to his Coke-bottle glasses, determining which part should be returned to the customer while inquiring as to people's business at the fair and telling stories about his years as a ticket taker.

"Been here seventy-one years." His voice echoed against the gatekeeper's shack, gravelly and rough, unnaturally loud, in a way that reminded me of my grandpa Florentino when his hearing aid batteries went dead. "Started when I was eighteen years old. A'course, I was a strappin' fella then. I helped set up them midway rides. Can't do that no more. Y'all be sure to take a ride on that Ferris wheel, y'hear?"

He paused to point a crooked finger at the teenage couple he was holding hostage in the gateway. "Met my girl on that Ferris wheel. Whoo-wee! She was a dandy, but she had a feller on 'er arm. I made me a plan with the ol' boy that was runnin' the ride, and when that girl stepped on the platform, I slipped right in beside her while her beau was givin' over the tickets, and I says, 'Pardon me, ma'am, I gotta test this here ride for safety. Mind if I go up with ya?' That seat scooped us in, and we stalled out at the top, and the rest is history." He tapped the young man on the shoulder. "You want to sweep a girl off her feet, son, you gotta be bold."

The girl hip-butted her boyfriend, giving him a pointed look, and he sheepishly tucked the ticket stubs into his pocket as they moved on.

The next customers stepped up, and the old man began telling the kids a story about the first time he ever tasted cotton candy.

A tic started in my left eye, and I looked up and down the fence, searching for another entrance. This was like a traffic jam on an LA freeway, only without benefit of radio, BlackBerry, cell phone, or other means of self-distraction and multitasking. If I had to stand here a minute longer I was going to . . . to . . .

I had what Oprah commonly refers to as a *light bulb moment*. If I had to stand here a moment longer, nothing was going to happen. I wouldn't explode, and Ursula wouldn't storm into my office telling me how inept I was and threatening to fire me, and David wouldn't holler that I was too slow releasing the jib and now the boat wouldn't come smoothly around, and my mother wouldn't go into a tirade about how I was always late for family gatherings.

I was here in Daily, Texas, on my own. A solo entity. Master of my own destiny, at least until tomorrow, when the crew arrived with Amber.

Today, I had no one to answer to but Manda Florentino, and actually, Manda was enjoying the bit of local color at the gate. She was thinking that, back when she was in news production, the ticket taker would have made an interesting human interest piece. No telling how much history, how many life experiences resided in that stooped-over body.

Never forget that everyone has a story, Grandpa Florentino said to me when I went into the news business. For as long as I could remember, Grandpa Florentino had told stories of his trip to visit family in the little Italian village where he met my grandmother when she was only twelve years old. He was eighteen and had just joined the army. He traveled the world and then came back to marry the girl with the beautiful golden-brown eyes. In all his years away, he'd never forgotten her. She remained the center of his universe ever after.

I had always wanted that kind of love, but over the years I'd come to wonder if it was possible in the jaded world of talk-show relationship therapy, high divorce rates, and temporary commitments.

The ticket taker smiled as I passed through the gate and handed him my coupon. "Goin' to the festival?"

"Yes, I am."

"Nice day for it."

"Yes, quite."

He stopped halfway through tearing my ticket. "You're not from around here, are ya?"

"No, I'm not."

"You one of them TV people?"

The muscles in my spine stiffened instantly. "Pardon me?"

He finished tearing the ticket, then held both pieces close to his face to examine them. "Them TV people. You ain't heard? Amber Anderson's got on Final Five of *American Megastar*, and they's gonna be lots of TV people. Supposed to be the biggest thing to happen since Elvis come to Daily."

"Elvis has been here?" Now, that might be an interesting bit for the Amber story. Maybe this was one of those middle-of-nowhere towns in which Elvis performed before he made it big. Perhaps that had something to do with the decorations in my room.

"Why, shore 'nuf." Tucking half of the ticket into the collection box, the attendant slapped a hand over the lid, then leaned on it. "Let's see . . . that's been ten, maybe twelve years ago."

I took a step toward the gate, reaching for my ticket stub. Considering that Elvis had been dead for much longer than that, this probably wasn't a lead worth pursuing. "Okay . . . well . . . I guess I should move on out of the way." Pinching the ticket between my fingers, I tugged and it slipped free. "Okay, well, thanks."

He lifted a hand and waved. "Have a great day. Don't miss the pony pull and the Ferris wheel."

"I won't." I turned around and hurried toward the giant metal cowboy, in search of Carter.

I found him outside the Kiddie Korral. He'd squatted down by the fence and was helping a little boy work up the courage to feed the goats.

"Like this," Carter said, and slipped his hand through the fence, holding his palm flat, with a few oats inside. "Put the food in the middle, and she won't nibble your fingers." A large white goat promptly demonstrated by politely eating out of Carter's hand.

The little boy giggled and bounced up and down. Beside him, his mother smiled adoringly—either at her son or Carter or both. She poured some animal food onto the boy's hand, and Carter's pupil quickly gained a new furry friend. The boy's mother tucked her hands into her back pockets, leaned close to Carter and said something, then graced him with a flirty smile. Grinning, he shook his head at whatever invitation she'd offered, then moved along.

I followed at a distance as Carter meandered down the midway, stopping long enough to buy himself a corndog, chat with a balloon vendor, enjoy a glass of fresh-squeezed lemonade, and watch a trio of kids take a camel ride. After the midway, he moved on to the rodeo arena, looking for all the world like a man enjoying a carefree day at the fair. If he'd come here with any agenda, he certainly hid it well.

As he stood at the fence, casually observing a horse-showing contest, I began, once again, to question my earlier suppositions. He hardly seemed to be scoping out locations, poking around for information about Amber, or waiting for her to arrive. He wasn't even answering his cell phone, which rang several times. He only checked the numbers with a seeming lack of concern, then tucked the phone back into his pocket. He appeared to have no agenda at all, which meant there was no reason for me to be following him. I did, after all, have work to do.

Even though I knew that was true, I lingered in the shadow of the bleachers, watching him brace a foot casually on the fence as one horse-showing contest finished and another one, involving old men in overalls and harnessed teams of ponies, began.

I found myself moving out of the shadows, wishing Carter would turn around and see me there.

Chapter 12

Imagene Doll

It's a good thing Donetta's nephew, Kempner Rollins, is the new coach at Daily High. Without Coach Kemp and his baseball team, the work on the hotel rooms wouldn't have come along like it did. Those boys came in there and got busy cleaning things out, lickety-split. Up and down the stairs they went, carrying Christmas decorations and boxes of leftover yard sale treasures. Donetta was in such a hurry to have the rooms cleared, she told them to throw that stuff away, wonder of wonders, because Donetta's a packrat to beat all. She's the only person I know who'd hoard the leftover junk from a three-day church rummage sale.

She wouldn't let the boys throw out the prom dresses and tiaras that were stacked in room 4-B, even though I wanted her to. Those things were the flotsam from the last hare-brained Donetta Bradford plan, which was hatched when Donetta heard that the ladies in Betty Prine's Literary Society planned to ride a float in the Founder's Day parade, dressed in red hats and purple feather boas, like one of them classy Red Hat Societies. Next thing I knew, Donetta'd decided the gals from our Friday night bunko and book exchange group ought to have a float in the parade, too. She borrowed a flatbed trailer, found us a driver, bummed some hay from the feedstore, and named us the Daily Tiara Bunko and Book Society. She cleaned out every Goodwill store within eighty miles, buying up old prom dresses and used tiaras so that we could ride in style, which we did. We paraded down Main Street like royalty, singing, "Zippity doo dah," all the way. We won the trophy for most entertaining float and put Betty Prine's snooty Literary Society to shame.

I thought maybe Donetta would give those dresses to the cheerleading girls when they showed up to help with the hotel rooms, but she put the cheerleaders to work cleaning trim, mopping floors, and getting the furniture dusted. Things progressed along fast, except for a short distraction with hauling out the prom dresses. When Coach Kemp saw his players coming down the stairs in gowns and tiaras, he put a stop to it real quick. He crossed his arms over that big chest of his and told those boys if they liked the fancy dresses so much, they could wear 'em to the baseball game against McGregor next week. The boys shucked their dresses and tiaras and got back to work.

It wasn't long before Verl had the crew rolling paint on walls. Verl took charge of those kids like he'd done it all his life, and they actually listened to what he had to say. That was surprising, considering that I'd seen more than one of them make fun of Verl when he was staggering drunk around town. Verl's own grandsons, Andy, Amos, and Avery, didn't even want him to come to sports events over at the school because his behavior embarrassed them so, and they had enough problems fitting in already. It can't be easy being the kid wearing hand-me-down clothes that smell like a house with a hundred cats locked inside. Having your grandpa pie-eyed and falling down the bleachers at the ball games doesn't help, either.

But today, Amos and Avery looked happy, and Andy looked about two inches taller than usual. Even though he was just a sophomore and kind of wiry and small for his age, he outworked the older boys, hauling stuff out to storage and then trotting up the stairs two at a time, looking for more jobs to do. His grand-daddy put him to painting, and he lined those edges along the trim boards just as careful and slick as a whistle. Pretty soon, Verl was using Andy as an example to show the other boys how to edge the walls. They took the lessons politely and called him *sir* and *Mr. Anderson*. Andy looked as happy as I'd ever seen him.

When I went downstairs to head back to the café for the sup-per rush, Donetta had just finished a set and style on a lady who lived up toward Waco.

"You done a good thing, DeDe," I said, and gave her a little hug. "How you got Verl so fired up is a mystery, but it's sure nice to see." I slipped back through the wall with a lightness in my step and a happy feeling in my heart.

All through the supper hour, I made a point to say nice things when the crowd made remarks about Donetta hiring Verl. Thanks to Betty Prine's gossiping, even the countertoppers were talking about it.

"Hope he don-don-don't take a snort or two and fall-fall-fall down the stairs, down the stairs," Doyle joked, and I gave him a dirty look. If there was anybody who should've had sympathy for Verl, it was Doyle. Doyle sure enough knew what it was like to be made fun of by other folks.

I turned on Doyle, feeling a little self-righteous, even though not a few hours ago, I'd been saying the same things myself. "Well, he's doin' a fine job, Doyle Banes, and we might all do well to remember the Golden Rule here." I looked hard at Betty Prine, over in the corner with that snoot-nosed husband of hers, Harold. "And besides . . ."

Doyle slid off his stool and started toward the front door. "I'll be uddd-dogged," he muttered, looking out the window. "Broth-brother Ervin, ulll-look at that, will-will ya?"

Both Ervin and Harlan Hanson swiveled around just in time to see a big RV truck tool down Main Street. It pulled around the corner beside the café, and we could hear it rumbling in the alley.

"Woo-wee!" Harlan whistled. "Shore 'nuf is a rig, ain't it? That's one of the bunch from Miss Lulu's place, I think."

Betty Prine stuck her nose close to the glass and tried to see around the corner. "Who's Miss Lulu got at her place?"

Brother Ervin ignored her and swiveled back around to the counter. "I imagine that's the people who was out by Caney Creek Church earlier. I hear they asked O.C. all kind of questions about the Andersons."

Betty cocked her head back, her lips puckering up. "What would a nice motor bus be doing out at Caney Creek, of all places?"

"Ulll-lookin' for in-information about Am-Am-Amber and her m-m-m-music, uhhh, music," Doyle chimed in, and I stuck a hamburger basket in front of him to shut him up. The last thing we needed was Betty Prine sticking her pointy nose into this Hollywood business.

Betty gave Doyle a look that could have fried an egg. "Those Anderson children never learned anything at Caney Creek Church but heathenism—all that clapping and stomping around those people do. It's blasphemy. Every time those Anderson kids came to vacation Bible school, I had to teach them how the Lord's music is *meant* to be lifted up. I'm happy to see she has remembered at least some of what I taught her."

"You been keepin' up with the *American Megastar* show, Betty?" No doubt Harlan said that just to annoy Betty. He knew there was no way Betty Prine would admit to watching a show filled with beer-drinking country songs and, even worse, rock-and-roll music.

"Why, no, of course not!" Betty's face got red, and she stood up, tossing her napkin on the table. Like a puppet on a string, Harold hopped to his feet and went to pay the bill. "What with being president of the Literary Society, I have *far* too much preparation to do, and besides, Harold and I confine our viewing to programs of moral value. We'd never allow one of *our* daughters to participate in such a show as that."

"It's a uggg-good thing th-th-they ain't been asked-asked then, ain't it?" Doyle said, then turned around and gave Harlan a big grin. Betty's two spoiled-rotten daughters were both so mean-spirited nobody'd ever want them on a TV show.

"Well, I think it's just wonderful what Amber's doing," I said. "Some folks might hear about all Amber's been through and hear her sing and decide to change their lives."

Betty spit through the gap in her teeth and rolled her eyes. "As if hearing a story is going to change someone's life, Imagene Doll."

"Hard to say," I answered as she gathered up Harold and headed for the door.

"The para-parables in the uuub-Bible are stories," Doyle pointed out.

Betty didn't answer. She just went out the door with her nose in the air and Harold trailing behind her.

"Good point," Brother Ervin agreed.

Harlan turned an ear toward the rumble of the motor home outside. "Wonder what they're doin' out there, parked in the alley."

Bob came back out of the storage room, where he'd gone when Betty mounted her high horse and charged into the conversation. "Can't tell," he said. "I just looked out the rear door, and they were unloading something from underneath their bus. I asked if they needed help, but I guess they didn't hear, or . . ."

The front door burst open before Bob could finish, and in came three people—a lady with short-cut blond hair and two fellas following behind her. Before we knew what was happening, they'd marched through the café all tangled in microphones and cameras, come right behind the counter, and caught Bob at the fry grill.

"Sir," said the lady with the spiky white-blond hair, "do you have any information about the rumors that Amber Anderson has been selected for the Final Five on *American Megastar*? Any word on plans to hold her hometown reveal during this weekend's festival?"

Bob stood there like a deer in the headlights, his spatula glinting in the evening sun.

The lady reporter shook the microphone in his face, then brought it back to herself and fired out another question. "Any comment on the rumors that, after a whirlwind romance, Amber is secretly engaged to Justin Shay and they will be arriving here together tomorrow?"

Bob just stood there with his eyes unblinking and his mouth halfway open.

The lady reporter wagged her microphone again. "What about the fact that Amber was recently seen with Shay at a Shokahna rally, and the claim by members of the Los Angeles–based religious sect that Amber intends to convert to Shokahna so the couple can be married in a Shokahna temple?"

Bob didn't have an answer for that, either. Nothing. Not a word. His lips moved and he made a little gurgle in his throat, but he was choked down like a hot tractor in a July wheat field.

I headed over to the counter. I was starting to feel bad for Bob. I could picture this on *Hollywood Undercover*, which was what the cameraman's jacket said. If I didn't do something, the world's first introduction to Daily, Texas, home of Amber Anderson, would be Bob Turner, fish-eyed with his mouth open and a little stream of spit dripping from the corner. People would think Amber came from a village of simpletons, and all her chances to make a good impression for America would be spoiled.

"Can I help you folks?" I said, and the reporter swung around so quick she almost boxed me in the nose.

"Ma'am, can we get a comment on the reports that Amber Anderson will be arriving here this weekend to film her Final Five show for *American Megastar*?"

"Well . . ." Squinting against the bright light on the camera, I saw my reflection in the lens. My hair was a little off-kilter, and my blouse—double knit with red rosebuds and blue daisies in little baskets—was bunched up above my boobs so that I looked like I had two pair. I was appalled, of course, so I grabbed the shirtwaist and pulled, then patted my hair.

The reporter waved the microphone in my face. I reckon she thought I was froze up, like Bob.

I gave what I hoped was a thoughtful yet friendly look. "I can't say that anyone in Daily has been contacted with official news that Amber has made the Final Five, but being as she's a hometown favorite, there has been some speculation. An *un*confirmed report, I believe you'd call it."

The lady reporter drew back, surprised, I guess, that folks in Daily knew proper TV terminology. "And what about her alleged secret engagement to Justin Shay and reports that her family members are angry about the marriage and have threatened to disown her should she convert to Shokahna in order to marry Shay? Do you think such a conversion would undermine her credibility as a gospel singer?"

"Well . . ." That bit about Amber taking up some flaky Hollywood religion got my back up. "I'd have to say that hearing such a thing certainly would be upsetting to her family and the entire town."

The lady reporter perked up like a barn cat hearing a rustling in the hay. Having uncovered the tail of a scandal, she was ready to dig down and get after the meat. "Can you elab—"

"On the other hand," I went on, and she swung the microphone back to me, wheeling her chin toward the cameraman to tell him, *Keep rolling—here's a lady with a big mouth.*

The camera came a little closer. "Of course, considering that we all know Amber, and have known her all her life, we Daily folks wouldn't be likely to believe such a thing. Amber Anderson is a fine young lady. There may be some things about city life she doesn't understand, and a young girl can have her head turned, but I'd stake dimes to dollars that Amber Anderson knows what she believes and no Hollywood playboy's gonna change that. When Amber sings them gospel songs, they come straight from her heart. She's got a God-given talent and a pure motivation, and I'm sure that bothers some folks whose motives maybe ain't so pure."

The lady reporter drew back so that she was a head taller than me. Her chin curled into her neck, and we had a moment of what's called *dead air.*

Lucky for her, I was on a roll. "It's a sad world when folks want to tear down a young girl who ain't done anything to anybody and is just trying to make the best of herself. Isn't that a sad thing? I don't reckon most of us would like to have our lives on the front page. I wouldn't, would you?"

The lady reporter choked on whatever she was about to say. The fire went out of her eyes, and she stood there looking almost as froze up as poor Bob, the microphone hanging slack in her hand. The cameraman chuckled, and the photographic equipment shook up and down on his shoulder.

"An . . . any other comments," the reporter muttered.

"No, ma'am, not a thing," I said. "Y'all have a real nice day, and thanks so much for stopping in at the Daily Café. Can I get you some coffee?"

Signaling to the cameraman to *cut*, the reporter heaved a sigh, then collapsed onto a barstool with her forehead in her hand, like she had a headache. "Make mine a double. To go."

"Coming right up." I started for the coffee pot, thumping Bob's shoulder as I went by. Stumbling forward, he belly-bounced off the counter, let out an *ooof,* then passed gas so loud it made the lady reporter jerk upright and stare in pure amazement.

Since Bob had her attention and he'd finally come out of vapor lock, he decided to introduce himself. He probably couldn't have picked a worse time. "Howdy, ma'am. I'm Bob Turner, owner of the Daily Café, president of the Chamber of Commerce, and former employer of Amber Anderson. Anything you want to know about Daily, I'm your man."

The reporter shut her eyes, muttering something about finally getting the chance to do a story on location, and this is where she ends up. I guess Daily wasn't exactly what she had in mind for her first big news report.

While she was waiting for her coffee, the countertoppers had decided to introduce themselves and see if they could get a little airtime. Doyle stuttered through a description of the lime quarry, told her she ought not to miss seeing those giant rock crushers at work, and offered to take her on a tour if she was looking to see Daily sights.

About the time I delivered her coffee, Harlan was starting into a fine story about how the town got its name. ". . . folks usually do wonder about it. Legend has it that the first thing built on this spot was an old trading post, and the fella that ran it put out a big sign that said *Daily Provisions*. The name stuck over time, everyone who moved here eventually bein' known as Daily folks, until finally they named the town that. While you're here, you won't want to miss seeing Boggy Bend Park. There's paintings down there done by real live Tonkawa Indians—'course they're not live anymore, but they was once. Great swimmin' hole. Spring-fed year-round. Never dries up. Did'ja bring yer swimsuit?"

Slapping a five-dollar bill on the counter, the TV lady grabbed her coffee, then left as fast as her red high heels would go. The cameraman trailed behind her, looking like he thought it was all a little funny. The reporter gave him a dirty look, then slapped open the door, stumbled over the stoop, and marched onto the sidewalk. Ramming her fist into her hip, she glared up and down Main Street, looking for her next victim.

The funny thing was, Amber Anderson's grandpa was working in the building right next to her and she never even knew it. Brother Ervin grabbed the phone and called around Daily, just to warn folks not to tell her anything.

At the counter, the regulars had a fine time reliving their brush with fame.

"That was a good one about the Indians, Harlan," Ervin congratulated.

Harlan gave a little bow. "Thank you, brother. I've got to say that the Academy A-ward goes to Doyle and his tour of the rock crushers at the lime plant."

Doyle nodded with the keen eye and straight face of a man who's gone a long way by being smarter than he looks. "W-well, uuuth-ank you, Erve. If that don't-don't-don't get her to ulll-leave town, n-nothin' will."

But out there on the sidewalk, that lady reporter wasn't going anywhere. As she headed down the street, she had the wily look of a prowling cat that was gonna dig and dig and dig until she snatched that mouse right out of the haystack.

At the counter, Bob went back to scraping the fry grill. He was in a sour mood about *Hollywood Undercover,* and he didn't feel like talking to anybody. His big chance to emerge onto the national spotlight, and he froze up. Things couldn't get much worse than that.

After the excitement died down and the supper crowd dwindled, Maria and Estacio took over the café for the evening. As usual, I dragged myself out the door, thinking that working three meals was too much for a woman my age. All the same, I wasn't looking forward to going home. Even before I'd made it to my car, I was already thinking about my house sitting there on the hill, dark and lonesome, with the yard kind of ragged and the flower beds gone to seed. Every evening when I turned in the driveway, I wondered for just a minute why the place was so quiet, then it dawned on me that, these days, there wasn't anybody to turn on the lights but me.

I wasn't ready to face that moment tonight, and there was still activity over at the beauty shop and hotel, so I went in and followed the racket upstairs. The baseball players and the cheerleaders were gone, but Verl was there with Andy, Amos, and Avery. The boys were sweeping the floors. Frank had come up to help after closing the auto shop downstairs. Everyone, including Donetta, looked like they were on their last legs—especially the boys.

Frank passed me in the stairway. "Those are some hardworkin' boys," he said. "You know, I was thinkin' I might ask them boys if they'd like to do some jobs for me at the shop from time to time. Verl, too, if he's of a mind. My place could use some paint and caulking."

I could've hugged Frank right then for being such a kind soul. That old greasy auto shop didn't need paint work any more than the man in the moon. "I imagine that'd be good." Down the hallway, little Amos leaned his chin on the broom handle and closed his eyes. All towheaded, with his freckled cheeks, he reminded me of my boys at ten years old. "Verl ought to take the boys on home. They're wore out."

Frank nodded in agreement. "Verl didn't want to quit until the job was done." He leaned a little closer to me. "I imagine after all day workin', he means to take the money by The Junction and tie one on tonight. No tellin' what shape he'll wake up in tomorrow."

"Mercy," I muttered, looking at the kids and thinking about what the rest of their day would be like. They would put themselves to bed tonight, wake up in the morning and scrounge around for some food and clean clothes to wear. I'd never really given it much thought before—how things must be for those Anderson kids, day to day.

Frank sighed, his face somber. "Verl ain't never had ten dollars in his pocket that didn't go at least half into whiskey. One day of work ain't gonna change a bad habit a man's carried all his life." Being an old rodeo man himself, Frank had been around enough to know a bit about folks.

"I reckon not," I agreed. "I wonder if Verl would let me take the boys on home with me for the night, since he's busy working and all." The idea formed in my mind, even as I was speaking it. "I could cook them a nice supper and wash up their clothes. Tomorrow's Saturday. They could sleep in late, and I could make a good breakfast."

Frank gave me a surprised look, but he didn't try to talk me out of it. Having been my Jack's best friend, all Frank ever wanted was for me to be happy. "Don't know, but I guess you could ask."

"I believe I will." I headed off down the hall, determined that tonight that big old house was gonna be lit up from top to bottom and filled with the one thing it needed most—the merry ruckus of little boys just being boys.

Chapter 13

Mandalay Florentino

Even after I'd concluded that Carter didn't seem to have any hidden agenda, I was still latently watching for him as I toured the fairgrounds late that afternoon, still scouting locales, looking for potential snippets of filler, soaking up the atmosphere, and trying to devise a means of slipping Amber and a camera crew into an extremely crowded location without inciting a riot. Walking her in through the front gate was certainly not a possibility. Pictures of Amber were everywhere—in the exhibit building, on a banner hanging above the fair office, gracing T-shirts on the midway. Right now, Amber Anderson was the most recognized face in town, and the air was alive with anticipation of a hometown girl becoming the next American Megastar.

It occurred to me, as I was taking in the plethora of *Vote for Amber* shirts on the midway, that Amber had an amazingly strong grassroots base pulling for her, and even though *American Megastar* had never seen a gospel singer make the top two, Amber might have a very real chance of being in the Final Showdown.

I found myself unwillingly being drawn into the current of Amber Anderson euphoria, and I was filled with a renewed excitement for her hometown show. Anyone with this many people believing in her was worthy of a little effort. Amber had been an underdog all her life, and maybe, just maybe, she could pull this off. A carefully crafted hometown show would go a long way toward giving her a fighting chance. If the rest of America could see Amber Anderson the way these people did, viewer votes would roll in by the thousands.

I, Mandalay Florentino, was going to awaken the slumbering crusader inside me and do the very best job I could to make that happen.

As the light started to fade and the midway lights came on, I stumbled upon an idea behind the cow barns. The rear area of the fairgrounds was crowded with livestock trailers of various types, some with horses tied to them, waiting to participate in the horse-showing competitions. The livestock parking area was inside the fairgrounds fence, and in fact, the trailers were entering the enclosure through a rear gate that was supervised by only one attendant, who checked the drivers' paperwork and then glanced briefly into the trailers to inspect the livestock.

The Amber entry plan jelled in my head as I watched one of the livestock haulers enter the gate, mosey through the rows of parked vehicles, and continue toward the rodeo arena.

What I needed was a trailer and a horse.

One of those large silver trailers might do nicely. . . .

Just to be sure, I climbed onto the fender of an empty trailer and peeked in the window. Perfect. We could put the horse in the livestock compartment, so as to pass inspection at the gate, and hide Amber and the crew in the front compartment, which was designed to hold saddles, rider clothing, and various other paraphernalia.

Bingo. Surprise entrance into the fairgrounds. Even our contact at the rodeo contracting company, who knew that a surprise performer would be arriving to sing at tomorrow afternoon's opening performance, wouldn't spot this one coming.

"Mandee-lay, you are so smardt," I muttered in Ursula-speak. I pictured her giving me my first-ever Uberstach compliment.

"Well, hey there, Amanda-lee."

That didn't sound like Ursula at all.

"What're you doin' out here?"

I turned to find Imagene and three half-grown boys watching me stick my head into some stranger's livestock trailer.

"You enjoyin' the fair?" Imagene glanced around, wondering, no doubt, why I was skulking around the back lot in the dusky evening shadows. "You on yer way to the pony pull?"

"Oh . . . uhhh . . . yes, I am." I stepped down from the trailer, and the oldest of the boys gave me a suspicious look. "Enjoying the fair, that is. I guess I'm lost, though. I . . . thought there might be some—" *come on, think of something*—"ponies out here."

The littlest boy lowered an eyebrow. He looked to be about the age of my youngest nephew, maybe ten or eleven years old. There was something vaguely familiar about him. "The arena's that way," he offered, pointing toward the high bleachers and enormous stadium lights—the ones even a blind woman couldn't miss. "Pony pull's over there."

I smiled in what I hoped was a pleasant fashion. "Well, that does make sense, doesn't it? I guess I should head that way. I wouldn't want to miss the pony pull." *What is a pony pull, anyway? Pony pull. Pony. Pull. Hmmm . . .*

"Yes, ma'am." The boy smiled, his brown eyes nearly hidden in a mop of tangled, overgrown hair. Even in the summertime when there was no school, none of my sisters would let their sons' hair get that long.

Imagene laid a hand on the boy's head, and he turned to look up at her. "That's real nice manners, Avery. Thank you." She smoothed the bangs out of his eyes and held his face between her hands. "You are a pure pleasure to take to the fair. I'm sure glad we decided to stop off here and get us a corny dog." Hugging Avery against her side, she turned back to me. "Boys, this is Amanda-Lee Forent-no. Did I get that right? She's from out of town. Amanda-Lee, these are Amber Anderson's brothers, Andy, Amos, and Avery." Pausing, she gave me a meaningful look. "I reckon you'd be interested in meeting them . . . all things considered."

Overhead, the streetlight flickered on, and it became very clear that Imagene Doll knew exactly why I was in Daily.

I attempted to hide my dismay by shaking hands with Andy, Amos, and Avery, who were polite but clearly confused about the reason for the formal introductions. Now that I knew who they were, I could see Amber in each of them.

Suddenly, the story of Amber's difficult childhood had a face— three of them. Andy, Amos, and Avery. I imagined Amber, just a little girl herself when her parents died, taking care of these three, fixing their meals, walking them to town to sell blackberries, making sure they did their homework at night. Something acute and moving struck me in the heart. This story wasn't just about Amber, it was about a family—four siblings, orphaned and struggling to stay together against all odds.

I swallowed an inconvenient lump of emotion. "It's very nice to meet you, Andy, Amos, and Avery. I hope we'll be seeing each other again soon."

"Yes, ma'am," Avery said pleasantly. Clearly Avery, the youngest, was the talkative one. Amos only smiled, and Andy, the oldest, nodded, looking slightly reserved and mildly suspicious of my interest.

Imagene tousled Avery's hair. "The boys thought, since we're here, we ought to go through the midway." Glancing over her shoulder, she laughed and laid a hand on her chest. "It sure is nice to be at the fair. I haven't come here since Jack passed away. You know, I feel so good tonight, I might even get on the old roller coaster. Jack always wanted me to try that thing and I never would do it. Seems like a person ought to try the roller coaster at least once before they die." A kindred look passed between us—the meaningful exchange of two people who would probably live and die having carefully avoided life's roller coasters.

"Why not?" I agreed, with false bravado. It's easy to tell other people to enjoy the ride. "You only live once."

"True enough." Imagene smiled, gazing toward the midway. "Jack would be proud of me if I did it. He never wanted me to miss out on anything fun."

"He sounds like a wonderful man." Would David care if I rode the roller coaster? After we were married, would he spend our years together making sure I didn't miss anything fun?

Imagene hugged Avery close. "He truly was."

Avery wrapped his arms awkwardly around Imagene's waist, interlocking his fingers on the other side. Andy and Amos focused on the carnival rides, seeming embarrassed.

"You guys have a good time," I said, feeling a vague emptiness. Maybe those heroic individuals like my grandfather, like Imagene's husband, didn't exist anymore. Maybe they'd died out along with larger-than-life westerns, Rodgers and Hammerstein musicals, and sappy romantic movies. In the era of self-help, self-esteem, and self-fulfillment, there was one common thread. Self. "I'll be anxious to hear about that roller coaster ride tomorrow."

Imagene wagged a finger at me, pursing her lips. "You ride it yourself, and we'll compare notes."

I laughed. "I will if you will."

"Deal." To seal the bargain, she grabbed my hand and shook it. "Be sure and ride the big Ferris wheel, too. We're real proud of our Ferris wheel and our roller coaster. The Ferris wheel's been in operation since 1936—put there for the Cotton Festival, back when there was money to be made in farmin'. That and the coaster are the only rides that stay as part of the park. The rest move on with the carnival." She motioned toward the slowly revolving wheel, its lighted spokes and brightly painted red seats circling in an unhurried rhythm. "The wheel sits on high ground, so it's quite a view. From up there, you can see the whole fairgrounds—heck, half the county, really."

"Thanks for the tip. I'll be sure to check it out." In my head, my mother's voice was warning that only an idiot would trust life and limb to a seventy-year-old midway ride. On the other hand, such a spot would be the perfect vantage point for taking in the complete layout of the fairgrounds. . . .

Imagene gathered the boys as I stood watching the wheel turn and listening to the voices in my head.

"Well, we'd best be off. Tell Miss Florent-no good-bye, boys."

I turned back to Amber's brothers.

"Good-bye," Avery chirped, tossing his head to get the overgrown hair out of his eyes.

"Bye." Amos pushed his hands into his pockets and focused on his shoes. Shifting uncomfortably, he added, "Have fun at the fair."

"I will, Amos. Thanks."

"Later." Turning to follow them, Andy pulled his bottom lip between his teeth. With his blond hair and blue eyes, he looked the most like Amber, perhaps because he was the closest to her age—fourteen, maybe fifteen. He had an intelligent, contemplative way about him. Walking backward a few steps, he lifted his chin and gave a half smile. "Say hey to my sister."

"Andrew, hush," Imagene whispered, snaking out an arm and grabbing his T-shirt. "That's supposed to be a secret."

I couldn't hear the rest of the conversation. I probably didn't want to.

I gaped after him as he followed his brothers away. The edginess that had been festering since the Amber banner incident yesterday came back with a vengeance. My presence here and Amber's entrée into the Final Five were the worst-kept secrets in history. Sooner or later, Ursula would find out about the information leak and my trip to Wonderland would end in disaster. *Off with her head.* Swoosh. I'd be just another casualty of *American Megastar*, season three.

Ursula would never buy the idea that this was not my fault— that I'd done nothing to cause the security breach.

Which brought up the question of who had. How could top secret results, known only to Ursula, me, and a few select individuals, have so quickly reached Daily? Even the employees of the Austin affiliate, who'd been gracious enough to provide me with the helicopter flyover, thought I was a producer from *48 Hours*, doing a piece on El Niño and erratic weather patterns in the southwest. The cover story seemed to have worked perfectly. What went wrong?

The Doom-o-meter whispered a low electric hum in my head, slowly growing louder, higher in frequency, harder to ignore. I took a deep breath, tried to think logically. *Calm down, calm down. Attack the problem, don't retreat. You can still pull this off. Make Amber's hometown show a success and Ursula won't have anything to complain about. The livestock trailer idea will work. It'll work brilliantly.*

Finally, I walked to the Ferris wheel and purchased a ticket, still mulling over the problem of finding a truck, a trailer, and some form of livestock. Before tomorrow afternoon. I was going to need help. Somebody local. Someone who knew where short-term rental livestock could be procured. Someone who could be trusted not to reveal the plan. . . .

Who?

The attendant took my ticket and I entered the Ferris wheel enclosure, then followed the line onto the platform as the ride unloaded, one seat at a time. I watched as Andy and Amos stepped off, followed by Avery and Imagene. Her puffy gray hair had been rearranged by the ride, and she was laughing while trying to smooth it back into place.

Maybe her?

Could she be trusted?

Would she be willing to help?

Clutching the guardrail, she waved at me as she started down the steps. "We're headed to the roller coaster! I'm going to do it."

"You go, girl!" I hollered, then gave her the thumbs-up. The entry line moved forward and I focused on boarding the Ferris wheel. A little twitter started in my stomach as I tipped my head and gazed upward into the maze of lights and girders. It looked huge from here, the highest seats seeming to touch the wispy clouds as they surrendered the final blush of sunset to a blanket of deep twilight blue.

I could hear gears grinding and bolts creaking. Overhead, the seats swayed with each movement of the wheel. A teenage couple kissed as they waited for their chair to descend. The seat jerked as the wheel moved again, and the girl clutched the bar, then laughed and snuggled into the crook of her boyfriend's arm. They looked as though they'd be content to stay there forever.

I missed David. I didn't want to be here, riding the Ferris wheel alone. I wanted to be half of a pair, curled up together, spinning slowly into the sky. With someone. Not with just anyone. With David. I wanted to be with David.

"Lady . . . lady . . ." The operator touched my arm. "Step forward, please."

Shaking off the fog, I moved into the loading area, looked over my outside shoulder, and waited for the seat. Breath caught in my throat as the basket slid across the platform, the wooden footrest making an almost inaudible swish. In another moment, I'd be on my way up.

"Pardon me, ma'am, I have to test this ride for safety. Mind if I go up with you?"

I turned around just in time to see Carter step into position beside me. The seat bumped me in the thighs, I landed awkwardly against the padded vinyl, a second operator slapped the safety bar into place, and we were spinning skyward.

I scooted gingerly into position, trying not to rock the chair as we went up. "I take it you've been talking to the ticket taker at the gate."

His eyes reflected the red light from the gyrating Mister Twister Rocket Ride next door. "Not much fun to ride the Ferris wheel alone."

Oddly enough, I'd just been thinking the same thing. "Well, considering that you saved me from the singing Elvis head last night, I guess I owe you one."

"You definitely do," he agreed.

"On the other hand, you led me into a life of crime."

He laid a splay-fingered hand over his chest, feigning innocence. "You said you were hungry. Would Little Joe Cartwright let a lady go hungry? I don't think so."

Our chair moved upward, then stopped as the last seats on the opposite side were emptied and rolled forward for reloading. I pressed a hand over my eyes, not so much afraid of heights as humiliated by the image of the night before. "I'm sorry about the *Bonanza* marathon. I don't know what was wrong with me."

"That's not exactly your normal hotel."

The gears below whined and squealed as the last baskets were loaded and the Ferris wheel started into a continuous backward motion. Carter leaned over the safety bar, causing the seat to tip forward.

I grabbed blindly for something solid. "Stop that, okay? This thing's been in operation over seventy years. It might not be that . . . strong."

His knee touched mine and the chair wiggled again as he leaned over the side. "I figured it was about that old. We had one like this where I grew up. My granddad worked over the summer helping to put it in so he could pay for Mawmaw's wedding ring."

Mawmaw, I thought. *He still calls his grandmother Mawmaw? How sweet.* "Where's that?"

"Where's what?"

"Where you're from."

"Down near Austin. One of those little spots on the map that's been absorbed by urban sprawl. When I was a kid, it was like this place, though." Our seat swept past the platform again and headed toward the apex. Carter gazed beyond the midway, toward the dim glow of ambient light surrounding the nearby town of Daily. "My folks moved into Austin a few years after my brother and I graduated from high school. They couldn't keep up with the farm anymore, and all the land around was going for development." He gave a somber, closed-lipped smile. "Kind of sad to see the old climbing trees plowed down for houses and golf courses."

"I guess that would be hard." I tried to imagine having that kind of attachment to a place. "My father's a real estate lawyer. He buys and sells properties, so we moved a lot. Always around LA, though. It was a fun place to grow up. A lot going on."

His gaze cut toward me, and he grinned. "Party girl, huh?"

"Hardly," I admitted. "My parents were gone quite a bit. The minute they'd walk out the door, my sisters and my brother would take off with their friends and threaten me with my life if I left the house. It stinks, being the caboose baby."

He laughed softly. "My parents were never gone. We used to *wish* they would go somewhere—not that it would have made much difference. There wasn't much trouble to get into around town. Our parents never needed to give us a curfew. They just figured we'd get bored and come home."

"Really?" I couldn't imagine teenagers getting bored and coming home before curfew.

"It was a good place to grow up, you know?" Even though he was looking at me, his gaze seemed far away, filled with private thoughts and old memories. "We'd take off in the morning, and as long as we were home by the time the streetlights came on in town, nobody worried about us. I feel sorry for my nieces sometimes. Kids don't have the same kind of freedom these days."

We swept past the platform and the waiting line of customers. I realized I'd momentarily lost track of the fact that we were going around and around on a Ferris wheel. "How old are they—your nieces, I mean?"

He smiled. "Eight, five, and two."

"Oh, they're cute at that age."

"They are that."

"So, is your brother older than you or younger?" Why I wanted to form the complete picture of his family, I couldn't say, but I was enjoying trying to figure him out.

"The same age, actually."

"You're a twin?" I tried to imagine Carter, times two. "Identical or the other kind?"

"My brother's adopted," he said flatly. "I am too, actually."

Heat rushed to my cheeks. "Oh, I'm sorry." *Open mouth, insert foot.* "I mean, I shouldn't have assumed . . . I didn't mean to pry." Actually I did, and my mother would have said, *This is where being nosy will get you, Mandalay Maria.* "It's none of my business. I have a bad habit of asking too many questions." I fanned a hand in the air apologetically. "It's one of those things my mother hoped to

173

cure me of before she sent me out into the world. Too late now, I guess."

Carter chuckled. "I think your mother did just fine." Grabbing my hand, he squeezed my fingers, then fastened them on the bar as the Ferris wheel reversed directions and started forward, spinning us toward what looked like the edge of the world. "Hang on," he said. "Here comes the good part."

Chapter 14

Imagene Doll

Standing in line for the roller coaster, I thought I'd have a stroke for sure. My heart raced, my breath came short, and my palms turned clammy and wet. Avery didn't seem to notice. He was hanging on to me for dear life. He'd never been on the roller coaster, either. He'd only been to the fair one time, when Amber took him, and after they paid to get in the gate, they only had enough money for ten ride coupons and a couple of caramel apples. Amber let him go on the rides while she watched, and to save on tickets, she told him not to pick rides where he'd need an adult along.

Avery was real excited to have a grownup to ride the roller coaster with him this time. Andy and Amos seemed excited, too. They didn't say it, but I had a feeling they'd never been on the roller coaster, either. The Lightning Snake was a pretty expensive ride. When I bought the coupons, Andy tried to give me the money he got paid from working at Donetta's, but I told him this was my treat. It embarrassed him a little. Andy was a good boy but kind of careful about getting too warm toward folks. I think he would have said no about letting me pay for the roller coaster, but he didn't want to cheat Amos and Avery out of the ride.

The closer we got, the bigger that thing looked.

Oh mercy, I thought, watching that train zip around the curves, turn almost sideways, then whip up a hill, rush down into the valley, go up again, and take another fall. The riders threw their hands in the air before the cars jerked sideways around another curve. *Fat as I am, I'll pull that thing right off the track and we'll all die.*

It came into my mind that there was probably a limit on how much riders could weigh, and when we got to the front of the line they'd tell me I couldn't get on. That'd be embarrassing, and one of the older boys would have to ride alone, since it was two per car, but at least they'd all get a turn on the coaster. I could sit and wait on the bench without looking like I'd chickened out.

I got a heavy feeling as I pictured myself left behind on the bench. Jack would sure be disappointed in me for sitting this one out. *"If I die, Imagene, I'm gonna die livin',"* he used to say. The day he died, he was out on horseback sunup to sundown, helping work some cattle at Frank's ranch. Jack came home tired and sore, and as happy as I'd ever seen him. He died in his chair sometime during the late show. When I woke up and went down to rouse him to come to bed, he was already gone. Everything changed so fast—just like that roller coaster whipping around the track—on top of the world one minute, racing downhill the next, and no way to stop or go back.

"Here it comes!" Avery said, and pointed as the blue train whizzed into the loading deck. The red one was still rushing around the other side of the track with folks screaming and girls' hair flying in the air.

If I got on the roller coaster, it'd ruin my hair for sure, too. It'd be silly to wreck my hair, since I'd had it styled only yesterday, after the buzzard . . .

"It's here! It's here!" Avery squealed, pulling me forward as the line moved. Andy and Amos were already headed through the zigzag of ropes to the platform.

"C'mon!" Amos turned around and waved at us with a big grin. "They're letting people on!" It was the most I'd heard Amos say all day, the first time he'd smiled like he meant it.

Avery bounced up and down on my arm, trying to move my dead weight. Next thing I knew, I was headed through the ropes.

I'll just go far enough until they tell me I'm too fat, and then I'll put the little guy on with his brothers. . . .

"Hurry, it's getting full!" Avery broke into a trot, and I had to step quick to keep up. A couple of teenagers slipped under the rope in front of us and cut in line, and Andy and Amos broke into a run, not wanting to lose their spot. They made it past the line-cutters and got the third to last car, the two teenagers plopped themselves in behind them, and a young couple took the final car. Next thing I knew, there stood Avery and me, watching the safety bars lock into place and the blue train click forward.

Andy looked around and realized Avery didn't make it, but by then it was too late. "You get the red one, Aves!" he called, and then away he and Amos went.

Lord, have mercy, I thought. *I can't let this boy ride the roller coaster alone.*

I started looking around for a friend or neighbor who'd be willing to share a car with Avery. The blue train made it up the hill and swooshed downward, and I heard Andy and Amos laugh and yell.

"Here comes ours!" Avery pointed as the red Lightning Snake swept by with a rattle and a crash, then whipped around and around the corkscrew inside the track.

I checked back down the line. There had to be somebody I knew. . . .

"Here it is! Here it is!" Avery tugged. "Come on, we get the front!"

I'm too fat. I'm too fat and too old.

"Come on! Come on!"

The red train glided into the unloading area, and right there in the third seat was Otis Charles. Pastor Harve was in the seat behind him with one of his little grandkids. If they'd let those two big lugs on the train, they'd put me on without so much as a by-your-leave.

I waved my hand and tried to catch O.C.'s attention. If I could get him to see me, he'd take Avery on the roller coaster.

The crowd was closing in, pushing us forward. I waved harder. "Otis Charles? Otis Charles?" O.C. looked around like he'd heard me, but then the blue train whooshed by and the sound was lost.

"Come on! Come on, let's get the front!" Avery pleaded, bouncing and pulling my hand as the red train moved forward for loading. "Come on, Mrs. Doll!"

"Avery!" Before I knew what was happening, I'd turned around and snapped at Avery like he was one of my own sons.

He froze in place, his mouth hanging open and his big brown eyes going wide.

"Now hold on a minute, son. I can't . . ."

Avery's little face melted like frosting off a cake. I looked at that boy, and I wondered how many times he'd had promises made to him only to be taken back later. Standing there on that platform, he didn't seem a bit surprised about the roller coaster. He looked like he'd expected things to fall through.

Imagene Doll, if you don't get on that roller car with this boy, you might as well lie down in your grave right now. You might as well be dead already.

Giving Avery's hand a squeeze, I squared my shoulders. "I can't get on that roller coaster without sayin' a prayer first." I closed my eyes and verses whipped through my head in rapid-fire. *"I am with thee, and will keep thee in all places whither thou goest"*—I hoped that counted for roller coasters. *"My flesh and my heart faileth"*—which was true enough. *"The Lord is my helper, and I will not fear what man shall do unto me"*—or little boys. *"But strong meat belongeth to them that are of full age"*—I qualified for that, sure enough.

"There, now let's go before somebody else gets our spot." The two of us hurried forward and Avery pulled me into the very front car of the red train. A lady in the blue train screamed bloody murder as it swooshed by and whipped around a corner.

The Twenty-third Psalm came to mind. *"Yea, though I walk through the valley of the shadow of death . . . Thy rod and thy staff . . . Surely goodness and mercy shall follow me . . ."*

"Oh mercy!" I heard myself holler as the safety bar clicked down hard over my knees and the train jerked forward. It seemed like the bar should be up on my waist. Real tight, so I couldn't fall out.

"Get ready to fly!" the attendant called, and I swiveled around to tell him to stop this crazy thing—our safety bar wasn't near tight enough. But it was too late. The Lightning Snake let out a big hiss, and we were headed up the hill.

I shut my eyes as the car moved upward—*click, click, click, click*. It reminded me of the old elevator at Woolworths when I was a kid. That thing rattled and squeaked and jerked up and down like it'd fall any minute. My mama hated it. We kids thought it was the berries.

I felt along the safety bar and closed my hand over Avery's. One way or another, I would hold us both in this car until we were safe on solid ground again. *Lord, give me strength. Help me keep us both*—

"What are you doin', Mrs. Doll?" I opened one eye, and Avery was watching me with the darnedest look on his face.

"Praying, Avery. I'm praying some more." I glanced over my other shoulder and the folks on the ground looked like chickens in a yard. We'd almost made it to the top of the hill, and from where I was sitting, it seemed like there wasn't a thing holding us up. I couldn't see the track or the trestle or anything. Down below, the blue car was going through the corkscrew and coming in for a landing. I wished Avery and I had gotten on that car, and it would all be over by now.

"How come?" Avery asked, and I turned back to him.

"Because I'm scared, Avery. I'm scared to death, and when you're scared the thing to do is pra-aaaaay!" Off we went over the edge. Tears whipped into my eyes on the way down, and I promised God if I survived this, I'd never gossip, skip Sunday school, doze off during a sermon, overeat, put more than a nip of rum in my eggnog, think a mean thought, or get on another roller coaster as long as I lived.

No sooner were we at the bottom than we whipped up again, and sideways around a corner. After that it was up, down, around, sideways, around, up, down, around, and around, and around. All the while, I was screaming as loud as I could. Sometime during the ride, I left off praying, and the screaming turned to something between a holler and a war whoop. I felt like I was a kid again, bareback on my old pony, Whirley, galloping as fast as we could along the cow trail that went up and down the earthen terraces in our south pasture. Each time Whirley topped a hump, his feet cleared the ground for a minute as he leapt down the other side. My rear end left his back as we flew through the air, and for a piece of a second, I was hanging on just by my fingers in his mane. It was the closest I'd ever come to flying.

The roller coaster was the next best thing. As we topped the last hill, I threw my head back and imagined I was that little brown-legged girl, my hair streaming out behind me as Whirley took flight.

The minute our train came in for a landing, I gathered up the boys and said, "That was the most fun I've had since I was little. Let's do it again." All three boys were game, and we rode the roller coaster two more times, right in a row. I couldn't believe I'd walked past the roller coaster for fifty years, and just now, nearly seventy years old, I finally gave it a try. It made me wonder what else I might've missed just because I was afraid.

When we got off for the third time, it crossed my mind that I did break my promise to God about not getting on a roller coaster again if I survived the first ride. I figured He would forgive me, though. I had a feeling He was the one who wanted me to take those boys on the roller coaster to begin with. Funny thing was, when I brought us all into the fair and bought the ride tickets, I thought *I* was doing a good thing for the boys. As it turned out, the boys did a good thing for me.

As we left the Lightning Snake behind, I could still feel the ground moving under my feet. The boys and I staggered a bit by the gate, laughing about how we couldn't get our balance, and when I turned around, darned if Betty Prine wasn't sitting on a bench in front of the fun house, watching me with her lips squeezed together, blinking like a bug-eyed goldfish. One of her grandkids tried to wave at her from the Lightning Snake line, but she didn't even notice. She was too busy curling up her nose at me.

"Hallooo, Betty!" I smiled real big and waved at her, because at that moment, even Betty Prine couldn't ruin my fun. I was as happy as a pig in poop. "You enjoyin' the fair tonight?" From the looks of her, the answer was no. Betty Prine never looked like she enjoyed anything. My mama used to say if you frown on the outside long enough, eventually you'll grow a frown on the inside, too. I heard on *Oprah* where they use that Botox on people's faces so they can't frown, and that gets them over being depressed. Betty Prine needed a gallon jug of that stuff.

Avery tugged my hand and hinted that it'd be neat to go in the fun house. Andy scolded him for asking, and Avery looked down at his shoes.

"That's a fine idea, Avery," I told him. "I don't see why not. I haven't been in a fun house in years."

Avery brightened up, and the three of us marched right over to the ticket booth by Betty Prine's bench. "Come on in the fun house with us, Betty," I said, and Avery, bless his heart, gave her a hopeful look. What a sweet boy.

"Oh, for heaven's sake." Betty tipped her nose in the air, pretending she didn't see Avery at all. "Imagene Doll, *what* in *heaven's name* do you think you're doing?"

"Goin' in the fun house," I answered, just as pleasant as you please. I was proud of how nice the words sounded. That'd really get Betty's goat. "After that, we might go on the roller coaster again, or maybe that crazy thing where you ride up in a chair and then drop on a big rubber band."

Betty's eyes got smaller and smaller—narrow, like a rat's. "Have you *looked* at yourself, Imagene?" She flipped a hand toward me as I finished paying for another book of tickets. "Going around in public like that. People will think you've *lost* your *mind*."

I leaned over and took a glance in the mirror on the fun house sign. The wind had pulled the curl from my hair and stood it up straight at a height of about four inches, all the way around my head. I had lipstick trails around my mouth, and somehow I'd picked up a smudge of grease from the roller coaster. It had stained my shirt and there was a dollop on my cheek. "Well, will you look at that?" I said. "Boys, ain't that a funny mirror? Let's go see what else is inside."

Betty glared fireballs at me as I herded the boys toward the fun house. The best thing was I didn't care one whit. *The folks who mind don't matter, and the folks who matter don't mind*—I saw that on a T-shirt someplace on the midway. Maybe I'd buy one for Betty.

"Don't think everyone doesn't *know* what you're doing, Imagene Doll," Betty hollered after me. "You and Donetta Bradford using those poor boys to try to get on Amber Anderson's hometown show. You ought to be . . ."

The fun house music drowned out the rest, and Betty Prine was gone by the time we came out. As we strolled up the midway, I spotted Amanda-Lee and Carter trying to throw Ping-Pong balls into a goldfish bowl to win a goldfish. The balls were bouncing everywhere, and finally one landed in a dish, and Amanda-Lee came away with a fish in a Ziploc bag. Carter tried to take it from her and she sidestepped away, laughing. Holding the fish at arm's length, she told him to win his own fish—this one was hers fair and square. He argued that it was *his* ticket that bought the Ping-Pong balls, but she said it didn't matter—it was her toss that landed in the bowl.

I stood there and watched the two of them for a minute, reliving the first time Jack and I ever walked down a midway, him a young soldier and me just a girl in my first year of college, on a trip to Galveston Island with my chums. I first met Jack down on the beach. He invited me to a winter carnival that was set up by the shore, and that was all it took. It didn't matter that I'd just started college or that he had two more years in the navy. He won a Kewpie doll for me, and I fell in love. Every time we were within ten feet of each other, there was lightning in the air.

When Amanda-Lee danced away from Carter, she had that look in her eye and so did he. The space between them was filled with enough electricity to light up the entire midway.

After the gold fish booth, Amanda-Lee and I ended up in the restroom together. I was headed out and she was going in. I'd stopped at the mirror to try to do something with my hair. She had a flush in her cheeks and a glow in her pretty brown eyes.

"Well, hey there, Amanda-Lee," I said. "You having a good time at the fair?"

She stopped and looked at herself in the mirror, smoothed a few wild curls of coppery hair back into place, then tried to get a towel out of the dispenser with one hand.

"Here, I'll hold your fish," I offered, and she handed me the bag with the little orange and black spotted fish inside. "Ain't he a cute little fella?"

Amanda laughed. She had a sweet laugh. "I wondered if you ladies might want him for the beauty shop. I doubt they'll let me take him on the plane." She frowned at the fish, like she really didn't want to leave him behind. "He'd probably starve to death at my apartment, anyway. I'm never home."

"That's kind of sad, not to be home enough to feed a fish." Maybe I shouldn't have said something so personal, but I was getting to feel an affection for Amanda-Lee, like she was one of my daughters-in-law, brand-new in the family. Strange how with some people, you just feel like you know them right off.

"Yeah, I guess it is, in a way." Just for a second she had a somber look, but then she shrugged it off. "One of these days, things will slow down a little."

She smiled, and I smiled back. "I rode the roller coaster. Three times, actually. I'm almost seventy years old, and it was one of the best things I ever did. I wish I hadn't put it off for so long."

Amanda-Lee took her goldfish and raised him into the air like we were toasting with fine champagne. "Here's to life in the moment."

"You betcha," I cheered. I wished I'd learned about life in the moment when I was as young as her. Jack and I would have sailed around the world and seen all those places he remembered from the navy. "Looks like Carter's having a fine time tonight, too. That sure does my heart good, considering."

Tossing a wadded-up towel in the trash, Amanda raised a brow. "Considering?"

"Considering all he's been through, I mean." *Imagene Doll, did you or did you not just promise the Almighty, not a hundred feet from here, that if you survived the roller coaster, you'd never gossip again? You better pull out your umbrella. It'll be raining brimstone any minute.*

Amanda-Lee cocked her head to one side and leaned up against the sink, setting the fish on the counter like she wasn't in any hurry to move on.

Maybe it ain't gossip if you've got good motivations. It ain't. It ain't gossip. "Well, you know, his brother having cancer and all. It's not every young fella who'd give up his job and his place—his whole life, practically—to move back home and take care of his brother's business and those three little nieces. It takes a man with a pretty sterling character to do that—one who understands what's really important. Not just anyone would make that kind of commitment."

Amanda blinked hard, taking it all in. Her face softened, and she swiveled toward the door, like she was looking through it and seeing Carter in a whole new way.

"He don't wear it on his sleeve, either," I added. "It's just that Donetta could worm the Christmas list out of Santa Claus. Folks will tell her anything, even folks she don't know. Of course, she was sure he was from Hollywood, coming to do Amber's show, so she was trying pretty hard to get infor—" I slapped my mouth shut, just a second and a half too late, as usual. The beans were spilt.

Amanda-Lee let her head fall forward and sighed. A heavy twine of silence stretched between us. "I know you're aware of who I am," she said finally. "And why I'm here."

There wasn't any point denying it. "Well, I think I do, but I wouldn't tell a living soul. I understand it's supposed to be top secret—until the Final Five gets announced and all."

She pulled her lips to one side and narrowed her eyes, like she was thinking hard. "Would you be willing to help with something? It's a strange request, and I'd need complete secrecy until it's over."

Pure intrigue tingled all over me. I felt like James Bond having an undercover meeting with Q in the bathroom. "Anything. You just name it. I'd do anything to help Amber's show turn out to be the best one of all."

Amanda-Lee blew out a long breath. "What I really need is a horse and a trailer. . . ."

Chapter 15

Mandalay Florentino

As I wrapped up my conversation with Imagene, I experienced an emerging hope that Amber's hometown reveal would come off as intended. Our plan was clear and sharp—in my mind, at least. Tomorrow morning, after Amber and the crew arrived in Austin, they would leave the airport and drive straight to the home of Imagene Doll. Her farm would provide a secluded country location, where we could prepare for Amber's grand entrance without the curious eyes of townsfolk and the potential interference of one roving reporter, whom Imagene had also seen roaming around town. Imagene assured me that the reporter had sufficiently offended the townsfolk by asking smutty questions about Amber, and no one would give her any information.

With silence from the locals and some strategic planning, we could keep a lid on the story until after Amber's big reveal at the rodeo arena. Once word of that got out, things would probably become frantic before her hometown reunion concert at the Daily community building, but right now, I could only attack one Amber issue at a time.

Imagene had committed to arranging for a suitable horse trailer and truck to be waiting at her house. She would also procure Amber's brothers, and hopefully her grandfather. When Amber arrived at the farm, we would shoot family reunion scenes and interviews, using Imagene's place as a down-home locale. With a little ingenuity, and about a thousand pounds of luck, it would work.

If Ursula found out I'd confided in one of the locals, she'd have my head stuffed and mounted on her wall. I could hear her screaming, even now. *Vhat? Vhat? Did you think these people couldt be trustedt, Mandee-lay? You leet-tle fool. Trust no one.*

"This has to remain absolutely secret," I whispered to Imagene as we prepared to part ways. Two teenage girls had come in and were giggling in front of the mirrors. I waited until they left to say anything more. "If word gets out, there will be paparazzi everywhere and this whole thing will turn into a fiasco. It won't be about Amber's singing anymore; it'll be about celebrity gossip. The only thing keeping Amber on the show right now are the viewer votes. If public opinion turns against her, she'll be out of the Final Five before she even has a chance. This hometown show is important." I left out the fact that the network powers-that-be didn't like Amber. Warren Entertainment, the studio that awarded the million-dollar recording contract, didn't want to be saddled with, direct quote, "a gospel music–singing bumpkinette with decidedly poor judgment and a penchant for stumbling into controversial situations."

Imagene appeared to have a clear understanding of the problem. "That business in the papers about Amber and that awful Justin Shay isn't true, is it?" She watched closely for my reaction. "Sometimes a young girl can fool herself, thinking that a fella who's never done right by a woman before will do right by her. I'd hate to see Amber fall into that trap. She's such an innocent little thing."

I tried to brush off the possibility. "My suspicion is that it's more media hype than anything. I can't picture someone like Justin Shay having a serious interest in Amber." On the other hand, there was Ursula's concern that Justin might actually show up in Daily with Amber. Surely Justin Shay had more important things to do . . . unless he really was in hot pursuit of Amber. He'd been known for obsessive whirlwind love affairs in the past.

Imagene nodded, looking relieved. "Well, that's what I told that lady reporter in the café—she ought not to be spreading rumors on national TV. Amber's a good girl." She glanced toward the door. "Shoot. I forgot I had the boys out there. They probably think I fell in." Hiking her purse onto her shoulder, she hurried toward the door. "I'll see you tomorrow. You got the directions to my place, right? Two miles west to the crossroads, take a left, then four miles on County Road 2103. Old white house with a big red barn, kind of sits back in the live oaks. There's a couple of antique horse-drawn plows welded into the gateway. You can't miss it."

"I'll see you in the morning," I said, then grabbed my goldfish from the counter and followed her out, mentally cycling through tomorrow's plans as she disappeared into the crowd. In the midst of the cyclonic spin of work-related details in my head, there was a small, persistent voice asking, *Where'd Carter disappear to?* I found myself standing outside the restroom, searching for him, even though he'd probably given up on me and moved on by now, and that was undoubtedly for the best. An emotionally unavailable soon-to-be-married young professional shouldn't be searching for some guy who was not her fiancé, still evasive about his reasons for being in town, and not part of her plan to salvage Amber Anderson's reunion show. A committed professional would be back in her hotel room, covering all the bases, plugging the laptop into the phone line to email tomorrow's plans to the crew, maybe giving David a call to say good-night, exchange *I love yous*, and perhaps ask said fiancé to skip the upscale hobnob with the wealthy *female* client up the coast. . . .

I spotted Carter sitting on a bench near the Lightning Snake, and the imaginary phone conversation fizzled. There was a giant blue stuffed gorilla on the bench next to him. He grinned and pointed to it as I came closer. "My prize is bigger than yours."

"Yeah, but mine came with a two-day supply of goldfish food." I held up my fish, and it twirled around in its watery bubble, the colored lights giving it a metallic sheen.

Carter looped an arm around the neck of the gorilla and glanced over his shoulder toward the roller coaster. "You ready for the . . . Lightning Snake?" He pronounced *Lightning Snake* with all the drama of a professional voice-over announcer, then stood up, issuing a silent challenge.

"With the gorilla and the fish?"

"Sure, why not?"

"Well . . . I'm not sure about the gorilla, but I don't think the fish would enjoy it." Holding up the bag, I inspected the fish like the concerned pet owner that I was. "He's looking a little traumatized from having Ping-Pong balls thrown at him all day, actually. He'll probably need therapy."

Carter chuckled. "We could leave him with the gorilla."

"He might get stolen." I watched the roller coaster zip down a hill and whip around a curve. Really, that didn't look tempting. No telling what kind of underpaid lackey tightened the bolts on that thing. "Besides, the fish doesn't even know the gorilla."

Holding the gorilla close to the goldfish bag, Carter performed cursory introductions. "Gorilla, Goldfish. Goldfish, Gorilla." The gorilla's black plastic eyes stared sightlessly through the bag at me, and I couldn't help laughing.

"I don't think they like each other."

Little dimples formed at the corners of Carter's mouth, followed by a smooth grin. "I think they like each other pretty well." Somewhere near the rodeo arena, fireworks exploded into the sky.

"I . . ." Whatever I'd been about to say flew from my mind. I felt lightheaded, out of body. "I guess you'd have to ask the gorilla."

"I already did. He said he'd be happy to sit with the goldfish while we go on the roller coaster."

"How about if I watch the gorilla *and* the goldfish while *you* go on the roller coaster?" I came back down to earth and surrendered to my own lack of chutzpah and the fact that I shouldn't be riding the roller coaster with some guy I met on a business trip. This escalating game of flirtation at the fairgrounds had to stop before I did something I'd be tempted to lie about later. I'd never lied to David about anything. We were completely open and honest with each other. The rules didn't change just because I was stressed out and a long way from home. "I'm really not a Lightning Snake kind of girl. I'm a both-feet-on-the-ground kind of girl. Thanks for the offer, though." I took a step back, putting a safe distance between us.

Carter tipped his head to one side, watching me from the corner of his eye. "There's no hidden agenda here, Manda. Just two friends on a roller coaster ride."

I blushed, embarrassed that I'd so clearly telegraphed my thoughts. "I know that." In the back of my mind, I was thinking *friends, he said friends. Even people in committed relationships have friends.* "Thanks for hanging out with me last night and everything, but I think I'd better head back to the hotel and get some work done. I need to plug my laptop in somewhere, clear up my email, and make plans for tomorrow."

Both Carter and the gorilla gave me the same blank look. "I think the phone's in my half of the room, along with the Care Bears and the light switch." He lifted both hands, swinging the gorilla into the air. "Afraid you're out of luck until I get back to the hotel. Might as well ride the roller coaster."

I held the fish bag against my chest. "We'll just wait for you to ride the roller coaster, big guy." I could feel myself falling into the dance again. Something about Carter was magnetic, even if I didn't want it to be. "Hand over the gorilla."

Carter and the gorilla backed toward the roller coaster. "Just one time, then we'll go. Even you both-feet-on-the-ground girls need to kick up your heels once in a while."

His gaze caught mine, and I felt warm, then hot, sort of tingly all over, like the time I put my hands on the Vandergrift Generator during high school science class and the current crackled over my skin, making my hair stand on end.

Carter took another step backward, and I followed, my resistance caving in. "Maybe just once."

"My treat," he said, pulling a pair of tickets out of his pocket. I surmised that he'd bought them while I was in the restroom.

"You didn't have to do that." It was an automatic response, one I didn't mean. The fact that he'd bought me a ticket was incredibly nice.

"It seemed like a good way to make up for getting you arrested last night." He had the sweetest smile, a contagious enthusiasm for whatever the moment dished up. "Besides, what kind of a friend would I be if I let you miss out on the fun?"

"He never wanted me to miss out on anything fun." Imagene's words about Jack came back to me and for a moment, all the lights and the noise and the crowds faded away. It was just Carter and me. Fellow convicts, partners in crime, temporary neighbors, roller coaster riders. Friends.

By the time we made it to the front of the roller coaster line, the warm glow of unlikely camaraderie had faded in the face of the whoosh and whine of the Lightning Snake. The cars came in for a landing, and Carter and I climbed in somewhere near the middle.

I tried to remember the last time I'd been on a roller coaster. Adventure Land when I was ten. That was it. I threw up when I got off the ride, and my sisters made fun of me.

I glanced out the side of the car, toward the gorilla and the fish, waiting on the loading dock with various backpacks and other bulky belongings.

"Hang on," Carter said, as the car clicked forward.

"I can't believe I let you talk me into this." We climbed the first hill slowly, and I once again had a view of the entire fairgrounds. The lights, the stars overhead, the heavy full moon lifting on the horizon combined to create an instant of peaceful perfection. I turned to Carter and saw a reflection of my emotions, but then the front car topped the hill and the rest was a blur. I screamed like a banshee. Sometime during the ride, Carter convinced me to let go of the safety bar, and I floated above the seat, laughing and screaming at the same time, exhilarated and terrified, completely alive in the moment.

When the roller coaster returned to the platform, I sat in the car, feeling lightheaded and floaty, like my body was still moving, even though we'd come to a stop. The safety bar lifted and I stood up, then fell clumsily back into the seat, laughing and trying to catch my breath.

Stepping onto the loading dock, Carter reached for me. I slipped my hand into his and staggered onto the dock, a dizzy Cinderella.

"Ready to take another spin?" His fingers squeezed mine just before he let go, and I felt it all the way to my toes. I wanted to ride the roller coaster with him again, but I knew it wasn't a good idea. I was already feeling wild and giddy, like a high school girl on a first date.

I tried to clear my mind as we wandered toward the railing where the gorilla and the fish waited patiently. "I'd better get back to the hotel," I said, the proverbial wet blanket. I picked up my fish, and the bag felt cold against the warm places his fingers had touched. "This was fun, though. I needed a little downtime." I motioned over my shoulder toward the roller coaster. "Or up and down time. That was great. I can't remember when I've laughed like that." Sadly enough, that was true. The realization settled over me like a lead cloak. There was a disconnect in my life lately—a growing chasm between the things I enjoyed and the things I did each day. I missed being with the local station, producing *Good Day LA*, effortlessly mixing cooking and fashion with the latest health and fitness news, segments promoting worthy charities, and human interest pieces showing the lives of people trying, in their own little ways, to make the world a better place.

Maybe reality TV wasn't for me. The chewing up and spitting out of hopes and dreams was good for ratings but hard on the soul. Maybe all those years of Episcopal school had more effect on me than I'd thought. Deep inside, a part of me felt a growing sense of restlessness, of unfulfillment, a nagging worry that maybe, just maybe, the God I'd visited in my stiff Mary Janes and itchy Sunday sweaters expected me to do something . . . *more* with my life.

Beside me, Carter sighed, as if my melancholy mood was rubbing off as we strolled along the midway. "This was good, tonight. Sometimes you just need to get away for a while, you know?"

"Yeah," I agreed, reminded of the things Imagene had told me about Carter. "I heard that you're taking care of your brother while he's going through cancer treatments. That has to be hard."

He quirked a brow at me, surprised, I guess, that I'd been investigating him.

"Imagene mentioned it when I saw her in the restroom. She was glad you were out here having fun, I think."

His lips parted in a silent *ah*. "Word gets around in a small, small town." That was a quote from a country song—I couldn't think of which one, but a contestant had performed it on the show sometime this season. We'd had a tough time getting in touch with the songwriter to secure all the necessary permissions.

I nodded in agreement. "That must take an incredible load off while he's going through treatment. A solid support system is a big part of recovery." The last bit sounded like TV drivel from some on-air medical expert, which it was. It struck me that I'd so often stood just off set, watching cancer victims and families pour out their hearts and experiences. I'd never once put myself in their shoes. My family was healthy. "I can't imagine what it would be like to have one of my sisters or my brother going through that."

Carter nodded, still looking away. "You don't know it until it happens. Then you deal the best way you can. I wanted to be the one to give bone marrow to Chris, but I wasn't a match, so I couldn't. I could come back home and keep his business going, make sure the bills get paid. I'm no sound and lighting systems engineer, but I can do the legwork for him—go out and look at the sites, get copies of the blueprints, talk to the customers. Chris does the design work from home or from the hospital. It keeps his mind off things." He chuckled as we walked past the giant metal cowboy and the Kiddie Korral, which was dark now. "He's pretty determined not to let this slow him down. Two weeks ago, he was doing the schematics for a new church building in Austin while they were starting a drip to get him ready for the bone marrow transplant."

"Schematics for a new church building in Austin." Suddenly, Carter's presence in Daily made sense. The pad for a new building had been cleared behind the Caney Creek Church. I felt an inordinate sense of relief, knowing there was a logical reason for his presence here, and that reason didn't have anything to do with *American Megastar* or Amber. "So is your brother going to do the sound and lighting for the little church out on Caney Creek?" He took his attention from the metal cowboy long enough to give me a quizzical

sideways look, and I added, "I passed by there the other day. It looked like they were clearing land for a new building."

He eyed me a moment longer, then switched the gorilla to his other arm, shrugged, and said, "We'll see. They're quite a ways from being ready. Hopefully Chris will be back on his feet by then."

And you'll be where? Where would Carter be once his brother was well? What was his life like before? What would it be like after? "Then what's next for you once your brother's back on his feet?"

"We'll see." He shrugged, and the gorilla moved up and down. "This past year, I've learned to just take life as it comes. You never know what's around the corner." He smiled at me as we exited the fairgrounds gate. "See you at the hotel." Walking backward a few steps, he lifted the gorilla's shaggy blue paw and waved good-bye. I laughed and strolled on to my car. I had the feeling he was watching me. I wanted to turn around and look, but I didn't.

We left the fairgrounds in a stream of departing vehicles. All the way to town, I found myself checking the rearview mirror, trying to decide which set of headlights was Carter's. By the time I'd parked in the alley behind the hotel and killed the engine, he was pulling in. Remembering my entrance into the darkened corridor the night before, I was glad.

He stopped beside my car and leaned out the window. "I'm headed to the Buy-n-Bye for a soda. Can I bring you anything?"

A quick pang of disappointment registered somewhere in the rebellious part of me that had been picturing us raiding the café again tonight. "No, but thanks." *Remind him that you have to work tonight, Mandalay. As a matter of fact, remind yourself. No Batman and Robin adventures around the hotel this evening.*

He waited to see if I'd change my mind, then pulled back inside the window. "Slide your computer cable under the door. I'll plug it in as soon as I get back."

"All right." Grabbing my purse, the fish, and my laptop case, I got out of the car. He waited, shining his headlights on the entrance while I fumbled for my hotel key and opened the door. Slipping inside the hotel as Carter drove away, I hiked my laptop onto my shoulder, then hurried past the moaning dumbwaiter and the closet full of Styrofoam heads, made a quick grab at the fresh cookies on the antique buffet, and rushed up the stairs. The hallway smelled of new paint, but within the realm of Suite Beulahland, the scent was still a mixture of aging plastic and flowery perfume like my grandmother wore.

I stood just inside the doorway, taking in the place—what I could see of it with the light from the hall—with a renewed sense of awe. In the morning when there was plenty of sunlight, I needed to snap some pictures of the room to show Paula. She, of all people, would appreciate the thematic collection of oddities in this place. She would find some deeper meaning in it.

I propped the door open and then tried calling her, balancing the cell phone on my shoulder as I transferred the fish to an empty water glass in the bathroom, then carried him to the bedside table, where he could enjoy Elvis from several angles. Unpacking my laptop, I slid the cord under the door.

Paula's home line rang unanswered, and her cell rolled over to voice mail, which probably meant she'd gone on one of her many online-arranged dates.

By the time I'd changed into my sweats, I heard Carter jogging up the stairs. A few moments later my light came on and he pulled the laptop cord taut under the door, leaving the computer tethered in the alcove between the rooms. Carter knocked three times, and I knocked back. Sitting on the floor with the computer on my legs, I listened as he moved around his room, then grabbed something from the bathroom across the hall and went downstairs. I resisted the urge to shuck the laptop and follow.

Waiting for the old-fashioned dial-up connection was arduous. By the time my email window opened, I'd closed my eyes and let my mind drift back to the fair. I was on the Ferris wheel, sailing over the top, falling off the edge of the world in slow motion.

"Hang on, here comes the good part. . . ."

"What kind of a friend would I be if I let you miss out on the fun. . . ."

A long, slow sigh passed my lips, and I laughed to myself. Then the email server beckoned, and I felt guilty. David was at home working and I was in Texas doing . . . what exactly?

I checked for David's name in my inbox. Nothing tonight. No doubt, he was busy catching up from his trip. On the way home, he had probably gone to the marina to check on the boat. Without regular together time, the boat became lonely.

Ursula was waiting in my inbox, along with flight schedules from our travel planner, questions from three different production assistants, an email from Rodney, who was planning to switch assignments so he could be my crew chief, and a whine from the wardrobe mistress, who hadn't been able to find Amber for her fitting today. Fortunately, as skinny as Amber was, she looked good in practically anything.

I put out a flurry of emails, answering questions, disseminating plans and travel schedules, and emailing driving directions to the crew. When that was finished, I took a deep breath and plunged into three messages from Ursula—one with useful information about the schedule for next week's show and two reminders that bad things would happen to me if the Justin Shay/Shokahna fiasco escalated and reflected badly on *American Megastar*. As if I didn't know that already. Fortunately, after sending the final email, Ursula had headed off on a flight to New York to supervise Cal Preston, her personal choice to be the winner of this season's contest. At least she'd be occupied with trying to make Cal's hometown show outshine the rest, and therefore she would be too busy to harass me and my crew this weekend.

I answered her email with a glowing report, telling her how well everything was progressing in Texas and that the groundwork was in place for a smashing reunion show. I left out the details, mostly because in print it would sound ridiculous. When the crew got here and heard about the horse and trailer, they were going to laugh me out of the county.

What if I couldn't pull if off?

What if, tomorrow, one nosy reporter morphed into many, and this whole project turned into a media circus?

What if the hopes and dreams of Daily and Amber Anderson were crushed beneath the tirelessly marching feet of a juicy scandal and the public's need to know?

My heart started racing. Setting down the computer, I closed the door and then walked to the window and checked Main Street in both directions. No unusual traffic. No sign of strangers hiding behind trash cans with long-range lenses.

Standing with my chin in my hands and my elbows resting on the window frame, I let my forehead fall against the cool glass and tried to get my thoughts in order. My earlier sense of peaceful euphoria hit bottom with a painful crash that left a big black splatter of reality—something like a Rorschach blot. Make of it what you will.

By the door, the laptop chimed, letting me know an instant message had come up. Probably Ursula, ringing in to threaten me from somewhere high above the central United States.

Pushing away from the window, I returned to the computer, sat down, and clicked the IM window to open it.

Hey, gurl, you OK? The screen name was Paula's. I relaxed instantly. A chat with my best girlfriend was just what I needed tonight.

Yeah, fine. How r you? Apparently, Paula wasn't on a date tonight. Strange that she hadn't answered her home phone or her cell.

Kind of wacked. You sitting down? NTTYS.

Need to tell you something? The last time Paula sent me an instant message with *NTTYS* in it, Bernie, the producer who'd mentored us through our college internships, had fallen victim to an aneurism and died right there in the newsroom.

What? You're scaring me.

Wasn't going to tell you til you got back. That's y I didn't answer the phone.

TELL ME WHAT? I sat staring at the cursor, the seconds seeming to stretch on forever as I waited for Paula's reply. When it came, I stared in disbelief.

Check out profile #21672 on Mydestiny.com.

I growled at the screen. *A date? You scared me to death 4 a date?*

Just look, K?

I opened a window, brought up *Mydestiny.com,* and entered the profile number. On dial-up, the search was slow, so I moved back to Paula's window. *It's slow. You have a date with this guy?*

Just messaged him, anonymously. He asked for my picture.

Wait. Here it comes. . . .

I switched to the Mydestiny window, watching as the page materialized, segment by segment, from top to bottom. A name came up on the banner. *David C. Single white male, 40,* followed by two pictures of David in the left center of the screen. Paula was playing a joke on me—sort of a strange joke, but a joke.

Why hadn't David taken his profile off Mydestiny yet? I'd removed mine months ago.

I flipped back to the IM window and typed in, *Very funny*.

The Mydestiny window scrolled onward, and a third picture came slowly into view. David on the boat with the wind in his hair. He'd just grabbed the mooring line, glanced up at the camera, smiled.

I took that picture. Three months *after* we met.

Acid gurgled into my throat.

You OK? The cursor flashed at the end of Paula's question. *OK? OK? OK?*

I couldn't formulate a coherent thought, couldn't remember how to type. I stared at the keyboard, unable to join letters into words that would make sense.

The past six months flashed through my mind—David and me on the boat, the two of us around town, hanging out at his apartment, eating at Gregorio's on his birthday. He was depressed about turning forty, depressed about his life, depressed because his ex-wife had remarried and had two kids within two years.

He asked me if I wanted to get married. I said yes, and he said, "Let's do it soon."

The next day, I started making wedding plans. He told me anything I wanted was fine. I left it to him to pick out an engagement ring. He never did.

Now I knew why. He was busy trolling online, waiting to see if something better would come along.

Hitting the Work Offline button, I slapped the computer closed. I didn't want to think about this. I couldn't. I had Amber's shoot tomorrow. I had to stay focused.

How could this be happening?

What if there was a mistake? What if I was jumping to conclusions?

What possible excuse could there be for his keeping a Mydestiny page? For stocking it with a picture I took? For requesting a photo when Paula contacted him?

Would he really do that?

My cell phone rang in my purse. For just an instant, I hoped it was him. I wanted him to make all of this go away, to explain everything. He probably could. David was a consummate salesman.

That wouldn't make it true.

In my heart, I knew what was true. He didn't love me. He was forty and trying to talk himself into the idea that it was time he got married again.

I was thirty-four and tired of being single in the city.

It was a lethal combination.

Grabbing the phone, I switched it to vibrate. It was only Paula. I didn't want to talk to anyone. I couldn't. All I could do was stumble across the room, climb onto the fuzzy bedspread, twist my fingers into the thick artificial fur, bury my head, and cry all over Beulah's pink satin pillows.

Chapter 16

Imagene Doll

In the morning, I didn't hear noises in the house and think about Jack. I was busy dreaming of the roller coaster, and I reckon Jack wouldn't have wanted to wake me up and spoil the ride. He joined me in my dream. Where Avery had been by my side as the Lightning Snake crawled up the first hill, now it was Jack. The sight of him filled me with joy, but I was confused, too, because he couldn't be there.

"They said you died," I told him. "They said you were gone."

He smiled at me, his eyes twinkling the way they used to when I prodded him to reveal what was inside my Christmas packages.

"You look good," I said. He did look good—like the tall, straight navy gent who stole my heart the first time I saw him.

The coaster made it to the top of the hill, and we hovered for just a minute at the crest. Jack put his fingers over mine on the bar, and even though I could see him touch me, I couldn't feel it. He lifted up his hand, and I let mine follow. The coaster started down the hill, and we threw our arms in the air and laughed and laughed.

I woke up sometime before the ride was over, and for a minute, I just laid there thinking about it. My first roller coaster ride with Jack. If the Anderson boys hadn't talked me into stopping by the fair last night, if Amanda-Lee and I hadn't made that pact to get on the roller coaster, it never would've happened. I couldn't have ridden the roller coaster with Jack in my dream, because I wouldn't know what the roller coaster felt like. Because I'd gathered up my courage and tried something new, it was like Jack got to do it, too.

It hit me that I hadn't been much fun to be with this past year—moping around the house every night, not wanting to get out of bed in the mornings, turning down my sons' invitations to go along on family trips and whatnot. I hadn't been showing Jack's memory a very good time since he passed on.

Throwing off the covers, I made up my mind that I would start doing better. Today was the beginning of it. Helping Amanda-Lee get Amber and the filming crew into the fair would be an adventure, for sure. Jack would love every minute of that.

Slipping into my housecoat, I crossed the room to shut the door, so as not to wake the Anderson boys while I was moving around getting dressed and puttering about the place. The old wood floor squeaked under my feet, and down the hall, one of the boys caught a breath and sighed, the bed squeaking as he turned over. That was Avery, probably, down in Jack Junior's room. Either Andy or Amos was snoring like a little old man in the bedroom across the hall. I stood in the doorway for just a minute, listening to the sounds and remembering the days when every inch of our house was full—full of kids, full of chores to be done, homework to be checked, dirty laundry needing washing. Full of life. It felt good to have the house alive again.

Once this adventure with Amanda-Lee was over and school let out for summer, I'd invite all the grandkids up for a long visit.

That would be fun. It was high time I opened the house for company again.

The phone rang, and I hurried to close the bedroom door and grab the receiver before the noise woke everybody up. Donetta was on the other end, and I knew right away something was up.

"GiGi, we got a problem," she said. Her voice was low, like she didn't want anyone to hear. "You still got the Anderson boys over there?"

"Yes, I do." I couldn't imagine why me having the Anderson boys would be a problem, since their granddad was probably still laid out somewhere, after a long night hugged up to a bottle. "The kids're sleeping. We went to the fair last night on the way home. I rode the roller coaster. Three times."

"I heard about that." Donetta didn't sound as surprised as I thought she would. "Betty Prine's already been on the phone this morning, telling everyone about you cozying up to the Anderson boys because their sister's gonna be famous."

The hackles rose on the back of my neck. Darn that woman. She could make a sow's ear out of a silk purse. "Oh, let her talk. I don't care. Betty Prine's not worth my time. Those boys and I had fun. They're real sweet children—grateful, and polite. Betty Prine can just—"

"I ain't got time to talk about Betty Prine this morning," Donetta said. "We got bigger fish to fry. Is there anyone out in your front yard?"

I sat down on the edge of my bed, scratching my ear through the nest of roller-coaster hair. "Donetta, did you slip and hit your head in the shower again? Why in the world would there be someone in my front yard? It's just me and the boys here, and they're all still asleep."

"Just check, GiGi. Just check if there's anyone in your front yard. Don't let them see you looking."

"Donetta, what—"

"Just check. Go look out the window." Netta was in no mood to mess around. When Donetta Bradford takes that tone, you get up and go look out the window if that's what she wants.

I stood at the curtain and pulled it aside, just a little. The yard looked quiet, all the way down to the front gate, and Hamby, my across-the-pasture neighbor's big cow dog, was lounging out under the oak tree. "Not a sign of anyone outside. Hamby's there under the tree. If there was someone around, he wouldn't just lay there like that."

Donetta blew out a quick sigh. I pictured it tinted with Rumba Red #5. "Good. They didn't find their way out there. Imagene, you got to stay at your house, and whatever you do, don't come to town."

"Donetta, what in heaven's—"

"Just listen. I don't have much time. Lucy's out front cussin' at people in Japanese. She's pretending she don't speak English."

"Donetta . . ."

"Listen," Donetta hissed, and I stepped back from the window. The last time Donetta got that sharp with me was when she came to make me get out of bed for Jack's funeral. "There's reporters and TV people, folks with cameras, and I don't know who else all over town. They're in the café, the hardware, the grocery, down at the Baptist church, and just now when Lucy opened up out front, they come bustin' in here, saying they knew *American Megastar* was here, and did we have Amber Anderson hidden upstairs? Forrest and Buddy Ray are headed over from the jail to come get these people out of here, and then I'm gonna lock the door and not let anybody in, except regular customers."

"Donetta, what . . ." My mind started spinning like the Tilt-A-Whirl at the fairgrounds, and my peaceful morning whiffed right out the window quick as a puff of smoke. I looked out at the front yard again, checked the bushes and the trees, and tried to see behind the stone pillars at the gateway. "How in the world? How could all that happen overnight?"

"Don't know. From the sounds of it, Verl hit half the watering holes in the county after he finished up here yesterday. He was at it pretty hard, and his tongue a-waggin' the whole time about how Amber was in the Final Five, and there was people from *American Megastar* in town, and he was gettin' rooms fixed up at the Daily Hotel for the rest of the crew, and Amber'd called him last evenin' saying she'd be home Saturday morning with a big surprise." She paused, and in the background I heard Forrest hollering, at least a half-dozen voices chattering back, and Lucy yelling in Japanese. "Lands, Imagene, there's no tellin' what that old fool said, and to who, but word's out. They're after it like hounds on a cottontail. They're lookin' to stake out anyplace Amber might come to and anybody she might plan to see. They're lookin' for Verl, they're lookin' for Amber's brothers, and they're lookin' for the *American Megastar* people."

"Oh mercy," I said, and Donetta added a quick *amen.* Pacing back and forth beside the bed, I tried to think. Somehow, we had to get this mess under control before Amber, Amanda-Lee, and the filming crew got to my house later this morning. "All right, DeDe, listen. I'm getting an idea, but it's gonna take some help."

"Whatever we got to do for Amber, you know we'll do it." Donetta would, too. Anytime anyone ever needed help, she was right there. She'd be the first in line with a shovel at a ditch diggin'.

I sat on the edge of the bed and started jotting down notes. The call waiting rang on my line—probably one of my boys checking on me, but I didn't answer it. "First of all, get that darned Betty Prine and lock her in a closet if you got to, but shut her up about the Anderson boys being with me last night. If the reporters track us down, everything'll be ruined. I got to tell you something top secret, DeDe. Promise me you won't tell a soul. Nobody. I mean it."

"GiGi, this ain't the time for games."

"Promise me."

"I promise. You know I'd never tell a secret." That wasn't exactly true, because anyone who talked as much as Donetta had spilled a secret or two, but never with the intention to hurt anybody.

"All right. The *American Megastar* crew is coming here later this morning. They're coming straight to my place from the airport, with Amber. They're gonna film her seeing her family again, and then we're gonna load her in a horse trailer and take her to do a concert at the fairgrounds. You can't tell *anybody*."

It took Donetta a minute to answer. "Imagene, you experiencin' any blurred vision, any headache, numbness in your extremities, any disorientation this mornin'?"

"I ain't havin' a stroke, Netta." It was aggravating that she didn't believe I was involved in the *American Megastar* plan. "Now hush up and listen. I called down the road last night and got a pickup and a horse trailer on loan from my neighbor who's been keeping old Magnolia for me since Jack died, but there's still things to do—we need someone who can drive the pickup, for one thing, because my neighbor's tied up this afternoon. Now, on top of that, we got these reporters to worry about."

I continued on, not giving her time to interrupt. "You call over to the café and tell Bob to keep them reporters busy as long as he can. Tell him to be slow with the food—get the countertoppers to brew up some wild stories about where Amber might be and when she might come in—anything that'll send them away from the fairgrounds and away from my place. Pass the word around town. Also, call Miss Lulu at the RV park and tell her that if she's still got that spiky-haired lady or her crew out there, go out and lock the park gate and pretend she's lost the key. That lady reporter sure enough knows where the Anderson place is, and we don't need her going out there and catching Verl half sloshed this morning—if she hasn't already."

I stopped a minute to write some things on my notepad, and Donetta started to talk. "Wait," I said. "I got more. Call Brother Harve and O.C., and ask them to check for Verl at home, and if he's not there, to hightail it over to The Junction. Verl's probably laid out in his truck in the parking lot, as usual. Tell Harve and O.C. I don't care if they have to pick him up and carry him here, I need him over to my place. They can't let anybody follow them. If they think they got a tail, they'll have to take evasive maneuvers."

"Good gravy, Imagene, you're making this sound like a spy movie. O.C. and Harve are gonna laugh me off the phone."

"Just tell them it's important. Tell them it's for Amber. Brother Harve's always had a soft spot for the Anderson kids."

Donetta sighed. "All right. I'll do it. Anything else?"

I stopped to think, looking at my list. "See if you can line us up someone who knows how to drive a pickup that's haulin' a four-horse slant trailer. Someone who ain't busy this afternoon. Don't tell them who it's for yet. Where's Amanda-Lee?"

"Still in bed, I think. I haven't heard a peep from her so far this morning. Carter passed through here on his way back from breakfast a while ago. He said he guessed she'd turned in early yesterday evening. He helped her plug her computer into the phone line when they got home from the fair, and that was the last he heard of her."

A sense of something not right tickled the short hairs on the back of my neck. Why would Amanda-Lee sleep past eight o'clock on the day her crew was headed up from Austin to film Amber's show? "Well, that don't seem right, does it—considering she's got a big day today and all?"

"No, it don't," Donetta agreed. "Reckon I ought to go wake her up? I haven't even heard a toilet flush up there or nothin' all morning. Women always go to the pot first thing."

"Donetta, for heaven's sake." Some of the things Donetta would talk about!

"Well, they do. That's always how we knew when to put out the breakfast trays—soon as the toilets started flushin'."

"That's just two things it don't seem should be associated—breakfast trays and toilets flushing."

"Well, you know, out one end, in the other."

"Donetta!" I couldn't help it, I laughed and DeDe laughed, too. For a minute, I forgot what we'd been talking about and why I was at the window with a notepad in my hand.

"You know, when she leaves here, she'll be followed." Donetta's words floated loosely around a thought about the low branches on the live oak trees needing to be trimmed.

"Who'll be followed?"

Donetta coughed into the phone. "Amanda-Lee. Wake up out there, Imagene. When Amanda-Lee leaves the hotel, these reporters are gonna follow. You shoulda heard them asking Lucy did we have the people from *American Megastar* registered here, and was Amber and Justin Shay upstairs, and so forth. They're hanging around by the doors, waiting for anyone to come out of the hotel. When they see Amanda-Lee's car pull out, they'll be hot on her tail."

"We can't have that. She'll lead them right here." I stopped to think about the problem. "All right, I got an idea. Give Harlan a call on his cell phone and find out how soon he's gonna be back through town on his mail route. Whenever he comes by the Hair and Body, he can go around back and pull on into the garage. Amanda-Lee can load up in the back part of the wagon and have Harlan drive her out here, and them reporters won't have a clue."

Donetta was quiet for a minute. I had a feeling she was staring at the beauty shop windows, trying to get a vision of whether or not the plan would work.

"It might do," she decided finally. "It just might do."

"It'll have to do. I don't have any other ideas. You?"

"If I did, I woulda said so." Donetta sounded a little peeved. It wasn't normal for me to be the one doing the planning and giving the orders. It felt good to be thinking on my own. All my life, I'd had someone else thinking for me—first my daddy, then Jack, now these last months Donetta and my sons. It was a powerful thing, finding out I had a mind of my own. I felt like I was on the roller coaster again—bold and free and full of life. "Have the counter-toppers get busy serving up some Amber Anderson stories. Maybe Brother Ervin can offer to show them the church where Amber used to sing, maybe even let them think she might show up there today—that wouldn't be a lie exactly, would it? To let them think that, I mean? Ervin could hint without actually saying so."

"I think it'd be all right. It probably ain't a sin to mislead reporters, anyhow."

"No, probably not, I reckon."

Donetta let out a long sigh, and I could hear her fingernails tapping the phone. "What exactly are you gonna be doin' while I'm calling half the county?"

"Well, for heaven's sake, Netta, I can't spend all morning on the phone. I got boys to feed, and then after that I got Hollywood comin' to my very doorstep. I need to get busy and clean my house."

Donetta just smacked her lips, huffed into the phone, and hung up, of all things. Even with all the years we been friends, there's times when Donetta Bradford can be just plain hard to get along with.

Chapter 17

Mandalay Florentino

The Ferris wheel sat waiting with one empty seat as David and I strolled through the fairgrounds, taking in the scent of funnel cakes and corn dogs, the richly blended sound of voices, the mechanical clicks and swishes of rides, and the tinny melodies of carnival music. By the Ferris wheel gate, the old ticket taker stood waiting, his body bent and wrinkled, a stark contrast to the smooth satin of his candy-striped vest and tall white top hat. He waved me over, and I tugged David's hand, pulling him toward the Ferris wheel.

David leaned away, laughed, and said, "What's the hurry?"

The ticket taker beckoned, and I tried to pull David closer. Any minute now, the gate would close, the Ferris wheel would spin upward, and we'd miss the ride. "Come on," I pleaded. "It's almost too late." High overhead in the seats, I could see my sisters, my nieces and nephews, and Paula in her bridesmaid's dress with her laptop computer, cruising *Mydestiny.com.*

Mydestiny.com. Something vaguely disturbing, mildly threatening, crept through my mind. I looked up at the blanket of night sky overhead. What could possibly be wrong here?

The ticket taker was closing the gate, his movements slow and deliberate. "Let's go," I said, trying to move forward. The gate was closing. David's fingers slipped from mine, and I didn't look back but ran for the opening, slipping into the last seat as it started upward.

"Pardon me, ma'am." I turned, and Carter was standing on the girders, riding the upward swell like a sailor on the rigging of a pirate ship. "I have to test this ride for safety." Swinging forward, he landed in the seat beside me.

"How did you . . . ? Where . . .?" I looked over the edge, and David was below, waiting in line to purchase food. He bought a caramel apple on a stick. A television crew walked up the midway with cameras, and David prepared to give an interview. Ursula slipped the apple from David's hand, took a bite, and smiled up at me.

"Don't worry," Carter whispered. "It's only a dream." I turned my face toward his, and he kissed me as we spun upward into a shower of stars.

The metal cowboy smiled, and atop his hat, the blue gorilla smiled, as well.

The gears of the Ferris wheel knocked, then buzzed, then knocked again, a steady, rhythmic sound. Someone below called my name.

"Amaaanda-Lee . . . Amaaanda-Lee . . . you awake in there, hon?"

The Ferris wheel, and the midway, David, Ursula, Carter all vanished. I opened my eyes and took in Elvis, larger than life on a black velvet tapestry.

I was vaguely aware of my cell phone vibrating toward the edge of the bed and someone knocking on the door. My face felt crusty, my eyes swollen and sore. My cheek was stuck to something furry and plush. For a moment I thought of the blue gorilla and drowsily considered the possibility that I'd fallen asleep with it.

"Amanda-Lee? Amanda-Lee-ee? Hon, it's Donetta. I just wanted to check on ye-ew. It's almost eight-thirty. Don't you need to be gettin' outta bed?"

Eight-thirty? I jerked upright, taking in the room, my computer on the floor, the fish in a bathroom glass, the anatomical alarm clock, flashing 8:30, 8:30, 8:31. My cell phone vibrated on the bed again and everything came back to me in a rush—the fair, the roller coaster, Carter, the fish, my computer, Paula's instant message, the painful revelation about David . . .

"Amaaan-da-Lee-ee, you all ri-ight in there?"

Pushing off the bed, I stumbled, stiff-legged, toward the door. When I opened it, Donetta was on the other side with cinnamon rolls and a glass of orange juice. "I thought ye-ew might want somethin' to eat, hon," she said, then inclined her head to one side and frowned sympathetically. "Ye-ew all right, sweetie? You don't look so good this mornin'. Ye-ew sleep all right last ni-ight?"

"Fine, thanks." I set the rolls on an ornate white and gold washstand by the door. "A little too well, I guess. Thanks for waking me up. I can't believe I overslept."

Donetta peered past me into the room, curiously taking in the fully made bed, the computer on the floor, all of my things in a compact pile by the chair, as if staged for a quick exit. "It's no problem at all, darlin'. We were just worried, that's all. Carter come by on his way to the café for breakfast and said he hadn't seen hide nor hair of you since yesterday evenin', and then I called Imagene, and she said you had a big day ahead today, and we figured I might-should wake you up."

"Yes, thank you for checking on me." I stepped back from the door, preparing to throw on some clothes, then get busy making final preparations for the day and checking on the crew's ETA.

That was probably the crew chief, Rodney, calling on the phone right now. Or Ursula.

I turned toward the phone as it buzzed a second ring. It could be Paula, calling about David. . . .

My stomach sank and fresh tears prickled against my throat, stinging like salt in an open wound.

Donetta's hand touched my arm, rubbed up and down with the faint scratch of long fingernails. "Is somethin' wrong, hon? You look like somebody died."

Somebody did. Me. Mandalay Florentino, happily engaged girl, killed in a train wreck of my own making. Scattered around the wreckage lay scores of details—wedding plans to cancel, a dreaded call to my family, an even worse call to David. What would he say? Would he deny everything, try to explain it away, or just admit that while I was planning our wedding, he was making sure there wasn't something better to be found. Some*one* better.

I wanted to crawl back onto the hairy bed and bury myself in it. Why was all of this happening at once?

Swallowing the tears, I gave myself a mental shove. *Time to pull it together, Mandalay Florentino. Quit marching in the pity parade; step up and salvage what's left of your life.* It wasn't too late to do a fabulous job on Amber's hometown segment, return to LA in triumph, and help Amber and her little brothers in the process. The personal wreckage would have to wait until I had time for it. At least I still had my career. For now.

"I'm fine," I assured Donetta. "I just didn't mean to sleep so late. I've got to . . . a lot to do today."

She nodded in a conspiratorial way. Glancing up and down the hall, she leaned close and said, "Can I come in for a minute, hon? I just talked to Imagene, and we've run into a little hitch this morning."

I stepped back, allowing her into the room when what I really wanted to do was slam the door shut. I couldn't confront one more hitch today. *Please, God, no more hitches, okay? My fiancé is trying to date my maid of honor over the internet. That's enough for one twenty-four-hour period, all right? Please?* I was surprised to find myself praying, but I probably shouldn't have been. Desperate times breed fervent faith, my grandmother always said. These were desperate times. If my career tanked today, I couldn't handle it. I couldn't. *Please help me make this segment a success. . . .*

Donetta must have sensed that I was close to the breaking point. She interlaced her fingers and folded her hands against her chest as if she were praying, too. "Imagene and I got it all figgered out. I been makin' phone calls, and everyone in town wants to hay-elp."

Making phone calls? To everyone in town? My mouth dropped open. Donetta took my hand between hers and patted and rubbed it vigorously. "Now don't panic, hon, but thay-re's reporters downstairs. A lot of reporters. . . ."

Panic, why should I panic? Just because Amber's hometown segment would be ruined, along with her chances of making it into the Final Showdown? Just because she and her brothers would continue to live in poverty? Just because Ursula would kill me, then terminate my employment, and I'd be lucky to get a job entering news copy into the teleprompter somewhere?

"We got a plan," Donetta went on. "It's gonna sound a little crazy, but we think it'll work. First of all, y'all go ahead and git yourself dressed and git your things together, then just wait here until I call for you. Don't dare go downstairs, and stay away from the windows, because if those folks see you, they'll be all over you like stink on a skunk. They're watchin' the hotel, the car, everything. Bob said some of them's hid out behind pallets and trash cans in the back alley, tryin' to figure out if Amber's in the hotel with Justin Shay."

She paused to check her watch, holding her arm out and squinting at the numbers. "In about forty-seven minutes, the mail wagon'll come through town and pull into the auto shop out back, and then . . ." She continued on with a plan that sounded like an ill-advised cross between a Grisham novel and a scene from *Petticoat Junction*. My mind rushed to keep up, hurriedly taking in details that included me stowing away in the back of a mail truck, O.C. tracking down Amber's grandfather, the Baptist pastor creatively misleading reporters into thinking that Amber might be marrying Justin Shay this afternoon at First Baptist Church in Daily, some woman named Lulu locking the gates to her RV park, a man named Doyle waiting until Amber and the crew had arrived at Imagene's house, then stalling a gravel truck in the road so as to prevent anyone who didn't know the back roads from getting to Imagene's farm.

I let my head fall back and exhaled slowly. "This is never going to work." Pacing a few steps toward the front windows, I peeked into the once-quiet street, now filled with cars, media vans, RVs, and satellite trucks with logos on the sides. Most of them weren't local. Overnight, the Amber-and-Justin story had mushroomed, attracting the interest of every tabloid newspaper, broadcast magazine, and entertainment show in the country. I didn't even want to think about what Amber had done to arouse such media attention. Maybe she really was planning to be Justin Shay's next wife, or victim, which was pretty much the same thing. He'd have her sign a prenup, and in a year she'd be left with nothing but a tabloid history, a broken heart, and a ruined life.

By the door, Donetta cleared her throat with determination. "Ye-ew just go on ahead and git dressed, and let us handle the rest. Some folks 'round here might not seem like the sharpest knives in the drawer, but I'll stack Daily people up against a bunch of outsiders any day of the we-eek."

She departed in a blur of big hair and red lipstick, leaving behind a cloud of perfume. My cell phone buzzed again, and I grabbed it as a text message came through. Paula. She was in a meeting this morning but she wanted to make sure I was all right.

I messaged a reply while fishing through my suitcase for clothes. *Doing OK. Big shoot today. Overslept. Talk later. Love you—M*

Paula sent back kisses and hugs, and three little words, girlfriend to girlfriend. *Men are scum.*

Apparently Paula's latest internet date hadn't worked out too well, either. When I got back to LA, it would be just Paula and me again, single in the city, eating dinner at some hole-in-the-wall restaurant she'd discovered and bemoaning the fact that the fickle butterfly of true love never seemed to land in our rose garden.

What a depressing idea. I didn't want to go back to hanging out with Paula, whining about the lack of decent, available men in LA in the over-thirty set. I didn't want to be unhappily unengaged. I wanted to rewind four days to Paula and me, jubilantly discussing bridesmaids' dresses and wedding plans over lunch under an umbrella in sunny California. This time, I'd stay away from Madame Murac and her hexed roast beef.

Ah, love awaits. Boy, was she ever wrong.

The phone blurred before my eyes as I checked the list of missed calls. Three from Rodney, my crew chief for the Amber segment, one from a number I didn't recognize, two from Ursula, and one from David early this morning. I thought of David, calling to say good morning, and my heart failed to do the engaged-girl handspring. Instead, it crashed against the pavement and lay bruised. David wasn't who I thought he was.

As soon as the sentence crossed my mind, I realized it wasn't true. David was exactly what I'd always feared he might be—an unsettled, emotionally disconnected, self-focused individual with one bad marriage behind him already. He wasn't looking to form a partnership of hearts and lives; he was looking to take someone into *his* life, without having to give up any part of himself.

The truth was that I'd known it all along. I'd lived in denial for six months. No matter how much I wanted it to be, our relationship wasn't love at first sight. It was two people trying to put together puzzle pieces that didn't fit, trying to ease the fear of growing older alone, lacking the faith to continue searching for that one perfect soul mate in a confusing world of possibilities.

I laid the phone on the vanity, wiped my eyes, and got ready to take a shower. I had to pull myself together before getting on with the business at hand. Rodney's calls undoubtedly meant something was wrong—Rodney didn't call just to vent and issue threats like Ursula did. Right now, the crew would be high in the air, somewhere over the southwest, with their cell phones turned off at the pilot's request.

By the time I exited the shower, the phone was ringing again. Wrapping the towel around myself, I picked it up and answered. The number on the screen was listed as unknown.

"Mandalay Florentino."

"Geez, Ms. Florentino, where've you been?"

"Butch?" The midwestern accent and the use of *Ms. Florentino* immediately revealed the caller's identity. Nobody except Amber, and her hopelessly polite former handler, Butch, ever referred to me as *Ms. Florentino.*

"Yes, ma'am, it's Butch. Where've you been? I've been trying to call you all morning on Rodney's phone."

"You're with the crew?" *Correct me if I'm wrong, but didn't Ursula fire you two days ago?*

"Not anymore. I'm on an air phone now." Leave it to Butch to hopscotch into useless details. Amber and Butch got along so well because they were equally clueless.

"Butch, what's going on? Why are you calling me? Where's Rodney and the crew?"

"They're on their way. I got an earlier flight to Austin. I'm about to land."

"Butch, Ursula said she'd fired you. Why are you flying to Austin?" My mind rushed to sketch out some scenario that made sense.

"I got rehired this morning. Right after they found out Amber'd disappeared."

"Amber did what?" *Please tell me you didn't say disappeared.* "Butch, where's Amber?" The line clicked and filled with static. I clutched my phone tighter, imagining that I could pull Butch through the ether. "Butch, are you there? Where's Amber?"

"Nobody knows. When the limo showed up for her this morning, she wasn't in her hotel room. The desk clerk said she went out the back door last night with her suitcases, and the parking attendant saw her get in a private limo. She left a message at the studio saying she had something to do and she'd be in Daily for the shoot Saturday noon. The paparazzi have gone nuts. I bet there's ten of them on the plane with me. Word on the street is that Justin Shay's private plane left the airport this morning and filed a flight plan for Texas."

Closing the toilet lid, I wrapped the towel tighter and sank down, my wet hair dripping little streams of water down my back. When I caught up with Amber Anderson, I was going to wring her scrawny neck. How could she do this? Didn't she realize how much was riding on this day?

Butch went on talking. "So, Ursula calls me this morning and figures maybe I can find Amber, and the next thing I know, I've got my job back."

"Ursula's in on this?" A tiny, foolish part of me had been clinging to the hope that, since Ursula was in New York for Cal Preston's segment, Amber's disappearance had been kept between Butch, Rodney, and the crew. I should have known better. The crew didn't breathe without first asking Ursula's permission.

"She's on her way . . . to Texas." The words were an apologetic whine. Butch knew that Ursula on her way to anywhere was not good news. He finished with a hopeful, "If she can get a flight out of New York City. They've got bad weather there right now—no planes taking off."

An impossible heaviness settled into my chest. This situation was falling apart faster than I, and the whole town of Daily, Texas, could rake it back together. "Butch, we have to find Amber before Ursula gets here," I said, secretly praying for airline delays, overbooked flights, more inclement weather between here and New York—anything that would delay Ursula's arrival or, better yet, prevent her from arriving altogether. This sweet, sleepy town wasn't ready for Ursula Uberstach, and more important, Ursula wasn't ready for Daily, Texas. The two would collide like opposing storm fronts—hot and cold air clashing somewhere high in the atmosphere, producing a disaster of global proportions. "Butch? . . . Butch? . . . Are you still there?"

He didn't answer. Static overtook the line. Undoubtedly, Butch's plane was coming in for a landing. Maybe he'd get lucky and trip over Amber at the airport.

I tried not to think about where Amber might be as I braced up my sagging moxie and called Ursula's cell number. Cold sweat beaded on my neck and joined the tiny rivers dripping down my back. One ring, two, three. The tidal wave of tension dissolved into a pool of relief when her voice mail picked up. Best to keep the message short and to the point, considering that the details would sound ridiculous. "Mandalay, checking in. Everything's set on location. As soon as Amber gets here, we'll start shooting. I talked to Butch. He thinks he knows where to find her. I'm headed to the location now, but I'll have my cell if you need to contact me." I couldn't think of anything else to say, so I quickly hung up, hoping Ursula was stranded on a tarmac somewhere.

With the obligatory Ursula call out of the way, I hurriedly dressed and prepared for the day. Standing at the mirror, clipping up my hair, still curly and damp, I had a sense of the surreal, as if all of this must be some sort of strange dream—one of those night-mares in which disaster looms and you try to run, but your legs won't move. Surely, any moment I would wake up, gasping for air with my heart pounding. I'd realize none of this was happening, and then I'd lie back down on the bed and wait for the morning to melt into focus.

The hinges next door squealed as Carter went into his room. Exiting the bathroom, I stood momentarily in the alcove. For an instant, I felt warm and settled. My cell phone rang again, and I answered it, thinking of Butch.

David was on the other end. I could hear an engine revving as he said hello. He was probably on the highway somewhere up the coast, headed for the posh party of his female client.

"Hey, baby," he yelled. "Hang on, let me roll up the window."

I waited for the background noise to quiet. Even after it had, I didn't know what to say.

David was in a talkative mood. He usually was when business had gone well, or when we were out on the boat. When David was in his element, he had the charisma of a politician and the charm of a Casanova. "Tried to call you earlier this morning. How's the Texas job going? Think you'll be home by Sunday? The boat's ready for a day out."

For a nanosecond, I considered not saying anything about Paula or *Mydestiny.com*. Part of me wanted to just leave things as they were, forget the past, concentrate on the future.

What kind of a future can you build on lies, Mandalay? I knew it was true. Any future David and I built would be like the biblical house constructed on sand.

"David, I have to ask you something important."

"Yeah? More wedding stuff?"

I took a deep breath, then let the words rush out. "No. Not about the wedding. I want to know why you still have a profile on *Mydestiny.com." Please, please don't lie this time. Please tell me the truth.*

He paused and I heard the car downshift. The engine quieted to a mild rumble. "Oh, that's old. No big deal."

Closing my eyes, I leaned against the wall, slid slowly down beside my computer, and flipped up the screen. The computer exited sleep mode and there was David's profile, still frozen in time from the night before. "Don't lie to me!" My voice echoed through the room. "It's not old, David. You're still answering inquiries to your profile. You answered an inquiry *last night*, for heaven's sake. How could you do that? How could you be trolling for dates online when our wedding is less than three months away?" The last words came out in a sob. Pressing a hand over my eyes, I tried to stop the tears from coming. I shouldn't have started this conversation. I should have waited. If Donetta came for me now, or if Ursula or Butch or Rodney called, I'd be a basket case.

David didn't answer. The car rumbled at idle, and I heard the whoosh of other vehicles passing by. Clearly, he'd pulled over to concentrate on coming up with an answer. "You were checking up on me?" He had the nerve to sound offended, as if *I* had invaded *his* space.

"In between traveling, working, and trying to arrange a location shoot?" I spat, pushing up the walls around my heart. "No, David, I wasn't checking up on you. I didn't think I had to. But since I did find out my fiancé is online looking for dates, why don't you just tell me the truth? How about the truth for a change?"

He took time to compose an answer. In the delay, my hopes sank further, seeped out of me, and pooled on the uneven wood floor. "It doesn't mean anything."

It doesn't mean anything? "Of course it means something, David. The question is what? What does it mean?"

"It's just . . . I'm a little more . . . skittish than you. We're at different points in life, Manda. I've been down this road before. I just wanted to . . . be sure."

"To be sure of what, David? To be sure you wanted to marry me? To be sure there wasn't something better out there? To line up your next sailing partner? What?"

"No . . . Yes . . . I don't know, Manda." He sighed, a slow, resigned sound, as if he'd known all along this moment would come. "I'm forty years old, Manda. I wanted to be sure I was ready to get married again. I know that things don't always . . . work out. I'm not some starry-eyed kid who believes in love at first sight, soul mates, and all the storybook stuff."

There it was, in a nutshell. Cards on the table. Nothing left hidden. This was it. The end. Opposite priorities. Irreconcilable differences. "The problem is that I do believe in it, David. I don't want someone who's just with me until things get a little too difficult, or something better comes along, or marriage isn't as much fun as it used to be. I want the real thing— for better or worse, rich, poor, sickness, health, forever and ever, amen."

"Manda . . ." he said softly.

"I have to go," I whispered. "I'm sorry, David. Don't bother calling me back. I won't answer."

"Manda, wait . . ."

"I can't, David. There's no point in waiting. There's no point in hashing it over again and again and again, or trying to explain. Don't you see? If you have to try to make it happen, it isn't real. You and I were never real. You obviously knew that all along, and now I guess I know it, too. We were just looking for . . . security, someone to be with, but I'm done playing let's pretend. I don't want to be with someone who's just looking for any port in a storm. I want to be with someone who wants to be with me forever. Anything else isn't good enough. Good-bye, David. It's over." Hanging up the phone, I curled my knees to my chest, rested my chin on them, and stared out the window at the cloudless Texas sky. Strangely enough, I didn't cry. I just sat and quietly waited.

By the time Butch called again to tell me he was on the ground in Austin, I'd stopped trying to figure out how my private life had become such a mess. The only thing to do now was focus on my job—prove to myself and the rest of the world that I wasn't the dewy-eyed idiot David thought I was.

Unfortunately, Butch had no idea where to find Amber. He'd tried to call her cell phone, but she wasn't answering, even for him. Reports were that Justin Shay's private plane had landed at a Vegas airport after having mechanical problems. Amber and Justin had been spotted briefly in Vegas, and speculation about a quickie marriage ran wild. The pair had left the city sometime during the night, pulling a clever switcheroo involving another private plane. They were headed to Texas, or were already here. No one knew for sure.

Butch had gained all of this information from a TV in the airport bookstore. The media were wild over the gospel good girl and the aging Hollywood bad boy. The right picture of the new Mr. and Mrs. Shay would be worth millions.

As we talked, I eased toward the window and peeked out. The street was clogged with vehicles of all sizes, cables, satellite dishes, monitors, receivers, reporters, and countless photographers, heavy laden with cameras and zoom lenses.

I peeked around the curtain, and at least a dozen lenses turned my way. Jumping back, I stood against the wall. "Butch, it's insane here. Whatever you do, don't come into town." It occurred to me that, with the aid of modern technology, people outside could even be listening to my cell conversation. I'd produced a morning news segment on wireless eavesdropping devices two years ago. "Butch? We shouldn't talk any more on this line right now. Call Rodney and tell him to strictly follow the directions in my email from last night."

"All right, Ms. Florentino. I'm on the mission." Butch's voice held an edge of excitement. "I just picked up a car and I'm headed out. I've got an idea. There's a place Amber told me about—somewhere she went to get away from everything. I think I can find it. She said . . ."

"Butch!" I cut him off, emphatically. "Don't tell me any more." What were the odds that Butch could actually track down Amber? "I'll try to call you back on a land line later. In the meantime, call Rodney. Tell him what I said."

"Roger, Captain. Over and out." Butch hung up. At least one of us was having fun.

Carefully avoiding the window, I moved to the alcove between my room and Carter's and knocked on the door. "Carter, I was wondering if I could borrow the phone. I can come around and get . . ."

To my surprise, the door lock clicked, the adjoining door opened, and there stood Carter, surrounded by Care Bears.

I glanced down at the lock, shocked to find out that he'd had the key in his possession all along. Had I known that on the first night of my stay, I wouldn't have slept at all.

"The front door key opens it on my side," he said sheepishly. "I thought you'd probably rather not know that until after I left."

Glancing past him, I noted the packed suitcases and the blue gorilla, ready for travel. The gorilla smiled happily at me, and a rush of remembered emotions came back. "You're not leaving . . ." The words surprised me as much as the realization that I didn't want him to go. I wondered if this was some sort of knee-jerk reaction to my breakup with David.

Glancing at the suitcase, he nodded. "I only had the room for two nights. Truth be told, you were supposed to have the whole suite all along. Now you'll have a phone *and* your own light switch." He smiled, and warmth slid over my skin like a thick, soft blanket. He was wearing a walkathon T-shirt from some hospital in Nashville, faded jeans, and cowboy boots. The azure shirt made his eyes an even deeper shade of blue. The first thing I'd noticed about him were his eyes.

"I don't mind. You can have the room. I just need the phone for a minute." I wondered what had come over me. I was acting like a heartsick schoolgirl, dumped by one boyfriend and looking for someone else to give me a class ring.

"A little too crowded around here for me." Shrugging toward the window, he leaned against the doorframe, crossed one leg over the other, and looked down at his boots, then back at me, his eyes twinkling mischievously. "It's been fun, though."

"It has been fun." All at once, I realized that was true. In spite of the setbacks, the work-related disasters, and the collapse of my personal life, I'd had more fun these last two days with Carter than in the previous six months put together. Carter was easy to spend time with. He had a relaxed way of dealing with people that was natural and comfortable. "Thanks for saving me from the ghost, helping me steal nachos, and talking me into the roller coaster. I know I probably wasn't very good company. It's been kind of a tough weekend."

A one-sided grin sketched a dimple on his cheek. "You were good company."

I scoffed at the compliment, then blushed. "Thanks for putting up with me."

"It isn't a hard job." He pushed away from the doorframe, preparing to leave, then he hesitated there, the smile fading, as if he might say something more. Finally, he shook his head and backed a few steps into his room. "Sure you don't want to trade the fish for the gorilla? Last chance."

I wondered what he'd been about to say before he'd brought up last night's carnival prizes. "You can have both. Maybe your nieces will have fun with the fish." Moving to the table, I balanced the Ziploc bag against a lamp and poured the fish into its travel container.

When I came back, Carter and the gorilla were waiting in the doorway, smiling at me, side by side. "Nah. I can only go for a fair trade. Give a little, get a little. It keeps the balance even."

I was struck by the comment, by the simple decency in it.

"Besides," he added, "if I bring the girls one more stuffed animal, their mom'll hang me. The fish, I might get by with. The fish is small."

I pictured him presenting the fish, my fish, to his nieces as they waited for their father to come home from the hospital, and my heart felt light. "I'd have to know where to check on the welfare of the fish."

His eyes met mine, and he raised a curious brow at the blatant request for contact information. The comment surprised me, as well. It was completely uncharacteristic, but I didn't care. Something inside me couldn't bear the idea of Carter simply walking out the door, never to be heard from again. I wanted to know where he was. I wanted to know whether his brother recovered, whether his three little nieces would grow up with a father.

A knock on the hallway door startled both of us. "Amanda-Lee? Amanda-Lee?" The door creaked open and Donetta's voice echoed through the room. "Ye-ew ready, hon? It's time. The mail wagon's down . . ." Before I could react, she was standing in the alcove, looking at Carter and me with no small amount of surprise. Taking in the gorilla and the fish, she frowned apologetically. "I forgot that key unlocks the center door, too. I'm sorry about thay-ut. I hope it didn't cause any—" blushing, she looked away for a moment—"problems."

"Not a one," Carter answered. "We were just about to make a trade."

Poking a long red fingernail through her puffy helmet of hair, Donetta scratched her head, then shrugged. "Well, thay-ut's real nice. It surely is." Squinting speculatively at Carter and me, she tapped the red fingernail to her lips. "Carter, hon, ye-ew in a big rush today? You think you might-could spare a few hours to help with somethin' rea-ul important?"

The trade would have to wait.

Carter shrugged good-naturedly. "I'm sure I could—unless you're going to ask me to go down there and help Buddy Ray with crowd control. I wouldn't take that on, even for you, darlin'."

Giggling, Donetta fanned her face, her cheeks turning red. "Oh, I declare, you are such a flirt. If I was forty years younger and not married, you'd have trouble on your hands." She glanced pointedly at me.

I blushed and looked away, wondering what in the world Donetta had up her sleeve. Clearly, this conversation was leading somewhere.

Donetta turned her attention back to Carter. "Hon, can you drive a stick shift diesel pickup and a four-horse slant trailer with a dressing room up front, because we got a little problem this afternoon. . . ."

All at once, Donetta's intentions became clear. Whether he wanted to be or not, Carter had just been drafted into the Daily, Texas, version of *Mission Impossible*.

Chapter 18

Imagene Doll

Seems like it never fails that when you're expecting company, something will go wrong. From the time Donetta called in the morning, it was one mishap after another. My old vacuum picked that very day to break down, so the boys and I had to sweep the floors the old-fashioned way and shake the rugs off the back porch. While we were out there, I noticed that the flower beds were a mess. I was trying to decide if there was anything we could do about it when my neighbor with the horse-hauling rig stopped by on his way to take his wife to the hospital to have their baby a week sooner than expected. He dropped off the keys to his truck and trailer and said Magnolia was waiting in his corral, but he couldn't be there to help us load her up. No sooner did he leave than Jack Junior called, and he was all in a stew because he'd seen the commotion in Daily on the news. He wanted to make sure I didn't get in my car and drive into that mess. I told him I was fine and he shouldn't worry, but he felt the need to keep me on the phone and chat a while anyway.

By the time I got off the phone, the Anderson boys had disappeared into the yard. When I went out, there they were, Andy trimming the bushes and the other two hard at work with the rake and the hoe. They'd spotted some bluebonnets and Indian blanket flowers blooming out in the pasture, and bless their hearts, they'd dug up a wheelbarrow full to plant in the flower beds.

It'd been a long time since little boys brought me flowers from the field, and I stood there on the porch, wanting to cry, because it touched me so. I didn't, though, because I figured it might scare the boys. They really were such good children—hard working, quiet, and sweet. They deserved a better life than they had.

Brother Harve and O.C. showed up in Harve's old Pontiac with Verl in the back, covered in hay, stinking of whiskey, and still wearing his dirty, paint-covered clothes from the day before. I wanted to grab him by the neck and shake him around until he thought twice before he took one more swallow of whiskey. At that particular moment, I think I could have done it. I was filled with what Brother Ervin called *righteous fever*. Any kind feelings I'd had toward Verl the day before were gone. I was holding the garden shovel, and I had a mind to do some rebukin' right across his skinny rear end. *Donetta gives him a day's honest work and this is how he spends the money. Imagine!*

Brother Harve was a lot nicer about it all than I would have been. He and Otis Charles got Verl out of the car real gentle-like and brought him up the walk, Verl stumbling along on O.C.'s shoulder, with his legs dragging and his head lolling on his neck. I started to send the boys inside, but before I could say anything, Avery ran up, gave the old drunk a hug, and said, "Hey, Peepaw, look at the flowers we dug up. We didn't hurt anything. They was just growin' out in the pasture."

Verl swished his lips around and blinked, trying to make out the flowers, which I'm sure he was seeing double or triple of. "Them's shhr-real nice, Aaa-ve-eee," he slurred, then leaned forward and planted a big whiskey kiss atop Avery's head. Staggering, he put his hand on Avery's shoulder, using the boy as a brace to steady himself. He had the nerve to grin at me with tobacco hanging all over his nasty teeth. "Mmm-mor-nnnin', Mmmiii-zzz Doll."

I'll good morning you, you filthy old drunk. I wanted to rip his hand off Avery's shoulder, tell O.C. and Brother Harve to let him fall in the flower bed and leave him there with the worms, the way he deserved.

Verl let his head sag forward, like all this talking was too much effort.

"We better take him inside and get him a bath," I told O.C. Being as there were kids and a pastor present, I didn't say the things that really should've been said. The idea of helping get that old fart undressed and in my shower was about more than I could stand. Maybe we could just stuff him in, clothes and all—wash everything at once.

I turned to head up the porch steps, and all of a sudden, there was Andy. "I've got it, Mrs. Doll," he said, then took O.C.'s place underneath Verl's arm. "I know how it works best. Y'all just go ahead and do the flowers." Pulling Verl away from Brother Harve, Andy said, "Come on, Peepaw," and started up the steps, cradling Verl's flopping head with his own.

Standing there on the walk, I felt myself shrinking smaller and smaller. Even after Andy had disappeared through the screen door, I could still see him, gently carrying that old man up the stairs with the kind of love that bears all things and keeps no account of wrongs.

Sometimes it ain't the drunk or the sinner who needs a shovel across the rear, it's the ones who could quote you chapter and verse about grace, but don't hand it out. The next time I got the urge to rebuke, I was gonna think of Andy and remind myself that love covers over a multitude of sins. In point of fact, it covers over them all.

Brother Harve clapped his hands together and rocked back on his heels, looking at the flower beds. "Well, how about we get this yard in order, boys?" His big, deep voice made the sentence sound like the benediction of a sermon. "O.C., you go out in the shed and see if you can get the lawnmower goin'." He waved toward the driveway and the yard. "Mow the tops off that spear grass and get it all in shape for Mrs. Doll."

"Y'all don't have to do all that, Brother Harve," I said, embarrassed to have someone else's pastor cleaning my yard. "The boys and I were trying to tidy it up a little, that's all."

Brother Harve just smiled, picked up a bluebonnet plant, and held it tenderly in his hands. "We'd be pleased, Mrs. Doll, truly pleased. I'm sure I can't think of a better use for a fine Saturday morning than to plant flowers in good soil. You just go on and attend to whatever you need to in the house." He turned his attention to the boys. "Now, dig those holes deep, boys. There's a certain way you've got to plant wild flowers for them to take root."

I went in the house to find some things for Verl to wear after he got cleaned up. All of Jack's clothes were still in the closet. Every time my kids had asked me about cleaning them out, I said I wasn't ready. But there was no sense in that stuff sitting there when Verl needed something to wear. Jack would get a kick out of old Verl dressed up in his clothes. Everything would be too big, but at least the clothes would be clean.

In the bathroom, I heard Andy talking to his granddad real gentle-like, helping him get undressed and climb into the bath, taking care of him just like Verl was a little baby. It was pretty clear that Andy did that a lot. Amber probably had, too, before she left. I couldn't imagine being just a youngster, having to take care of the person who was supposed to be taking care of you. Widow or not, I'd lived a pretty fortunate life. Maybe that was why the Lord had let me lose Jack sooner than I planned—so I'd have a few years to learn about struggles on my own.

When Verl sobered up, maybe I'd have a talk with him. Maybe there was something I could do or say that might make a difference.

I thought on the problem as I went down the hall and into our closet. All Jack's things were still lined up in neat rows. I could picture him in that closet, could say what day of the week he might wear each outfit—suit for Sunday, trousers and a shirt on the weekends. If he planned to take a ride on our old horse, Magnolia, or if the rodeo was in town, he'd wear his plaid cowboy shirt and those black polyester western pants he'd bought at the Cheyenne Frontier Days in 1974. The kids were ashamed to be seen with him in those.

Thinking back to the old times, I chuckled to myself. Seemed like it was only yesterday. A life goes by fast. Maybe that was what I'd tell Verl. Maybe I could make him see that those three little boys outside would be grown and gone before he knew it, and the way things were going, none of them would have much worth remembering.

Maybe after the rodeo today I'd keep old Magnolia at home instead of taking her back to the neighbor's house. It'd be good to see her in the pasture again, and maybe the Anderson boys would like to come over and feed her and take her for rides. Every boy ought to have the chance to get on a horse and head out to pasture and pretend he's a cowboy or a Knight of the Round Table.

I started to pull out a pair of overalls, but then I thought about that article in *The National Examiner* and the picture of the bearded gun-toting hillbilly they wanted everyone to think was Amber's grandpa. I thought of that spiky-haired reporter in town asking nasty questions about Amber. It wouldn't do for Verl to go on TV today in old gardening clothes. I was going to pick out the best thing Jack had that might fit. By the time I got done with Verl, those reporters wouldn't know him from the justice of the peace. If I had to put ten gallons of coffee down him, I'd get him sober, as well. After the boys finished with the flower bed, I'd give them a little spit-shine, too. When Amber got here, they'd look just as respectable as the Downtown Browns. Then let those reporters try to say what backwater white trash Amber came from.

I pulled out a suit first, a black one Jack wore for weddings, funerals, and Easter Sunday. Even if I could get Verl into that, with his old wrinkled face and pasty skin, he'd look like a corpse in need of a coffin. He should have something with some color . . . something bright that would make him look lively.

Lord have mercy, was there anything that could make Verl look lively? Maybe I was expecting too much from a change of clothes.

I settled on the pastel-colored golf shirt and pants the girls at the office gave to Jack for a joke at his retirement party. Taking the clothes with me, I went and knocked on the bathroom door. "Andy, just let your granddad soak in there a minute, and I'll have some clean clothes for him to wear," I said. "What size shoe does he take?" Shoes might be a problem. Jack was a size twelve, double E. No way Verl was a twelve.

"He says about a nine," Andy answered, then he asked something else of his grandpa. I tried to hear Verl's answer, to decide if he was getting any more sober, but I couldn't make it out clear enough. I'd just have to hope for the best. There might be some old tennis shoes in the closets of the boys' rooms. Grabbing Verl's coveralls, I measured up the inseam, then hurried to my sewing machine and tacked up the new pants.

When I came back to the bathroom door, Andy told me that sometime while Verl was passed out, he'd soiled his underwear and he'd need a new pair. Andy said it just like it was an everyday matter. As I went to Jack's bureau for some clean socks and underwear, I thought about poor Andy. I bet sometimes he wished he could just do the things a normal fifteen-year-old boy did.

No wonder Amber was trying so hard to win *American Megastar*. There wasn't much waiting for her here. All these years, I'd let myself believe it was charity enough to buy blackberries from the Anderson kids, or teach them in vacation Bible school, or offer a ride home when their granddad left them stranded at a football game. What a lazy, foolish notion that was.

When I brought Andy the clean underwear, Verl started to get ugly. He wanted boxers instead of briefs, of all things. The thought of seeing Verl Anderson's pickled body in either one was enough to give me the hives, but I cracked the door a bit anyhow and poked my nose close to the opening. "Verl Anderson, you stop giving that boy trouble and put them clothes on right now, you hear me? You don't have them clothes on in three minutes, I'm gonna come in there and put 'em on you myself. And you ain't gonna like it."

Verl sputtered, then stood up and thumped around the bathroom. He hacked up a big nasty cough, then I heard him sit back down on the pot. "Them ain't ssshmy drrrawers!" he roared. "I ain't wearin-iin' shomeone elshe's drrrawers."

Well, heaven's gates, there was Verl Anderson in my bathroom, worried about hygiene. "Them drawers are clean, Verl. Now you get them on or I'm comin' in there." I wanted to add, *You soiled your drawers, Verl. You got fallin'-out drunk and soiled your drawers like a little child. Aren't you ashamed of yourself?*

Verl muttered something to Andy, and I rattled the doorknob just to give him a good scare. "I mean it. This is your last warnin'." I felt like it was thirty years ago and I was trying to get the boys out the door for church.

Verl grumbled some more, but I could hear Andy helping his grandpa into the clothes. Finally, the door opened and there sat Verl atop the pot, red in the face from all the work but looking almost human. The shirt hung over his frame like a coat on a rack, and the pants were too big, but it wasn't so bad. A belt, some shoes, a shave, and about ten cups of coffee, and we'd be in business.

I reached in the drawer and grabbed a comb to do something with Verl's hair. I'd long since thrown away Jack's old tubes of fixative, so I took my Aqua Net out of the cabinet instead.

Verl shied away. "You ain't shprayin' that shtuff in my hair!"

He couldn't go far, being hemmed in between the toilet and tub, so I just went on with what I was doing. "Oh, yes I am. You might as well shut your mouth or it's gonna get in there, too, and your teeth'll stick shut." Not a bad idea, actually. "I get done with you, Verl Anderson, you're gonna make Amber proud." Dousing Verl's head, I started through his thick gray hair with the comb. "Land sakes, Verl, when's the last time you had a real haircut? You need to come by the Hair and Body."

Verl's head flopped back and he gave me a hateful look through one glassy blue-gray eye. "I ain't got no monnn-ey for no hairrr-cut." The words hung in a cloud of whiskey breath that was at least eighty proof.

I wanted to say, *Well, if you'd stay away from The Junction, you'd have enough for a cut and shave, now wouldn't ya?* But instead, I said, "I'm sure Donetta would trade it out for some more work around the building. There's a lot still needs to be done there."

Verl opened both eyes and looked at me like somewhere in that foggy brain of his, the idea was trying to take root.

"There's lots of folks need work done." I gave Verl a few more sprays with the Aqua Net. Verl had a nice head of hair, actually. "Like me, just as a for instance. All this mess around the yard and the barn, not to mention keeping up the flower beds. I can't do all that at my age. Maybe Andy, Amos, and Avery could come and help me some. Maybe you could, too. I want to plow and plant the garden patch this year. I miss having my fresh vegetables. Maybe you and the boys could come do that for me, and then when the vegetables come up, I'd do the canning and we'd split what we get. Maybe we could do that."

Verl blinked hard. "I like themmm home-canned tom-maters. Shhhtore-bought ain't the same thhh-ing."

"That's a fact," I said, and a little lightness came over me. I could picture how me and the boys, and even Verl, could grow a garden this summer.

"Merna cannn-ed them to-mmmaters real good." Merna, Verl's wife, had run off with another man way back when Amber's daddy was a teenager. Verl fell apart after she took off and left him with a child to raise.

"I'd sure can some tomatoes for you," I told Verl. He tipped his head back, and I wagged the comb in his face. "But I'll tell you somethin' else. You start that garden and don't keep it tended, you're gonna have one mad woman on your hands." Setting down the comb, I fished a plastic razor out of the drawer and held it ready. "If you're coming here, you clean yourself up and shave. You ever show up at my house in this kind of condition again, you're gonna think them boiled, skinned, and packed tomatoes has a pretty easy life."

Verl's jaw dropped open, and I took advantage of the opportunity to throw some soap on there and start shaving. By the time I finished, he didn't look half bad.

"Help me get him downstairs for some food and coffee," I told Andy. He'd been standing quiet the whole time, leaning against the wall with his hands in his pockets and his chin ducked. I wanted to tell him to hold his head up. All this trouble with Verl wasn't his fault, but you can't convince a kid of that.

"Yes, ma'am," Andy said, then moved around me and got under Verl's shoulder. "In the kitchen?"

"That'll be fine," I answered, and checked my watch. In a little over an hour, the TV crew was supposed to be showing up. I hoped the mail wagon would get here soon with Amanda-Lee, and I hoped Donetta had found us a driver for the horse rig. With everyone busy at the Reunion Days, it wouldn't be so easy.

While I rustled up a belt and some shoes, Andy helped Verl, smelling better and not weaving around as much as before, down the stairs. By the time I got to the kitchen, he was slumped in a chair, his eyes closed like he was all wore out.

Andy put his hands back in his pockets, looked at the floor, and frowned. "I'm sorry, Mrs. Doll."

"Andy"—the word come out so sharp that Andy jerked upright—"this ain't your fault one little bit, and don't you forget that. Your granddad's a grown man, and he ought to know better than to get like this." I glared at Verl, but he just rolled his head to one side, so I focused on Andy instead. "You don't worry about a thing. I'll get him woke up and acting like he should. You just go on outside and help Brother Harve and Otis Charles with the flower beds. When those Hollywood people get here, you hold your head up, you hear? You're a good boy. Not every young man would take care of his granddad the way you do, and look after his brothers, and help an old woman with her flower bed without a complaint. Lots of those kids you go to school with that come drivin' in with the fancy cars their daddies bought, if they got asked to do something for somebody else, they'd act like it was the end of the world."

Andy looked at me for a minute, chewing his lip, his blue eyes thoughtful under the mop of blond hair. "It ain't hard fixing flower beds," he said finally. "I'd help you with the garden this summer. I'm getting my driver's license next month. I could bring Amos and Avery." He gave a glance toward his granddad—sort of a sad, hopeless look, like he knew Verl wouldn't be sobering up and appearing at my door with a rake and a hoe anytime soon.

"Andy, we're *all* gonna work on that garden this summer," I told him, and I meant it. If I had to sit on Verl's head and drive him by the ears until he sweated ninety proof all over my yard, I was gonna make it happen. "Just don't you worry. I'll see to it."

Andy smiled like he believed maybe I could, then he turned and went out the door, whistling a little tune under his breath.

Chapter 19

Mandalay Florentino

The mail wagon was clearly not built for passengers. The cargo compartment of the remodeled army jeep was filled with mail containers, packages of all sizes, two huge rolls of what appeared to be plastic sheeting, aluminum cans gathered from the side of the road, and a supply of dog biscuits in blue buckets marked Small and Large. Some of the dog biscuits had spilled, so that the floor was a crunchy mixture of dog food and dribbled soda pop. A skinny black kitten was moving warily around the compartment, licking dried soda and eating crumbles of dog biscuit. In the cab up front, a basset hound scratched at the sliding window and licked his chops, hoping to make a meal of the kitten. When it wasn't searching for food, the kitten arched and hissed at the dog.

"Sorry about the animals," the postman, Harlan Hanson, apologized as he ushered Carter and me into the back with the kitten. "Sheriff's wife called and said her dog, Flash, was on the lam again, and if I saw him, could I pick him up and drop him back at home?

The little cat was stuck in a cardboard box out by the county line. So far he and Flash ain't gettin' along too good."

Picking up the kitten as Carter and I climbed into the cargo area, the mailman examined it momentarily, then handed it to me, saying, "Here. He's a skittish little thing." Then he shut the tailgate as we perched atop the plastic mail containers. Checking the lock, he rapped twice on the window, which was opaque with dust. "Stay down and hang on," he ordered before moving to the driver's seat. The vehicle started with a cough and a wheeze, and muted light flooded the compartment as the auto shop owner threw open the garage door. We squealed backward onto the street, did a *Miami Vice*–style one-eighty, and sped down the alley, honking while dodging obstacles and news crews. A hail of obscenities flew after us, and in the cab, Harlan yelled, "Yeeeeeee-haw! Take that, you nosy buggers!" as we fishtailed onto the street.

The kitten dug into my arm until finally I pulled him loose and tucked him in my lap atop the Prada handbag that only days ago had been one of my major concerns. Now the Prada seemed like a shallow symbol, a trapping I'd hoped would make me into something I wasn't.

The mail wagon whipped around a corner and flew over what felt like a speed bump. The cat, the Prada, and I went airborne and landed mostly in Carter's lap. A second turn sent the Prada rolling to the floor, where it fell with a dull thud into a puddle of goo. Carter's arm caught my waist, saving me from the floor, and we hovered in what might have been a romantic clutch if not for the cat squalling between us.

The postman opened the sliding window, and Flash stuck his head through, barking. Cat claws went through my bra, into my skin.

"We got a few on our tail," the postman hollered over Flash's barking. "I'm gonna slow down and do some deliveries. By the time we run the riverside loop and drop Flash at home, they'll git bored and move on. Y'all just lay low back there and keep out of sight."

Both Carter and I glanced at the dust-coated back window. Not much chance of anyone seeing through that.

"Hit the deck!" the postman hollered. "They're comin' around the front."

Carter and I fell back against the rolls of plastic, with the cat suspended spread-eagle between us.

Sucking in a breath, Carter pulled his shirt, and the cat's claws, away from his chest. Overhead, the window slid shut, Flash quieted to a dull whine behind the glass, and the vehicle slowed.

"I bet you're wondering what you've gotten yourself into," I said, carefully unhooking the kitten from my beautiful periwinkle silk summer sweater, another designer leftover from Wardrobe. The vehicle rolled along the roadside, moving in the slow stop and go of mail delivery.

"The thought did cross my mind." Carter's attention strayed to the kitten. Holding it and his shirt suspended in one hand, he rolled onto his side and braced an elbow, waiting patiently for me to break the link between us or for the kitten to relax, whichever came first. "All I caught on the way downstairs was that Amber Anderson's on her way to town and we're headed somewhere to meet up with her before the horde of reporters finds her. Somehow, there's a gravel truck and a horse trailer involved. I don't quite have that part figured out yet."

"You're probably better off not knowing," I said, and he chuckled. I felt the warmth of his breath on my neck, and a tingle slid over my skin. Our position suddenly seemed intimate, cozy despite the bouncing packages and the kitten. It should have felt strange being here with him, but it didn't. "If I told you the plan, I'd have to kill you."

Repositioning his hand, he held the cat a little closer to me. "You could just swear me to secrecy." The words were warm and comforting, like a promise. Somehow, even lying on a roll of sheeting in the back of a mail truck, not knowing where he was headed, he oozed confidence—not the arrogant sort, but the kind that made me feel like the day would somehow turn out all right.

The next thing I knew, I was sharing the plan, including the fact that, right now, Amber was AWOL and my tyrannical boss was headed this way. "So now my life is in the hands of a twenty-four-year-old college intern who's been fired once already and thinks he knows where Amber might be," I finished, thinking that for all any of us knew, Amber could be halfway across the country right now, or halfway across the world, getting married to Justin Shay in Paris, Rome, or back in Vegas at the Love Me Tender Chapel, tying the knot as an Elvis impersonator crooned "Wedding Song." They could honeymoon in the Beulah suite, all three of them. I wouldn't need it once Ursula—

"It's not your life, Mandalay." I felt Carter's words as much as I heard them. "It's just your job. There's a difference."

The tide of my emotions turned abruptly, like a rogue wave striking shore, then slowly draining back out to sea. Carter was right. Whether we bagged the Amber Anderson segment today or not, the sun would still rise tomorrow. "You're right," I said, feeling shallow and artificial, a Hollywood girl who'd built the core of my existence on superficial things. Compared to what Carter's family was going through, a job failure didn't amount to much.

Suddenly humbled, I pretended to be busy working the cat claws out of my sweater.

"I'm not lecturing," he said softly. "It's just that this last year has opened my eyes a little, made me realize how easy it is to get . . . caught up in things." I imagined his face as he said those words—the subtle play of light and shadow, the earnestness in his eyes. "When something happens like what's happened to Chris, you don't have any choice but to quit fighting the sails and let the wind move the boat—drift on faith for a while."

I looked up at him, felt myself being drawn in by his close-ness, by something else I couldn't explain. *Drift on faith*. Amber had rehearsed a song with that line in it for show number eight. It was a metaphorical tune about little boys building leaf-and-twig ships and sending them down the river, dreaming of where the wind and the water would take them. I'd closed my eyes and just listened as Amber's voice filled the rehearsal room, weaving a story of childhood dreams, of growing up, losing yourself to the world, then searching for the truths of your own soul.

Amber's voice coach vetoed the number, saying it was too soft and the judges wouldn't like it. That week, Amber sang "Wind Be-neath My Wings" instead. She dedicated it to her brothers. There wasn't a dry eye in the house, and the judges loved her. Even so, I wished she'd performed the song about the boats.

"Here," Carter said, handing me the kitten as it relaxed and released its hold on his T-shirt. "I think it likes you better." He glanced toward the window as the kitten curled up on my chest and started purring. The vehicle had stopped. Up front, the post-man was trying to convince Flash to disembark.

I stroked the kitten, still thinking about Amber and the song. I realized now that I had wanted Amber to sing that song not be-cause it displayed a particularly outstanding vocal range or ability, but because the lyrics were capable of evoking emotion, of making people think. Amber's one true advantage in the competition was that despite all of her shortcomings, she had a sense of purpose deeper than just winning a million-dollar recording contract and making herself a star. She wanted to say something to people. She wanted to make a difference.

I suddenly knew why I'd been pulling for Amber all season, even though her naïveté was such a liability. Once upon a time, I was the girl who believed one person could make a difference. I was going to take the news business by storm, rise to the top, use my power to expose wrongdoing, stamp out hatred, promote understanding, end homelessness, improve education for LA's inner-city kids. Back then, the list was endless. Every story was personal to me, every job advancement a chance to have a bigger impact, move a step closer to my goal.

When had the goal become just about advancement and not about changing the world? What had happened to the idealistic schoolgirl who felt an inner calling? When had my life become a quest to prove that I'd left behind the shy, knobby-legged, imperfect little sister with the Coke-bottle glasses and the big ideas? Somewhere during the past few years, I'd forgotten the things that girl dreamed of. I'd convinced myself she and I were not the same person and the sense of inner fulfillment she yearned for didn't matter.

I'd let my boat drift into a tiny whirlpool of self—self-need, self-doubt, self-satisfaction, self-advancement. I'd surrounded myself with an ocean of people who spun in their own little pools, who made me feel all right about my life.

The truth was that I was drowning in my self-created vortex, and that was why, when Amber had drifted by, I'd grabbed on without wanting to, without meaning to, without even realizing it, really. I wanted someone, something, to pull me out of the pointless spin. Amber was a breath of fresh air, a person motoring along on a direct, if somewhat naïve, and lofty course, following a calling.

"This segment seemed like a chance to make a difference," I admitted quietly, focusing on the kitten and not on Carter. "I wanted to come through for Amber and her family because they need the break, because Amber's music is about more than just hitting the recording-contract jackpot. But the truth is, I also needed it for me. I needed this job to count for something." It seemed strange to admit something so close to the center, so newly realized and fragile. Carter would probably laugh. He'd think I was kidding, considering that I worked in reality TV. Hardly the place for such idealistic talk.

He reached across the space between us and scratched the kitten, his hand touching mine. "It'll work." As usual, he spoke as though he believed it, believed he could find Amber, defeat a horde of reporters and paparazzi, and make the show turn out all right just because he said so.

I turned my hand over and his fingers interlaced with mine. It felt natural, as if my hand were created to fit perfectly in his. I looked into his eyes and felt myself falling. The whirlwind of thoughts in my mind, the shifting packages, the gentle rumble of the engine idling, even the purring kitten seemed far away. "Thanks for coming," I whispered.

"I wouldn't have missed it." The words seemed intimate. His face grew contemplative, as if something were on his mind and he was trying to decide whether to say it.

I wanted to know what he was thinking.

Up front, the truck door slammed. Carter and I jerked upright like a couple of teenagers caught making out. The window slid open and the postman poked his head through. "All righty, now we're on our own. Y'all dig in your spurs and hang on, because we're runnin' late and I'm gonna take the back way. It'll be a bumpy ride down about five miles of dirt road." Closing the window, he revved the engine and we left town behind in a squeal of burning rubber, the jeep whipping around corners and up and down hills like a San Francisco taxicab, while Carter, the cat, and I bounced and rattled around in the back.

By the time we reached our destination, I was starting to feel sick, the package compartment was filled with a fine haze of dust, and the kitten was stuck to my sweater again. When the postman opened the door, Carter and I tumbled out unceremoniously. The kitten jumped for solid ground and made a break for it, bolting through a newly planted flower bed and disappearing under a white two-story farmhouse that was just as I'd hoped it would be. Blinking in the sunlight, I took in the old red barn, the aged whitewashed fence around the yard, the towering, twisted live oaks with their long branches starting high on the trunks and bending toward the ground. I suddenly felt better about the day. If we could find Amber, my plans just might work out after all. So far, I hadn't heard from Ursula, which meant she was still en route somewhere. With any luck, we could have this thing bagged before she found her way here.

Overhead, the cloudless April sky seemed to promise that everything would turn out all right.

The cell phone rang in my purse, and I rushed to dig it out as Harlan headed toward the front porch, looking for Imagene. Carter wandered a few steps away to study an old iron-wheeled tractor that was sitting like a rusty statue outside the barnyard.

I checked the number on the phone. "Butch . . . hello?" Static obscured the line, and I moved away from the house to see if it would improve. "Butch, are you there? Did you find Amber? Butch?"

"Hey . . . Ms. Florentino? This connection's not . . . ery good." Butch's voice was a thin ribbon of sound, a tiny ray of hope. I grabbed it like a lifeline.

"Butch, have you found Amber?"

Static, and then ". . . thing yet. I just went by Amber's house, and there's photographers camped out front, but I've . . ."—Butch faded into the ether again—". . . more places to look. Is Rodney there with the crew yet?"

"No, no one's here yet. Butch, you have to find Amber," I hollered into the phone, as if that would make the connection more viable. "Butch? Butch?" He was gone again. The line didn't disconnect, so I waited. "Butch?"

". . . ere's a car out here." Snatches of Butch's voice floated through the static. ". . . see anybody . . . climb over and walk . . . believe this place. Oh man, there's . . ."

Butch was gone. I hollered his name into the phone, even after the line disconnected. My stomach twirled and clenched, and I pressed a hand over it. The reality of the situation, the one I had been trying to avoid all morning, seeped through me like a gallon of ice water. Everything here was beyond my control. There was nothing I could do to make it turn out all right. I was as helpless as a little leaf-and-twig sailboat, drifting at the mercy of currents and the wind.

I looked at Carter, busy investigating the old tractor, and the full understanding of what he'd said in the mail wagon poured over me with an intensity that raised gooseflesh on my skin. *"Quit fighting the sails and let the wind move the boat—drift on faith for a while."* It's hard to drift on something you don't acknowledge. Over the years of my adulthood, I'd strayed so far from a childlike confidence in God's ability to guide the tide of human events that there was nothing left to buoy me when the storms blew in. I'd treaded water to the point of exhaustion, and now I could either sink below the surface or stop swimming, let go, and allow the current to carry me along.

Closing my eyes, I took a deep breath and abandoned myself to the belief that there were no accidents. Everything that had happened, from my being put in charge of Amber's segment, to Amber's disappearing with Justin Shay, to Carter's being in the hotel room next to mine, had happened for a reason. I was here for a reason. Just because I didn't create the plan didn't mean a plan didn't exist.

The idea wrapped around me like a warm, soft blanket—something old and well used, pulled from the abandoned storage spaces of childhood, a little too small to cover me now, but a good start. I remembered how it felt to put my trust in something larger than myself. I wanted to feel that way again.

"Doesn't look like there's anybody here," the postman said, startling me from my reverie as he came down the steps. "I reckon they went on over to the neighbor's to see about the horse trailer. I better git back down the road before Doyle blocks it off with the gravel truck. Gotta finish my route. Y'all just make yourselves to home. I'm sure they'll all be here directly." He climbed into his truck as I thanked him for the ride.

"Well, that was purely my pleasure, ma'am." Sticking an arm out the window, he shook my hand. "I'll call later and apologize to Imagene about the kitten. I reckon he's probably made hisself at home under there already." He nodded toward the house. "She needed a little somethin' around here to keep her company anyhow." Firing up the engine, he put the jeep in gear, waved out the window while making a loop in the yard, then careened down the driveway.

Carter watched the jeep disappear as he walked back from the tractor. "Guess we're on our own."

"Guess so."

We wandered toward the house and sat down on the steps next to a freshly planted flower bed. The air was heavy with the honey-sweet scent of flowers. A gentle breeze stirred the freshly mowed grass and combed the leaves of the live oaks, causing the shadows to shift and dance. All around, there was a sense of spring, of old things giving way to new beginnings. Anything seemed possible today.

"It's nice here," I said.

"That it is," Carter agreed. "Kind of makes you realize a day that didn't start out looking too good can still turn out all right. It looked like it might rain first thing this morning."

"It did?" How could I have slept through an oncoming storm, on top of everything else?

Chuckling, Carter braced his long legs on the steps, rested his elbows on his knees, and sat twirling a purple wild flower he'd picked somewhere. "The clouds put on a pretty convincing show earlier. Sent the reporters running for cover, and the fry cook in the café was worried the rodeo might be a washout."

I groaned under my breath. "Good thing I slept through it. I don't think I could have handled one more unexpected contingency today."

"Nah, don't worry." He watched the flower petals move. "Donetta foretold a perfect day for the rodeo. She *sees* things in the beauty shop window, you know. Visions." Glancing sideways at me, he raised an eyebrow with an exaggerated air of mystery.

His expression made me laugh. "Did she happen to tell you how Amber's location shoot would turn out?" Even though I was joking, a little voice inside me whispered, *The last time you got mixed up with the soothsaying shop owner, Mandalay, it did not go well. Leave this one alone.*

"Didn't say," Carter admitted. "She told me I shouldn't pack up and go so soon."

Actually, maybe Donetta's prognostications weren't so bad after all. "Why were you leaving?"

Glancing sideways, Carter studied me for a moment, then said noncommittally, "It seemed like the right thing to do."

"Why?"

He turned his attention back to the flower. "Hanging around flirting with someone else's fiancée probably isn't the best use of time, for one thing. Last night when I didn't see you around the hotel, I figured you were, well . . . pointing that out, in a nice way. I'd finished what I came here to do, so I thought I'd do the gentlemanly thing—pack up and leave you to your work." He grinned and held the flower out to me, his eyes catching a dash of passing sunlight. "The guy on the phone is an idiot, by the way."

"The . . . guy . . . ?" I stammered, dumbfounded as he slipped the flower into my fingers. "What . . ."

"The guy on the phone this morning," he said again. "The online Romeo."

Suddenly, everything was humiliatingly clear. I wanted to sink into the steps and disappear, hide somewhere underneath the house with the cat. "You heard that? You . . . you heard me talking to David?"

He shrugged apologetically. "The walls in that old place aren't very well insulated. I think they probably heard it downstairs in the café." At my look of utter mortification, he softened and added, "Just kidding, but yes, I heard it. For what it's worth, the guy's a fool." Our gazes caught and held, and I was suddenly aware of the smallest things—the shallow breath in my lungs, the slow, steady beat of my heart, the heat of a blush in my cheeks, the color of his eyes, sky blue, but darker near the centers, his fingers touching mine, the velvety leaf of the flower brushing my wrist, the realization that he was going to kiss me, and I wanted him to, and then he did.

Every other thought turned to mist in my mind. There was only an awareness of him, of us, an explosion of sensations like nothing I'd ever felt before.

Skyrockets.

Chapter 20

Imagene Doll

The last thing I expected to see when we drove up to the house was Amanda-Lee and Carter kissing on the porch steps. It must have been some kiss, because they didn't even notice my car pulling in. It wasn't until my neighbor's old truck and trailer rattled through the barnyard that the two of them broke away, and then they looked a little dazed, like they couldn't figure out where they were or what'd happened.

I waited a minute to leave the car, pretending to be busy gathering my purse. Avery opened the door and popped out of the back seat, then ran to the barnyard to open the gate for the horse trailer. It'd been against my good judgment to let Andy drive the truck over from the neighbor's place, since he only had his learner's permit, but he'd promised he could do it just fine. I'd finally said maybe it'd be all right, if they went slow across the tractor lane through the pasture.

Verl, pickled as he was, had offered to drive, but I'd told him not a chance. He did turn out to be a help with getting old Magnolia loaded in the trailer, though.

"Here, let me try," he said after the boys and I had all tried and Magnolia wouldn't go anywhere near the trailer.

Being frustrated and in a hurry to get back to the house before Brother Harve and O.C. came back with my potatoes and bagged ice from town, I wasn't in the best humor. "Verl Anderson, what in the world do you know about horses?"

He had the nerve to look offended. "Mrs. Doll, for fifteen years I was a cowboy on the Four Corners Ranch out in the panhandle." The food and coffee had started to clear up Verl's speech, finally. "But I broke my back, and we moved here because I couldn't ride no more." Taking the lead rope from my hands, he stroked Magnolia's muzzle. "I may not be good for much, but I still know how to get on with a horse." Verl talked to that old mare, and darned if she didn't put her head right in Verl's chest. The two of them just stood there for a minute, like they belonged together.

That was exactly the way Carter and Amanda-Lee looked on my porch—like they'd just found a powerful connection and were more than a little surprised by it. It was nice to know my ability to spot a good match hadn't gone south along with my memory and my figure. Amanda-Lee had the glow of a woman who'd just seen fireworks go off in broad daylight. I knew that feeling. I had it the first time Jack kissed me.

Amanda-Lee blushed and got embarrassed when she saw me walking up, probably because she was supposed to be engaged and all. When we got a minute alone, I'd have to tell her the story about Jack and me, and then she'd see that some things are meant to be.

"Well, we got the trailer here," I said, just to start a conversation. Neither of them came back down to earth and answered me, so I tried again. "Carter, are you our driver?" I knew he was because Donetta'd already called and told me so, but I thought

I'd give Carter a question that would be easy to answer, since he looked a little dazed.

"Yeah," he said finally, and blinked twice. "Yes, ma'am."

"Well, that's real fine." I patted him on the shoulder and sort of pointed him toward the barnyard. "Why don't you go on and help Verl and the boys unload the horse and put her in the corral until we're ready to head to the fairgrounds after lunch? One of the trailer tires is pretty soft. I think it needs some air."

"All right," he said and wandered off, looking like he didn't know which way was up. It sure was cute.

Amanda-Lee gazed after him as he went. She finally caught me watching her, turned the other way, and blushed even deeper red. "The crew's . . . ummm . . . not here yet."

I couldn't tell whether that was a fact or a question, so I said, "No, hon, I guess not, but I'm sure they will be soon. Long as they don't miss the exit off the interstate, they really can't get lost, coming here from Austin. They just follow Bee Hollow Road, then take a right at the four-way like the directions said, and they'll get here."

"Rodney's good with directions," she muttered absent-like, and stole another glance toward the barn. "I hope Butch finds Amber."

I wasn't sure what she was talking about, but I slipped my arm in hers and guided her toward the door. "Come on inside, hon. I got a roast in the oven and some crust ready for apple pies. O.C. and Brother Harve went after some potatoes and ice in town. After that drive from Austin, I figure your people will show up hungry."

Amanda-Lee followed me into the house, and we walked slowly through the entry hall, past the staircase toward the living room and the kitchen in back. She looked up at the high old ceiling my mama complained about after those low-roofed houses came in style. My daddy would have no talk of remodeling it. He valued things with some history to them.

"Now, there's plenty of light in here," I told Amanda-Lee as she stopped to look back at the staircase. "It ought to be fine for filming. I'm sorry the place is a mess. I don't keep house as good as I used to now that it's only me living here." Of course, I'd been housekeeping all morning and the place looked all right, but it's always good to apologize for the condition of your house so folks will think it normally looks better.

"It's beautiful." Amanda-Lee's voice was wistful and dreamy. With the state she was in, probably everything had a little halo around it. My house isn't beautiful. It's old and homey and well-used, which is fine with me.

"Well, y'all just make yourselves to home when your crew gets here," I said. "Now, I mean that. You go in any of the rooms, move things, do whatever you want to do. You need anything, just ask me. Don't open any of the closets, though. That'd be taking your life in your hands. The Anderson boys and I cleaned in a hurry this morning."

Amanda-Lee laughed. "You should see my apartment." She seemed to be coming back down to earth a little bit. "I can't even *get* to the closets."

"I always thought it'd be fun to live in an apartment in the city somewhere," I told her as we walked into the living room, where the stained glass windows cast colorful strips of light over the bridge table, my recliner, and the blue corduroy sofa Jack bought when he retired. I hated that sofa from day one, but I put up with it because Jack thought it was comfortable.

Lately, I'd noticed how good the old picture of him in his navy uniform looked next to that sofa. The picture was one of those that had been hand colored years before Polaroids. The photographer got Jack's eyes just right. "That's Jack," I said when Amanda-Lee looked at the picture. "He was wearing that uniform the day we met, and oh mercy, my heart just fell at his feet when I saw him across the pier. He smiled at me, and I just stared at him. I couldn't move or breathe. I'd never had anything like that happen to me, ever."

I laughed, picturing how smitten I must have seemed. Watching Amanda-Lee and Carter brought it back to me. "There was a winter carnival down the way, and he asked me to go with him. I forgot all about the girlfriends I came to Galveston with, and I said yes, and that was that. I never had eyes for another man again. Even when Jack was gone far away in the navy, all I thought about was him coming back and us starting a life together. People say love at first sight doesn't happen, but it does." Amanda looked at me, long and soulful, like she wanted to believe such things weren't just for storybooks.

I went on talking as we moved into the kitchen. "The funny thing was that all my girlfriends, and my folks—just about everyone—had a pure conniption fit right at first. There was a fella waiting back home for me with a ring. Everyone knew it, and so did I. We'd already talked about getting a ring at Christmas and having a wedding here at the house in the spring when the bluebonnets were blooming in the yard. It would've been a beautiful wedding, but once I met Jack, I knew it wasn't the right thing. I knew I'd only said yes because I felt it was time I got married, and I'd found a good boy who liked me, and I thought that was enough. But the first time Jack kissed me, the world shifted under my feet." I stopped by the window, then turned back and looked into Amanda-Lee's face. "Not everybody gets the chance to feel that."

Tears sparkled in her eyes, and it was like looking in a mirror. I could see myself all those years ago, standing in that very spot, trying to decide if I had the courage to do something that wasn't what I'd planned.

"That's a sweet story," she said. Turning away, she pretended she had something in her eye.

"Oh, it ain't a story, hon, it's real. Don't let anybody ever tell you the good Lord don't have certain plans for folks. When you run onto one of them plans, you know it. He planned for me and Jack to be together, and I guess He planned for Jack to go on to heaven and me to have this time by myself." I opened the oven to check the roast, and my glasses steamed up. "It's taken me a while to accept that, but I guess He wanted to give me a few years to find out what I could do on my own—like riding the roller coaster."

Amanda-Lee nodded, and I truly felt that she understood. "How about we get these pies finished up?" I suggested, and she seemed willing enough. I stirred the cinnamon and sugar into the apples, then she held up the bowl while I scooped the filling into the crusts. "Feels good to make apple pies. I haven't had occasion to do that in a long time. It's my own fault, though. Just this morning, it came to me that all I been doing this past year is sitting around my house missing Jack. He would sure be disappointed in that."

"It takes some time," Amanda-Lee said as we started pinching in the top crust. "To adjust to the loss of a spouse, I mean—about a year on average. There are some changes in the chemistry of the brain—it's not all just emotional."

I stopped for a minute, surprised. "Lands, I didn't know that. All this time, I just been thinking there was something wrong with me. The doctor gave me some pills, but I don't know if they really help."

"Medication can be a key part of treatment, but it's also important to realize that grieving is a process. It doesn't stop just because the family wants the parent or grandparent to get on with life." Amanda-Lee finished her pie and dusted off her hands.

"I think my kids get frustrated with me sometimes." I hadn't admitted that to anybody, not even to Donetta, but I could tell calling twice a day and driving down on the weekends to mow the lawn and take care of things was getting to be a strain for them.

"Family members are often just frustrated that, no matter how hard they try to provide companionship, take care of chores, and so forth, they can't replace the person who's gone," Amanda-Lee said sympathetically. "When the grieving spouse talks about that person, the children and grandchildren take it as a complaint or a signal that they're not doing a good enough job. The reality is that the grieving spouse just needs someone to talk to, someone to reminisce with."

I stood there with my mouth open, thinking she'd surely been a fly on my wall. "Why, that's it exactly. I feel like the boys get their feelings hurt when I talk about Jack or say how much I still miss him. You hit the nail right on the head."

"I did a show on it once," she said, glancing up at me in apology. "I'm sorry. I don't mean to be sticking my nose in where it doesn't belong."

"No, goodness, this makes me feel a lot better—knowing other folks have gone through the same things. It makes me think it'll get better, eventually."

"It will." Amanda-Lee poked down a bubble in her pie.

"You're pretty good with those pies, too," I pointed out. "You must have a mama or a grandma that bakes."

She shook her head, watching me cut slits in the top crusts. "I was in news production for ten years. I always enjoyed the cooking segments on the morning show. One of these days I'd like to learn to cook."

"Watch out for 'one of these days.' " I shook a finger at her and smiled as I opened the oven, and we each picked up a pie. "You'll end up an old lady, wishing you'd got out and done more things."

We put the pies in, then I got the meat fork and a hot pad to check the roast.

Amanda leaned up against the counter. "When I was taking care of my email, I saw an ad for a seniors' cruise that departs from Galveston and goes to five different ports of call. You can snorkel, take a rainforest tour, visit ancient ruins. I thought about you."

I stood back and closed the oven, then pulled off my glasses because they were fogged up again. "Me? Why in the world?"

She looked out the window, watching Carter and the other fellows looking at a tire on the horse trailer. "You mentioned that your husband had wanted to take you on a cruise and you wished you'd gone. You could still do it."

"Oh goodness, I'd never . . ." I stood there feeling flustered, with the kitchen blurry around me. For a minute, I forgot all about my glasses being in my hand, and I couldn't figure out why I couldn't see. "I'd never go off on a ship like that, all by myself. With a bunch of strangers. I don't think I'd ever do that." I remembered my eyeglasses and put them on, looking around for something that needed to be done. Imagine the idea of me getting on a big boat and setting sail!

Amanda-Lee cut a sly look my way. "You never know. It might be like the roller coaster."

The screen door opened, and Otis Charles came in with the potatoes and a couple bags of ice. I took advantage of the distraction and introduced him to Amanda-Lee, but they'd already met before out at Harve's Chapel.

"Amanda-Lee's in charge of the *American Megastar* show," I said, and she gave me a panicked look, then glanced over at O.C. "Oh, it's all right, hon," I said. "O.C. won't tell anybody. He plays football for the University of Texas. Got a full scholarship."

Amanda-Lee frowned and stuck her hand out to shake O.C.'s. "Mandalay Florentino," she said, even though I'd already told him her name. She sure had a strange way of saying that name. The way she said it, Amanda-Lee sounded almost like a foreign word.

"Nice to meet you . . . again," O.C. answered. "The guys in my dorm watch the show, especially since Amber's on it and all. You think she'll win?"

"I hope so," Amanda-Lee answered. "I'm going to do everything I can to give her a good shot at it."

O.C. nodded. "Sure is a lot of excitement about it in town. There's people everywhere."

Amanda was concerned. "That's part of the problem. We don't want crazy. We want natural. A media frenzy isn't going to win votes for Amber. The hometown segment is a big part of the Final

Five." She raised a finger like she'd just had a thought. "Would you, by chance, be willing to do a short interview, maybe tell the story about you and Amber and the calf . . . what was it . . . calf wrestling or something? I overheard you talking about it at the feed store."

Otis Charles took a step back. "The calf scramble?" he asked, with a funny look. "You mean the time I stole Amber's calf? My grandma Beedie pretty near tanned my hide that day." He grinned, and I started to laugh. I could still see Miss Beedie dragging that big old boy through the fence by his ear, him already a foot taller than her but looking scared to death of that little old woman.

Amanda nodded. "Would you mind our using that story in Amber's segment? We could get you talking about it—you know, reminiscing about growing up here and that kind of thing."

Otis Charles shrugged. "Yeah, sure," he said, then looked at the ice bag dripping on his shoe. "I'll put this in the cooler, then go see if I can help get the tire changed on that horse trailer. I think they got a flat out there."

"Oh mercy," I muttered. "I hope the spare's good."

Amanda looked like she might faint. I gave her the potatoes to get her mind off things. "Here, hon, why don't you wash and fork these and put them in the microwave? They're not very good that way, but we don't have time for much else."

Amanda moved to the sink and started in washing the potatoes. Every few minutes, she'd stop, walk to the hallway, and look toward the front door. Finally, she gave up and stayed at the sink.

I couldn't imagine what she was so worried about. "If your people get lost, they'll call, I'm sure."

Amanda let out a long breath, her shoulders sagging. "It's not the crew I'm worried about. It's Amber. She left LA in Justin Shay's private plane last night instead of coming with the crew today, and nobody knows where she is. Right now, one of our interns is driving all over the county, trying to find her. He thinks she might be at some secret place she used to go to when she was a kid." She closed her eyes, like she'd finally done all the pie making and potato scrubbing, small talking, and waiting she could. "If I don't find her in the next couple hours, we're dead in the water."

"If Amber's supposed to be here, she'll be here. She's a good girl, and in all the time she worked at the café , she never once called in sick or showed up late. I don't believe all that hogwash about her carrying on with that Justin Shay, either. Amber would never do such a thing, and certainly not with the likes of him. She's a good Christian girl." I felt sorry for Amanda-Lee, worrying about where Amber was and when the crew would get there, and whether the filming would go all right. "If Amber's around here, she's probably out at the old Barlinger ranch. Many's the time I drove by there and saw the Anderson kids climbing around that old house, playing in the barns and whatnot. Used to really get my hackles up, because it wasn't safe for little kids to be at an old empty farm with junk everywhere and the weeds up to your waist. It's a wonder none of them ever got snakebit out there, and . . ."

Amanda-Lee turned from the sink and grabbed my shoulders like she was going to hug me off my feet right then and there. "You know where Amber's special place is? Can you show me? Can you take me there?"

"Hang on a minute," I said as she headed for the front door. I trotted after her, not sure what to do. "I got pies in the oven. I can't just leave."

Amanda-Lee spun on her heel. "Can I borrow your car? Can you tell me how to get there?"

"Well . . ." I looked past Amanda-Lee, and outside a glimmer of sunlight on glass caught my eye. "I might just be able to save you the trip, 'cause there's a bunch of folks pulling up in the drive right now."

Chapter 21

Mandalay Florentino

I burst onto the porch as a car, a Cadillac SUV, and three vans stopped in front of the house. Momentarily blinded by the glare, I hurried down the steps and ran along the walkway, trying to see who was inside. Butch! Butch was driving the lead car, and in the passenger seat, a blond head, a pair of wildly gesticulating arms, long bouncing ringlets of hair . . . was that Amber? My knees, which had been locked all day, went weak as I ran around the car. It was! It was Amber. Thank God!

The driver's side door opened, and the next thing I knew, I was giving Butch a bear hug and babbling incoherently, "You're here! You're here! You found Amber. Butch, you found Amber. You found Amber. Butch found Amber. Amber's here." The words repeated over and over in my mind as I tried to assimilate the reality. From the first moment I'd set foot in Daily I'd been preparing for the eventual collapse of the Amber segment. It was hard to grasp the concept of potential success, the brass ring suddenly within reach.

I released Butch, and he stepped away sheepishly, eyeing me like a boy who'd just had his cheeks pinched by a senile relative at a family gathering. "Uhhh, hi, Ms. Florentino."

I took a yoga breath and blew out as the crew exited the vans, grabbing camera equipment, cables, lighting, boom microphones, and reflectors. Luckily, everyone was so busy they hadn't noticed me mugging Amber's handler.

Still inside the vehicle, Amber leaned toward the open car door. "Hey, Ms. Florentino. How are ye-ew this mornin'?" Her voice jingled with her usual zippity-doo-dah rhythm. "Ye-ew look ni-ice today. That sure is a cu-ute sweater."

I wanted to reach through the door, grab her by the neck, and squeeze. Instead, I clenched the window frame and leaned in. *Be calm. Be calm. Don't make the talent cry. When she starts crying, it goes on forever.* The last time the director had screamed at Amber for missing her mark during rehearsal, the rest of the day was a wash. She couldn't concentrate on anything. "Amber, where have you been?"

"Oh, well, it's a long story. I told Butch all about it." Amber glanced at Butch and then back at me, her blue eyes enormous, round, soulful, saying, *You're not mad at me, are you?* "Ya'll shouldn't have worried about me, Ms. Florentino. If there's one place I do know how to get to, it's Daily, Texas."

"Amber, you took off from LA without telling anyone."

Amber blinked innocently. "I left a note."

I clenched the window frame harder, my fingernails digging in until it hurt. "You were supposed to come with the crew. It takes days to put all the travel plans in place, Amber. You can't just take off by yourself." I felt like a parent, telling a toddler why she couldn't follow the bouncy ball into the street.

Amber blinked her long lashes in earnest surprise. "Oh, I wasn't by my-say-ulf," she drawled cheerfully. "I was with Justin. He said he could fly me in his play-un, but then a while after we got in the air, it started to have some trouble, and we had to land so the pilot could have it checked out." If Amber was the least bit concerned about any of this, it didn't show. From the corner of my eye, I could see Butch slashing a finger across his throat, trying to give Amber the *cut* sign. Clearly he'd already heard this whole story and thought I'd be better off without it. I flashed a dirty look over my shoulder, and he froze midstroke, then pretended to be scratching his ear.

Amber went right on talking, oblivious, as usual. "Justin told the pilot, 'Let's land in Las Vegas so we can see the sights,' so we did, but there were photographers everywhere. There's always photographers everywhere Justin goes. Justin said since we had such a big audience and all, why don't we just duck on into the weddin' chapel and get married? So we did." She slid out the driver's side door and grabbed my arm when I stumbled backward. "Just kiddin', Ms. Florentino. You're white as a sheet. We did go through the weddin' chapel, though. Justin's bodyguards kept all the reporters away, and we went out the alley, back to the airport. The plane wasn't fixed, so Justin got a new one, right there in the middle of the night, and . . ."

The nonstop barrage of chatter started to seem farther and farther away, as if it were part of a dream—a long, strange dream of planes, helicopters, automobiles, and paparazzi in hot pursuit. Somewhere in the story, Amber and Justin Shay ended up in Austin, where they attracted more media attention, forcing them to escape in a newly purchased Cadillac SUV. They ditched their pursuers by driving cross-country through a nature preserve and a network of back roads. Eventually, wonder of wonders—Amber threw her hands in the air palm up to illustrate their miraculous good fortune—they ended up on a road she recognized, which was near one of her favorite childhood places, the old Barlinger ranch. Since it was still fairly early in the morning and she'd wanted to show Justin the ranch anyway, they stopped in—all of which would have been fine if they hadn't locked the keys and both cell phones in the SUV. Fortunately, just when things were looking desperate, Butch showed up and the problem was solved by calling OnStar to unlock the SUV. Wasn't that just the most amazing timing?

Lifting her hands toward the shiny new SUV behind her and the line of trailing vans and crew members frantically moving equipment into place to capture the homecoming, Amber smiled broadly. "Then, when we got to the four-way, about two miles down, Butch called Rodney, and the crew was just about a mile down the way. We waited, and in a minute, there they were and we all drove in together. It worked out just perfect. Isn't that awesome?"

She paused, as if she expected me to answer. I'd been rendered temporarily speechless, so finally she went on. "I kept telling Justin all morning, even after we got locked out of the car, I had faith God wouldn't let me miss being here when I was supposed to be." She motioned toward the SUV as Justin Shay stepped out and surveyed the area, the farm reflecting off mirrored aviator-style sunglasses that probably cost more than I made in a month. I wanted to snatch them off his face, throw them on the ground, and jump up and down on them until there was nothing left but tiny pieces.

Justin gave Amber a quick chin bob. "You and Bubba get it all worked out, babe?" Motioning vaguely in Butch's direction, he swaggered toward us, flashing a perfectly straight, perfectly white, perfectly practiced smile. I'd seen that trademark Justin Shay smile in the romantic scenes of at least a dozen action-thrillers. It was about as real as his interest in Amber's well-being or his concern for her rapidly dwindling chances of becoming the next American Megastar.

"It's . . . it's Butch, Mr . . . Mr. Shay," Butch babbled, hopelessly starstruck.

I could feel my temper shooting toward a boiling point I usually only reached about twice a year. So far this year, I was over my quota. "No!" I exploded. "Everything is not *all worked out*. We're trying to put together a location segment here—a happy, whole-some hometown reunion that could, quite possibly, make or break Amber's chances on *American Megastar*. Thanks to you, we've got a media circus in town, paparazzi skulking behind every bush, and until five minutes ago, Amber was lost in the woods."

Justin drew back, shocked and offended, as my frustration, sim-mering in a pressure cooker for three days now, reached critical mass and exploded. "This isn't one of your pathetic Brat Pack weekends in Malibu, where you can screw up and buy your way out of it later. This is real life—real people who have real jobs to do, a segment to put together, and only one chance to get it right." Justin didn't move, only coughed in indignation, his expression saying, *Someone tell this . . . this . . . creature it can't speak to me that way.*

I tumbled completely over the edge, waving a finger at his car and screeching, "This is my project, and I want you and your stupid SUV *out* of here!" My voice echoed off the house and the barn, reverberated around the farmyard, and startled a flock of birds in a tree by the porch.

Backing up a step, Justin pulled off his sunglasses and blinked. He glanced at the car, then at Amber, back at me, and at the car again. He seemed . . . wounded? Disappointed? Momentarily human and vulnerable?

I felt a surprising stab of guilt. He looked like the dorky kid on the playground, being chased out of the kickball game by a schoolyard bully.

Amber shook her head, blinking her big blue eyes in complete dismay. "Oh, it's all ri-ight, Ms. Florentino. I invited him. I was a little nervous about the hometown reveal, and Justin said he'd come along and be moral support. He left off everything he had to do for the weekend to help me out. I thought that was sweet."

Sweet? I thought. *Sweet? Justin Shay has never done anything sweet in his life. He only wants you to be his babe of the week. Please, oh please tell me you haven't fallen for the misunderstood-bad-boy-who-*

just-needs-a-good-woman routine. That only works out in country songs. In real life, bad boys stay bad. They shop around on Mydestiny.com *while you're planning the wedding. . . .*

I wanted to grab Amber's slender shoulders, shake her, and scream, *Don't fall for it, Amber! Don't be stupid.*

Justin dropped his glasses back into place, braced his hands on his hips, and struck the pose of an action hero. "So what do we do first?"

I could think of a dozen answers to that question, but Imagene beat me to it. She stepped into the middle of the disagreement like Gandhi and invited everyone into neutral territory—the kitchen for lunch. Justin patted his well-sculpted abs enthusiastically, and the crew looked hopefully toward the house. Clearly, everyone thought lunch was a good idea.

It was my job, of course, to be the party killer. "Let's get a few shots of Amber reuniting with her family first. They're in back by the barn."

Amber's hands flew to her face. "They're here? Oh my gosh, they're here?" Before anyone could stop her, Amber was headed around the side of the house with the camera crew scrambling behind her. Following along, I glanced at Butch and wondered what they'd been talking about in the car. Clearly, he hadn't debriefed Amber on the plan for the day.

Amber rounded the corner, and the magic began the moment she spotted O.C. behind the house. "O.C.!" she hollered, throwing her arms open and launching herself toward him like a running back breaking through for a touchdown.

O.C. caught her in a cross between a hug and a football block, whipped her around in the air as easily as if she were a long-legged rag doll, then set her on her feet and stood back, his big hands clenched around her shoulders as she jittered up and down, asking rapid-fire questions, as the camera crew rushed into position.

"How's football? I couldn't get but one UT game when I was out there in California. It was the Rose Bowl. You did real good. That coach shoulda played you the whole time, though. I told Marta, the cleaning lady at the hotel, 'He's from Daily, and in a few years, he's gonna be a famous Dallas Cowboy, just you watch.' She thought you were awful good, too. You gonna bulldog in the rodeo this afternoon? I saw Booger turned out in your pasture last time I was home, and he was limpin' like something was wrong with his hoof. Did he get better?"

Before O.C. could answer, Amber spotted Brother Harve coming out of the barn. "Oh, hold on a minute. I've gotta go say hi to your granddaddy." She jitterbugged across the yard, shook Brother Harve's hand, then hugged him shyly. "Hey, Brother Harve. Are you feelin' better? When I talked to Andy last time, he said you were in the hospital with pneumonia. I'm so sorry about that. You hadn't ought to go fishing on those mornin's when it's so cold. You know that."

Brother Harve smiled benevolently, his weathered hand trembling as he cupped the side of her face. "Oh, I'm fine now. Fine as frog hair, don't you worry. We all been watchin' you sing on TV, and we're just as proud as who'd-a-thought-it! You're doing a good job out there in California. I think up in heaven, the choirs of angels are singin' along, Amen?" Pointing a finger upward, he added dramatic emphasis. "You don't let nobody tell you the world doesn't want to listen to music with something good to say, you hear? You just remember what it feels like to hurt. There's always somebody out there hurtin' for need of hope."

Amber nodded, her shoulders sagging solemnly. "I'm trying, Brother Harve. There's so much . . . stuff to keep in mind." She glanced at me, momentarily aware of the cameras, and the crew, and the heavy load of expectations trailing behind her. "I messed up again today." She turned back to Brother Harve, and for an instant, I had a sense of what it would be like to stand in the tiny

LISA WINGATE

red cowboy boots of Amber Anderson—nineteen years old, far from home, trying to spread good in a world that fired back with nasty newspaper articles and stressed-out, screaming TV producers. Trying to keep the faith while surrounded by flash and cynicism.

She'd done amazingly well so far. Standing there with Brother Harve, she looked worn, slightly lost, but she still believed she could make a difference. Somewhere between local news and *American Megastar*, I'd lost that dewy-eyed sense of conviction. Watching Amber, I wanted it back.

Avery came out of the barn, spied his sister in the yard, and ran back inside, yelling, "Amber's here! Amber's here!" The cameras swung toward the barn as Avery and Amos bolted across the yard, followed by Amber's grandfather and finally Andy. Within moments, the Andersons became the picture of a family reunion. They hugged, laughed, cried. Amber wrapped her arms around her baby brother so tightly I thought she might never let go. Closing his eyes, he buried his face in the soft golden ringlets of her hair and they stood like statues in the sunlight, their bodies melted together in a silent embrace.

"Oh, you're so big," she murmured finally. "You got so big while I was away. I missed you so much." Opening her arms, she took in Amos and her grandfather, and finally even Andy joined in, completing the circle.

The cameras caught it all. The scene was perfect. It was everything I would have planned, and more, because it was real. The emotions weren't staged or forced—they were genuine. The joy was complete. It surrounded us, flowed over the onlookers like a soft, warm breeze. Imagene sniffled, and Brother Harve slipped an arm around her shoulders. O.C. looked away and wiped his eyes.

I thought about my family. It had been too long since we were all together in one place. Busy schedules, holiday commitments to in-laws, complicated lives and distances kept us apart far too often. As soon as I got home, I was going to call my mother and tell her we needed to plan something for Easter, even though that gave us only a week. An egg hunt, maybe, or a family volleyball game at the beach. The kids were probably all too old for egg hunting, but volleyball would be fun. We needed to spend more time together.

The scene in the yard made me realize something else. The circumstances may have been different—different part of the country, different income bracket, different sizes and shapes, but the language of family was universal. Amber loved her brothers and her grandfather as much as I loved my family, and in a way, even more. My sisters, my parents, my grandparents, and I didn't depend on one another. We didn't have to. We lived self-contained lives that intersected during holiday gatherings, births, deaths, weddings, and funerals. Amber, her brothers, and her grandfather had no economic safety net to fall back on. They needed one another for survival, for everything.

"This is gold," Rodney muttered in my ear, motioning one of the cameras closer. "This is perfect. Bag this, lunch, and the rodeo, and we're halfway there."

For an instant, I felt guilty for coldly discussing the marketing of something so real, so tender and heartfelt as Amber's homecoming. Reminding myself that all of this was in Amber's best interest, I slipped into work mode and pointed out Brother Harve and O.C. "There's some pretty good filler over there. Brother Harve runs the church near Amber's house—the one where she learned to sing Southern gospel. His grandson, O.C., grew up with Amber. Ask him about the time they were in the calf scramble together. It's good stuff."

Rodney glanced sideways at me, seeming properly impressed. "Sounds perfect. Anything else?"

"Not yet," I admitted. "I wanted to do some interviews in town, but there's no way. The minute this Justin Shay thing broke, there were paparazzi everywhere. It's a zoo, basically." I glared across the lawn, trying to vaporize Justin Shay with my death ray.

Unfortunately, he didn't disappear. Bored with the family reunion, he strolled toward the corrals to look at the horse. Watching him pass the barn, I wondered momentarily why Carter hadn't come out.

Rodney frowned. "What about getting Amber into the rodeo? Is it going to be a problem?"

I affected what I hoped was an air of supreme confidence. "We'll do it just the way I described it in the email last night. I think we can get away with sending Butch and a camera operator in as advance. They can hide the equipment in a duffle bag, check in with our rodeo company contact, then pre-position somewhere near the press box on the west side. Everyone else will have to move in with Amber. We're only going to get one chance at it. There's no room for mistakes. As soon as the paparazzi finds out she's here, it'll be a circus. I don't know about the concert plans this evening. We'll just have to see."

Rodney scratched a sneaker back and forth over the new spring grass. No doubt he was calculating the difficulty of transferring everyone from the dark interior of a horse trailer into position before the crowd went wild. "It's always a circus with Amber," he admitted dryly. "Has anyone heard from Ursula yet?"

Ursula. Just the mention of her seemed to evaporate the hopeful possibility that this day would end well. I couldn't admit that to Rodney, of course. "Not since this morning. Butch told me she's headed this way. I had some missed calls earlier."

Rodney lifted his head and sent a puzzled look my way. "Where were you this morning, anyway? Ursula's on the warpath, Amber's gone, I'm trying to move a crew, at what, may I add, was a ghastly hour of the morning, the press are all over us, and I can't even give you a buzz to let you share the love? I almost turned in my union card and quit right there."

"Very funny." Even the thought of losing Rodney was terrifying. Rodney was an icon, a pioneer of reality TV. He'd forgotten more about the genre than everyone else knew, combined. "Rodney, if you quit, I'll kill you. I'll kill you and I'll tell everyone I went temporarily insane."

Rodney's lips twisted in a wry sideways smile. "Not a long trip today."

"No, it's not. I'm halfway there already."

"You're all right, love," he said, and moved a camera operator again with a subtle twist of his chin. "You're better than you think. Just look at that." He pointed, and I returned my attention to the ongoing family reunion, where Imagene was now gathering everyone for lunch.

"That's perfect," Rodney muttered.

"You're right." Whether it was luck, fate, divine intervention, or just the hapless magic of Amber Anderson, everything had come together at exactly the right time, in just the right way. As the Anderson family started toward the house, Amber with her arm around Amos, Avery stretched between his sister and grandfather like a human chain, and Andy in front of them, walking backward and chattering on about the ongoing baseball season, I knew the goose had just laid the golden egg.

On the back steps, Amber held out her arm to help her grandfather struggle upward with one good leg and one that swung stiffly at his side.

That scene was going to melt hearts all over the nation.

Chapter 22

Imagene Doll

Lunch didn't turn out anything like I planned. It was mostly the Andersons, Brother Harve, O.C., and me eating, while the TV people flitted around, taking film of us and the food and the kitchen. One of the boys put his motion picture camera right over the table between Brother Harve and Verl and took a close-up picture of the roast before Brother Harve sliced it. Then that boy went over and got some film of the apple pies. I didn't know if he was just hungry or if the roast and the pies was gonna get a starring role in Amber's show, but I was glad the pies looked as good as they did. I'd forgot about them in all the commotion of Amber driving up, but it turned out all right, because apple pies take a long time to bake. That cameraman must have thought they looked pretty good, because he filmed them for a long time, then rested the camera on his shoulder, closed his eyes, and took a long sniff.

"I can go ahead and cut you a piece if you want," I offered, and the crew boss, a dark-headed fella named Rodney, gave the camera boy an aggravated look. Rodney was kind of a quick-moving, impatient man, it seemed like. He was tall and thin as a rail, like he didn't stop to eat much. Those kind of people make me nervous. I wished he'd stop moving those kids around the kitchen, let them sit down for a bite, and have one himself, too. Thin as he was, he could use it. I always like to feed skinny people.

"Just do what you'd normally be doing. Just act natural," he kept saying. "Act as if we aren't here." That was a fairly tall order, considering that the kitchen was a tight fit, with all of us, all of them, and their equipment. The Anderson kids were pinned up against the wall, because we'd had to scoot the table back some to make room for the extra lights, and by the door, O.C. was hunched over his plate, because people kept hitting him in the head with microphone poles and cords and big reflectors that looked like giant pieces of stiff tin foil. It was a good thing Carter'd stayed out in the barn to work on the spare tire. I didn't know where we would have put him. I felt bad about him not getting a plate, but I figured I'd send Amanda-Lee out with a tray in a while, since Carter was pitching in like a real trooper, trying to use Jack's old tire-plugging tools to get either the flat or the spare fixed and aired up so the horse trailer would be ready this afternoon for the rodeo.

Every so often, as the lunchtime filming was going on, Amanda-Lee glanced out the window, like she was wondering about the horse trailer, or Carter, or both. When the filming was done, we got up and let the crew sit down, and Amanda-Lee disappeared out the door before I could give her a plate. After serving everybody and cutting the pies, I started fixing a little food to take to the barn for Carter and Amanda. I didn't get in too big a hurry, mostly for selfish reasons. It made me feel good, having all those young folks around my table, going on about how good the food was. One of the camera boys said he used to work for the *Good Morning America* show and if I'd like to tell the rest of the world how to make a real apple pie, he could probably get me on TV.

I was so flattered, I turned red in the face. "Well, I might do that. I just might," I said, and tried to imagine me, plain old Imagene Doll, riding an airplane all by myself, all the way to New York to cook on TV. Betty Prine and the ladies of the Daily Literary Society would sure drop their dentures over that, and wouldn't Jack get a kick out of it?

I wrote down my phone number and handed it to that boy. "You just have someone call me when you're ready," I said, and he tucked the number in his pants pocket, like he'd really do it. He thanked me again for the lunch, then he and the good-looking baby-faced kid they all called Butch got up, got their things together, and asked me for directions to the fairgrounds, because they were planning to go on ahead of everyone else. I pointed out that it was still two and a half hours until the rodeo, but that didn't seem to bother them. They wanted to look over the arena while it was empty, they said.

"Y'all can't wait a little while?" Amber asked, and a glance passed between her and Butch. I'd intercepted that look a couple of times at the table. There was something going on between them, some private conversation underway. I wondered what was behind that, seeing as Amber was here with Justin Shay, who even in spite of his bad reputation, did have pretty good table manners. He complimented my pies twice and said he'd eaten in the best restaurants all over the world and didn't know when he'd ever tasted anything finer. He winked at me and asked what he'd have to do to talk me into moving to Hollywood and cooking for him. I wagged a finger and told him I was too old for all that, but he could come into the Daily Café anytime, because I was the one who baked the pies there.

He said he just might, and then he watched another private look pass between Amber and Butch and his grin turned upside down real quick. When Butch came over to tell Amber good-bye and to knock 'em dead at the fair, Justin leaned back, crossed his legs, and looped an arm over the back of Amber's chair. "She'll be awesome. She's always awesome." He flashed another smile at Amber before he turned back to Butch. "You get enough to eat there, Bubba . . . I'm sorry . . . Butch. It's Butch, right?" Patting his flat, tight stomach, he looked down his nose at Butch, stopping at the point where Butch's tummy drooped over his pants just a little bit.

Everyone at the table froze up, and I decided right then and there I didn't like Justin Shay. It was bad enough that he'd taken a shine to Amber, who was too young and innocent for a rich dandy like him, but it was another thing to be hateful to poor Butch in front of everybody. Butch was a nice young fella. He probably had a real good mama somewhere who'd raised him right and taught him to show proper manners, especially in someone else's house. In all the news articles about Justin Shay, I'd never seen one single mention of his mama. With all the rigmarole he was into all the time, his family probably didn't claim him anymore.

Like usual, Amber couldn't stand to see anyone get their feelings hurt. She stood up, gave Butch a big hug around the neck, and said, "Thanks, Butch. I guess if it wasn't for you, we'd still be stuck out at the old Barlinger place."

Butch turned red as a beet, then went out the door looking like a barnyard rooster puffed up to crow at the sunrise.

I fixed plates of food for Carter and Amanda-Lee, then headed out the back door. When I got closer to the barn, I could hear laughing inside. I didn't mean to spy exactly, but I did tiptoe around the end of the barn aisle. Amanda had the lug wrench and she was holding it away from Carter, who was squatted down by the trailer, trying to get the tire back on.

"All right, this is war," she said, giving him a flirty smile. "I'll have you know that I *do* understand what a lug wrench is for. My father wouldn't let me get my driver's license until I'd learned to change a tire. I'm not the helpless urban girl you think I am."

Standing up, Carter rested an elbow on the truck, looking like he was enjoying the conversation. "I don't think I said that, exactly. I just said you probably didn't want to get your nice clothes dirty." He waved a hand toward her cute blue sweater and black slacks. Standing there in the barn, she looked as out of place as a flower in a hogpen. Carter seemed to appreciate that fact.

"I might," she said and moved the lug wrench like she was thinking about getting down there and showing him how it was done.

"Now how would that look, a bigtime TV producer like yourself down here changing tires?" Pushing off the truck, Carter circled around and trapped her against the fender.

"You'd be surprised what producers do," she said.

"I'll bet I would," he agreed, his voice low and soft. The two of them looked into each other's eyes for a minute, slowly swaying closer together before he slipped a hand into her hair and kissed her. She let the lug wrench go, and neither one of them noticed when it hit the dirt and clattered against the tire.

A heat rose in my cheeks and I backed out of the barn aisle, figuring neither one of them probably had much appetite for food at the moment. Whenever they got finished in the barn, they could have a plate at the house. In the meantime, I had a little reconnoitering to do about the situation with Amber and Justin Shay. That match had no business happening, and I was about to see that it didn't.

When I got back to the house, the kitchen was empty, Justin Shay was sprawled out on my sofa with a pillow over his face, and the film crew was busy on the porch, setting up lights and those overhanging microphones on long poles. They had Amber's brothers and Verl out there in the rocking chairs, and they were telling them not to be nervous, just act natural and talk about Amber—how she was as a child, funny things they remembered about her, how she'd always liked to sing, and that sort of thing. Brother Harve and

O.C. were waiting just inside the screen door, so I guessed maybe they were next in line to get on camera.

Amber came out of the laundry room with a stack of dish towels. "Sorry, Mrs. Doll. I couldn't find any in the kitchen." She kept her voice real quiet, so as not to wake up Justin, or bother the filming, or both.

That was just like Amber to be cleaning up the kitchen when she was supposed to be the star of the show. "Sweetie, you give me those rags. You shouldn't be doing dishes." I reached to get the towels from her. "You go rest or watch the camera crew or whatever else you need to do."

She shook her head and kept the dishrags. "Oh, that's all right, Mrs. Doll. I need something to help me pass the time." She stole a glance toward the screen door. "It's weird sitting around, listening to everybody talking about me."

"I guess that would be strange." I slipped an arm around her shoulders and watched with her as the camera crew moved Verl to a seat near the edge of the porch. The sun sparkled against his silver hair. Verl really did have a good head of hair, when it was washed and combed.

Amber seemed to be thinking the same thing. "I guess you helped get Granddad cleaned up. He looks real nice."

Suddenly all the effort seemed worth it. "Goodness, it was no trouble at all."

Amber ducked her chin like she knew that wasn't true. "Thanks for doing that. He doesn't cooperate so good sometimes."

"Oh, he's no match for me, sugar. Don't you worry."

She sighed as the bright lights lit up the porch and the helpers with the big foil sheets and the microphone poles moved into place. "I didn't want people to make him look bad, to make fun of him on TV. People can be real mean that way sometimes."

She turned to me, and there was a little tear drawing a line down the side of her cheek. I wiped it away, then cradled her face in my hand and looked into her pretty blue eyes. "Don't you worry about that, sugar. You just keep your own sweet spirit and do right yourself."

"Yes, ma'am."

On my sofa, Justin Shay snorted in his sleep.

"How about we go do the dishes together?" I suggested, figuring that, being as everyone was occupied, this might be a good time to talk to Amber about a few things.

When we got to the kitchen, Amber started right in on the dishes at the sink. I took the towel to dry and waited a few minutes before I said too much. Over the years, I'd only spent a little time with the Anderson kids during vacation Bible school or around town or when Amber was working at the café. It wasn't like I was her gran or an auntie or someone she was used to getting advice from, but since getting involved with *American Megastar* and keeping Amber's brothers overnight, I felt closer to the family.

Still, I didn't want her to think I was another hanger-on trying to stick my nose in her business. She always was kind of a shy kid, and every time anyone ever asked her if she and her family were doing all right, she just smiled and said everything was fine, just fine. She'd tell about a big holiday dinner they'd cooked, or how she and her brothers and her grandpa'd played a baseball game out in the back yard, and it was so much fun. I always knew those were stories she made up so no one would feel sad for her, and maybe to hide how bad things were at home. I never had any real idea what it was like for those kids until I saw Andy carrying his granddad up my steps. I should have known how things were, because I knew—everyone knew—about Verl, but it's easy to mind your own business when someone else's business looks like too much trouble.

Even though Amber and I worked side-by-side at the café a lot of days, I never even knew she was trying for *American Megastar* until I saw her on the audition show. She didn't tell a soul she'd tried out except Buddy Ray, who, I found out later, drove her to Dallas for the audition.

I laughed, thinking about the look on Buddy Ray's face the other night when he locked his keys in his car. Poor thing. He never could seem to do anything right, bless his heart. And now, from the looks of it, he was losing his girlfriend to a slick city fella with a smooth white smile. I never would've thought Amber'd carry on with another boy behind Buddy Ray's back. "You know, Buddy Ray darned near arrested your producer her first night in town," I said, and watched to see how Amber'd react to me bringing up Buddy Ray.

Amber looked heavenward, like she wasn't surprised, just embarrassed for Buddy Ray's sake. "Oh no. Did Forrest find out?"

"I'm not sure how much Forrest knew about it, exactly. It did go out over the radio, because that's how I heard. By the time I got there, Buddy Ray had jumped to some pretty wrong conclusions, but in his defense, nobody told him the Daily Hotel was open for business again. It all worked out okay anyhow."

Amber leaned over the bean pot in the sink and gave it a good scrubbing. "Was Ms. Florentino mad?"

"I don't think so," I said, walking to the cabinet to put away a pie plate. "She didn't laugh outright, but I think she saw the humor in it."

Holding the bean pot under the rinse water, Amber got the bubbles off and handed it over. "She's been real nice to me, helping me get my mark in rehearsals and get extra time with the voice coaches and stuff. They think I don't know it, but a bunch of them at the studio have a bet going about when I'll get kicked off the show. Ms. Florentino didn't ever bet in it, though."

"I wouldn't think she would," I agreed. "That's a terrible thing for those people to be doing."

Amber shrugged. "I don't pay it any mind." She went on with washing pots, then, in a minute, turned the conversation back to where we'd started. "I hope Buddy Ray didn't get in trouble with Forrest. He was already in hot water for calling me in California on his work phone. He didn't do it when he was on duty—just when he'd stopped for coffee or something to eat, but Forrest was mad. I told Buddy Ray he shouldn't get himself in trouble just to call me."

Since the door was open, I went on and stepped through it. "How are you and Buddy Ray doing? I guess it's hard, you being out in Hollywood and all."

Finished with the last pot, Amber drained the sink, grabbed an S.O.S. pad from the soap basket, and started scrubbing the greasy mess left behind by the water. "Oh, Buddy Ray and me broke up a long time ago. We just didn't say anything because—" pausing, she glanced over her shoulder and checked the doorway for listeners before she whispered—"he's sweet on Cassidy Martin, but if her daddy knew that, he'd have a fit, her still being in high school and supposed to go away to Baylor in the fall and all." I gasped in surprise, and Amber added, "Please don't say anything to anybody. I don't know how it'll all end up, but Cassidy's eighteen, so it's really not anybody's business but theirs."

I couldn't help but think about Jack and me, and how my parents weren't happy about me quitting college to marry a boy who had almost two years left in the navy. I wasn't in much of a position to pooh-pooh young love, but on the other hand, I wondered if Amber was also saying that, her being nineteen herself, it wasn't anybody's business but hers if she wanted to get involved with Justin Shay. "Well, sure enough, if she's of legal years, it is her choice," I allowed. "But naturally, her daddy would be concerned about the age difference. Buddy Ray's twenty-five. He's been to school in Dallas and lived in Waco, had a job and such. He's . . . worldly, and she's just a girl only beginning to see things."

Amber's eyes blinked wide when I called Buddy Ray *worldly*. It was a stretch, but of course, I wasn't really talking about Buddy

Ray. I was talking about that smooth-talking lump in there on my sofa.

"Sometimes you meet somebody and you just know," Amber said. Letting the dish towel rest on the side of the sink, she gazed out the window with the wistful look of a girl in love.

Oh dear. Now what? "Well, sometimes, a young girl can get her head turned by a fella—you know the type that's got a nice smile, a big name around town, a pretty way of talking? You know *that* kind of man? Sometimes a girl can get her head turned and think she's in love, and the fact is that fella's no more right for her than . . . well . . . Don Juan. Some men just like to see if they can turn a girl's head. They like to . . ." Gracious, being the mother of four boys, I wasn't very good at this particular conversation. I'd never thought through anything like this before. ". . . unwrap a pretty girl like a shiny new toy at Christmas, but then pretty soon that toy ain't new anymore, and he's on to other things, and the girl is left behind in a bad way. You know there's fellas that do that kind of thing."

Amber didn't answer at first. She was concentrating on something out in the yard. "Oh, he's not like that," she answered kind of absent-like, and my heart sunk to my shoes. Poor girl really did have herself fooled. There she was, defending Justin Shay's character. "He's not like people think he is."

"My daddy used to say a man doesn't get his reputation by accident."

"There's a lot of stuff about Justin people don't know, either." Amber's shoulders got stiff and defensive, and I could tell I was pushing too far. "There's a lot of stuff about him people don't see."

I probably should have kept my mouth shut, but I couldn't. "There's a lot people *do* see, too, hon. Once you show your hind end in public, it's hard to get folks to see anything but. That's a bad old pun, but it's true. Justin Shay's had an awful lot of blessings fall in his hands, and he hasn't done much with it except buy big houses, wreck fancy cars, get himself arrested for drugs and drinking, cheat on his women, make kids he's not raising, and get himself into the newspapers. He may have been nice to you so far, but his past ain't much of a recommendation."

Amber folded the dish towel without looking at it, then set it on the edge of the sink. "I hate those newspapers. They never tell stuff the way it really happened. They make it look like I don't have half a brain."

I smoothed a hand over her hair. It felt like yellow silk under my fingers. Even though I loved my boys, I'd always wanted a little girl with long blond curls. "There's usually a lot of gossip about people who are famous. Folks want to know all about someone who's pretty and talented and on TV, and what they don't know, they make up sometimes. It's not right, but that's the way it is. I reckon it makes regular people feel better about their own lives when they know somebody famous makes mistakes, too."

Turning on the water, Amber cupped her hands under the stream and washed the last of the crumbs down the sink. Then she stood there with the water running over her fingers. "I almost didn't come for the concert today. I maybe wouldn't have, if it wasn't for Justin coming."

I kept stroking her hair, letting it slide between my fingers and over my palm. She leaned into my hand, like somewhere deep inside her there was a little girl who remembered a mother's touch. "Why in the world would you miss your big homecoming show after you worked so hard to get into the Final Five?"

She stared into the sink for a long time, watching the water run over her small, pale hands. "I don't know if I want to be famous. Justin says you get used to the things reporters say and to having people stop and take your picture on the sidewalk and cameras following you around. He says you learn what things not to say, but I don't know. Sometimes I think it'd be easier not to try—to just come home and live a regular life, you know?" Resting her elbows on the sink, she kept turning her hands over and over in the water, like she was trying to wash something off.

I thought about what it must be like to be just a teenaged girl, with so many choices to make, so many hopes resting on her. The weight must've seemed like more than she could bear. No wonder she was easy prey for a man like Justin Shay. Many a desperate young girl had latched onto an older man who promised to take care of her. "Oh, honey, you deciding not to sing would be like hiding a lamp under a pot—you remember when we studied that verse in the book of Luke, way back in vacation Bible school? We've got to be the salt of the earth, and we can't do that if we hide ourselves away in places where we feel safe and comfortable, and sure no one's going to say mean things to us." *Like you been doing, Imagene. That's just what you been doing—staying where you know you'll be safe.* "To salt the earth, we got to go out into it, to use all the tools God gave. He gave you that beautiful voice for a reason. Anytime you sing, there might be someone out there who's feeling sure enough lost, and they might say, Look at that pretty girl, and my what a voice she's got. I wonder where she learned that song."

Amber gave a halfhearted little smile over her shoulder. "I think about that sometimes." Turning away, she looked off into the yard. "The song I wanted to do on the show a couple weeks ago was from a CD I got in the airport here, and it was recorded right in Texas. My voice coach wouldn't let me do the song on the show, but I called the company to see if maybe we could have a meeting about me recording CDs for them. If I did that, I could be back at home, and probably all those reporters wouldn't care about me anymore. I've been trying to get in touch with the man who owns the company all weekend, but he hasn't been answering, so then I thought, maybe that's because I'm supposed to stay with *American Megastar*. I just don't know what to do."

Turning off the water, she dried her hands on the towel and looked at me to see what I thought. There was a part of me that wanted to be kind, to make things easy on Amber and say it'd be just fine for her to quit *American Megastar*, move home, and record her songs. But there was another part of me that thought of how hard Amanda-Lee had worked to produce Amber's show, and how the mayor and Brother Ervin had hung that banner across Main Street a couple days ago, and how everyone in town had hopes and dreams tied to Amber. That part won out and found my voice. "Amber Anderson, don't you sell yourself short. You're as good as anybody on that show—better, even. Ms. Florentino believes in you, and so does everybody in Daily. If we have anything to say about it, you're gonna be the next American Megastar."

Chapter 23

Mandalay Florentino

The afternoon was golden, sunlit and perfect, filled with new grass and wild flowers. No one had heard from Ursula, and Butch called from the fairgrounds to say that, other than the normal festivities, things looked quiet over there. From what he could gather, rumors of an Anderson-Shay hometown wedding had spread like wildfire, and the media presence was now focused on the Daily Baptist Church in town. A local florist showed up with silk bouquets and a wedding arch, the owner of the Daily Café wheeled in a catering wagon full of fried chicken, and the minister was waiting in a black suit with a boutonniere on his lapel, helping to fuel speculation that nuptials were imminent.

Meanwhile, back at the ranch, the interviews on the porch were proceeding swimmingly. The conversations with Brother Harve, O.C., and Amber's family were funny, charming, touching. They painted a picture of Amber, not as the recent press fiasco had made her appear, but as she was—a young woman raised amid loss and deprivation, yet filled with hope.

As the afternoon sun caressed the tall, golden spires of last year's grass, Rodney moved the equipment to a field of wild flowers behind the barn. In her jeans and T-shirt, her bare feet cuddled among tender green shoots, Amber sat surrounded by a sea of blue flowers as bright as her eyes. She talked about her dreams—a singing career, a family, a big place in the country where foster children whose lives were hard and dangerous, and filled with fear, could come to breathe clean air, to pick blackberries, plant a garden, and experience peace.

"We didn't have a lot of things, growin' up," she said, her fingers absently combing the bright red petals of an Indian paintbrush. "But we didn't ever have to be afraid to walk out our front door, either. Sometimes, I'd pack a backpack, and we kids would hike off down the creek for miles and miles, just to see what we'd find." Pausing, she looked up, not at the camera but past it, toward Justin Shay, who was hanging around under an oak tree, getting in the way. "Every child ought to have the chance to do that. If they could, the world would be a better place."

Justin smiled—not the practiced smile, but one that was almost tender.

Rodney called it a wrap, and Justin trotted through the posies, helped Amber up, gave her a hug, telling her how well she did. I wanted to be sick.

"I wish he'd fall off a cliff," I muttered, and Carter grinned sideways at me as Amber and Justin strolled off, shoulder to shoulder.

"I think you'd better get used to having him around," Carter said. "Any minute now, they'll pack a knapsack and hike down the creek."

"Over my dead body."

Carter leaned close to my ear. "*We* could pack a knapsack and hike down the creek."

A warm tingle ran from my head to my toes and lit up all the nerve endings in between. Everything in me wanted to chuck the day's work, tiptoe through the tulips, and find out what it would be like to spend more than just a stolen moment with Carter.

Rodney turned my way, and I came out of the floaty, feathery blue, then sank back to earth. Rodney gave me a look that said he'd caught the exchange between Carter and me. "How long do we have to get packed up for the fairgrounds?"

I checked my watch. "Twenty minutes."

The crew chief wheeled his hand in the air. "All right, people, get everything loaded in the horse trailer. We're on the road in twenty."

"Guess I'd better make sure the lug nuts are on tight," Carter said, and started toward the truck and trailer.

Rodney fell into step with me on the way back to the house. "What's with the cowboy?"

"I'm not exactly sure." It was a surprisingly honest admission.

"That's not the darling new fiancé I met at the Christmas party—the one with the, uhhh . . . let's see . . . sailboat, wasn't it?" Rodney rubbed the flap of pallid skin under his neck, eyeing Carter contemplatively.

"Not." I couldn't hide the touch of humiliation. I'd been babbling about wedding plans for weeks.

Rodney shrugged. "The cowboy looked familiar. I thought maybe he was the fiancé."

"There is no fiancé anymore." How Rodney could even remotely confuse David with Carter was beyond me. They were polar opposites in looks and everything else. David was abrupt, intense, quick, and a careful dresser with perfect hair and all the latest accessories smacking of money and success. He'd tried to sell Rodney an investment plan at the studio Christmas party.

Carter was slow, easygoing, casual and comfortable, with an apparent affinity for collecting free T-shirts from fund-raising events. His hair had a mind of its own—slightly wild and out of control, unpredictable, like he was. He didn't need to command the room or attract attention to himself. He hadn't bothered to introduce himself to the crew after he finished working on the trailer. He just stood on the fringes, watching the show.

"I won't be getting married and sailing the coast this summer."

Rodney patted my shoulder in what might have been an actual show of affection. "Most of the time, marriage is overrated. I didn't like the sailboat man anyway. Too anal."

I laughed and Rodney strode ahead to scold one of the grips for dragging something expensive through the dirt. "Let's go, people. Let's get this baby on the road."

As usual, the crew jumped into action. Within fifteen minutes, Amber's grandfather had led our token horse into the front of the trailer, the crew had loaded their equipment in the back, and we were locked and ready. After a short debriefing on the porch, we called Butch one last time to get a final report, Rodney finished his instructions to the crew, and everyone squeezed into the small dressing room in the nose of the trailer.

Amber walked out of the house with Justin Shay trailing her and the wardrobe girl still arranging hair and patting on Amber's makeup. Her glow was gone, and Amber was clutching Justin's hand. "Did you talk to Butch?" she asked me, hesitating at the trailer door.

"Butch says everything's fine at the fairgrounds," I assured her in the calming, situation-under-control voice I used when contestants succumbed to stage fright. "The plan is in place, the stage is ready in the arena. The rodeo band knows that a guest artist is coming to sing, but they don't know it's you, so when your name and your new status as an *American Megastar* finalist is announced, there will be a lot of commotion and excitement. We'll bring you out of the trailer, under the bleachers, and onto the stage quickly, before the crowd has time to react and move forward into the aisles. You're doing the national anthem, 'God Bless the U.S.A.,' and then the two you wanted to do—'A Wanderer's Road' and 'The Hand.' The music will cue up as quickly as possible to try to minimize crowd movement. You don't have to worry about a thing except your songs."

Amber's face went pale. "I . . . I can't remember the songs. I can't . . . remember the words."

Grabbing her shoulders, I gave her a leveling look. "Yes you can, Amber. You know the songs."

"Come on, babe, you were just singing them for me in the field," Justin chimed in. For once, I was grateful for his presence. Now was not the time for Amber to have a meltdown.

"I think I'm sick," she moaned, and wobbled in my hands.

"You're not sick, Amber. You're not sick. Just take a few deep breaths. Come on, deep breaths with me. In . . . out. In . . . out. That's it."

The color slowly began returning to Amber's cheeks. In my mind, I was counting down the minutes, my wristwatch ticking like a time bomb. If we didn't leave now, we wouldn't make it. The rodeo crowd would be in place, the band would be ready, and Amber wouldn't be there.

"Come on, Amber. You can do this. It's just like performing on the show. You go out, hit your mark, and sing."

She nodded weakly. "I didn't think it'd be so hard to . . . come back home. I'm sorry, Ms. Florentino."

"It's all right, Amber." I braced up her shoulders. "Most of the contestants have a hard time with the hometown show. It's a lot of pressure, hitting the Final Five and coming back home for the big reveal. You'll be great. These are your hometown people.

The Dailyians, remember?" Amber laughed at the quote from the purple T-shirt.

Justin slipped an arm around Amber's waist. "Come on, babe. We'll go over the songs again on the way. You're gonna be awesome." He helped her into the trailer, and I stepped back, surprised by what seemed like a genuine show of support. Maybe even Justin Shay wasn't beyond the reach of Amber's magic.

Justin helped Amber to a seat, and Carter closed the door, leaving Amber and Justin reviewing lyrics while the crew pored over details. Carter and I climbed into the cab of the truck. In front of us, Imagene, Brother Harve, O.C., and Amber's family packed into their cars, and with a chug of the old Pontiac's engine, a whinny from Magnolia, and the rattle of horse trailer doors, we were on the road for Project Amber Final Five Reveal.

I checked my watch. Not too bad. Only two minutes behind schedule. So far, everything was going well enough. With any luck, we'd keep it that way.

The plan fell into place with astonishing precision. Within fifteen minutes, we'd arrived at the fairgrounds gate, the cars had parked out front, and Carter was sweet-talking our way past two guards and a livestock inspector, despite the fact that we had no veterinary paperwork for the horse. The livestock inspector was female, which may have aided in our success. Carter gave her an apologetic smile and said, "You know, we didn't even think about those papers, but we're just here for the rodeo and then we'll be heading back out. I promise our passenger back there is healthy as a horse." He winked and grinned, and the livestock inspector rolled her eyes. Bracing her clipboard on her hip, she stood back and looked at the horse, then squinted at Carter.

"I know you," she said finally, waving her pen at him. "You look cuter without the beard thing, though." Circling a finger around her mouth, she drew an invisible goatee, then wrote something on her clipboard and stepped back from the truck.

"You're not the first one to make the observation." With a sheepish grin, Carter shifted the truck into gear and glanced in the rearview mirror.

The inspector waved us through.

"What was that all about?" I asked as we bounced past the gateway into a parking lot crowded with trailers and saddled horses.

"Who knows?" He flashed the same smile he'd used on the livestock inspector.

"You used to have a *beard thing*?" I mimicked the livestock inspector's hand motion.

Focusing on squeezing the rig through a gap between two haphazardly parked trailers, he muttered, "Not recently."

"You've been to Daily before, then?" The mystery of Carter Woods gnawed at the back of my mind. Something wasn't adding up here. How did the livestock inspector know he used to have a beard?

He glanced sideways, one eyebrow rising. "Manda . . ."

A tiny cowgirl in a pink hat bolted from behind a trailer, and Carter slammed the brakes. My heart jumped into my throat as the girl froze in our path, and our rig squealed and vibrated to a sudden halt as the little girl's father raced out, scooped her up, and waved at us apologetically. Inside our trailer, people, or equipment, or Magnolia thumped against the walls.

"That didn't sound good," Carter muttered as we started forward again.

"Just get us to the arena." I focused on the task at hand. No more distractions. "There's our contact with the stock contractor." I pointed ahead to where a tall man in a black hat was waiting with Butch at his side. When we reached the gate, they waved us through, then walked in front of the truck, clearing crowds of horses and rodeo patrons so we could drive past another gate behind the bleachers.

"It's showtime," I said.

Carter gave a quick twist of his head and a ready-for-adventure grin that reminded me of the night we'd broken into the café. "Let's go."

Opening the trailer, we found the crew and equipment in remarkably good shape, considering. Rodney took charge of his people, and Amber disembarked bright-eyed and ready to sing. Justin Shay stumbled out afflicted with motion sickness and sank to the ground, too green to get in the way. The cameras rushed into position, our rodeo contact cued the MC, and we hurried Amber up the ramp beneath the bleachers just as her Final Five announcement lit up the arena. A collective gasp went through the crowd, the band started the national anthem, the crowd rose to its feet, and Amber took the stage. Her voice floated into the cool evening air and drifted heavenward.

Everything was perfect. I stood on the exit ramp with Carter, watching Amber's moment of triumph from behind the stage.

"She's amazing," I said.

Carter's fingers slipped over mine. "Yes, she is." He was looking at me, his voice low and intimate. An invisible current pulled us together, drew me into his arms, into his kiss. My body flushed hot, crackled with the excitement in the air, with the bliss of a moment when all was as it should be. Somewhere far away, Amber's voice rose to a crescendo and the crowd burst into thunderous applause.

When Carter's lips parted from mine, Amber was already halfway through her second song. I turned around, and Butch was coming up the ramp, eyeing Carter and me in a way that made me wonder how much he'd seen. It wasn't the most professional behavior, making out under the bleachers during a location shoot.

I gave Butch the high sign and quickly brought up a new subject. "Good job on the advance, Butch. It went off like clockwork. She sounds great."

"She sure does." Straightening his glasses, Butch gazed adoringly toward the stage. "Man, I love to hear her sing. There's nobody on the show that can touch her."

"I think you're right," I agreed. "If the rest of this hometown segment goes this well, she'll have a real shot at the top."

Butch blinked in surprise, then studied me narrowly, chewing his bottom lip like he wanted to say something but didn't know if he should. He glanced curiously at Carter.

"Carter drove the horse trailer for us," I said, and Butch blinked rapidly, as if I'd just bombarded him with something that wouldn't compute. His gaze darted back and forth between Carter and me.

The vague uneasiness needled at the back of my mind again. What was up with Butch? What was that look about?

On stage, Amber finished "God Bless the U.S.A.," and for several minutes the thunder of applause drowned out everything else. When things finally quieted, we stood listening to her next number.

Butch studied Carter with several quick sideways glances, then finally stuck his hand out and introduced himself. "Butch Logsdon."

I quickly apologized for not having performed the introductions myself. "Sorry, you two. Butch, Carter . . . Carter, Butch." The two shook hands and I added, "Butch is one of our interns . . . in charge of helping Amber, mostly."

Nodding toward the stage, Carter smiled. "Seems like that wouldn't be too bad a way to spend an internship. She's a talented girl."

"Yes, she is," I agreed, and Butch dropped his head forward, gaping at me as the song ended and applause drowned out everything else. When the applause died, there was more than the usual jostling in the bleachers overhead. "Sounds like we might be getting some extra guests already," I said. "As soon as Amber's done with the fourth song, we need to move her back to the rig. Maybe

we can make it out of here before the paparazzi block the gate."
It was probably too much to hope for. In the days of cell phones
and instant messages, word traveled at the speed of light, and the
fairgrounds were only a few minutes from town.

Somewhere near the gate, a siren wailed and I envisioned hordes
of reporters beating down the arena gate.

On stage, Amber made a joke about the noise, then the band
cued up and she started her last song.

My cell phone vibrated with a message. Taking it off the clip, I
glanced at the text. It was Rodney, telling everyone there was a crush
at the gate and the sheriff was trying to keep the intruders out.

We're rolling as soon as the number's over, I keyed in, sending the
reply to the entire crew.

Carter started down the ramp. "I'll go turn the trailer around."

"Thanks." I paced back and forth until the number was over and
the rodeo crew hustled Amber off stage. Waving to the fans hanging over the railings, Amber made her way to the ramp entrance,
where two burly cowboys blocked pursuers. After signing a few
autographs for fans, Amber turned our way, squealed, and broke
into a run with her arms open. I prepared myself for an exuberant
hug, but before I knew what was happening, Amber had wrapped
herself around Butch, and I was standing there with my arms in
the air and my bottom lip down around my knees.

"I did it! I did it! I did it!" she cheered, her face buried against
his neck. "That felt so great. Oh, that was just the most awesome
thing."

"You knocked 'em dead," Butch cheered, then swept her off
her feet before setting her down again. He wrapped her in his arms
a moment longer, then backed away and glanced guiltily at me.
"I'll go see if the trailer's ready." Leaning over, he kissed Amber on
the cheek, whispered something in her ear, then jogged down the
ramp, leaving Amber and me standing against the girders, out of

range of the zoom lenses and the flash bulbs exploding like fireworks outside the fence.

Amber peered toward the trailer, then let her head fall back against the cool metal. "You were right, Ms. Florentino. That felt so good."

"It looked like it." I nodded toward the ramp, where Butch had disappeared. "What's going on with you and Butch?"

Eyes falling closed, Amber smiled slightly. "Butch is awesome. He's so smart and so . . . strong, and he knows so much more than anybody gives him credit for. It's like I told Mrs. Doll—he's not like people think he is."

I stared at Amber, trying to make sense of what she'd said. "Amber, I thought you and Justin Shay were—" *a couple, a duo, a romantic pair* "together."

A puff of laughter burst past Amber's lips. "Ms. Florentino, you've been reading too many newspapers. You know all that stuff they say isn't true. Justin's a nice guy, and he's my friend, but that's it. For one thing, he's way too old for me."

I felt like I'd suddenly been dropped into an alternate universe—a place in which Amber made sense and I was the one who was nuts. "Then what's he doing here?"

Opening her eyes, Amber held her hands palm-up. "He's here because he flew me out on his plane, remember?"

"But *why*, Amber? Why would he do that if you two aren't . . . together?" Justin Shay was known for a lot of things, but a charitable nature wasn't one of them. If he was spending time with Amber, there was a reason.

Crossing her arms behind her back, Amber rested against the girder again, staring into the darkness beneath the bleachers. "Did you ever meet somebody, and right from the first, you knew there was a reason that person was in your life, but you didn't know why?"

I pretended to consider the question, but in truth, I was thinking about the night I met Carter—how comfortable, how natural it seemed when we were together. I was thinking about Imagene and the day we stood in the rain, talking about the fear of drifting far out to sea. "Everyone has that feeling sometimes."

Amber's lips twisted to one side. "You remember that night I went with the people from Studio 10? Remember Butch had to come get me when everybody got drunk, and then I ended up in the newspaper and they said I was partying all night?"

"Yes, Amber, I remember." How could I forget? The Studio 10 incident was one of Amber's more notorious Hollywood fiascos.

"I wasn't partying, Ms. Florentino. I was talking to Justin. At first, we were just talking about Hollywood and the show and stuff. He wanted me to go see his beach house in Malibu, but I said I'd better not."

She finished the words with an acuteness that told me she was more savvy than anyone gave her credit for. "I told him he didn't have to stay there just to keep me company, and he said he didn't feel like partying, because it was his birthday. So I asked him why didn't he want to celebrate, and he said he never liked birthdays, because it was his birthday when his mom took off with his little sister, and he never saw them again. She just dropped him at the video arcade and never came back. Can you imagine that—leaving a boy Avery's age alone in a strange place?"

Moisture rimmed the corners of Amber's eyes, and I felt myself getting choked up over the life of Justin Shay. I'd never heard that story about his mother.

Amber continued talking. "So I got to telling him about my brothers and the day my mama and daddy died, and the county split us up and sent us to different foster homes down around Austin while Peepaw was trying to get custody of us. And the thing was, Justin knew exactly how it felt, going into a place where you don't know the people, and sometimes they're mean, and sometimes they're all right, and sometimes the other kids beat you up and take your stuff, and nobody even notices it." Even now, I could see the sadness of those realities in Amber's face. I suddenly understood why, in spite of her grandfather's failures, Amber and her brothers were so determined to maintain a life together.

"I told Justin about how I used to sit out at the old Barlinger house and dream that someday I'd make lots of money, and I'd buy the whole ranch and make a place where kids can go with their brothers and sisters while the courts decide things. There'd be computers to help search for family members they might've lost touch with, and horses, and fishing poles, and a swimming hole at the creek so they could just go outside and be kids and not have to think about the pain in their lives.

"In the summer, the place would be like a camp, and kids who've been separated in foster homes could come and spend a couple weeks with their brothers and sisters. There'd be a chapel where the kids could learn that God loves you no matter what your parents did or what foster home you're in. We could show them how to write notes and draw pictures back and forth to their brothers and sisters, like I did with my brothers when we were separated." Exhaling a quick sigh, she turned to me, her eyes filled with a greater vision. "Don't you think that would be an awesome kind of place?"

"I do think it would be." More than ever before, I understood the magic of Amber Anderson. It was so much larger than one nineteen-year-old girl from a seedy trailer on a bare-dirt farm. She had the glow of a true believer. "You know, Amber, if you make it to the top two, you'll have the power to do things like that. You'll be in a position to make a difference." Even though the winner got the million-dollar recording contract and the major publicity, the runner-up always received offers and enough notoriety to begin a recording career.

Amber shrugged, uncrossing her arms and picking at a finger-nail. "I figure Justin Shay's already got what it would take to do it. He's got so much money, he just spends it everywhere, and he's got friends with money, and he's in the newspapers all the time. I think it might be nice for him to be in the paper for something good for a change. Maybe he won't be so empty inside. Maybe he'll see that we're given stuff so we can do something that matters. That Shokhana place he gives his money to isn't a church—it's a big glass temple where you have to have a lot of money to even get in."

She flicked a glance my way, perhaps to see what I was thinking. "I'm sorry, Ms. Florentino. I knew when I invited Justin that having him come here would probably mess up my hometown show, but I figured there's a pretty good possibility I won't make it very far in the Final Five and then my chance to talk to somebody like Justin Shay would be gone. Nobody'll care what I've got to say anymore, so I brought him here to see the Barlinger place."

My throat prickled with emotion. "Amber, you have every chance to make it to the top of the Final Five."

She looked at her hands again. Long ringlets of hair fell across her cheek, catching a stray beam of sunlight and turning golden. "Ms. Uberstach doesn't like me."

Denying that would have been a paper-thin lie, so I didn't bother. Ursula didn't like Amber. Even Amber knew it. "It's not up to her, Amber. Ultimately the decision comes down to viewer votes. You can get the viewer votes—if we can finish up this segment. We need the concert at the community building tonight and a few more interviews, then we'll have what it takes."

Leaning away from the rail, Amber peered toward the grow-ing commotion at the bottom of the ramp. Flashbulbs went wild. "We'll never get out of here. You wouldn't believe what those people will do to get a picture. They bury themselves in the sand by Justin's beach house at night and stay there all day, waiting for him to come out so they can jump up and take pictures. It's crazy and they won't stop, no matter what you say to them. They'll ruin the concert tonight."

"You let us worry about that. You just get ready to sing." I said it as if I had a plan, which I didn't. The cacophony below was getting louder—voices yelling, horns honking, chain link clanking against the poles, the blast of a police siren. On the ramp above, the two cowboys were having trouble holding back the crowd. If we didn't get out of here soon, we'd be mobbed.

A moment later, Butch was running up the ramp. He didn't stop as he reached us, just hollered, "Holy mackerel, he's actually doing it!" His voice cracked on the high note as he skidded to a stop at the entrance to the bleachers. For some reason, the crowd there had cleared and the two burly cowboy bodyguards were gone.

"What in the world . . ." I muttered.

Butch motioned for us to follow. "Come look at this!"

Amber started up the ramp at a trot, then broke into a run with me a few steps behind her. By the time I reached the top, she and Butch were engrossed in watching something below in the arena. They seemed completely oblivious to the fact that the bouncers had disappeared and we could be swamped by the crowd at any moment.

"Amber, wait!" I called. Knocking Butch sideways as I passed, I reached for Amber and grabbed the back of her rhinestone-studded jacket the way a parent might snag a toddler about to disappear into a crowd.

"Amber, what are you doing?" I screamed, pulling her back. Overhead, the crowd had grown deafening. "You can't go that way, Amber!"

She whirled toward me in a flash of blond hair and sunlit rhinestones. "Justin's down there! Look!"

Still clutching her jacket, I inched forward so that I could see the arena floor. The chaos in the stadium took a moment to register.

Around me, spectators streamed toward the railings. Paparazzi and news crews were rushing to push through the onlookers, moving cameras and equipment over barricades to reach the front of the crowd.

On the arena floor, the sheriff's young deputy, Buddy Ray, was chasing a suspect, screaming, "Halt, police! Halt, police!" His quarry, a man wearing nothing but a nice suntan and red satin boxer briefs, dashed though the deep sand, evading Buddy Ray with the speed and skill of an action hero. As he ran, he flipped gate latches, allowing calves, horses, and a herd of sheep into the arena. Slinging his shirt over his head, he hollered, "I'm running with the bulls! I'm running with the bulls!"

I suddenly realized the man wearing nothing but his boxers and a smile was Justin Shay.

"Justin!" Amber screamed, but her voice was lost in the chaos. "Justin!" Whirling toward Butch, she pushed her hair from her face. "What's wrong with him? What is he doing?"

Butch reeled up his bottom lip and came to his senses. "It's all right. He did it on purpose. He's distracting them so we can go." Amber blinked at him doubtfully as Butch took her hand and pulled her toward the vehicle. I looped my arm around her from behind, and we hurried away.

Rodney met us halfway up the ramp. "Let's go! The crowd's cleared for some reason."

A belly laugh caused Butch to stumble sideways. "You won't believe why . . ." The words ended in a wheeze, and Butch reached into his jeans pocket, searching for his asthma inhaler.

"Tell me later," Rodney barked, then took control of Amber and hustled her away.

"Go on. I'll ride with Butch," I called as Butch wheezed harder, searching his pockets.

"I've got the crew," Rodney yelled. "See you back at the house." As they rounded the corner, Amber glanced back at Butch with concern. He waved good-bye, still wheezing, then finally fished his inhaler from his shirt pocket and took a puff. He was trying to say something, but between laughing and wheezing couldn't catch his breath. Finally, he started down the ramp, motioning for me to follow.

We'd found our way to the back gate and reached his car before he'd managed to compose himself. He was laughing so hard he had tears streaming down his cheeks. Taking the keys, I told him to get in the passenger seat, and we left the chaos of the fairgrounds behind.

Butch wiped his eyes as we turned onto the rural road and the sirens faded into the distance. "That was priceless." His voice squeaked like an adolescent's. "I can't believe he actually did it."

"Butch, what are you talking about? What happened back there?"

Turning to look over his shoulder, Butch started laughing uncontrollably again. I resisted the urge to slap him back to his senses. "Butch, I said, what happened?"

"I . . . I told him . . ." Butch chugged between puffs of laughter. His face was splotchy red and gray, still wet with tears. "I told him to . . ."

"Butch!" The car teetered off the pavement and strafed a patch of sunflowers along the side of the road. "Get it together already."

"All right, all right." He sniffed again and swallowed hard, then shook his head, bending down to look in the side mirror. "You have to sort of picture it." He raised his hands, like a director sketching out a scene. "We're throwing stuff in the trailer and trying to figure out how to get Amber out of there. There's press and paparazzi everywhere—they're, like, beating down the fence, shinnying down the bleachers, and there's Justin, getting in the way, and they're all screaming questions and going crazy to get to him. He's so busy posing for the cameras, he knocks one of our units off the trailer fender, and Rodney about hits the roof and hollers, 'You're out of here now, you bleep-bleep-bleepin' bleep!' Then, it's like they're going to get in a fight, and I can just picture that in the papers tomorrow, so I tell Justin if he really wants to fight, why doesn't he go slug the deputy down by the gate, get himself arrested, and take the heat off of us so we can get Amber out of there. I didn't think he'd really do it."

My mouth fell open and I turned to Butch. "He punched the deputy?" The car veered off the road again.

Butch's hand jerked toward the steering wheel. "Do you want me to drive, Ms. Florentino?"

"No, I don't want you to drive." I slapped his hand away. "Justin punched the deputy?"

Butch shrugged, like he didn't care either way. "Who knows, but he's sure about to get arrested. No big deal for him. He gets arrested all the time. That was pretty cool, though—the running with the bulls thing. That ought to make the papers." Butch started laughing again, a chuckle first and then a full-blown guffaw. "Man, that was funny. Did you see . . ." He went on recapping the scene, but I tuned out. A new complication had begun working its way into my mind. For the moment, we were free and clear of paparazzi, but the jail, where Justin Shay was undoubtedly headed, was adjacent to the community building. We couldn't possibly have Amber's welcome home concert there tonight. With Justin Shay's arrest, the paparazzi would multiply like cockroaches.

"We have to find somewhere else for Amber's welcome home concert." I was talking as much to myself as to Butch. "We can't possibly have it in town tonight." Drumming my fingers on the steering wheel, I tried to think. The fairgrounds were taken up with the fair . . . Imagene's house was too small . . . the barn, maybe . . . a barn . . . concert . . . not very practical. The place was full of old tools and tractor implements. Even with help, we couldn't clean it out in time . . . "Harve's Chapel!" The idea dawned in my mind like a sunburst in the darkness, and the producer in me started turning the wheels in overdrive. "It's ideal—out of the way, intimate, a place where Amber has history. Imagene mentioned a choir practice there tonight. . . ." I smiled to myself, struck with a mental *Wow*! "We can get Amber singing with the choir behind her. In the place where she learned to love gospel music. It's perfect." I fished for my purse and cell phone on the floorboard, then remembered it was in the truck with the crew. "Butch, can I borrow your cell? I have to make some phone calls and set this thing up."

"Mine's dead," Butch said with a distinct lack of concern. "I might have my car charger back there in my duffle bag. Do you want me to get it?"

"Of course I want you to get . . ." I glanced sideways, and he was eyeing me with the strangest look—not the naïve, gullible, college-kid Butch expression, but one that implied critical thinking and a high degree of skepticism. "Butch, why are you looking at me like that?"

He considered me for a moment before answering, then looked down at his hands and chewed his bottom lip. "To be honest, Ms. Florentino, I'm wondering why you're working so hard on this. I mean, I know why I'm working so hard on it—I want Amber to go out in style, but why are *you* working so hard on it?"

I drew back in shock. Was this Butch—baby-faced, mealy-mouthed Butch, the *intern*, critiquing my work ethic? "It's my segment, of course I'm . . ." The second half of what he'd said suddenly registered. "What do you mean '*go out in style*.' Amber's not *out*, and if we do this segment right, she's not going to be *out*."

With a rueful laugh, Butch turned his face away and surveyed the blue wild flowers on the roadside. "You can drop the pretense, Ms. Florentino. I know. I heard Ms. Uberstach. Why do you think I got fired?"

A strange queasy feeling stirred in the bottom of my stomach. I'd never, ever seen Butch act like this. Butch was always bubbly and enthusiastic, filled with positive energy. "Know . . . what? Heard what, exactly. What are you talking about, Butch?"

"Come on, I'm not stupid, Ms. Florentino. I was in the media closet, and Ms. Uberstach didn't know I was there, and I heard her talking to someone on her cell phone. I heard her say it." His chest rose and fell, and his Adam's apple bobbed up and down. "I didn't have the heart to tell Amber, but I think she's pretty much got it figured out. She's smart about people."

Stomping the brakes, I skidded the car to a halt in the middle of the gravel road. "What are you talking about, Butch? What did you hear Ursula say?"

He turned to me slowly, studied my face, squinting one eye, his lips pressed together in an expression of disbelief—the sort of expression characters on cop shows use while patiently soliciting confessions from perpetrators. Finally, his eyebrows flew upward and his mouth dropped open. "You really don't know, do you? I just figured you had to be in on it. I mean, you're an associate producer. You'd have to know . . ."

"Know *what*? What did you hear Ursula say?" I repeated. "What?" I felt like a tornado victim, watching the storm come my way, unable to move.

"I heard Ursula promise that Amber would be off the show in week one of the finals—the recording company didn't want a gospel artist on their label, *period*, and they couldn't take the risk of letting Amber get into the Final Showdown, when the vote would be more closely monitored. Ms. Uberstach said Amber would be out next week. It was all arranged."

"Ursula doesn't have that kind of power," I muttered, searching the road ahead, trying to decide how Ursula would pull off something like that. Even if she did arrange things with the judges . . . "Each week's show is decided by viewer votes."

I heard Butch snort. "And what *counts* the votes?"

"Software," I muttered. "Dysterco software."

"Exactly," Butch said, and suddenly so many things made sense. I'd seen the president of Dysterco in Ursula's office at least a dozen times this season. He and Ursula came and went from lunches, dinner meetings. Ursula had just hired his niece to oversee our in-house system.

The reality crashed over me like the leading wave of a flash flood, laden with debris. Ursula was planning to get rid of both Amber and me at the same time. When Amber's hometown segment tanked, it would appear my incompetence, my inability to keep the location confidential, was to blame.

"I'm sorry, Ms. Florentino." Butch's voice was a low hum somewhere on the fringes of the storm, like the buzzing of downed electrical wires. "I thought you knew. I figured that was why you were hanging out with a music producer. I figured you were, like, working a deal under the counter for Amber to get on the Higher Ground label."

I turned back to Butch, tried to tune in, but my mind was spinning in hyperdrive. "Music prod . . . what?" Ursula's earlier admonishment that Amber might be secretly negotiating with a recording company other than the sponsor of *American Megastar* came to mind. "Who are you talking about, Butch? What guy?"

"J. C. Woods," he said, and I felt myself hit a brick wall. "He doesn't host 'Mason County Line' for the Country Network anymore. He moved back home to Austin and started his own record label—Higher Ground. They specialize in folk and gosp—" The look on my face brought Butch to a stop midsentence. He let his hands fall into his lap and muttered, "Geez, Ms. Florentino, don't you read the trades?"

I sat stunned in my seat, blindsided as the wreckage of my life tumbled down around me. I couldn't think about the trades, or anything else. All I could think was *J. C. Woods . . . J. Carter Woods . . .* the writer of at least one of the songs Amber had performed on the show and apparently a music producer, as well.

My boss had set me up and so had Carter, and I'd stood blindly by and let it happen. I had to be the biggest fool in the history of television.

The numbness of shock slowly left me, and I awoke like an accident victim coming to consciousness, suddenly aware of a blinding pain, a seething anger that painted a fine red sheen over the tranquil blue sky, the puffy white clouds, the fields of lazily waving wild flowers. The car idled forward, and I realized I'd taken my foot off the brake, begun moving into action.

"Ms. Florentino, are you okay?" Butch's voice was clearer now. "Ms. Florentino?"

I stomped on the accelerator and the rear tires fishtailed, then the car lurched forward, careening up a hill and around a corner.

In the passenger seat, Butch took a white-knuckled grip and offered to drive.

I put both hands on the wheel, tightened my fingers until the nails bit in. The Chevy whizzed around an S curve like a car on the Lightning Snake, then splashed through a low-water crossing, hit bottom, and rocketed out the other side.

Butch again offered to drive. By the time we wheeled into Imagene's driveway, he was looking green in the passenger seat. We'd caught up to the horse trailer, and the crew was just disembarking near the barn. Amber, her rhinestone jacket glinting in the sun, was chattering blithely to the grips as they unloaded equipment and prepared to carry it back to crew vans in front of the house. As usual, Rodney was in the lead, cracking the whip and barking orders. I pulled up near the vans, threw open my door, and got out.

"I'll . . . get . . . the keys," Butch muttered.

I didn't answer, just headed across the yard and intercepted Rodney. He grinned, said, "Ah, love, that was brill—" Catching the look on my face, he stopped.

"Did you know?" I ground out. Rodney blinked in confusion, and I added, "Did you know about Ursula's plan?"

Rodney was unflappable, as usual. "What plan, love?" He glanced at the crew members passing by, then toward Amber and her family, silently indicating that if we were going to argue, I should keep my voice down.

Clenching my teeth, I tried to rein in my emotions. What I wanted to do was yell so loud the reporters would hear it in town. Instead, I lowered my voice, leaned closer to Rodney. "Her plan to manipulate viewer vote counts and take Amber off the show next week."

The revelation won an incredulous look, then the realization slowly dawned in Rodney's eyes, as if some loose puzzle pieces were finally fitting together. "If I knew of a plan like that, I wouldn't be here, would I?" He glanced over his shoulder at Amber, who was still chattering away to one of the grips, explaining something about the horse, which had apparently refused to come out of the trailer. "Ursula wanted me in New York. Cal's a bore, so I switched assignments with Tony. The little country kitten's more interesting." He shrugged toward Amber, who had just spotted Carter getting out of the truck. Carter, his attention focused on the commotion in the trailer, never even noticed Amber fanning her hands and heading his way at a giddy trot. She overtook him, grabbed his hand between both of hers, and began trying to yank his arm off.

Her voice, high and brimming with enthusiasm, jingled across the yard. "Oh my gosh, Mr. Woods. It's so good to finally meet you. I'm such a big fan. I'm sorry I didn't say anything earlier. I didn't know it was you until Butch told me after the concert at the rodeo arena. Didn't you used to have a beard? I'm such a big fan. Of you, not of beards. I love your songs. They're just . . . awesome. I've been trying to call you all weekend, and . . ."

The roar in my ears drowned out the rest as I crossed the yard. Amber had her back turned, but Carter saw me coming. He looked like a man who wanted to be anywhere but here.

Amber finally picked up on the change in his demeanor. She turned around, and her face went pale, her mouth dropping open. "Ms. Florentino, I . . . it's not what it looks . . . I didn't . . ."

"We'll talk later," I ground out. Amber started to protest, to attempt explanation again, but I stabbed a finger toward the house. "Leave."

Fidgeting uncertainly, she glanced at her grandfather and brothers, then at the confused grip behind the trailer. "I didn't . . . I'm . . . I'm sorry."

"Later," I said again. "Just go in the house, Amber."

Tears filled Amber's eyes. She hesitated a moment longer, then spun around and ran for the house. Her family went after her, the frightened grip slunk quickly away, and inside the trailer Magnolia quieted, as if even she sensed a powder keg about to blow.

I turned on Carter, the heat of fury, of humiliation, rising in my face. "You played me."

He raised his hands palm-out, trying to placate me. "Manda, it's not like that. It's not what you think."

"Oh really? Really?" My voice reverberated through the yard. Clenching my fists, I fought to regain self-control, to rein in the volume. By the vans, the crew stood frozen in place. "How? How is it *not* what I think? You *weren't* here to meet with Amber? You *weren't* scamming all of us to get close to her? You *weren't* using me to . . ." An enormous lump rose in my throat, shattered, and I felt tears rushing in. Swallowing hard, I closed my eyes, tried to breathe. I wouldn't break down here in front of everyone. I couldn't.

"I wasn't using you." Carter's voice was soft, intimate. It washed over me like the warm waves of a peaceful shore, lapping at my feet, trying to lure me into the surf, where a dangerous riptide of need, and fantasy, and loneliness lay hidden beneath the surface.

"Don't." My voice quivered, started to bend. "Don't bother." In my mind, he was David, trying to gloss over the reasons for cruising *Mydestiny.com*.

Carter had even been smart enough, ruthless enough to use my breakup with David to sucker me in. *"The guy on the phone is an idiot, by the way. For what it's worth, the guy's a fool."*

I was the fool. Like every good scam artist, Carter had found the tender spot. He had discovered the place where I was weak. He had put sweet-smelling salve on the wound, and I'd been putty in his hands.

He closed the space between us, tried to touch me.

"Don't," I hissed, my voice trembling with an overspill of emotion. I had to get out of there. I had to get out of there before I fell apart in front of everyone. Turning around, I hurried across the lawn to the crew vans, climbed into the front one, started the engine, and took off, headed nowhere, somewhere. Anywhere but here.

Chapter 24

Imagene Doll

Watching Amber take that stage at the fairgrounds was one of the highest points of my life, not only because Brother Harve, O.C., the Andersons, and I were on the very top of the bleachers, but because when Amber belted out the national anthem and the flag unfurled high above the stadium, it was a moment of pure glory. I could feel my Jack, and all the other soldiers who'd passed on, standing right there with us. They probably had to wipe away tears of pride just like I did. Life has only a handful of perfect moments, and that was one of mine.

And then, no sooner had Amber got off stage than there was Justin Shay, running through the arena in nothing but red shorts, trying to get everyone to look at him. Heaven's gates! Why he did that, I couldn't imagine, but at least he got arrested for it. When Buddy Ray took him into custody, Justin Shay was arguing at the top of his lungs, saying no redneck deputy could take him to jail, and he was gonna call his lawyers, and if those reporters wanted a show, they better come to the sheriff's office to see it.

The reporters went, all right. Harve, O.C., and the rest of us got trapped in the traffic trying to get out of the fairgrounds. Those newspeople drive like they're on an episode of *NASCAR*.

By the time we got back to my house, the *American Megastar* crew was crashed in the living room. Amanda-Lee and Carter were nowhere to be found, and Amber was in the kitchen all alone, wearing a sad look. She was fixing some leftover roast and sliced bread on a tray for the crew to eat. When I walked in, she sniffed and wiped her eyes with the back of her wrist.

"Well, land sakes, sugar," I said, putting my things on the counter. "You ought to be happy as a fly in fresh butter right now. How come you look like your dog just died?"

Amber's shoulders trembled up and down. "I messed up. I always mess up. I'm so stupid. I always open my big mouth at the exact wrong time." The last word shuddered like the end of a sad song. She stabbed a knife into the pickle jar, pulled out a pickle, and started after it like she wanted to cut it to bits.

I was afraid she'd chop her finger off, so I took the knife away. "There now, hon, don't take it out on that helpless pickle. Tell Mrs. Doll what's wrong."

"I screw everything up," she blurted with a little hiccup and a sob.

I rubbed her back, and we stood side by side at the meat tray. "Now, that's not true. No way that's true. You couldn'ta done better at the rodeo arena. It was a sight to behold. It's too bad Justin Shay had to go crazy and run around in his unmentionables like that. Is he smokin' some kind of drugs or something?"

Sniffing, Amber shook her head. "Huh-uh. Justin did that for me so we could get out of there without all the reporters following us."

"Well, I'll be dogged." *Time to repent. Lord, in the future, I'll not be so quick to think the worst of people.* I'd jumped to the complete wrong conclusion about Justin Shay.

Amber sighed and wiped her eyes again. "Butch says it's no big deal—with the lawyers Justin has, he'll be out by tonight."

"Well then, what are you worried about? He did a nice thing for you—almost like one of them movie heroes he plays. I bet it made him feel real good to do that, don't you figure? He maybe didn't know he had it in him to put someone else ahead of himself. You know that down at the jail, Forrest and Buddy Ray will treat him real good." My pep talk didn't seem to be cheering Amber up one little bit. "Buddy Ray's probably in hog heaven, having all those reporters see him make an arrest. Heck, he might even make *The National Examiner* or the *Austin Statesman*. Who knows?"

That won a little smile from Amber, but it didn't last long.

"What's really the matter, hon?"

Groaning under her breath, she walked to the hallway door and peeked through to make sure no one was there. "Ms. Florentino's really mad and it's my fault. I didn't mean for it to happen . . . I didn't know her and Butch were back. I thought they were farther behind us, but she came around from the front of the house and she heard me talking to Mr. Woods. She told him off right there in the yard and then she got in one of the vans and took off out of here. He borrowed Butch's keys and went after her, but it won't do any good. I've only seen Ms. Florentino that mad once before, and it wasn't pretty."

I had to think for a minute to get all that news into a column. "Who's Mr. Woods?"

She pointed through the window toward the horse rig. "The guy who drove the truck and trailer for us—Mr. Woods."

"You mean Carter?" I said, still trying to get things in a row. Sometimes, talking to Amber was like herding cats. "Honey, what in the world would you have said to get Carter and Amanda-Lee in a fight? The two of them seemed to be getting along awful good—*real* good, if you know what I mean."

Amber threw up her hands and let them slap back against her thighs. "That's what makes me feel so bad. Ms. Florentino's always all uptight and stressed out. I mean, I like her and all, but some people, you know, just don't seem happy. Then, today when we were having lunch and stuff, she seemed really happy. When Mr. Woods brought the horse trailer out of the barn for us to go, I could see why. I thought, dadgum, no wonder Ms. Florentino's in such a good mood, since she gets to ride up front with a guy who looks like that. And you know, I thought I knew his face from somewhere, but I couldn't place where. I didn't know he was J. C. Woods until Butch whispered it in my ear at the rodeo arena." She held out her hands like she was pleading for me to believe her, which wasn't a problem, being as I had no idea what she was talking about.

"Whoa, there. We're gonna have to back up a little bit, sugar. Who's J. C. Woods?" That name seemed familiar, but I couldn't place it.

"J. C. Woods, from the Country Network?" Amber's voice tilted upward, like she couldn't believe I didn't know the name right away. "He hosts the 'Mason County Line' show, where they have all the big time singers and songwriters on and stuff—I mean, he doesn't anymore, but it's still in reruns sometimes, except on the show he has longer hair, and a goatee."

I scratched my head. "Carter's a TV star?" At my house, I only got regular channels, but I was surprised Donetta hadn't picked up on it, since she watched cable TV all the time. I hadn't pictured Carter as a TV star. Even though he was sure good-looking enough for it, he seemed like a pretty normal young man. Nothing like that Justin Shay, who I guess wasn't all bad, either, come to find out.

"Yeah," Amber went on. "He's a songwriter and stuff. I sang one of his songs on *American Megastar* a while back. I wanted to do another one—this song about little boys with toy sailboats, but Ms. Uberstach wouldn't let me. Ms. Florentino liked it, though."

"Well, it seems like that'd give the two of them even more in common—Carter and Amanda-Lee, I mean. I can't figure why they'd have any reason to fight about something like that." What girl wouldn't want to be romanced by a country music TV star with a poetic nature?

Amber's eyes flicked to one side, and her lips tilted downward. "Except she didn't know who he was, and he didn't tell her, and he probably didn't tell her because I've been trying to meet with him about recording for his music company, Higher Ground." Looping her arms over her chest, she darted another look my way, then fidgeted from one foot to the other. "I wasn't trying to do anything underhanded, Mrs. Doll, and I didn't mean it against *American Megastar*, or Ms. Florentino. It's just that . . . well . . . I guess I could have waited to contact J. C. Woods until I was actually off *American Megastar*, but once you're off, you're not news, you know? It seemed smart to do it now, so when I found out I was coming home this weekend, I set it up to meet him here in Daily. I been trying to call him ever since yesterday, and he didn't answer his cell phone, so I figured maybe he wasn't interested after all, and I was kind of downhearted about it. Then, when I found out he was actually here—I mean *right* here—I went a little nuts and blabbed the whole thing right where Ms. Florentino could hear." She stopped to take a breath and stood there twisting and untwisting her arms like a little girl confessing in the principal's office. "I really screwed it up bad. Now probably both of them will hate me, and I'll get kicked off *American Megastar*, and I'll be back here working at the feed store. I'll just be stupid little Amber Anderson again."

She started to cry, and I opened my arms and took her in. "Ssshhh, now, there's nothing stupid about you, Amber. You're a good girl. You didn't have a way in the world of knowing this would happen. It was a smart thing, you trying to make use of your opportunities and look to the future."

"I really wanted . . . I wanted Andy to have money for college, and . . ." She gulped down the rest of the sentence in a sob, and I felt my shoulder getting wet. "And I wanted . . . I wanted to make a place for kids who don't have anybody, and I wanted . . . I wanted . . ." She choked on the words again, and I smoothed my hands over her hair, patting like I would have when my boys skinned a knee or had a fight with a bully at school.

"Hush, now. There's a good girl." Laying my hands on her shoulders, I pulled her back so I could look her in the eye. "You got to remember that when things are out of our hands, that doesn't mean they're not in God's. I've got it written right there on my refrigerator, see? On that football magnet there by the ice dispenser? One of my sons put that on the coffin at Jack's funeral. It says *God's ball* on it because Jack told that to our oldest when Tim had his heart broke over not getting a football scholarship years ago. Jack sat him down and explained how sometimes in life you carry the ball, sometimes you just run along, and sometimes you're flat on your back, but just because *you* don't have the ball don't mean it's not moving toward the goal. There's a whole team of men and angels at work in every life."

Amber looked at the football and nodded like she could see Jack's point. I turned her loose and grabbed a napkin from the table. "Here now, you wipe your eyes. One way or another, we'll make this turn out."

The phone rang and I grabbed it, knowing it would be Donetta, because I'd just been thinking of calling her to help me straighten out this mess. Whenever I'm about to call Donetta, she calls me first.

She didn't even say hello, just, "Imagene, what in the world's going on? First, you let Amber make her big surprise appearance at the fair before your best friend can get out there, and then I find out that Justin Shay's been arrested for riding a bull naked at the rodeo, and you don't bother to call and tell me that?"

"No one was naked on a bull, DeDe." One thing about a Daily story, no matter how fantastic it is to start with, it'll be even better by the time it gets around town. "He ran around the arena in red silky boxers, that's all. Kind of like them things pro wrestlers wear. He wasn't naked."

"Even so—" Donetta clicked her tongue to let me know she still had a knot in her tail—"you coulda called. I had to hear it from Betty Prine, of all people. She come by here with her feathers up because she knew the gossip and I didn't. How do you think that made me feel?"

"I'm sorry, Netta, I—"

"I wouldn't leave *you* out of somethin' newsworthy, Imagene Doll. Like just now, I got Amanda-Lee and Carter about to tear each other up in the back alley, and what am I doin'? I'm callin' you."

"Good gracious," I said, stretching the phone cord around the corner into the pantry and cupping my hand over the receiver. "What are they saying?"

Donetta smacked her lips to let me know she was double disgusted. "Well, if I knew, I probably wouldn't tell somebody that doesn't bother to call me, would I?"

"Donetta." Sometimes I wanted to beg forgiveness from Donetta and pull her hair all at the same time. "We been in the middle of a top secret operation all afternoon."

"Are you sayin' I can't keep a secret?"

"Of course not. I wasn't saying that."

"Half the county heard about Justin Shay goin' wild before I did."

I started rearranging the cans on the bean shelf out of frustration. "Yes, I know, Netta. I'm sorry. We got caught in the traffic leaving the fairgrounds and I clean forgot to call you. You know how foggy I am sometimes, especially days when I miss exercise class."

That made Donetta happy. "I been telling you exercise is good for the mind."

"It is. I know it surely is. You were right."

"No reason we got to get old, fat, and addle-brained all at once."

"There surely isn't. Two out of three's bad enough."

There was a long pause on the other end of the phone, then finally, "Oh mercy, I forgot what I called you about."

"Amanda-Lee and Carter having a spittin' match in the back alley. Is everything all right now?" I grabbed onto the tiny hope that maybe this situation might have worked itself out on its own, because I didn't have the first idea how to fix it.

"I wouldn't say that, exactly." I pictured Donetta fluffing the back of her hair like she always did when she had to deliver bad news. She always said bad news goes over best with good hair. "Just now, she stormed in the door, hollering that she never wanted to see him again, and he walked off down the alley, I think. Then she went back and hollered something else out the door, then slammed it again. Now she's headed up the stairs, and I don't know where he's gone. Maybe he got in his car and left. Anyhow, it looks like the romance is over, which is a shame, too, because I had a feeling about that pair."

"Oh lands," I muttered. "I better get my keys and get over there."

"You'd best wait a minute." I heard the squeak of Donetta going through the door into the back hallway. "Amanda-Lee don't know it yet, but she's got company up there. Her boss showed up a while ago, in a taxicab all the way from Austin. A real cranky lady. Tall, like one of them fashion models. Has some kind of foreign accent, that's for sure. I couldn't understand a word she said. Hang on a minute." Donetta put her hand over the phone, and I heard the muffled sound of her hollering up the stairway. "Yoo-hoo, Amanda-Lee-ee. You've got company up there, hon. I say, you've got company up there, hon. . . . Hon?" The line hung up, and I figured Donetta'd hit the button by mistake. It didn't matter. I had a pretty good idea of what was going to happen next.

Chapter 25

Mandalay Florentino

"I can't believe I've been so stupid!" I screamed, yanking open the back door of the hotel. Manda Florentino, producer, wanted to step back into the alley and punch him out, while Manda Florentino, victim of romantic stupidity, wanted to run away sobbing uncontrollably. I settled for screaming from the doorway and throwing a crumpled Coke can as Carter tried to exit the car he'd borrowed for our ridiculous high-speed chase from Imagene's house to the Daily Hotel. Next time I saw Butch, I was going to smack him for giving Carter the keys. "You're a liar, Carter . . . J.C. . . . whatever your name is. I guess you can sit back now and have a good laugh. You conned me and I fell for it, but if you think I'm going to let you get your slimy mitts on Amber Anderson, you've got another think coming."

Carter grimaced, pretending as if the truth actually stung. "Manda, it's not what you think. . . ."

"Yeah, I'll bet." Jerk. What a jerk! How could he do this? Was there an invisible sign on me that said, *Go ahead, tell me anything—I'll believe it.* "You should give up music producing and go into acting. 'Church sound systems,' the whole small-town Texas boy thing, and the brother with cancer, the poor little nieces back home. That was priceless. You deserve an Oscar."

He blinked, like I'd caught him by surprise, rendering him speechless.

I called him a name my mother wouldn't have approved of, slammed the door, walked three steps, then went back, yanked open the door, and hollered something else that would not have made my mother proud.

She would, however, have applauded my uncovering Carter for the shark that he was and telling him exactly what he could do with his music company. During her years in Hollywood, my mother had learned how to handle sharks. She'd warned us girls about two-faced lecherous show-biz men. I knew better than to fall for a guy who was too charming, too smooth, too . . . perfect. Too good to be true.

I knew better.

Why had I been so stupid—about Carter, about David? Why was I so gullible lately? Why was I willing to split with David and fall right into Carter's arms, into his trap? Was I that desperate, that blind, just because I was thirty-four, not married, and I hated my job? The reality pinched some tender place inside me as I dashed up the stairs. Donetta hollered something from below, but the words were too faint to distinguish over the roar of self-recrimination.

Why had I let myself become such an idiot, such a sap?

Why did this hurt so much? Why did I feel hopeless, as if I'd never find my way to something good, to someone good, to a life, a relationship, that meant something?

I wanted to lock myself in my room, lie down in bed, and never get up. It wouldn't matter if I did. My job, my existence, was pointless, so much so that I was trying to convince myself the results of a reality TV show really made a difference in the grand scheme of things—that it was my sacred duty to uphold justice, compassion, and the dreams of a little country girl who wanted to make it big. But the truth was that Amber was looking after Amber, and Carter was looking after Carter, and Ursula was . . . sprawled out on the furry bed amid a sea of pink satin pillows.

I stood in the doorway blinking, hoping she would disappear, hoping I'd finally gone over the edge and the Ursula image was an anxiety-induced hallucination.

She rolled onto her stomach, raised her head in a lithe maneuver, and raked an outstretched claw through the thick white fur of the bedspread like a lioness marking her territory. Her hair, hanging in the disheveled remnants of a bun, tumbled around her with a life of its own, and deep rings of smudged mascara gave her pale blue eyes an icy glow. For Ursula, she was a wreck.

"Hello, Mandee-lay," she purred, stretching her fingers into the bedspread again, then drawing them back, the thick white fuzz bulging between her fingers. "The patroness below showdt me to the room. I hope this izz my bed. It izz deee-vine."

She waved vaguely toward the adjoining door, still open from this morning. "The room with the lee-tle bearzz suits you, daah-ling."

I glanced at the door, pictured Carter standing there, laughing and agreeing to be our driver for Operation Amber. No wonder he was so quick to sign on. He had an operation of his own underway.

I'd let the wolf in the door and never thought twice about it until he blew down my house of straw. I wasn't going to make that mistake again. I didn't care if it cost me my job, my livelihood, my reputation. I didn't care if Ursula ruined me in LA. For once, I was going to come out on top.

The she-lion would not be leaving me bleeding on the floor today.

"I'm surprised you came." I crossed the room to the adjoining door, pushing it closed to shut out the memories. The blue gorilla sat in Carter's chair, smiling as the lock clicked into place.

Something twisted painfully just below my ribs.

An empty Ziploc bag lay dripping on the lamp table by my bathroom. I picked it up, swallowed hard, felt air squeeze from my lungs. *I won't break down in front of her*, I told myself. *I won't.*

Ursula turned on the bed and reclined against the pillows. "There was a lee-tle fish in the bag. It wazz dead, so I didt away with it." She flipped a single finger toward the bathroom. "I do not like lee-tle fish."

A sense of loss, disproportionate to the missing goldfish, stabbed inside me. I wondered if the fish was really dead or if Ursula had derived some perverse pleasure from flushing it, watching it wriggle and squirm and try to fight the current. Down the toilet, like the rest of my life.

Anger seeped in where the hollow ache had been, filled me until I felt like I would burst if I didn't wrap my hands around Ursula's long, jewel-encrusted neck and squeeze, very hard.

Patience, give me patience. My father's most important life advice to me when I started into the working world—when you're tempted to do something stupid, step back and ask for patience.

Or in the words of a Chinese fortune cookie, *He who dances with the devil must watch his step.*

"It was important that the situation here progress . . . as plannedt." She tilted her head solicitously, resting her chin on curled fingers.

"Of course it was," I bit out, forcing a crocodile smile to match hers. I was through groveling before the throne of Ursula Uberstach.

"Wouldt you like to give me a report?" It wasn't a question, of course. It was a command to stand and deliver.

I'd like to give you a lot of things. A nifty little report isn't one of them. "Things are going well. I tried to call and save you a trip out here. I know how *busy* you are." Busy making back-room deals, busy trashing me, busy ruining the lives of perfectly innocent people, busy sleeping with the president of Dysterco, busy plotting to commit fraud.

Fraud . . . An idea began to form in the recesses of my consciousness, a divine inspiration. Maybe, just maybe, I could salvage this situation yet.

Ursula's mask cracked for the barest instant—like a tiny nuclear reaction far out in space. A flash, then nothing but silky-smooth darkness. Emptiness.

For the first time in a long time I didn't envy even the tiniest part of her. She was powerful, successful, gorgeous. Gorgeously vacant. Successful only because she used people like toys, because no one mattered to Ursula but Ursula. She wasn't trying to change the world—she was only trying to make it revolve around herself. No matter how many impressive credentials, or how much power was attached, I didn't want to be like her. Ever.

She shifted on the pillows, sat a little straighter, scenting a change in the wind. "My case wazz stolen in the airport, with my phone and my identification. This delayedt me momentarily."

Not long enough. I'd never wished identity theft on anyone before, but I wished it on Ursula. I hoped some hairy-shouldered man in a greasy tank top was charging a new above-ground swimming pool to her Visa right now. "That must have been difficult." There was a flippant undertone even Ursula couldn't miss.

Her eyes narrowed. "Yes, but I am here now. I understandt you have experienced some problems? I have seen the press coverage."

I'll bet you have. "Nothing I can't handle."

"The segment of Am-beer is very . . . important. Your job here is very important." She stroked a finger across her perfectly tanned chin, rested a long red fingernail against her lips, trying to read me.

"Why, exactly?"

Her eyebrows shot up, then lowered. "Mandee-lay? Do you care to explain?"

The muscles in my jaw tightened. My teeth clenched, and I forced words through the barricade. "Why would Amber's segment matter when she's off the show next week anyway? As a matter of fact, wouldn't it be more convenient if Amber's segment was a complete botch job—if, say, someone tipped off the paparazzi and they swarmed the place?" *Boom. Boo-yah. Bombs away.* Direct hit, right over downtown Ursula-ville.

She looked remarkably calm, disturbingly so. For a flicker of an instant, I thought, *What if I'm wrong? What if this is all a figment of Butch's really vivid imagination?*

I pictured his face in the car. He didn't seem the least bit unsure of himself. I'd never ever known Butch to lie about anything. Why would he lie about this?

Ursula's chin lifted and she watched me coolly from beneath lowered lashes, her eyes narrow slits of frosty blue. "Mandee-lay. I suggest you explain yourself."

You first. "I think the question's pretty self-explanatory. Wouldn't it be easier to take Amber off the show next week if her hometown segment was a flop—if there was a plethora of negative media about her coming here with Justin Shay and turning the town on its ear? If she's not the little hometown good girl anymore, then everything she sings about, everything she claims to be is a lie, isn't it? She's a hypocrite, and hypocrites don't get viewer votes."

Ursula shrugged, tracing the red fingernail over her lips again. The usually flawless manicure was chipped. She paused to inspect it. "Mandee-lay. What are you suggestingk? I think perhaps you have been in this dreadful Texas climate too long. Perhaps you have become dehydratedt. Otherwise, I know you would not say something so . . . ill advised."

"Why don't we cut the pretense, Ursula?" *To borrow a line from Butch.* "I know what's going on. You promised to have Amber off the show next week. Period."

She winced. Barely.

Ah-ha. A crack in the ice . . .

"Butch should not hide in closets listeningk." She fluttered a hand in the air, like a queen dismissing peasantry. "He izz a boy. He misunderstoodt. I toldt him this when I gifted his job back to him. He seemed to understandt."

"I think he understands very well."

"Butch should not frighten Am-beer with this foolishness. She is, after all, such a fragile lee-tle thing. Like the fish." Her gaze drifted toward the bathroom, and she smiled slightly. "Sometimes a quick departure is . . . merciful, no? But this . . . this conversation Butch speaks of was only idle talk. Butch should not be troublingk you with such . . . foolishness."

"He was trying to do the right thing." *A concept you would know nothing about.* "I imagine he thought I should know I was being set up."

"Man-dee-laaay," Ursula admonished, looping an arm around the full-body Elvis pillow. Her elbow compressed the neck so that the head bulged forward—no doubt illustrating what she planned to do to me. "You must not listen to a silly boy. Why wouldt I bring Butch back to hizz job to find Am-beer, if not to save this segment . . . for you."

Hmmm . . . let me think. . . . "Maybe so that Butch would tell Amber about her imminent exit from the show and she would bail on her own? How's that for a scenario? That would save you from taking the risk of manipulating viewer votes, wouldn't it?"

The lazy sweep of her gaze stopped, shot back to me. "I have no control of viewer votes. You know this, of course."

"But Dysterco does. Convenient that you're sleeping with the president of the company, isn't it?" *Bingo.* I'd struck a nerve there. Ursula sat up, bent Elvis in half, and fired a visual laser bolt at me.

"I could have you terminatedt for such talk."

"Go ahead." Hopefully, she only meant terminated from my job. What were the odds that Ursula had connections with the Swedish mafia? "But I'll tell you what's going to happen first." No point stopping now. Might as well go all the way. If I was headed down in flames, I was going to take as many of Ursula's plans with me as I could. "I'm finishing Amber's segment, and it will be good. I have the crew at a secluded location, and you won't be contacting them. We're filming Amber's welcome home concert tonight, and I'm not telling you where. When the show airs, you will not, I repeat not, in any way manipulate the viewer votes. You know, and I know, that Amber has talent, and she has public interest. With a good hometown segment, she's got every chance of making it to the Final Showdown. Ultimately, Cal Preston has the greater fan base, so in the end he probably comes out on top, but either way, it'll be fair, and having made the final two, Amber will have offers from other labels." *Like Higher Ground.* It occurred to me that by doing this, I could be giving Carter Woods exactly what he wanted—what he'd scammed me for.

One troll at a time, Mandalay. Knock out the big one first, cross the bridge, then worry about the rest.

Ursula swung her legs lazily over the edge of the bed, dropped Elvis, stood up, and towered to her full five-foot-eleven-inch height. She smiled. Murderously. "And how, lee-tle fish, do you expect to accomplish this thing?" Pinching her thumb and forefinger together, she held her hand in the air, recreating the motion she must have used just before flushing the goldfish. My goldfish.

I'd never come so close to contemplating murder in my life. I pictured the scene, like something from a horror movie. Vampira, the evil, blood-sucking boss, taken out by a stake through the heart.

"Watch me," I said. "If I see any, I mean any, indication over the next few weeks that the viewer tabs have been tampered with, I'll go public. I'll blow the whistle so loud you'll be able to hear it all the way to the FCC and the federal courthouse. I don't care how well you and Dysterco think you've covered it up; between my testimony and Butch's, we'll get attention. The last time I checked, fraud was a crime."

Ursula scoffed, took a few steps in my direction, then stopped, seemingly to investigate a *Birthplace of Elvis* platter on the wall. "You will never prove anythingk." But there was a little tic in her cheek that indicated otherwise. She knew that if Butch and I went public, given the notoriety of the show, there would be an in-depth investigation. The media would go wild.

"I won't have to. The scandal will be enough. It'll be 'Quiz Show' all over again. The studio won't want the notoriety, and neither will the network." In an industry where public opinion was everything, public scandal was the kiss of death. If the viewers found out they'd been duped by *American Megastar*, the show would be history.

Ursula's eyes widened, then narrowed. She was temporarily speechless. Finally, she stammered, "You . . . you vill be ruinedt if you do this thingk. You vill never work in television again."

"And neither will you." *Ka-ching. Little fish has the money cards, baby. Read 'em and weep.*

She turned to me, appraising my determination. I was determined, more so than I ever thought I'd be. I was ready to go all the way to the mat. If Ursula wanted a fight, she'd get one. I was through being everyone's patsy.

Her chest rose and fell with a long breath. She blinked slowly, then again, as if she were seeing me for the first time. Manda Florentino, fire-breathing dragon, the Rocky Balboa of reality TV. I felt larger than life. Later, I would probably second-guess this moment, but right now I was shielded by an armor that even Ursula and her career-killing sword of doom couldn't penetrate. For the first time in a long time, I was doing the right thing, standing on principle. It felt . . . exhilarating.

"Mandee-lay." The word was almost a plea. A plea, from Ursula. Any minute now, the world would be coming to an end. "Think of what you are doingk. In four weeks, the season will be finished and you vill never see this girl, Am-beer, again. She izz not worth the demise of your career."

It was my turn to inject the conversation with a rueful laugh. "Wasn't the demise of my career part of the plan anyway? A little fringe benefit? Amber's not the only one being set up here."

"It does not needt to be so." Ursula dangled a carrot to see if I would bite.

Backing away a step, I opened my purse and took out the skeleton key for the room. "You have my terms. I'm not changing my mind."

Letting her arms fall open, Ursula lifted her hands, her expression one of utter confusion and complete disbelief. For once, she couldn't have exactly what she wanted. She couldn't have me. "Mandee-lay, why will you not hear me? Why wouldt you do this . . . this foolish thing?"

Opening the hallway door, I stepped into the threshold. There was no going back from here. "Because it's the right thing, Ursula. You should try it sometime." Slipping through the door, I closed it behind me, then stuck the skeleton key in the lock and turned it. I backed away with the key in hand and hurried down the stairs, leaving Ursula imprisoned in a one-room palace of Elvis memorabilia. The thought was delightfully satisfying.

By the time I reached the bottom landing, Ursula had already started to pound on the door. A mixture of threats and Swedish obscenities echoed along the corridor.

Donetta gave the commotion a look of concern when I passed through the downstairs hallway.

"No matter what she says, don't let her out." I pointed up the stairs. "It's for her own good. For Amber's good."

Donetta took in the racket with an unconcerned flutter of false eyelashes. "I was just closin' up for the evenin'. I don't hear a thing, hon." Her deep red lips curled upward into two circles of blusher.

"Good," I said, starting toward the beauty shop with her. "I need your help. We've got a concert to put on."

The dumbwaiter moaned as we passed by. A chill ran up my spine, followed by a palpable sense of satisfaction. I hoped the ghost of the Daily Hair and Body was preparing for a very active night.

Chapter 26

Imagene Doll

When the town of Daily, Texas, sets its mind to something (good Lord willin' and the creeks don't rise), it'll happen. We wanted to put together a welcome home concert Amber'd always remember, and by golly, we did. The ladies got the funeral casseroles, coffee cakes, and banana breads out of their deep freezes. Bob kicked all those reporters out of the café, closed it down, and set to work frying all the chicken nuggets he could, with only two hours' notice. Harlan and Ervin borrowed tables and chairs from the fellowship hall at the Baptist church. Doyle and Frank helped Miss Lulu dig out the two big canopy tents she uses every year for the Fourth of July party at Boggy Bend. Betty Prine (if you can believe it) and her literary society even brought over fresh flowers, table linens, and some fancy French hors d'oeuvres and crumpets they had left over from their First Tuesday Tea. Even though her house is right across the street from the jail, Betty didn't say one word to the press about the plans for Amber's welcome home concert. She was mad at those reporters because they parked on her lawn and ran over her hydrangea bush.

It's not easy getting dozens of casseroles and a whole community of people out of town right under the noses of a bunch of nosy reporters, but Daily folks are resourceful. People snuck out of town a few at a time while Forrest and Buddy Ray kept the press milling at the jailhouse. They told the reporters there'd be a big news announcement from Justin Shay's lawyer at eight that evening, which was thirty minutes after Amber's secret concert was supposed to start out at Harve's Chapel. At seven forty-five, Forrest and Buddy Ray dressed the prisoner up in a deputy's uniform, and the three of them left out the back door, pretending to be headed off on patrol. I imagine those reporters had a long night before they figured out Justin Shay's lawyer wasn't even in town and the jail was empty.

In the meantime, the Dailyians gathered for the biggest party we'd seen since the highway department put a historical marker out at Boggy Bend. There wasn't enough room for everyone in the little church building, but nobody seemed to care. Folks set up their lawn chairs and blankets on the grass outside, Brother Harve threw open all the doors and windows, and Caney Creek saw the biggest choir practice it'd ever had. The music of the gospel band and the choir and Amber's clear, sweet voice lifted into the night and covered us all with a sheen of glory.

In all my life, I never did see a girl look happier than Amber was right then. Her tiff with Amanda-Lee was over. She had her brothers watching her from the front row and that cute little Butch giving her a shiny smile and all the filming crew looking pleased, despite the tight quarters. Amber even coaxed old Verl up onto the stage, and the two of them performed a rendition of "Danny Boy," an old song Verl comforted the kids with when they were little. I never even knew Verl could sing, but listening to the two of them, I could see where Amber got her voice. Verl sure must have felt good when that crowd of folks, who'd always thought he was nothing, stood up in their seats, clapping and wiping their eyes. I almost couldn't take it all in, but it brought to mind that verse about the least being the greatest and the greatest being the least. Verl was humble, even when the crowd went wild with applause. He just blushed and waved off the attention and went back to his spot on the front row. I couldn't help thinking he sat a little straighter after that, and beside him, Andy, Amos, and Avery looked proud of their grandpa. It was a far sight from the times he'd staggered down the bleachers at the football games, that was for sure.

Halfway through the concert, the spiky-haired reporter—the one who'd been the very first to arrive in Daily—showed up with her cameraman. Amanda-Lee gave a worried look as the lady squeezed her way in the back door. Doyle got up and offered his seat, and wonder of wonders, that reporter just sat down real nice to watch the show. I guess even she could see the night was magic all on its own.

Amanda-Lee relaxed, but she still seemed down-in-the-mouth. In fact, she was the only one in the room who didn't look happy. I knew why, of course. She was thinking about Carter. I sure wished we could have located him and got those two kids together to talk things out, but during the commotion of everyone preparing for the concert, he disappeared. Donetta called the phone number he listed when he rented the hotel room, but no one answered, so she left a voice mail, inviting him to the concert. She made sure to add that Amanda-Lee would be there. All during the preparations and the concert, Donetta and me hoped Carter would get the message, turn around, and head back to Daily. If we could get him and Amanda-Lee together, I was sure the magic of the night and that big old Texas moon would do the rest. Sometimes situations look different in a softer light. There was many a time Jack and me got in a wrangle over things that turned out to be mostly a misunderstanding. I tried to tell that to Amanda-Lee and suggest that she could get Carter's phone number from Donetta, but she wasn't in the mood to listen. She said it didn't matter and she had work to do, but thanks for the offer. Then she went on watching the concert and looking sad.

As Amber finished her last song and left the stage, Donetta and me stood outside the church, feeling plain bushed. Folks gathered around to congratulate Amber and visited with one another on the lawn and filed to the food tent.

"Not likely we'll have another day like this one anytime soon," Donetta sighed.

"Don't know if I could take another day like this one," I admitted. "I feel like I could sleep till spring."

"It is spring." Leave it to Donetta to point out the obvious.

"Next spring. I could sleep till next spring, I'm so tired."

Donetta nodded, squinting out into the live oaks, where the rising moon cast a speckled shadow over the cars, the Dailyians in lawn chairs, and way in the back, that reporter's big motor home. She'd started to interview folks in the crowd now, but she was being real polite-like. She asked some questions about Amber and Justin Shay, but not in such a mean way, and she didn't bother Amber while Amber was talking to the crowd of friends and neighbors. I had to chuckle as the reporter worked her way through the church yard, though. Justin Shay was standing not five foot away, and she didn't even know it was him, on account of the police uniform. He pulled his hat low and gave me a smile as the camera passed him by. I think he was enjoying being just regular folk for a change.

Donetta blew out a long breath. Her lipstick had rubbed off on her front teeth, and I made a motion to let her know it, just in case she got on camera later. She finger-brushed and gave me the once-over, too. Real chums do things like that for each other. You know you're best girlfriends when you check each other's teeth without even thinking about it.

I slipped my arm around her, and we laid our heads together. "It's been a real good day."

"It certainly has," she agreed, patting my hand on her shoulder. "I sure wish Carter woulda come back, though. I like that boy a lot."

"Me too. I hadn't done any matchmaking in a while. Maybe I'm a little rusty, but I had a feeling about those two."

Donetta made a regretful *tsk-tsk*. "I did, too. I thought I saw it in the window that first day after they both came to town, but maybe I was wrong. Guess I'm gettin' old. What good's a hairdresser who can't spot a real match anymore? Might be time for me to just go on out to pasture, start spendin' my time playing dominoes at the old folks' home." Donetta sounded almost as down-in-the-mouth as Amanda-Lee had, her vision having failed to come true and all.

I swatted her fingers. "Donetta Bradford, we are neither one of us getting old unless we decide to let ourselves. I was thinking, maybe we could take one of those cruises that sails out of Galveston—go see some things we never seen before."

Donetta craned back and broke the link between us, her neck growing three inches longer and her eyes bugging out. "On a boat?"

"That's the only kind of cruise I know of."

"You don't even swim, Imagene."

"I could learn." I braced my hands on my hips, getting a little aggravated with her acting like we both had one foot in the grave. "We could take Lucy, and all three of us get on a big boat and sail off to Timbuktu—like that movie Thelma and Louise, only we'd have two Louises and we'd use a boat, not a car. And we'd have a happier ending. It's time we did some things. Had some adventures."

Donetta gazed up at the moon, thinking about it. "Maybe so . . ."

I started feeling a little hopeful, and a little scared. *No time to stop now, Imagene*, I told myself. *You need to set this plan in ink while you got your courage up. Lots of senior folks go on those boats, and you can, too.* "Where is Lucy, anyway? We could ask her right now."

"Over in the tent serving food, I think." Donetta squinted at the moon, like she was trying to imagine what it'd look like from the water. "If there's work to be done, you know Lucy won't be standing around. I'd better go help, come to think of it."

"All right," I said, figuring it might be best to let that cruise idea settle on Donetta a bit so she wouldn't out-and-out say no. A piece of me couldn't believe I was so determined to go through with it, but in the very back of my mind, I could see me, Imagene Doll, in a big pink sunhat far out at sea.

Donetta headed for the food tent, and I turned and walked into the church to see if anything needed to be done there.

The place was empty, except for Amanda-Lee, packing up some equipment by the stage.

"I thought I'd let the crew go get something to eat," she said and smiled, but I could see in her face that she didn't feel much like a party. "We have the footage we need. I think Rodney and I are going to catch the red-eye back to LA so we can get this into production. . . ." She took a peek toward the door as a set of headlights flashed by. "The more time we have, the better we can make it. We have some good material to work with, thanks to you."

"Lands, I didn't do anything." I felt my cheeks go red. It'd been a long time since anybody gave me credit for doing something important, other than baking the pies at the café. To the countertoppers, a good pecan pie was important. "It was nothing any neighbor wouldn't do for another, anyhow. We take care of our own here in Daily."

"It's a nice town," Amanda-Lee said, and the conversation ran dry for a minute. She picked up a clipboard and rearranged some papers on it, then smiled at me a little sadly. "I'm going to miss the Dailyians, I think."

All of a sudden, I felt like one of my own kids was moving clear across the country. I was going to miss her and all the excitement *American Megastar* brought to town. "You come back and visit, y'hear? Whenever things get too busy there in the big city, you just hop on a plane and head this way. Don't feel like you have to call ahead, even. I got lots of guest rooms and not near enough guests."

She seemed kind of surprised by the invitation at first, then her face brightened, like she was thinking she'd really come back. "I might just take you up on that."

"I'd enjoy the company." A meddlesome part of me figured that if she came back, maybe we could find a way to bring Carter here at the same time. Brother Harve said Carter was helping with some part of the wiring for the new Caney Creek Church building. Maybe Brother Harve could give him a call and tell him there was a problem back in Daily he needed to look at. It wouldn't really be a fib. Not exactly . . .

Amanda-Lee started taking down some kind of lights that looked like what Jack used to keep out in his shop. I moved around to help her. "On second thought, though, you might want to call before you come, just to make sure." If she gave some notice, we'd have a better chance of getting Carter here at the same time. "I'm thinking of taking one of those cruises like you saw on the internet. I figured I'd get my boys to help me find one. They're a whiz with computers."

She stopped halfway through folding up the light stand, smiled at me, and nodded. "Good for you. I bet you'll have a great time."

"It'll be different from anything I ever did before, that's for sure." A queasy feeling stirred in the pit of my stomach. Telling Amanda-Lee I was going to take the cruise made it really seem like a commitment. "But I just got to thinking, life's like that plate of fancy French nibblets the literary ladies brought tonight. There's lots of things on there that look a little strange, but you'll never know if they're good or not if you don't try something new. No telling what I missed out on because I let myself be afraid. You helped me figure that out, Amanda-Lee. You and the Lightning Snake."

Amanda-Lee looked at me for a long minute. I had a feeling she was thinking about that night at the fair when she and Carter rode the Lightning Snake together and she asked me to be part of her plan to make Amber's show the best.

"I want to thank you for doing right by Amber," I said. "She was sure upset when she thought you were mad at her."

Amanda-Lee went back to folding up the light holder. "I'm not mad at Amber. I already apologized for losing it with her."

"You seem kind of down-in-the-mouth tonight, though," I went on, trying to act like I was just making chit-chat.

She untied the cord and retied it. "It doesn't have anything to do with Amber. She was great tonight. The show will be great."

"She'll be glad to hear that." I was hoping the conversation would slip around to what'd happened with Carter, but so far, Amanda-Lee was being careful not to drift that direction. "Amber admires you a bunch. She really wants to make you happy."

"It'll be a good show," she said, but there wasn't much feeling in the words. She looked as blue as any little girl I'd ever seen. "That's all that matters."

"I suppose so." I tried to look casual by moving into the choir loft and picking up some empty water bottles. "Guess it was meant to be, the show turning out just right and all, especially after so much unexpected excitement. Amber was sure worried you'd quit her after she spilled the beans about Carter." I glanced over at Amanda-Lee, and she stiffened like a board the minute I mentioned his name.

Since the topic had come up, I grabbed it and dove on in. "You know, it's a funny thing. Amber told me she'd been trying to call J. C. Woods about his music company all weekend, and he wouldn't pick up his phone. Seems like if he was *really* here to steal her over to his company, he would have answered his phone . . . unless something'd happened to make him change his mind about meeting up with Amber." I moved on around the choir loft, stacking up music books and letting the idea sink into Amanda-Lee's head for a minute. From the corner of my eye, I saw her stop what she was doing and slowly turn toward me.

She didn't answer at first. I guessed I'd gone too far and made her mad. "It doesn't matter now," she said finally. "After this hometown segment, Amber will have a good chance to make it to the Final Showdown, and if she does, the decision about where to eventually go with her recording career will be up to her. She can make her own choices."

"Oh, I know that." I hovered there for a minute with the trash in my hands. *Leave it be, Imagene. You're pushing your nose in where it doesn't belong again.* But of course I couldn't help myself. I really did like Amanda-Lee, and it was a shame for her to be so sad, and for her and Carter to be at odds, being as they had so much in common. "I just meant that sometimes things aren't what they look like. I don't think Amber or Carter Woods really meant to do anything . . . well . . . anything underhanded. Seems like Carter was a lot more interested in other things than he was in Amber . . . if you ask me." *Which she didn't, Imagene. Butt out.*

I slipped out the choir loft door to go dump the bottles into the trashcan behind the sanctuary. When I came back in, Amanda-Lee was standing stock-still on the matted-down spot of carpet where the pulpit would normally be. She was watching someone walk up the stairs outside the front door. His face was hidden in the shadows, but I could tell by the cowboy hat and the Hawaiian shirt who it was.

My hopes rose up like Lazarus, and I looked up at the ceiling, sending out a silent *Praise the Lord* and *amen.* Then I slipped out the back and left things in bigger hands than mine.

Chapter 27

Mandalay Florentino

Air caught in my throat, the room seemed to shrink around me, and my heartbeat slowed. The moment stretched like a cartoon imprinted on Silly Putty. For an instant, I had the thought that maybe something was wrong with me physically. I'd produced news reports about overstressed young professionals who experienced sudden heart arrhythmias, strokes, and anxiety attacks. The brain, lacking oxygen, chemically imbalanced, misfired in its internal connections, and convinced the eyes to see things that didn't exist.

I blinked, focused on the stained-glass window high in the peak overhead, then looked back at the entrance. He was still there. Not coming or going, just standing in the darkened doorway, his face hidden in the shadow of his cowboy hat.

Maybe it wasn't him. . . .

Every grain of my existence wanted it to be him. I didn't know how to feel about that. All afternoon, I'd been fighting to push away the thought of Carter, trying to focus on work, to do the job that needed to be done, to make my business life a success even if my personal life was a wreck. I'd built up a defensive wall, brick by brick, hoped it would protect me tonight when things were quiet, when I was alone and some random image of my time with Carter, some flash of memory ignited a yearning that could only end in self-recrimination. *You sure know how to pick 'em, Mandalay Florentino,* I'd tell myself then. *You made a monumental fool of yourself. You're just lucky Butch clued you in. . . .*

Even that was humiliating—the fact that fresh-off-the-turnip-truck Butch had discerned Carter's identity and cracked Ursula's secret code before I had. *I* was the Hollywood-savvy news producer, after all. Once upon a time, I could look in the mirror and see a woman who was accomplished, sharp, competent, nobody's fool. Today's revelations had rocked me to the core, left me feeling broken and uncertain of everything, including my own judgment.

My only salvation was the whisper-thin belief that, from the beginning, the unexpected trip to Daily, Texas, had knocked me slightly off center. I'd been preoccupied with the rapidly escalating Amber crisis and the collapse of my relationship with David. I'd been looking for any port in a storm. Otherwise I would have pegged Carter as a fraud from the very beginning. Once I got home, I would feel more like my old self, my *real* self. Amid the humiliating buzz of canceling wedding plans and getting back the belongings I'd stored at David's apartment, these few days in Daily would be just a distant memory, a tiny little sound I couldn't hear. Carter would be nothing but a silly vacation romance, a folly, a mistake. I would morph into Mandalay Florentino, defender of the little guy, too consumed with fighting evil Ursula and her Dysterco death ray to have a broken heart.

Beneath all the postulating, there was a nagging question. Why did I feel Carter's betrayal so deeply? Why did it seem as if something important, *someone* important had suddenly dropped out of my life? Why was I desperately hoping that the shadowy figure outside the door was Carter, not someone else in a cowboy hat and Hawaiian shirt?

My heart fluttered into my throat, inconveniently exhilarated by the idea that he'd come back. To see me? To talk things out? To try to sign Amber for Higher Ground? If it was really him, why was he here?

My mind rushed to assimilate Imagene's revelations. *Amber told me she'd been trying to call J. C. Woods about his music company all weekend and he wouldn't pick up his phone.* Was that true? I'd heard Carter's cell ring several times. I'd seen him check the number and tuck the phone back into his pocket. *Seems like if he was really here to steal her over to his company, he would have answered his phone . . . unless something had happened to make him change his mind. . . .*

Had something happened? Was I foolish to think so, to hope for it, to believe that he was here now to talk to me rather than to promote some scheme that would advance his recording interests? Was I setting myself up for another fall? Only a few days ago, I'd been telling myself that David and I didn't have any secrets from each other. I'd been convinced that the separate-but-together life he offered was what I wanted. I'd told myself I could fit happily into the mold, be his shipmate, roommate, walk down the street together looking like the perfect power couple. Even now, in spite of everything I'd learned about David, a part of me liked the picture. A part of me desperately wanted to be half of a whole, a partner, a soul mate.

Was I trying to paint a new picture, hastily writing a fresh duet because the future I'd imagined with David had been shattered?

I looked hard at the doorway, tried to decide, tried to see the picture. But with Carter there was no picture. I couldn't imagine, couldn't presuppose what it would be like with him. There was no mold for me to squeeze into. Nothing about him fit the artificial scenarios I'd envisioned. Carter was an enigma, a mystery yet to be solved, but the details seemed insignificant. There was only the way I felt when I was with him, the way he made me laugh, his willingness to watch cheesy westerns late into the night, his lack of unrealistic expectations and demands. Carter made me feel like it was good enough, more than good enough just to be myself, just to spend time together. He made me feel . . . perfect.

Had I ever experienced that kind of peace, that sense of rightness before? With David? With anyone?

I could feel him watching me from the doorway. Ducking his head, he pushed his hands into his pockets, and something in the motion let me know for certain it was him. He was waiting there in the darkness, giving me time to consider his presence here, allowing me to make the first move if I wanted to.

Before I heard it in my thoughts, I felt the glimmer of an answered prayer, a tiny grain of faith, a holdover from childhood or the years of Episcopal school, or perhaps something new, sprinkled there by Daily folks, Amber Anderson, or some magical combination of everything. Perhaps some things *were* meant to be and the only chain keeping me prisoner was the fear I'd allowed myself to build. If this wasn't real, if it wasn't meant to be, how could I possibly feel it so deeply?

I started up the aisle, a few steps at first, then faster, until I was just inside the door and he was outside. Only the threshold separated us.

I hesitated, unable to cross. A stubborn, wounded part of me felt the need to slow the situation down, to control it, to yield beneath the burden of the heavy chain of questions, of worry and trepidation. A whisper of apprehension told me that as much as I wanted the shadow man to be Carter, he was really J. C. Woods, someone I didn't know at all. *Be careful,* a voice in my head warned. *Don't put yourself out there too far. What if you're wrong? What if there is no grand plan? What if it's all just wishful thinking? Remember what happened with David. . . .*

I hovered on the threshold, teetering between a chasm of fear and a bridge of faith.

Crossing his arms over his chest, Carter leaned against the railing and rolled a stone beneath his boot, waiting for me to say something. I had the sense that he would wait there all night. However long it took. As always, he was patient, like the boy in his song "Drifting on Faith," aware that the river, not he, was in control of the boat.

Finally, I couldn't bear the silence. "You could come in." I wanted to see his face, to look into his eyes and know, once and for all, who he was. When I saw him, really saw him, would I know?

He turned toward me, but his expression was hidden. "I wasn't sure it was safe." I could picture him smiling just a little—a soft, fond smile, as if this were all just a misunderstanding and we would solve it soon enough.

"It could be."

He chuckled under his breath. I loved his laugh. "I didn't want to leave things the way they were." There was no laughter in those words, only a tenderness that seemed heartfelt, that pulled and tugged deep in my chest.

I don't want to leave things this way, either. I don't. Hope swelled inside me, as fragile as a soap bubble. I stood uncertain of whether to cradle it protectively or pop it before it grew any larger.

Could I withstand one more shattering of trust?

Did I have the courage to take the risk, to throw off the chains and cross over?

"No telling what I missed out on because I let myself be afraid. . . ." Imagene's words repeated in my head. Why was it so easy for me to tell her to set her concerns aside, to jump on a boat and sail out to sea? Why couldn't I find the backbone to do the same thing? What if I never did? What if I played it safe today, tomorrow, forever? Would I become the woman hiding in my house alone while life passed by outside the window?

Crossing the threshold, I stood in the darkness, saw Carter's face in the moon glow. "I'd like to know the truth. Carter . . . J.C. . . . Which is it, anyway?" There was an edge of bitterness I couldn't banish, a remnant of the wall I'd worked so hard to build. It was easy to cling to it, to hide behind it—so hard to let go, to stand in the open, vulnerable.

"Carter to friends and family, J.C. for business."

"Which one am I?"

"The first, I hope." His fingers drummed against the railing, his chest rising and falling. His eyes were deep blue in the moonlight. "Manda, what you and I . . . I wasn't using you to try to get to Amber. I'll admit that at first, I was a little—" he paused to search for the right word—"curious. I wanted to see what kind of situation I was dealing with. No offense, but your show's got a reputation for chewing up bright-eyed kids and spitting them out. I figured there wasn't much chance that a country girl singing faith music and southern gospel was really going to get the million-dollar record-ing contract. Truthfully, I figured Amber was just being used for publicity—the butt of a highly profitable joke, more or less. The entertainment business is rough, even where I've been, and reality TV is a whole new level of dog-eat-dog. So yes, I was interested in talking to Amber about Higher Ground. But I met you first, and you weren't what I'd expected. It didn't take me long to discern that Amber was in good hands, so I left the situation alone. I let you do your job. You're good at it. I figured I'd call Amber next week and tell her to stick where she's at for now—that Higher Ground would be there later, if *American Megastar* didn't work out."

My instant reaction was to be self-righteous, to defend my territory, to defend the show. In the wake of that impulse, an inky black guilt slid over me. The truth was that he was right. Everything he'd said, all his fears about *American Megastar* and the show's intentions for Amber were spot on. "*American Megastar* wasn't going to work out for Amber." In spite of everything, it hurt to voice the truth. "While I was here trying to put together a good hometown segment, my boss was in bed with the maker of the tabulation software, planning to have Amber voted off next week."

Carter didn't seem surprised. Clearly, he knew more about the underbelly of the entertainment business than he'd let on. Shaking his head, he sighed. "And?"

"And I think I have it under control for now. Of course, when the season's over, I'll be out of a job. If not before." The reality sent a queasy feeling through me. I had an apartment to pay for, a car, bills. There was the issue of medical insurance. I wouldn't be getting married and adding my name to David's policy. I was a single girl. I had to support myself. "It's worth it, though." I wasn't sure if I was trying to convince myself or him. "It feels good to do the right thing for once, you know? I hope I'll still feel the same way when I'm standing in the unemployment line."

I forced a halfhearted laugh, but a touch of self-pity prickled in my throat like a sand bur. What had I done to deserve this? My whole career, I'd tried to do the right thing, to be someone my family and I and even God could be proud of in a business that didn't always value integrity. All I wanted was a job in which principles and hard work counted for something, a relationship in which I could be myself, be loved, be protected, trust and be trusted. Why couldn't I find those things? Other people did. My sisters were all happily married with fulfilling careers—why not me? "I got into broadcasting because I wanted my work to count for something. I used to feel like it did, but lately . . ." I knew I was rambling, trying to prop myself up, talking about work so I could avoid the real question, the one I still needed to answer. Was this thing between Carter and me more than just a chance meeting, more than just a sudden and powerful attraction? If so, where did we go from here? He lived in Texas and I lived on the west coast. The truth was that we barely knew each other.

"I know a little recording company in Austin that could use somebody with production experience and big-time connections in the LA scene."

I looked up, momentarily shocked, then suddenly fluttery and uncertain. Was he asking me to come back?

Adjusting his hat, he scratched his ear, seeming to have embarrassed himself with the sudden suggestion. "Just a thought."

It's now or never, Mandalay, I told myself. *You either get on the boat or stand on the shore and watch life sail on by.* "I might take you up on that."

He tipped his head to one side, studied me. His grin broadened finally, a soft white line in the darkness. "You know where to find me."

"Actually, I don't."

Slipping a hand into his pocket, he retrieved a business card. "Now you know where to find me."

Our fingers touched and a tingle of excitement, a blossoming sense of something new, something profound slipped over me as I took the card and tucked it away. "I guess I do." I wanted to tell him what I was really thinking, to admit to the powerful connection I felt with him. He would probably think I was crazy, some desperate thirty-something woman playing relationship bingo.

Pushing off the rail, he stepped closer, and I felt my body quicken in response. I wanted to throw myself into his arms and kiss him, whether it made me look overeager or not. Overhead, the trees stirred and a lover's moon hung low, as if in anticipation.

Carter stroked a finger alongside his lip, came closer yet, so that only a step separated us. "Of course, I have to be out in LA next week to negotiate a cut for a movie soundtrack. I could look you up."

"You could," I agreed, and then finally I found the courage to step aboard the boat and cast off from shore, let the current take me where it would. "You'd better."

He laughed deep in his throat. "In that case, plan on dinner. You pick the place."

Suddenly, I was looking forward to going home. I wanted to show Carter everything, to share with him all the spots I loved best, to stand on the pier together and watch the sun go down as ships combed the horizon. "Are we going to pay for the meal or wait until the place closes and break in?"

"Your choice." The words were intimate, an invitation drawing me to him. "We could get arrested again."

"Tempting . . ." I knew I would do anything to be with him—even get arrested by Buddy Ray again. "But how about a walk on the beach instead?"

"That's good, too." He reached for me, and I slipped into his arms, felt a sense of hope, and promise, and perfect symmetry like nothing I'd experienced before—as if this moment, the two of us, had been predestined long before I ever knew it. Suddenly, the work to be done on Amber's segment, the questions about my job, the battle with Ursula, the uncertainties of bills and medical insurance felt far away, insignificant.

His lips met mine and all seemed right with the world.

Somewhere deep within me, beyond the passion, beyond the beauty of the night, that little spark of Daily magic ignited in me again, began burning in a place that had gone dark and untended, that had yearned to be bright and warm. I felt it now, something old, something new, something complete. Perhaps it had been there in me all along—the belief that there is a plan and a purpose, that God whispers into every life some things that are beyond the scope of the mind and can only be felt with the heart and the spirit.

Those dreams, the ones that are dreamed *for* us, not by us, are the truest of all.

Chapter 28

Imagone Doll

Amber's shindig continued on as the moon rose high overhead. During dinner, the band moved their equipment outside to one of the tents. Brother Harve and O.C. made us a bonfire out of some leftover construction materials, and everybody went to dancing. Amber took the floor with that cute little Butch, and she even danced with Buddy Ray some, for old time's sake. He looked pretty proud of himself, out there cutting a rug with Daily's first certified superstar. O.C. danced every number with a little girl he'd invited home from college. Watching O.C. and his sweetheart, I got a feeling about those two.

Donetta had more fun than I'd ever seen. She couldn't get her stick-in-the-mud husband out of his chair, so she decided to teach Andy, Amos, and Avery how to dance. They took to it pretty good, and finally even old Verl agreed to a spin. With Verl in Jack's golf clothes and Donetta in her favorite pink shirt and the pants with the lime green palm trees, they made a colorful pair.

There must have been some bona fide magic in the night air, because Doyle even got up his courage to ask Lucy to dance. It took him a while to spit out the question, but when he did, she left the food service line like a rocket and I took her spot. Doyle and Lucy shined up the floor in the swing dance. Who knew old rawboned Doyle could move like that?

Things were just getting into full blush when Amanda-Lee and Carter finally found their way outside of the church with the rest of us. I guessed she'd changed her mind about being in such a hurry to head for the airport, because she and Carter got some food and sat down to watch the band. I was glad she stayed to see our celebration, since it all happened because she came to Daily. I told her so as she moved through the food line, and she smiled and said she couldn't have done it without me. It made me feel real special.

As Amanda-Lee and Carter settled in at a table just off the dance floor, I had the satisfaction of a job well done. All the Hollywood business had come out fine, and it seemed that I hadn't lost my touch for matchmaking after all. Amanda-Lee and Carter looked starry-eyed and happy, like they were on top of the world. After they finished eating, he asked her to dance, which was pretty brave of him, considering that Miss Lulu and the choir ladies had just got ahold of Verl and the Anderson boys and the dance floor was getting rowdy. Carter didn't seem worried. He just grinned at Amanda-Lee's protests, then dragged her from her chair and took her off to a patch of moon shadow under an oak tree. They danced there like they didn't know anybody else was around.

The sight of them made me smile as I wandered off and sat down on Pastor Harve's old swing, where the glow from the church window fell soft and golden on the grass. I tipped my head back, and high above, the man in the moon spread out his cape of stars just for me. The band toned it down for a slow song, and the clear, sweet notes of "Sentimental Journey" floated on the night air. That was our song, Jack's and mine.

I let myself slip into a memory of the night I first danced with Jack. In my mind, I could see him, tall and straight in his uniform. He smiled and bowed low, offered his arm. I put my hand in his and he swept me to my feet, and we danced on an old wood pier nearby the midway of the winter carnival. Below, it was high tide, and the waves caught the stars in pieces, then turned them loose again as they kissed the shore.

An ordinary person doesn't see too many glorious moments like that in a lifetime. I'd sure thought my glory days, and Daily's, were over, but maybe I'd counted us both out too soon. Just when you think a place doesn't have any life anymore, it yawns and stretches, catches a fresh breath, and looks out with new eyes. Then you realize that the plain kind of places, the ones like Daily, where folks are friendly and a good story will buy you a fresh cup of coffee any day of the week, don't ever really die. They only doze off like sage old hounds sleeping away the hot afternoon, awaiting the cool of evening to get up and throw back their heads, lope through the hills, and bay at the moon.

As I opened my eyes and looked at my friends and neighbors dancing on the lawn, at Amber laughing with her family and Amanda-Lee in the arms of her beau beneath the shadows of the live oak trees, I felt full inside. Of all the Reunion Days past and yet to come, this one, when a bunch of country folks outsmarted Hollywood, helped make a sure-enough superstar, did a little matchmaking, and threw a whale of a party to boot, would be remembered in Daily history.

Surely this was a gathering folks would relive for years to come, the sort of moment when the night falls quiet, and soft, and deep, when the air is filled with the warmth of people who love one another. Overhead, the angels swoop down low to be near. God breathes a sigh across the heavens, the blessings shower down like falling stars, and the cup overflows with light.

About the Author

Lisa Wingate is a popular inspirational speaker, magazine columnist, and national bestselling author of several books, including *Tending Roses, Good Hope Road, The Language of Sycamores, Drenched in Light,* and *A Thousand Voices*. Her work was recently honored by Americans for More Civility for promoting greater kindness and civility in American life. Lisa and her family live in central Texas.

Visit Lisa at her website, *www.lisawingate.com*

Questions for Conversation

1. *Talk of the Town* is a "fish out of water" tale. Have you ever been forced into a situation where both people and place seem alien to you? Do you ever end up feeling comfortable, and what changed to make that possible?
2. Why do you think that we, as a nation, are so obsessed with Hollywood? Is small town life more "real" or "authentic" than Hollywood? Have you gotten caught up in the reality TV craze?
3. Have you ever lived in a small town, and if so, what was it like? If not, does the idea of living in a small town like fictional Daily, Texas, appeal to you?
4. Have you experienced members of a community pulling together in an effort to help one of their own?
5. In what ways is Mandalay changed by her weekend in Daily, Texas? How did characters Imagene, Amber, and Carter each affect her differently?
6. In what ways is Imagene changed by her friendship with Mandalay? Have you ever met a new person and felt an instant connection?

7. Imagene takes some risks at the end of the novel. If money and time weren't an obstacle, what risky thing would you attempt?
8. Imagenc believes two people can be meant for each other. Do you believe in love at first sight? Have you ever seen it happen?
9. Do you think Amber will end up being compromised and changed by Hollywood?
10. Amber asserts that Justin Shay might feel better about life if he used his vast resources to do something good. Do you believe this? Have you ever found a sense of purpose through an act of service?
11. *Talk of the Town* also celebrates friendship. What makes a friendship that lasts over time? Talk about your truest friend and the ways in which that person has supported you.

Be the first to know

Want to be the first to know
what's new from
your favorite authors?

Want to know all about
exciting new writers?
